For the joy of words.

Tony Andermaas

In the Name of Honour

Tony Vandermaas

iUniverse, Inc.
Bloomington

In the Name of Honour

iUniverse books may be ordered through booksellers or by contacting:

iUniverse
1663 Liberty Drive
Bloomington, IN 47403
www.iuniverse.com
1-800-Authors (1-800-288-4677)

ISBN: 978-1-4697-6887-8 (sc)
ISBN: 978-1-4697-6888-5 (e)

Printed in the United States of America

iUniverse rev. date: 2/15/2012

For my grandchildren.

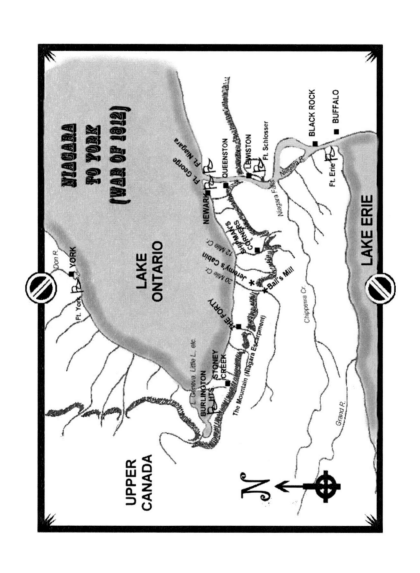

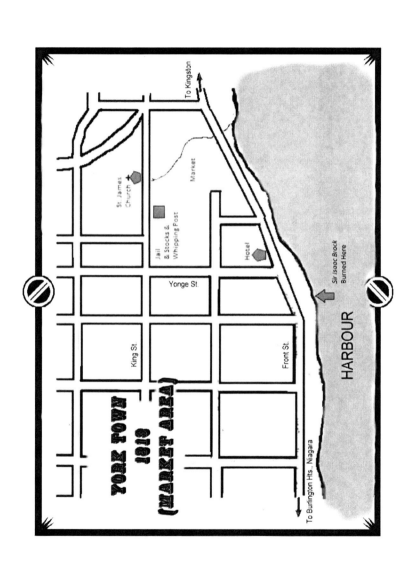

YORK TOWN
1813
(MARKET AREA)

To Kingston

St. James Church

Jail & Stocks & Whipping Post

Market

Yonge St.

King St.

Hotel

Front St.

Sir Isaac Brock Burned Here

HARBOUR

To Burlington Hts., Niagara

The Cast of Characters

Historical Characters (in alphabetical order):

Canadian/British:

    Bisshop, Lieutenant-Colonel Cecil – one-time commander of the forward post at Shipman's Corners, died after raid on Black Rock, N.Y.

    Fitzgibbon, Captain James – "The Green Tiger," leader of the irregulars officially called "The Green Tigers," better known as "The Bloody Boys"

    Merritt, Captain William Hamilton – leader of irregulars known as the Provincial Dragoons, future builder of the Welland Canal

    Murray, Colonel John – commander of the Forlorn Hope, sent to take retribution for the burning of Newark

    Riall, General Phineas – commander of British forces at Lewiston

    Simcoe, John Graves – Lieutenant Governor of Upper Canada from 1791-1796

    Strachan, John – Anglican Minister who took charge in York during and after attack by Americans

American/American Sympathizer:

    Chapin, Dr. Cyrenius – leader of American "irregulars"

    Mallory, Benajah – Willcocks' second in command

McClure, Brigadier-General George – commander of the Americans in Niagara

Porter, Captain Peter – militia Captain who rebuffs British at raid on Black Rock, N.Y.

Willcocks, James – leader of the group of mostly traitors known as the "Canadian Volunteers" – former politician, newspaper editor, etc.

Fictional Characters (in alphabetical order):

Canadian/British:

Davidson, Oliver – Jeremy van Hijser's distant cousin

DuLac, Josef – Caughnawaga Indian and friend of Jeremy

Halberson, Colonel James – acting commander at Burlington Heights

Halberson, Davis – the Colonel's nephew and one of Jeremy's group

Renforth, Capt. Howard – Army doctor who helps Jeremy

Van Hijser, Jeremy – trapper, hunter, farmer and hero of this story

The other Caughnawaga Indians – Maurice, Giles, Gilbert, Tomas – members of Josef's group

American/ American Sympathizer:

Billings, "Parson" Phineas – brother-in-law of Dorian Williamson, Canadian Volunteers

Sims, James Archibald – "antiquities trader" who has the map

Williamson, Dorian – one of Willcocks' group leaders

Also fictional are all characters not listed as historical.

The Places

Ancaster – town on the Niagara Escarpment (The Mountain), now part of the City of Hamilton, still known by that name

Beaverdams – now a part of the City of Thorold, still known by that name

Black Rock – now a suburb of Buffalo

Burlington Heights – now in the City of Hamilton, the base would become Dundurn Castle after the War of 1812

Chippewa – now a part of the City of Niagara Falls, still known by that name

Fort George – still exists as an historical site in Niagara-on-the-Lake

Fort Niagara – still exists as an historical site on the American side of the Niagara River, across from Fort George – originally a British Fort before the American War of Independence, the two forts were built to control entry of French ships into the river

Lewiston – across the Niagara River from Queenston, it retains its name

Newark – former capital of Upper Canada, by this time formally renamed Niagara, but still commonly referred to as Newark, now the Town of Niagara-on-the-Lake

Queenston – still known by that name, but now part of the Town of Niagara-on-the-Lake

Shipman's Corners – also known at the time as The Twelve, became the City of St. Catharines

St. Davids – still known by that name, but now part of the Town of Niagara-on-the-Lake

Stoney Creek – still known by this name, although it has been amalgamated into the City of Hamilton

The Forty – now the Town of Grimsby

The Twenty – became the Village of Jordan, now part of the Town of Lincoln

York — capital of Upper Canada after Newark, now the City of Toronto, it's original name

Prelude

Young Oliver Davidson sat serenely on a tree bole which curved out over the Niagara River, watching the tiny eddies created by his fishing line as the dark waters flowed past. The sun had not yet risen completely and he savoured the solitude, barely caring if he actually caught anything.

At sixteen, Oliver was considered to be an adult. He certainly looked and acted the part, standing five feet, ten inches tall, with muscles tempered by the chores on his mother's farm as well as the daily work at loading and unloading wagons at the natural harbour created by the ebony rock that jutted out into the Niagara, giving the town of Black Rock its name. This being the Lord's Day, however, he was free – free to loaf until called to church by its bell, whose peal could be heard for some distance around. He had completed his chores for the morning, those that were allowed in his mother's rather strict observance of the Sabbath. Now no one would disturb him, as he was fully a half-hour's walk from town.

As he drowsed on the broad tree trunk, luxuriating in the pure idleness of the pastime, he heard a splash behind him, followed shortly by the sound of muttered and whispered voices.

"We're too far downstream," one of the voices proclaimed in frustration.

"Aye," responded another, "but the main body has drifted off even further."

Oliver slipped cautiously from the tree and, once firmly on the riverbank, proceeded cautiously toward the sound of the voices, keeping low among the bushes. There was a war on after all, and one just never knew even if the American side of the Niagara had never yet been involved to any degree.

"Never mind then," said the man who obviously in charge of this group of more than two score men. "The plan was to attack straight away upon landing and that's exactly what we'll do." The men had a military bearing, appearing even in the poor light like battle-hardened veterans, and they quickly grouped around the speaker, obviously waiting to move out on his command.

The leader, no doubt an officer, although he wore no insignia, looked all around, stopping as he looked in Oliver's direction.

My God, he's seen me, Oliver thought, his heart racing. He dropped to the ground and froze there, afraid to move or make a sound, hoping desperately that he was wrong. I hope they didn't hear me landing, he thought, the pressure of suffocating panic rising in his chest.

"Right then, lads," the officer said. "Let's be off, shall we? We have some time to make up." The man was now pointing in Oliver's General direction, making Oliver's heart skip a pair of beats. "That's the way, there."

Oliver allowed himself to begin breathing once again. I haven't been spotted after all, he thought as he watched as the men head off toward town, at a mild trot and in single file, making barely a sound.

Oh, God, he suddenly thought! Whatever am I doing lying here? I should be off to warn the town!

Oliver scrambled to his feet, filled with shame at his cowardice. Taking a less pronounced pathway along the river's bank, he ran as quickly as his legs could carry him toward Black Rock. He arrived, gasping and sweating profusely, more from panic than from heat and exertion, at almost the same moment that the British soldiers were disarming the pickets not far from where he emerged. He watched powerlessly, since he could not pass without detection, fervently hoping that they would move along.

He could take it no more when he noticed that several of the enemy lighting firebrands and walking purposefully toward the blockhouse and militia barracks, obviously intent upon setting them aflame. "What in God's name do you think you're doing?" he shouted out suddenly, stepping out from his hiding place. Then, "What am I doing?" he asked himself aloud, fully realizing that he had given himself away.

"Lieutenant!" the man closest to Oliver shouted to the man in charge. "This boy wishes to know what it is we're about." This remark was accompanied by a howl of laughter from those closest to him.

The man referred to as Lieutenant closed on Oliver in several long strides and grabbed him by the arm. "Corporal," he called out.

There was a man guarding the pickets they captured, and he now looked toward the sound.

"Take this lad and place him with your prisoners, will you?" he said. "We wouldn't want anything to accidentally happen to him if he happens to wander into our path."

Oliver was guided to the militiamen who were to have been guarding the town — eight embarrassed men in all — and was ordered to sit on the ground with them. "What do you intend to do with me?" he demanded in a sudden burst of false bravado.

"We intend to leave you here," the Corporal replied in an Irish brogue, and tied Oliver's hands firmly behind him. He nodded in the direction of the now fully involved blockhouse and barracks. "And a nice cosy fire to keep you warm while we're away," he added.

"And just leave us here?" Oliver shouted, at once indignant, frightened and mortified.

The Corporal turned and grinned at the young man. "You don't think that we have the time to be minding the young for the Americans, do you?" he teased, and ran off to join the others, who were well on their way through town on their way toward the army camp at Fort Gibson.

Oliver sat helplessly stewing as he watched as the foreign troops dashed down his main street, bugle sounding. "Why isn't anyone coming to meet them?" he asked the militiaman closest to him.

"I just saw quite a number evacuating toward the south," the man answered glumly.

"Why don't they stand and fight?" Oliver came back, incredulous. "Do we live in a nation of cowards?"

The man looked at Oliver, his eyes hard. "If I wasn't tied up," he growled angrily, "I'd give you a smart cuff across the back of the head." Then, in a quieter voice, he added, "They've just gone to get their families safe. They'll be back," he finished, his voice sounding more hopeful than confident.

Oliver held his tongue, but looked disappointedly at the abandoned main street. That's not the news that's been circulating, he thought. All we hear of is the cowardice of our troops, turning and running instead of fighting battles. The talk is that in Washington, they're calling for the heads of our Generals for their cowardice.

Realizing there was nothing he could do, or even say, to make any difference, Oliver shrugged his shoulders uncomfortably and squirmed within his bonds to find a more comfortable position. A slight breeze had arisen from Lake Eire and the smoke from the blazing structures burned his eyes. Yet he could not avoid watching the sack of his town, as much as he could from where he sat.

The prisoners were off to one side of the main street, and they could see the backs of some of the buildings. Suddenly, one of the men sitting with Oliver straightened up, peering intently along that viewpoint.

"I think I see some movement down there," he said tentatively. "Yes, there it is!" he shouted, his excitement building. As an afterthought, he remembered his situation and glanced about to see if any enemy were nearby to hear him.

"You're right!" someone else piped up. "Someone's coming out of the back window! Say…isn't that old man Porter?"

"It is," said one of the others, chuckling. "And he seems to be having a time getting on that horse."

It was indeed Peter B. Porter, Quartermaster General for New York State, who struggled to mount his horse. Clad only in his nightshirt, he finally managed to get the animal under control and rode off at full speed.

"Where do you think he's headed?" one of the men asked.

Oliver watched the man disappear around a bend and muttered thoughtfully, "Probably to Buffalo to rouse the militia. At least, that's the way he's headed."

Another man snickered cynically. "Do you think we'll see him back before tomorrow morning?"

"Of course we will," said an older man, who had been silent until now. "He'll want to protect his supplies in the warehouse."

Oliver concentrated upon loosing the ropes that bound his wrists. Working them back and forth until his skin burned as though they had been in fire before them, he began to make headway. Fortunately for him, the soldiers had taken it easy on him since he was but a lad, as he heard one comment.

"You might as well stop your infernal squirming," the man next to him snapped. "They tied us well. You may as well save the skin on your arms and wait for release. After all, we're only militia. They won't take us away, but just parole us, and we won't be allowed to fight in this war." He looked over at the others. "And thank God for that," he added, eliciting a round of chuckled agreement from the others.

At the moment that his neighbour completed the sentence, Oliver's hands finally worked free. "Well, you layabouts can stay here until the war ends if you wish," he commented to a group of gaping mouths. "If you wish, however, I'll untie you and we can try to keep the bastards from destroying our home."

One by one, Oliver freed the men from their bonds. He tried, without complete success, to ignore the sheepish expressions they wore on their faces, and they huddled together to attempt to discern a plan of action. Their discussion was shortly interrupted by cries coming from the river itself.

"Come on men! We don't want Fitzgibbon and his Bloody Boys to have all the fun, now do we?" shouted a British officer in full uniform.

As he stepped aside, sword raised, well over a hundred uniformed British soldiers poured from a number of boats that were being poled into position behind the tavern nearby, and broke onto the road at a run. These must be the others to whom the first group's leader had been referring, Oliver thought. He and the pickets stepped back into the bush and the soldiers, in their haste did not seem to notice them at all.

"So much for liberating Black Rock from John Bull," the older man remarked wryly after the last of the soldiers had streamed by, using the term Americans had used for Englishmen since before the War of Independence. "I somehow doubt that we shall be able to disarm them all, especially without weapons.

"Let's then try to put out the fire before it burns the whole forest and the town as well," shouted one of the other men. "Are you coming, too?" he shouts at Oliver, who stood watching as the British began to load all the town's military stores onto the waiting boats.

"What?" Oliver asked, snapping his attention back to the man who was speaking to him. "Oh, of course."

The nine men proceeded to attempt to contain the fire, which by now had mostly finished with the military buildings, but was threatening to spread through the brush. Wetting their jackets in the nearby creek, they began to beat out the nascent flames and kicked dirt onto embers where possible.

Oliver sensed a change in the fortunes of war, and he turned about to see a man the others called Fitzgibbon addressing the officer in a loud voice, striving to be heard above the noise of the loading.

"Colonel, we really must leave before the Americans manage to rally their militia," Fitzgibbon urged. "Most of the boats have unloaded and returned for the men."

The Colonel, an officer of patrician bearing, shook his head. "Not until we get the salt loaded," he replied. "I am told there are eighty or more barrels here, and I intend that we shall load them for our men."

There was a short period of inaction as most of the troops huddled about the riverbank while the rest loaded the precious salt, so necessary for preserving meat and other foods for the long winter ahead. Suddenly, the site became pure bedlam as hundreds of American militia and a few dozen Seneca burst forth on both British flanks. Oliver and the pickets were themselves nearly shot in the fervour of the attack.

"Load the salt!" the British Colonel shouted to his troops. Then he proceeded to round up a number of men. "You men come with me!" he ordered, as he moved up to fight a forward action against the charging Americans.

The balance was but a blur to Oliver as he watched the militia, led by the same Peter Porter they saw leave from his bedroom window, rush by him. The man must have ridden to every farm, he thought absently. But he would have little more time for thought, as he was jolted into action as a gun was jammed into his hands.

"Here! Take this!" someone shouted. "I have two!"

Oliver followed blankly into battle, screaming loudly with the rest and running toward the British. The latter, contrary to local propaganda concerning their fighting prowess, were holding their own against the undisciplined hoard roaring toward them. One man fell beside Oliver, and then another in front of him, tripping him and sending him sprawling into the dust of the main street. Immediately behind him, another man fell as well, and Oliver could not make out whether a ball meant for him had hit the fellow, or if he had tripped as well.

"The officer's down!" Oliver heard himself scream wildly, in reference to the Colonel, and not knowing that he was the only one who could hear the cry. He watched as the Colonel was lifted and half-dragged, half carried, to one of the last boats to leave from the riverbank.

"Don't let them get away!" someone screamed in a bloody fervour.

"Kill John Bull and his band of murdering thieves!" cried another.

Oliver reached the riverbank as the last of the boats pulled clear of the protection of the black limestone outcropping and into the river's current. He stood there and fired aimlessly at the vessels, which were quickly leaving effective range. Mindlessly, he fired, reloaded and fired again, to what effect, he did not know.

Out of the corner of his eye, he saw a man lying in the dirt, a growing stain betraying the fact that he had not just tripped and would quickly rise. The cut of his clothes suggested that this man was reasonably well off. Perhaps he should make sure that the man was beyond help.

He rushed over to the fallen man and shook him firmly by the shoulder. "Mister, Mister, can you hear my voice?"

As he jostled the man where he lay, he noticed a piece of paper in a pocket. However, before Oliver could remove it, a figure burst into his line of vision and bent down to the body. Without ceremony, this newcomer flipped the body on its side and reached into the fancy coat pocket, pulling out a folded document that appeared to have illustrations on the piece Oliver could see.

"Do you live near here?" the man shouted, above the din of victorious American revellers. Getting no response, he tried once again. "I asked you boy, if you live far from here."

This time, the question registered. "No, sir – that is, I live just down that road there," he replied, pointing down a rutted road that led away from the Niagara River.

"Here then," the man shouted, handing Oliver a document with the same hand with which he had freed it from the dead man's pocket. "I'm sure this'll have the man's name and where he lives. Find his family and let them know he died a hero to his country."

The newcomer rose to leave, and Oliver was aware that their eyes met and their gaze locked momentarily. The man seemed about to say more when several militiamen, intent in their celebrating, insisted upon including Oliver and dragged him away from the scene.

Oliver looked back to see the stranger staring after him, but soon thought no more of it as he became one with the mob that surged back toward the bank of the Niagara. There, they all became caught up in celebration and taunting the backs of the fleeing British, the insults become more ribald with each passing moment.

The dead man and his letter soon melted into Oliver's subconscious and were forgotten.

★ ★ ★

By now, the British had reached the Upper Canada side of the Niagara River near Fort Erie, and the American men stopped firing and celebrating they became fully conscious of the results of the raid. They stood quietly staring across the water at the men who had escaped their wrath with all their stores. The U.S. Navy's schooner, the Zephyr, was merrily burning down to the waterline near shore and the militia and naval barracks and guardhouse were but smouldering embers.

Oliver finally sat down hard upon the ground, exhaustion overtaking him as the bloodlust and celebration died. He looked around, surveying the destruction all about. The moans and screams of the injured and the dying and stench of the loosed bowels of the already dead assailed his senses as he looked upon the broken and bleeding bodies lying in the dust on Black Rock's main street. Almost all were their own men, for the British had carried off most of theirs as they left.

"Well fought, young Davidson," said an older man, clapping him on the shoulder. "Well fought."

"I know so many of these men," Oliver muttered in reply, although the neighbour had already moved away. He rose to his feet and stumbled off into the woods, where he surrendered to the simultaneous urges to vomit and cry, allowing the horror to wash over him and away.

When the tears ceased, Oliver sat up and looked back out of his hiding place into the street. "And all of this over a few boatloads of stores," he mumbled wearily to no one. "If the militia had but arrived a few minutes later, no one would be dead or hurt, on either side, and all that would have been lost is a few boatloads of stores."

Oliver rose to his feet, feeling somewhat ashamed that he had been overtaken by the same bloodlust that had infected the others. He looked about him one last time before he noticed that he still had the gun in his hand. He stared at it stonily for several long minutes and then tossed it into the street before turning away from the scene for good. "This is yours, whoever you were," he said aloud. "I only hope you're still alive."

"Is this the glory of war of which our leaders speak?" he asked the still-settling, smoky, dusty air about him, as he trudged, drained and sullen, for home.

Chapter One

Jeremy van Hijser approached his home near the Twenty on the King's Highway that shadowed the Niagara Escarpment. In spite of the late autumn cold, he was soaked with perspiration and bone weary from yet another hunting foray that could at best be described as moderately successful. Over the span of these past several November days – of how many, he was not exactly certain – he had shot but one deer near the Thirty and sold it to an army unit that happened by on its way to Shipman's Corners to re-supply the British contingent there. They had taken both the meat and the hide and, while hardly profitable, at least saving Jeremy from the onerous task of hauling the carcass back home.

The hunting in this area was not what it once had been, or at least not what Jeremy remembered it to be. There were just too many people about in these troubled times; British and American regulars and militia, the Indians fighting each on their respective side, and the men of the Canadian Volunteers, whose role seemed at least to Canadian settlers to punish the personal enemies of their leader, Joseph Willcocks. With all these various groups roaming Niagara, and all requiring food and pelts, much of whatever game had not been killed off had fled for safer territories.

On this trip as on all recent occasions, Jeremy had been paid in military scrip, which promised to pay the bearer at some time in the future. Hopefully that would be some time soon, before this interminable war ended, he thought wryly. This war, which had begun in 1812, was now about to end another year and his cash funds were shaky.

The scrip was considered by most to be worthless, but was traded for goods and services that could not be bartered. Often, those transactions were discounted to allow for the uncertain value of the pieces of paper. About the only places where the scrip was worth its face value was at military establishments, but little could be purchased there except occasionally powder and lead for musket balls, and then only if the particular unit had supplies to spare. More than a year of warfare in the Canadas and overtaxed by the seemingly infinite war against Napoleon on the Continent, the British were hard pressed to supply their own troops these days and were increasingly unlikely to sell to civilians.

More often than not, simple barter was being used to complete transactions, especially among neighbours who could keep running tallies. Coins or gold were demanded in the case of strangers whose trustworthiness was not known.

Jeremy trudged wearily along the King's Highway toward his home. Before he reached the final bend before his destination, however, he turned left the muddy trail and climbed the Mountain and cut across the slope toward the rear of his small two-room cabin. Experience had taught him the hard way not to approach head on. As long as the Americans occupied Niagara, there would always be people who might yet be looking for him with scores to settle.

He crept almost noiselessly down until he reached the well that sat a short distance from the back of the cabin. As always when he passed the stone structure with the bucket atop it, he could not help but remember the woman who had owned this house before him. They had loved each other with a passion and even been engaged until the renegade Dorian Williamson murdered her. That had only been a few months past and the pain of the memory was yet fresh. At least he had killed the bastard without a flicker of remorse and sent him to Hell where he belonged.

And that was why Jeremy now edged his way carefully along the east wall; his senses alert to any anomaly that might justify his inexplicable feeling that something was out of place. Once at the forward corner, he peered cautiously around, screened by the bush growing there.

As difficult as it seemed for him to believe, Williamson had friends, or at least allies. They would make attempts on his life from time to time, thinking they must eventually catch Jeremy with his guard down.

His caution had paid off. As he unslung his custom German-made over/under from his shoulder, Jeremy studied a figure which sat quite unconcerned on the worn old plank bench in front, an even older gun resting carelessly across his knees, as though he had no intention of using it, or at the very least had little experience at it.

Jeremy studied the trespasser carefully, attempting to take the fellow's measure, although there seemed little enough in the young man to measure. Indeed, the chap sat tossing pebbles nonchalantly toward the road and stared off into the near distance as he waited, seemingly unconcerned, for something or someone. To all appearances he seemed rather harmless, but Jeremy rarely had strangers come to call upon him here and he had learned that appearances could be deceptive and dangerous indeed.

Jeremy took a moment to study the stranger. The young fellow appeared to completely guileless, a farm boy or such, and he could not help but wonder what this apparent child was doing here on his property. To all appearances, he seemed reasonably intelligent, having none of the dull appearance in the eyes that one normally associated with an idiot. He was good-looking, as Jeremy understood the concept, with a strong chin, brown wavy hair, and green eyes. It was difficult to guess his age, for his innocence cried child, but his well-defined muscles, broad shoulders and firm strong hands spoke of some years of hard work already behind him.

Whoever he was, Jeremy was not about to take a chance. For all he knew, the youth on his doorstep might be a new recruit belonging to one of the groups that Jeremy counted as enemies and might be here to make a name for himself. His inexperience could well be quite dangerous as his reactions would be unpredictable.

"Put your gun on the ground and then step away from the front of the house," Jeremy said evenly as he aimed his own weapon at the intruder from his place of concealment.

"What?" the young man gasped as he started, and then fairly flew from the bench. In the shock of the moment, he seemed to forget all about the gun he was holding, for it clattered loudly onto the rocks at his feet. "Don't shoot, wherever you are…whoever you are! I did nothing wrong! I'll leave if you want me to. Just please don't shoot!"

The expression of absolute terror on the trespasser's face made Jeremy want to laugh out loud as he stepped cautiously from the brush, looking about to see if there might be others and all the while keeping a careful eye on the boy. "I'll be the judge of that!" he snapped, somehow maintaining a straight face.

The youth visibly seemed to screw up all the courage he had yet available and risked a question of his own. "Excuse me, sir, but would you be Jeremy van Hijser?" the youth asked timidly.

"Never mind who I might be," Jeremy replied evenly. "What's most important at the moment is who might you be?"

"My name is Oliver Davidson," replied the young man with a gulp. "And if you're Jeremy van Hijser, I'm your cousin from Black Rock."

The last caused Jeremy to stop dead in his tracks. "My cousin?" he repeated dumbly. "As far as I know, I have no cousins. Explain yourself."

"Well, the truth be told, I'm not completely certain what our relationship is but I'm your second or third cousin, however such counts are made but my great, great, great grandfather – actually – I'm afraid I've forgotten how many greats there are – was the younger brother of the man that inherited the family business and then died of consumption or something." The young man blurted out in one rambling sentence, seeming almost to believe he might die if he did not rush the explanation to Jeremy's ears.

"That's quite some story," Jeremy replied, scratching his head in mild disbelief.

However, it did have a ring of truth to it. His family had once been fairly wealthy, owning a large tract of land in New Amsterdam that was based on a system much like the French Seigniorial. They had managed to keep the land after the British stole it from them and renamed the colony New York. When his ancestor came back from fighting for England in the French and Indian Wars, he found that he had been bankrupted by the incompetent and larcenous manager he had left in charge. As a result, he took a land grant in Niagara as payment for his service in the wars and they had been here since.

"How do you come to know of me? I've never heard of you."

"My mother kept track of such things," Oliver replied. "Don't ask me how, but she knows of all of the few relatives we have left in our entire extended family. When I found myself in dire straits at home, she sent me to Beaverdams to find you, since you're the closest relative I have in the area. I looked all about there for you, but then I met a neighbour who told me you'd moved away. Why did you leave?"

"When my wife and unborn baby died and then some traitors burned the farm buildings, I felt that there was little reason left to stay," answered Jeremy plainly and with a finality that brooked no further explanation.

"Well, no one seemed to know where you'd gone until a soldier in green came looking for me and told me where I'd be likely to find you."

"Good for you, and how nice of your mother to send you to someone who had no reason to accept your sudden appearance but for blood relation, a thin reason in my opinion," Jeremy remarked wryly. "I don't know what kind of trouble you're in, but I'm not certain you'll be safe here with me. In any case, I haven't the time to be minding the youngsters of others."

Oliver bridled at being referred to as a youngster. Was he not after all a man now, blooded in battle and out on his own? "You needn't worry about minding me. I'm quite able to look after myself and I fully expect to carry my own weight."

"I'm quite sure you can, Oliver, and in that you'd have no choice, but I've always preferred to work alone. I hunt by myself and then, when I'm done hunting, I live by myself. I've no place in this tiny cabin for any others, family or no." Jeremy plodded heavily to the front door and dropped to the bench beside the youth. "I honestly don't think I can help you except to give you one piece of advice. Turn around and head back home. Upper Canada is no place for a young American to be wandering around in." He sat back with finality, all the while studying the boy.

"I can't," Oliver replied, suddenly apparently deflated by this unexpected turn of events. "I can't go back home."

Jeremy sat slowly forward, mild surprise showing upon his exhausted and weather-beaten face. "And why would that be? Your folks toss you out? Are you a shirker perhaps?"

Oliver obviously bridled at that question. "I wasn't tossed out and I'm certainly no shirker. I worked hard and kept my Ma and myself well enough. And one way or another, I intend to send her enough money to keep her going in my absence."

"I don't quite know how you'll do that," Jeremy sighed. "What little money I get is usually in British military scrip, and I don't imagine they'll thank your mother for trying to buy things with it on the other side of the Niagara."

"I'll figure something out," Oliver asserted. "One way or another I must, for there's someone back home that wants to kill me, and I don't even know the why of it, or who he is, or whether there is but the one." The young man then proceeded to tell Jeremy the entire tale of the battle, the letter, and the threatening ultimatum.

"Why don't you just give them what they want?" Jeremy suggested.

Oliver looked off toward the road and seemed for a moment to be peering along through the trees that lined the route. "I would if I knew what it was," he muttered quietly. "But I have no inkling of it. I think the other man that spoke to me over the body may be the one who has what they want, for he searched the man's clothes, but they'll never believe me. They seemed quite certain that I have possession whatever it might be."

"Well, Oliver," Jeremy sighed, "I guess I'll have to let you stay here until I can figure out what to do with you. You can bunk down in the back storage room. I prefer to sleep in the front, where I can reach the door quickly if necessary." He turned to go in and then stopped. "I have a question, which just now occurred to me."

"And what's that?"

"The battle at Black Rock was in July. Where have you been for the past four months?" Jeremy asked, the realization of the time discrepancy causing him to experience a sudden pang of suspicion.

Oliver blushed strongly, quite obviously embarrassed. "I didn't know exactly where to find you, for my mother didn't either. She knew only that your family had settled in Niagara," Oliver explained. "I was never sure whom I could trust to ask, and when I did finally question someone, they either didn't know you or knew you well but didn't know where you live or didn't seem to think they should tell me. The closest answer I could get is that you travelled for unpredictable periods of time and no one was sure where you could be found at any given moment. It would appear that I'm not the only one who isn't sure whom he can trust."

Jeremy chuckled, but there was more regret than amusement in the sound. It was good to know that his neighbours still looked out for his welfare. "War does that to people, especially this one," he said simply. "Now, why don't we head inside?"

"But why..." Oliver started, but his question hung in the air unfinished, for it was interrupted by a loud report, followed by the distinct impression of something flying near his head. He sensed, more than heard, the thud of musket ball bouncing from the sturdy wood of the cabin.

Oliver stood rooted in place, seemingly not understanding what was happening.

Jeremy took a firm hold of his coat and he dove to the ground in front of the cabin, rolling to one side and lying there in the dirt, straining to determine from where the sound had issued, a task made all the more difficult by the repeated echoes. He scanned about the area, looking for any sign that would give away the source of what had obviously been a gun shot.

"Over there," Oliver whispered, pointing to a face barely visible above a fallen tree, not much more than fifty yards away. The assailant's position had been given away by traces of smoke which yet drifted in the nearly still air above the unruly tuft of hair which now could be seen to stand out stubbornly atop the head.

Jeremy barely nodded in reply. He put his hand momentarily on Oliver's shoulder to signal that the younger man stay in position and then silently crawled away on his belly as their attacker ducked below the cover of the deadfall to reload his weapon.

He approached quietly and barely heard the pop of the stopper as the would-be assassin pulled it from whatever container held his gunpowder just as Jeremy gained the cover of the trees. He waited momentarily to listen for any sign that the man had been alerted to his movement. When he heard the rasp of steel on steel, he knew the ball and patch were being rammed home in through the barrel of the man's musket. He would be ready to fire once more in just a second, he thought.

Jeremy edged forward through the trees with agonizing caution, carefully watching the placement of his feet and the way ahead at the same time. A snapped twig or rustle of dead leaves might, if his assailant were paying attention, give away his position and cause great risk to his life. Although it was doubtless a short time in actuality, it seemed to take an eternity before he found himself positioned at the one end of the fallen tree, looking down the assassin's barricade from end to end. He saw the object of his hunt couched there; a dirty little man carefully placing his musket on the tree in preparation for taking another shot.

The man seemed extremely confident considering that he did not seem to have noticed Jeremy's absence. He was taking his time adjusting his body position and aiming, a definite advantage from Jeremy's point of view. For one thing, the shooter was concentrating so completely on the shot that he was not paying sufficient attention to his surroundings to notice Jeremy. For another, a calm man was reasonably predictable. It would have been difficult to gauge his actions had he been nervous.

Jeremy decided to press his luck no further. He brought up his over/under slowly and carefully into firing position. He hated to shoot from here so low to the ground, for the kick could be considerable and it could knock him of balance. However it simply could not be helped. To stand up would risk extra noise, since it would require him to push up through the dry branches of the young trees in order to acquire a proper for the shooting stance.

He slowly pulled back the hammer so that he would not throw off his aim. When it clicked into place, he immediately squeezed the trigger evenly until the hammer dropped forcefully onto the flint. This resulted in a deafening report and smoke billowed around him as the powder exploded, sending the rifle slug flying toward the would-be assassin's hiding place.

Before Jeremy's missile could find its target, however, it became apparent that the would-be assassin had heard some sound, possibly the click of the hammer locking into position, causing him to break from his concentration. He unexpectedly whipped his head around, a movement that startled Jeremy.

Jeremy heard a crack as the slug blew a small branch from the fallen tree. He swore under his breath at his luck, certain that the shot had entirely missed its mark. Then, however, a curse issued from Jeremy's would-be target as the shot deflected from the same branch and somehow still managed to find living flesh.

The man fell back onto the ground and then, still cursing loudly, clambered tentatively to his feet, using the deadfall to help pull him up. Then he seemed all at once to remember his situation and realize how exposed his position was and he pushed off from the log, staggering away as quickly as he could down the road in the direction of Shipman's Corners while holding onto his stomach.

Jeremy's intention was to give chase but, as he tried to stand up, he became entangled in overhead branches. He lowered himself back to his knee and pulled out a new cartridge for his gun, ripping it open with his teeth and pouring the powder in through the muzzle, followed closely by the ball. But was all for naught for, as Jeremy drove the ball home with the rod, he could hear the pounding of horse's hooves issuing from around the road's curve not far distant from his cabin.

Chapter Two

Confident that the danger had passed with the sounds of the fleeing horse, Oliver jumped up from where he had been lying and started to run for the road. But Jeremy's voice from the brush cut him short.

"Where do you think you're going, idiot?" The sound reverberated off the escarpment, treating Oliver to multiple repetitions of the final "…idiot?"

The younger man turned to see Jeremy still kneeling where he was when he reloaded, gun at the ready and looking in the direction the fleeing attempted assassin.

"You're not going to let him escape!?" Oliver shouted back at his cousin in disbelief.

"And just what is it you intend to do?" Jeremy replied, a slight grin showing on his face. "Do you think that you'll be able to run down that horse we just heard?"

"I thought I might be able to get out to the bend and shoot at him in the straight stretch, if you hadn't stopped me," the younger man replied petulantly.

Jeremy could not help but laugh out loud at this remark. "Shoot at him with what? Do you intend to reload your gun on the run?"

Oliver pointed his gun toward the ground and pulled the trigger. There was noise as the powder exploded in the pan and smoke resulting from that explosion, but nothing else happened. No kick as a ball was launched by the reaction and no hole in the ground just beyond where it would have exited. He looked sheepishly at his gun barrel and then back at his cousin, who now was roaring with laughter, a result of both the release of tension and the look on Oliver's face as he realized he had an empty weapon in his hand. The younger cousin's face turned a flaming crimson as he realized his mistake.

"How did you know that the musket was empty?"

"Quite simply," replied Jeremy, still laughing. "Look."

Oliver followed his cousin's finger to the place where he had been seated and where he had dropped his musket when Jeremy had startled him. There, just beyond the rocks in an open patch of dirt, lay the ball."

"I hope this has taught you three things, young Oliver."

"And what might they be?

"First of all, don't drop your gun on the ground," Jeremy explained, his laughter now calmed to a grin. "And second, make sure you keep the muzzle up."

"And what might the third be?" demanded Oliver, becoming angry now as his embarrassment gave way to annoyance with Jeremy for the fun he was having at his expense.

"Third, make sure that you cut the right size patches for the ball, so it won't fall out quite so easily."

"Thanks," replied the younger cousin petulantly. Then his expression abruptly changed to one of puzzlement. "How did they know when to strike? How did that man know to wait for you on this particular day if, as you say, no one is quite certain when you'll be back?"

"I truly have no answer to that," Jeremy replied, shrugging his shoulders as if to dismiss the question. "It might be that someone saw me earlier and raced ahead to tell my enemies. It is also a possibility that he merely sat there for as long as it should take before I should return home."

"He must truly hate you if he would have that much patience to make an end of you."

"Possibly," Jeremy replied, grinning. "Else the man was paid a fair coin to do so."

Oliver stood as if lost in thought at that remark.

"Well, I'll hand you this, young Oliver – a coward you're not. However, a brave corpse will be of use to no one, least of all you. If you had done that in battle, or if that man had brought help, you'd be lying before me bleeding from a dozen holes. And what's worse, you'd be leaving me here to fend for myself." Jeremy lowered his over/under and waved to Oliver. "Come inside. I believe we need to discuss some matters."

The two entered the cabin and closed the heavy plank door. Jeremy directed his guest to a simple wooden chair near the lowly banked fireplace. He himself remained standing, leaning casually on the mantle.

"Now, let me see if I understand. A fellow combatant removed a piece of paper with a name and address and gave it to you." Jeremy knit his brow as he recalled the tale. "It would seem possible that the ball wasn't meant for me but for you."

Oliver blanched at these words. "For me? Why would you think that?"

"Well, like you said, nobody knew when I'd be back, so it's more likely that you were tracked here. And that someone who tracked you here or their agent believes that paper to be something more important than you describe. As you've told me, someone threatened your life over it, and now you can't return home. Have I missed anything?" he asked.

"No, that's how it was exactly."

"And now I'm to take you on for some unknown length of time, until all of this sorts itself out, is that right?"

Hearing the irony and annoyance that had crept into Jeremy's voice, Oliver's stubborn streak came immediately to the fore. "You needn't worry about me. I can carry my own weight."

Jeremy stepped away from the fireplace and strode to a window. He said nothing as he looked outside, the world beyond the walls of his cabin returned to its natural quiet self. "I'm quite sure you can," he sighed, "but that isn't really the problem at hand for, you see, I quite doubt that you'll be any safer here with me." He turned once more to look Oliver in the eyes. "What just happened outside there, a few minutes ago, is a more than an occasional occurrence here."

"Why? Who are they?"

Jeremy turned another chair about for himself so that the low back was facing him and he swung his leg in an effortless arc onto the seat. "That could be quite the long tale. Have you ever heard of the Canadian Volunteers, led by one Joseph Willcocks?"

Oliver nodded, obviously puzzled by the question and where it might be heading. "They're considered quite the heroes on our side of the river."

Jeremy grimaced. "I quite imagine they are. But on this side they're referred to as traitors, for most of them lived here under the protection of the Crown and on the Crown's free land. But worse than that, they aren't mere soldiers for the enemy. Much worse, they use the protection of the U.S. troops to plunder farms and wreak havoc upon the personal enemies of Mr. Willcocks. He was, at one time, a member of the Upper Canada Legislature, you may know, and started out the war serving under British General Brock at Queenston Heights."

"But why are they after you?" Oliver asked. "Were you once one of this Mr. Willcocks' political enemies?"

"No. And my problem isn't so much with Mr. Willcocks himself, although I keep careful track of his whereabouts when he's in the vicinity. My problem is actually with a particularly vile splinter group of the Volunteers." Jeremy stopped to gather his thoughts and looked down at the floor as unwanted memories flooded in.

"The blackguards of which I speak took me prisoner and tortured me, burned down my farm, desecrated the graves of my wife and stillborn child, and murdered my fiancée. This very cabin was her home." Jeremy stopped, obviously distressed by the telling and he choked back the tears that burned his eyes. "She was going about, inviting neighbours to our wedding when…" He had to stop once again to gather his composure. "…when those bastards set upon her like the pack of mangy curs that they are."

Jeremy yet knew the unspeakable grief that had come over him when the local pastor told him of what had happened, a grief magnified ever more greatly when he was the man hinted at the condition of the body. He also remembered running blindly away and shutting himself off from the world, at first not eating and then existing like an animal until a storm had brought his life – and his anger – into focus.

He put his head momentarily down onto his arms, which rested upon the back of the chair. Oliver made no sound, allowing him the dignity of his grief.

Finally the older man looked up once again. "I dealt with their leader and much of their group was decimated by the American soldiers, for this bunch had become too evil for even them. But another leader emerged, a man I met while imprisoned, one of those who had beaten me daily. He had no trouble recruiting others willing to be equally as inhuman towards others for the promise of booty."

"And they are still after you?" Oliver asked. "Why? Are you yet a thorn in their side?"

"No," Jeremy replied, the word coming out as an ironic snicker. "The leader can't stand that I won. I retired to this property and have tried to remain uninvolved in the war and its more disgusting and dishonourable side but, as it turns out, there is a personal vendetta involved well."

Jeremy looked up at his cousin, an enigmatic smile on his lips. "It seems the original leader – who I killed – was the new leader's brother-in-law."

★ ★ ★

Oliver had no immediate reaction to what he had been told. In truth, he was momentarily stunned by both the content of Jeremy's tale and the emotion with which it was presented.

He studied at length this relative who he only just met while the man succumbed to his memories. Like he himself, Jeremy did not look at all like the stereotypical Dutch boy. He had a darkly tanned and weathered face and light brown hair with hazel brown eyes, not the fair skin, blond hair and blue eyes that he continually heard he himself should have had as the descendent of a Dutchman. Jeremy was a hair over six feet tall and was plainly muscular without being obvious and his boyish good looks had not been diminished despite his twenty-seven years of frontier life

Finally, after what he considered to be a reasonable amount of time, Oliver felt he had to break the awkward silence.

"To stay here would yet be a less certain death than if I were to return home," he said with quiet desperation. "At least we can each fight the others' enemies together, without endangering my mother further."

Jeremy once again studied his younger cousin. "Very well, you can stay with me until we can think of a more permanent arrangement for you. In the meantime, you can hunt with me and do most of the heavy lifting."

"You want me to do the heavy lifting?" Oliver asked with feigned disbelief. "I thought perhaps you'd wish me to carry my share."

Jeremy laughed. "If you are to be my burden, you will do as I say," he said with mock gravity. "Of course, if you consider the work load to be too much for a boy like you, you can always ask your mother to find other relatives to inconvenience."

"Very well," answered Oliver with a mischievous grin. "This 'boy' will carry the load so the old man can rest his tired bones."

★ ★ ★

Only a mile from Jeremy's house, a man looked anxiously down the road from his perch on a large rock that occupied the corner of some farmer's land. That he could sit at all was a marvel, for it seemed to him that he had been waiting interminably for just this chance. And waiting had never exactly been his strong suit. With this paid assassin whom he had brought up from Pennsylvania for just this purpose, he would finally conclude this particular piece of business. Then he could carry on with the task his brother-in-law had started – becoming rich and powerful and putting into their place those who had looked down their noses upon him over the years before the war.

Besides, there was another item that needed attending to and he needed to attend to them before the others did. It would have helped if only he had known who the others might be.

The sound of a horse approaching broke into these thoughts. He stood up, peering down the road impatiently and waiting for the source of the sound to materialize from among the trees in the rapidly developing twilight. After what seemed like an eternity to the anxious man, he saw the rider hesitantly approaching. It was obvious that something had gone wrong, for there seemed to be none of the bombast that the assassin had displayed as he was leaving.

"What the devil's the matter with you?" he bellowed at the man, grabbing hold of the horse's reins as it seemed it might walk right past him. "I told you to come right back and tell me about it when you were through! Now, you've been gone this half day, with me waiting all the while!"

When the rider did not reply, the waiting man lost what little remained of his temper. "Well, is he dead at last?"

The horse nickered in annoyance at the stranger's tone and the feel of a strange hand upon the reins. But the only sound that issued from the throat of the rider was a groan as he pitched seemingly in a slow-motion arc from his mount and landed heavily on the ground. The assassin for whom the waiting man had paid so dearly and counted upon for so long lay there upon the ground staring up at his irate employer. Only an expression of pain was evident in his face and the blood which appeared to have ceased flowing long before was glaringly plain on the whole front of his shirt.

"Where have you been?" the employer shouted, ignoring the obvious suffering of the fallen man. "I sent you to kill van Hijser more than five hours ago! That was long enough to kill half the people in Niagara! Did you decide that a celebration was in order and go drinking?"

The injured man managed with great effort and pain to roll over just far enough to spit a mouthful of blood on the other's boots. He insolently wiped his mouth with his sleeve and as his arm flopped back down to his side, he grumbled through a sea of pain. "The only thing that I've been drinking…is my own blood, you bastard!" he managed before gasping and groaning heavily at the agony of effort. "The man had someone with him…one of them…managed to catch me…lucky deflection."

"Well, where have you been since then?" the man in charge demanded, without any trace of pity. "And did you get van Hijser?"

"If you must know…it takes rather…a long time to climb…back onto the horse after falling off…unh…when you've been gut shot. And then…figure that over the countless times… I fell off and had to… climb on all over again. And no, you bastard…he's still alive. I'm done for now…makes me wonder…why I even came back."

"No doubt it was to give me back the money I paid you to kill the man," his employer said as he stalked angrily toward the stricken man. Kneeling, he reached down and coldly opened the wounded man's jacket, pulling out the cash that he had seen placed there earlier. "You failed at the job I'd given you so I believe this is yet rightfully mine."

Then the man stepped back and stood looking down at the suffering would-be assassin, his eyes displaying an almost demonic rage with the dying man for failing to meet his objective.

"Aren't you going…to do something for me? Or do you intend…just leave me lying here?" the man on the ground whispered, his voice now barely audible, his ability to speak diminishing by the second.

"Of course." Calmly the man pulled his pistol from his belt and levelled it at the injured man. "I'll put you out of your misery. And, I might add, mine as well." He casually pulled the trigger and, as the echoes of the thunderous report faded into the forest, he stood staring down the road toward the cabin he could not possibly see from his vantage point. He absent-mindedly cleaned and reloaded the pistol and tucked it back into his belt.

Then he leaned down and rifled through the man's clothes until his fingers came into contact with that which he had been searching for. He withdrew his hand and looked at the bag of gold coins. Then he smiled wryly and dropped them inside his own shirt.

"You're not immortal, van Hijser," he muttered bitterly. "I will see you dead yet."

Chapter Three

While he had the help available to him, Jeremy had decided that it would be the perfect opportunity to enlarge the old well. He had been intending to do so since he had acquired the property but there was simply too much of labour involved for just one man. Especially in light of the short periods of time he had before leaving on his hunts each time.

In addition to the physically daunting nature of the task, every time he approached it, he was deluged with memories of Elizabeth. Of the men she had fought off just as he had arrived there. Of her smile and the laughter that had accompanied their tasks about it. Of the passion that had grown rapidly to true affection for her and the horror of returning home to find that she had been murdered by his arch enemy as she went about telling neighbours of their upcoming wedding.

And the terrifying things that had happened to his mind in the aftermath as he withdrew from the world, almost allowing himself to die at the hands of the elements. And as he thought of these things, he could feel the paralysing anxiety once again taking over his very being.

He counted upon the help of another working alongside him to distract the demons and hold him to his task.

Jeremy had sent Oliver down into the hole to dig shovels full of muck from the sides above the water line while standing upon a trio of wedged planks. Each time the bucket was filled Jeremy hauled it to the top and poured the soil on top of the small and now barren garden he kept behind the cabin. It was a time-consuming chore, becoming ever slower when they finished cleaning the well and began to dredge the bottom of the well to deepen it. Then would come the added back-breaking task of clearing and possibly breaking such rock as they might encounter.

After what seemed an eternity of labouring in the dark hole, Jeremy called down. "The sun is setting and it will soon be too dark to find the hole, much less work in it. Come on out, Oliver. It's time to surrender to the night."

Jeremy and Oliver abandoned the task and headed to the cabin for the night. They could smell what Jeremy termed his "eternal pot" even before they opened the door. This was the answer to Jeremy's desire not to do any more cooking than was absolutely necessary. He continuously kept a pot of stew warming in the fireplace, sometimes for days at a time, whenever he was near home. He added meat, vegetables or water as the consistency demanded and availability of ingredients allowed. Added to this, he always kept bread in various degrees of freshness on the table to dunk in the result which sometimes appeared generally unappetizing but always satisfied his hunger.

They settled in at the table, which consisted of nothing more than several planks nailed onto cross-pieces, with four legs attached to the entire assembly. Seated upon the backless benches which sat one to a side of the table, they each tore a piece from the remainder of the bread loaf and wolfed it down along with the stew which had been ladled onto old tin plates. Had anyone seen the men devour the modest meal, one would think that the time elapsed since their last meal could be measured in weeks.

Swallowing the last bite of his supper, Jeremy leaned back in his chair and looked thoughtfully off into the distance. "Have you any theory as to what that piece of paper may have been?" he asked idly, not actually expecting an answer. "Oh, by the way, would you like some tea?"

Oliver nodded. "Yes, thank you. As to the paper, it may well have been a map of some sort, or a diagram," Oliver offered through his final mouthful. "I thought I saw some lions on the page." He swallowed hard to clear the last morsel.

"Perhaps they were of a military nature," Jeremy said thoughtfully. He shook his head lightly as if dismissing it from his mind. "In any case, I doubt we shall ever know."

"True. It's not likely that Mr. George MacPhail will rise from his grave to tell us," Oliver sighed, then wiping his mouth with his arm.

Jeremy perked up at his cousin's words. "Did you say George MacPhail?" When Oliver nodded, he added, "George MacPhail, who lives just outside of Black Rock down by the small creek?"

Again Oliver nodded. "Yes, that would be the man. Did you know him?"

"I can't truly say that I knew him, as one might know a friend or neighbour. But, before the battle at Beaverdams, I would sometimes hunt on the other side of the river. In my travels, I occasionally came upon stories or pieces of information that I would pass on to Captain Fitzgibbon."

"You mean you were a spy?" Oliver broke in, a youthful romanticism leaving him just a little wide-eyed at the prospect of having a daring spy in the family, even if it had been to the benefit of the British.

Jeremy noticed the water was hot. He rose and poured some into the old teapot that his late fiancée, Elizabeth, had left behind in the cabin. Using a battered tin strainer, he poured the tea into tin cups he had acquired from the military. No dainty china for him. At any rate, he'd broken most of the more fragile items that he had found in a matter of weeks after moving in.

"Not a spy really," Jeremy replied, smiling at the younger man's youthful romanticism and his deflated appearance at the denial. "I was more of a gossipmonger, bringing back in my own time the whispers I heard and letting the British military men sort out their significance."

Oliver took a careful sip of the tea, not wanting to be scalded by it. As he pulled his lips away, he grimaced. "What on earth is that?!"

His cousin laughed heartily. "Oh, hadn't I warned you?" he asked with mock innocence. "I guess I should have, but then you might not have tried it. I know it takes some getting used to."

"What is it?"

"Hemlock," replied Jeremy simply. "That's why I didn't tell you right off. It tastes bitter at first but one gets accustomed to it rather quickly. It's been rather difficult to get our hands on real tea of late, what with the war and all. Although, I suppose, the wealthy aren't doing without. Here," he added, sliding over a small bowl. "Put some of this in it. It' will help, I promise."

"And what is this?" asked Oliver, suspiciously eyeing the brownish crystals in the bowl.

"It's sugar made from maple sap. Have you never had it before?" Seeing Oliver shake his head, he continued. I traded half a deer for that last winter and that bit's what's left. Very dear it is, if you'll ignore the play on words, so I use it sparingly."

Oliver stirred a tiny bit into the hemlock tea. He nodded in appreciation.

"So how did you meet Mr. MacPhail?" he asked, curiously pursuing the previous line of questioning. "Surely, he didn't travel in the circles or inns frequented by hunters and the like."

"No, George was more of a solid contact, an actual spy," Jeremy replied. Every few months, I would go to his house to sell him venison or whatever I had, and he would supply me with information to take back."

"Why did he buy game from you?" Oliver asked, obviously puzzled. "Mr. MacPhail was a fair hunter in his own right."

"He resold them," Jeremy replied matter-of-factly. "I couldn't very well sell to the U.S. military, now could I? Even if we weren't yet at war. Your government has never looked kindly on the British since your revolution." He laughed. "In fact, if any of the men had taken ill, I expect I would have been shot as agent trying to poison them. It was just easier that way and it gave George an extra income."

"When was the last time you saw him?" Oliver asked.

"Back in the spring," Jeremy replied. "I wasn't able to safely cross the river without a chance of being recognized once my trouble began with the Volunteers."

"So the paper I saw was probably some important information he was waiting to hand over," Oliver said, his excitement obviously building. "And that man that gave me the address was trying to fool someone into thinking that was on the piece of paper!"

"Likely," Jeremy concurred, nodding his head slowly. "But yet someone else, who knew or suspected that the dead man was a spy, saw the exchange and thought that you had it now. It looks like you've been tossed into the middle of something, cousin."

"So now what are we to do?"

"I think that, at first light, we should head for Beaverdams and find Captain Fitzgibbon, so that he'll be warned his spy is dead. That way, no one can send false information in MacPhail's name, in case anyone knew of his, er, hobby shall we say?" Jeremy answered thoughtfully. "But, when we get there, don't tell them you're an American, agreed?"

"I think that I should be able to remember that," Oliver replied with a grin.

★ ★ ★

"This is the part of my day that I always enjoy most," Jeremy sighed, as he stepped out of the house, the early morning sunlight barely filtering through the multicolour late autumn leaves. "As negative as I may seem at times, I can find no wrong with the things not made by man."

Oliver looked over his cousin as he stood taking in the morning air. While he himself carried his gun and wore a skinning knife in his belt, Jeremy wore what Oliver considered to be quite an arsenal.

In Jeremy's hand was the ever-present German over/under. Hanging within easy reach in a sling behind his head designed especially for that purpose was a steel tomahawk, honed to a razor edge. In the sash he wore about his waste were an ornately etched pistol that he explained he had "inherited" from a man who tried to kill him, a knife, and a bayonet in a homemade scabbard.

"Were you armed thus when I met you yesterday?" Oliver asked.

"I'm always armed thus when I travel," Jeremy answered. "You mean you hadn't noticed? It seems to me that the very first lesson you have to learn is to notice the things about you, but especially those weapons a man carries when you meet him. Your life may depend upon it. Now, we're off to Beaverdams. Normally I'd take the trails along the Mountain as we call it, but I want to let Mrs. Jarvis know that I'm off again. She gets a certain level of comfort from knowing when I'm gone, for some reason."

"How would she know you were back?" Oliver asked, honestly curious.

"I always stop there before I come back here to the cabin," Jeremy replied. "Her husband passed on recently and I like to bring her some small game when I return."

"I'd like to get to know your neighbours," Oliver sighed wistfully. "Back home, I knew everyone for miles around."

Jeremy gave the young man a sad smile. "And so it was where I lived in Beaverdams as well. But things are a bit different here," he sighed, looking off into the distance. "And the times are different, too. No one is quite certain what side their neighbours are on at times, for there are many recent American immigrants here. They came for the free land and lack of taxes, but now that the United States is trying to take us from the British, many of the newcomers have cast their lot with the country they abandoned." His eyes visibly clouded over. "And some just take whatever side looks like it's winning at any given moment in time or will enrich them the quickest or frightens them most."

"Well, let's be off," Oliver suggested. He was somewhat anxious to avoid this talk of loyalties, for he was conflicted as to his own at present. "Which way do we go?"

"Right. Well, it's on the way towards Beaverdams," Jeremy replied, indicating no specific direction.

"I don't know where that is," Oliver admitted sheepishly, having wandered about so much that he had lost his bearings.

"That's the second lesson then," Jeremy declared with a grin. "It might be helpful if you could find your way around the extended neighbourhood. Wouldn't do to get lost every time you head out, now would it? When we return, I suppose I shall need to draw you a map."

★ ★ ★

Oliver and Jeremy stopped briefly by the Jarvis property and had just continued on their way, heading for the woods. But before they could reach the green anonymity of the forest's cover, they heard a voice hailing Jeremy by name. They stopped and looked over their shoulders, Jeremy almost imperceptibly shrugging off his gun, when he recognized a corporal. His green clothing identified him as one of Captain Fitzgibbon's Green Tigers, sometimes known as the Bloody Boys.

"Well, if it isn't our favourite spy, er, trapper," the soldier welcomed Jeremy, grinning aat his own joke. "I recognized your unmistakable style of slinking off into the trees from all the way back on the road."

"That's favourite spy, er, trapper, retired, Jack," Jeremy shot back good naturedly. "I've had quite enough of your war now, thank you, even if elements of it yet seem to follow me around from time to time. As you know, that's why I find that I must slink into the trees, as you put it, whenever possible." It was obvious to Oliver that the two shared a bond that could only be forged in fires of battle.

"And who's this, van Hijser?" the corporal asked, nodding toward Oliver. "You've taken yourself on an apprentice, have you? Getting too old to do the carrying anymore?"

Jeremy laughed, and then feigned insult at the remark. "Never mind," he snapped. "This is a long lost cousin of mine. In fact, he was so lost, I didn't know until yesterday that he existed. He came looking for some action and adventure."

"Well, he might get some here soon," the soldier replied, now serious. "I'm going to Burlington Heights to find the Captain to tell him something's in the wind. We don't know just what, but we understand that the Americans may be about to move against us soon. There is a great deal of activity going on at Fort George."

"In addition, Willcocks has become ever more belligerent toward the citizens, threatening to burn people's houses down and it doesn't bode well. Thus far he's been kept in check by the U.S. Army and your old friend Dr. Chapin. You two wouldn't be headed in the direction of Burlington Heights, now would you?" he asked hopefully.

"Well, we were heading over to see Lieutenant Fitzgibbon, but you say Captain?" Jeremy asked.

"That's right, promoted for his service at Beaverdams."

"Well, I guess I shouldn't be surprised. In any case we were off to see him, but I suppose there'll be no sense in going to Decou's house if he's at Burlington Heights."

"If you don't mind carrying the message for me, I would be greatly appreciative," the corporal urged. "It would be best if I were here if something does happen."

"Jack, you know I'm trying to stay out of the war these days," Jeremy started. However, seeing the look on the other man's face, he shrugged. "And what makes you think that I would travel all that way?" He paused for a respectable period of time before sighing in mock surrender. "Very well, then. I suppose we could just as well hunt in that direction as any. But in case I don't find Fitzgibbon, or in the event that someone brings you information from George MacPhail, it might do you well to be suspicious. George has apparently been dead for some time."

"Very well, I'll keep that in mind. You're a good man, Jeremy," the corporal shouted as he turned his horse sharply about. "And while you're there, ask them if they can send the army along this way. They're no bloody good to us sitting on their duffs at the other end of the lake."

Before Jeremy could reply, the soldier and his mount thundered off across the Jarvis farm and disappeared down the road, no doubt on his way back toward Beaverdams.

He looked at Oliver and shook his head. "Well, take me for the fool that I am. "Somehow, I keep allowing them to volunteer me. Oh well, let's head toward Burlington Heights then. We can just as well hunt on that route as any other."

He noticed the confused expression on his cousin's face. "I know, you don't know where that is," he chuckled, and the two headed west to carry the message.

★ ★ ★

Late the next evening, Jeremy and Oliver arrived at the junction of the Niagara, York and Chatham roads near the crossroads known as Burlington Heights. All three roads were former Native trails, widened but little improved for white man's use. In general, they were muddy when wet and consequently rutted when dry, with roots, rocks and fallen trees and branches constant obstacles to those who travelled them.

Jeremy was not accustomed to the time it had taken them to reach here for generally he moved quickly unless hunting. On this occasion, however, he had decided to remain as close to the mountain as possible that they might avoid contact with any who might wish them harm. Most people stayed to the recognized roadways, not least for the fact that most would be lost on the Mountain. Jeremy had also decided that it would not do for locals to mention their hasty passing and, if Volunteers should chance upon Jeremy, they might decide it easiest to kill the cousins. They also were hampered by the fact that Oliver, although a strong young man, was not accustomed to the long periods of travel on rough terrain required to negotiate the Mountain trails.

Chapter Four

"I don't why, but he's suddenly arrived here."

The military man looked hard at the one who was bringing him the news. He hated to deal with him or, for that matter, anyone at all. But this one was worse for he knew the man wanted a piece of the prize when he was done and, moreover, that there was a certain amount of legitimacy in his claim for that piece.

He was dreadfully uncomfortable here in this place, but meeting in camp was definitely out of the question. He simply could not be associated with this man should anything go wrong. All the same, skulking about in the Upper Canadian wilderness like this in the damp and cold of a November day did nothing to improve his disposition.

"What do you mean 'here'?" he growled, looking directly at the unkempt younger man. "Do you mean at Burlington Heights?"

"Exactly right. Well, yet on the Mountain, but heading down even as I left to let you know. I've been following all the way and that American boy and the trapper he has traveling with him are approaching this area as we speak."

The soldier looked away, staring across the marshes toward the escarpment. He was struggling to formulate a plan to deal with this dangerous new twist.

"Why have you let him get so far? It's a long distance from the Niagara River. Why haven't you killed him by now and taken it?" At times like this, he could scarcely credit this colonial's self-proclaimed reputation.

"I'm intending to take as few risks as possible," the man replied. "I see no reason to get killed over this and I had no men to turn the odds in my favour."

"How many men do you require to kill a boy?" the military man asked impatiently. "Never mind answering that! Do you have the men now?" He longed to get back to the camp and near a warm fire and this maddening fellow before him was doing nothing to improve his humour.

"Yes I do. They arrived just before I did."

"And can you trust them?"

"Certainly. I made sure of that. They won't speak if they're caught." The man started to chuckle. "I have the best assurance possible. You see, they know nothing but that they're to shoot those whom I tell them to shoot and they'll be paid handsomely for it."

The soldier rose from the log upon which he had been uncomfortably perched and brushed his pants as though they were dirty. "Well, you know what you need to do. I don't know the reason why he ended up here, but I expect you to eliminate him and get the instructions before they can be used."

"Actually, as I said, he is now 'them'," the man interrupted. "He's picked up someone near the Twenty. I'm not sure who this other man is, but he seems to have taken our boy in quite willingly. And he is well armed, I might add."

"It matters not a whit who the other man might be. Kill them both. We went to great lengths to hide the prize and I shouldn't like to need to move it now. It's simply too dangerous." He started to walk away and then turned, as if his actions required some kind of explanation. "Now, I must return to the camp before someone notices I'm missing and begins to ask uncomfortable questions." As he turned to go there was a flash of light reflected from the officer's insignia on his uniform.

The younger man rubbed his two days' growth of facial stubble as he watched the soldier leave. "There goes a great pompous ass," he muttered to himself. "If only he need not be involved in this."

He knew he had no choice in the matter, however. The officer was involved. In fact, the officer knew more about the subject than he did. He would need to play along until he saw his opportunity.

★ ★ ★

The two cousins had headed down the Mountain, following the ravine of Big Creek all the way down to the faster and more direct Niagara road now that they were clear of territory in which Jeremy figured he would be recognized. Besides, after this the Mountain would curve ever farther away from Burlington Heights. Once on this more open pathway, they headed approximately westward toward their goal. Since they had climbed down from the escarpment, they had passed few signs of settlement save for the occasional half-cultivated farms.

Now that they had reached this crossroads, they came to the ultimate frontier sign of civilization – a tavern. This was Smith's Tavern in fact, and stood in a key location due to the intersection of the roads and because the British army were stationed at nearby Burlington Heights.

"Are we going in here?" Oliver asked, somewhat nervously.

Jeremy turned, surprised at the question. He had never known a young man to be reticent about entering a tavern. "I don't know if we are, but I know that definitely I will be seated in this fine establishment in moments."

"But why?" Oliver sputtered uncomfortably. "My ma made it quite clear that such places are the refuge of the Devil himself, and all manner of evil takes place in there, such as drinking the demon rum."

Jeremy stared at his cousin for what seemed a long time, wondering at the faith in his mother and his religion that urged him to think this way, since Jeremy himself had not been burdened with religion in some time. While he held with the rules that kept society together as much as it was possible, he had drifted steadily away from a belief in a higher being since his family died in childbirth. However, he was not about to interfere with the young man's faith, as long as Oliver did not interfere with his lack of it.

"This is the best place to ask where I might find Captain Fitzgibbon," he explained. "And if, in the process, some demon rum should cross my lips, well, I guess I will be forced to exorcise it next time I relieve myself. Now…are you coming or staying out here?"

Oliver looked about at the questionable men coming and going and staring at him as if he were on exhibit. He had no desire to be left to his own devices outside the tavern under these conditions any more than he wished to go in. Wallowing in conflicting feelings about the entire matter, he nonetheless swallowed his reservations and followed his older cousin into the tavern. He stood momentarily rooted just inside the door, taking in the unfamiliar atmosphere of the place. His immediate impression was one of incredible noise – clinking glasses, sliding tables and chairs, loud unintelligible voices. People seemed to fill every square in of this building that seemed much too small to accommodate them.

He saw soldiers in various stages of dress and sobriety, a few obvious farmers, trappers, and militiamen who were either coming or going back home. It was all rather suffocating to the young man, unaccustomed as he was to this environment. He looked about as if in a daze, trying to determine exactly where Jeremy had pushed off to through the crowd.

While scanning about for his cousin, he noticed someone watching him from the badly lit gloom of a back corner. The man immediately looked away as he realized that his attention had been noticed and tugged futilely at his hat brim, trying to pull it down over his eyes.

Knowing that he was being watched in this suspicious manner by such a character, he looked about some more, now with an even greater sense of desperation weighing on his mind.

When finally he spotted Jeremy standing at the long wooden bar, Oliver pushed his way through to a chorus of protests as he invariably and obliviously knocked aside both drinkers and drinks.

"Jeremy! Jeremy! I think I just saw him!" he shouted out, hoping to be heard above the din and pulling excitedly at his cousin's shirt.

Jeremy appeared to be somewhat annoyed as he excused himself from the soldier with whom he had been talking and turned to face Oliver. "What is it you want, boy? Did your mother not teach you any manners, specifically about interrupting when a man is talking? Just who was it that you think you saw?"

"It was him! I'm sure it was! I'm sure it was him!" Oliver shouted excitedly, ignoring the fact that Jeremy was talking down to him.

Jeremy grasped the younger man firmly be the shoulders and shook him hard enough to get his attention. Then he shouted, "Calm down! Who are you talking about?"

Oliver pointed toward the far corner of the room, not visible from their position. "It was the man that took the paper from Mr. MacPhail's pocket! He was just there, in the shadows, watching me, and when he realized I saw him, he slouched down and pulled his hat down low!"

Jeremy pushed his way through the heavy crowd with Oliver in tow. As they reached the indicated corner, however, they found no one there.

Nudging a man who sat on a bench beside the corner table, Jeremy shouted to be heard above the din. "Did you see a man here at this table, just a few minutes ago?"

The man was dirty and wet, due either to travel or work, with at least a weeks' stubble of growth on his ruddy face. He looked blearily at the table as if noticing that there was one for the first time ever, and then looked slowly back up at his inquisitors, his eyes bloodshot and his purchase on the bench tentative. "Hey, there's another table," he slurred drunkenly. "And you know what? There's no one at it. Did I see anyone? I see lots of people. And sometimes they're not even there," he said swinging his arm loosely across the front of his body, guffawing ludicrously at his own attempt at humour. "Which one did you want?"

Jeremy sighed, although certainly no one could hear it. "Let's go outside where we can talk," Jeremy suggested loudly, taking Oliver by the elbow.

Once outside, the two took a seat on a bench against the outside wall of the tavern. "That's much better," Jeremy muttered. He was unused to the level of the noise inside as well. "Now, are you sure it was the same man from Black Rock? That corner was quite poorly lit."

"I'm quite sure," Oliver replied. Then he hesitated and finally said, "Not completely. But I did see the same man at Shipman's Tavern on my way down, asking directions I believe."

"You didn't tell me you saw also him at Shipman's before, when you came to my place," Jeremy admonished. "Don't you think that I might be interest in such a tidbit, especially after we'd been shot at in from of my own home? Besides, what were you doing at Paul Shipman's Tavern? I thought you were rather averse to establishments of strong drink."

Oliver appeared chastened, but he felt the need to grasp for an excuse nonetheless. "I – I was even less sure of who he was then," he stammered. "I didn't actually go inside then, just noticed him through the open doorway. And that was different anyway. Shipman's Tavern is a major point of transfer for the stage coaches. It wasn't until I saw him in this tavern that I realized it might be the same man."

Jeremy smiled at this convoluted line of reasoning, as confused and uncomfortable as it sounded, but did not comment upon it. "Be that as it may, have you any other bits of information you had initially thought unimportant, and neglected to tell me? Bear in mind that our lives may be at stake."

As Oliver resolutely shook his head, Jeremy looked off down the road toward Niagara, not actually focussing on the darkness, lost deeply in his thoughts. "Just think hard about that before you answer," he said. "Well, let's assume for the moment that it was he," he said thoughtfully. "Why would he be following you here? He has the paper, so of what use could you be to him?"

"Well, I am a witness," Oliver suggested slowly. "Perhaps he knows someone tried to force it from me and he wishes to prevent me from telling anyone else what he looks like."

"Perhaps," Jeremy conceded, "But why not waylay us on the road then? Why follow us to a busy military camp before he takes action?"

"I'm at a loss. Can you think of a better explanation?"

"No, I cannot," Jeremy sighed. "However, something tells me that there is another story to this. In any case," he said, rising suddenly from the bench, "We had best not take any chances tonight and sleep with our eyes open." He saw a disbelieving look on the younger man's face and chuckled in spite of the situation. "Not to be taken literally, Oliver. I mean sleep lightly in a defensible place."

"Do you think we might be able to room here?" Oliver asked, looking at the tavern with a great deal of discomfort.

Jeremy laughed at the suggestion. "Well, now, it seems my cousin is a wealthy man. And he's much too good to sleep on the ground at night."

"That isn't what I meant," Oliver replied defensively. "I thought perhaps a room in a tavern would be more defensible than a campsite."

"It might seem so, but you don't get a room to yourself, unless you're independently wealthy. It's very busy in there and it's possible that there might be others about much of the time to bump up against you and possibly leave a blade to remember him by," Jeremy explained. "Don't forget that as yet we don't know if your man is working alone or with others. I really think it would be best if we made a camp well away from the road, without a fire I might add, that we might challenge anyone that came near. Trust me, lad, it also will smell much better and be much quieter. Now, let's be on our way."

Before they could rise to leave, they heard the tavern door open and close and a man who had exited walked quickly up to them. "I know not what it might be to you but, as to the man you were asking me about, I overheard him asking questions of others about York," he said.

Jeremy peered through the shadows cast by the man's broad-brimmed hat. "Aren't you the man we just spoke to inside?" he asked suspiciously. "The man who was too drunk and confused to give a straight answer? I don't know what magic elixir they offer in the tavern, sir, but that is a remarkable feat of sobering." Jeremy laughed lightly, all the while watching about himself for a trap.

"I didn't want to say too much in there," the man replied, nervously looking around as he spoke. "There are strangers and spies all about during this war, and sometimes it's difficult to decide who one can talk to."

"Well, how do you know that we're safe?" Jeremy asked.

"I've seen you here before, sometimes with British officers, sometimes delivering meat to the tavern or the camp," the man replied, apparently believing for some reason that any man seen with British officers could be trusted. "I thought I could take the chance, especially since the man you were asking about was acting quite strangely."

"At any rate, you say this man was asking about the town of York?"

"Aye, and the former governor's house, too," the man answered. "He was asking about Simcoe's house and how he might find it."

Jeremy looked a little perplexed by the man's information. "Why would he be asking about Simcoe's house in York? Tell me, sir, did he seem to be alone, or were there others asking about with him?"

The man open his mouth to answer, but no reply would be forthcoming. An explosion, seeming almost deafening by the open road, issued from the brush on the other side of the forks. The man's eyes opened wide, as if in surprise and even in the darkness Jeremy and Oliver could see as he pitched forward a rapidly growing dark stain spreading rapidly across his shirt over his back.

As their informer fell to the ground, Jeremy sprang into action. "Stay here with him! But stay low!" he ordered Oliver. "Try to get some help, although I fear he's long for it." With that, and before the younger man could protest, he was across the road and had vanished into the brush.

Chapter Five

As Jeremy was swallowed up by the near darkness, he could hear the sounds up ahead of another body crashing through the brush. Presumably this would be the man who was attempting to escape him. He moved as swiftly as he could while yet keeping his senses alert to the possibility that there could be more of them lying in wait.

It was glaringly obvious that whoever he was chasing was not making the chase terribly difficult. He was leaving broken branches and trampled weeds in his wake, and he was making enough noise to awaken every corpse in Niagara. This was not the mark of a man trying very hard to disappear unless he had no experience in woodcraft whatsoever, a doubtful proposition in this frontier region.

The other man's carelessness made Jeremy extra cautious. There was no doubt in his mind that this was just too easy. Surely his quarry must know that, in this thick brush and in the dark of night, all he had to do was to find a spot relatively free of brush and weeds and wait for Jeremy to pass. Once the trail was lost, it was unlikely anyone could pick it up quickly without some source of light. It was doubtful that the man could be that inexperienced at such things. Anyone, ignorant or not, would have left the trail at some point in the hopes of losing his pursuer.

Jeremy loped easily along in the direction of the noise, saving his strength for the confrontation that he was certain would come. Even so, he could tell by the noise that he was gaining on his quarry. After less than five minutes of this apparent cat-and-mouse game, the noise came to an abrupt stop. The darkness seemed to close in tightly in the sudden absence of sound.

He stopped where he stood and listened closely, not wishing to rush into whatever trap may have been set for him. Then there was an audible splash not far ahead. Apparently the person he had been chasing had found that this particular path had abruptly ended at one of the many swamps of this particular area. And now the man was be attempting to use the water to lose his stalker, or at least to make Jeremy think so.

Jeremy maintained his high level of caution, however, for it seemed suspicious to him that the crashing through along would stop for several seconds before the sound of the splash. While it was possible that the man had stopped, seen the marsh and weighed his options before deciding it was his best route, Jeremy decided it would be wise to tread carefully and keep his senses sharp as he moved forward.

Approaching the swamp, Jeremy could readily see where the other had entered the water. In fact, despite the fact that he had been heard to stop, apparently to decide his next step, it appeared the man had yet literally stumbled onto the wetland and fallen in, for the reeds and rushes were flattened over a large area.

But now the trail ended. Jeremy stopped and listened carefully but he could hear nothing. His quarry had finally gone to ground, or perhaps he had drowned out there, Jeremy thought hopefully. Some of these wetlands were unpredictable, with sudden drop-offs of sucking mud, but then surely he would be calling for help. Jeremy waited, listening to every night sound for something untoward. Considering the man's previous lead-footed haste, if he was yet alive he might take flight once more and there would again be there would be some sound created by the resumption. So he waited, thankful at least that the season for mosquitoes had drawn to an end.

It took less than ten minutes for Jeremy to hear another sound, but it was not what he was expecting.

"James! Is he still there?" someone whispered from nearby in the rushes.

"Shut up you fool!" the curt response came from close behind Jeremy.

So, there had been another after all, Jeremy thought. And this headlong rush into the swamp had been an ambush attempt. Unfortunately for them, Jeremy had been waiting patiently without making a sound for some time and they were beginning to wonder if he had turned back without them noticing. He hoped the man in the swamp was enjoying standing in what he knew to be cold water for all that time.

Obviously the man behind Jeremy was the more competent of the two, for Jeremy had not heard any sound behind him despite keeping his ears attuned to unusual noises about him. Likewise, he had not seen or heard any sign of anyone waiting for him to pass as he chased the other here. This other, then, must be the first to be dealt with. The first was a mere decoy, and not a terribly intelligent one by all evidence.

Slowly and silently, Jeremy backed into the marsh rushes that abounded here, being careful to leave as little evidence of his passing as was possible. Cautiously he circled around behind the location of the second voice, where he believed the ambusher to be secreted, based upon the direction of the short burst of whispered annoyance directed at his co-conspirator. He was slightly off, but not by much. Not three feet away he finally saw the dark shape – more of a shadow really – of a man hidden just off the trail that Jeremy and the man's partner had followed in the course of the chase. He was obviously waiting, either for Jeremy to resume the chase, thereby giving away his position, or to return the way he had come.

Jeremy crept closer, his breath slowed almost to a stop, as he pulled his bayonet slowly from its sheath. His progress seemed to him to be excruciatingly slow and his every muted breath yet sounded like a roar in his ears. It was taking so long in Jeremy's mind that he was beginning to fear that the man would decide either to give up the chase or to turn around just as he closed in. But he did not wish to give himself away, so he continued with his exercise in patience and self-discipline.

Finally, situated less than an arm's reach of the back of his target, Jeremy spoke quietly. "Are you looking for me by chance?"

The startled man spun around, trying hopelessly to bring his musket to bear on the voice behind him. In that same moment, Jeremy stepped forward and drove the razor-sharp point of his bayonet deep into the man's chest from below his sternum. He could hear the rattle as blood from the punctured heart poured into the equally opened lungs and he held his hand firmly across the man's mouth to assure that no alerting sound would escape. Finally, pulling the weapon free, he removed all the weapons he could find on the man and laid them quietly in the tall grasses.

Now Jeremy walked casually back to the edge of the swamp and cleared his throat.

"James! Is that you?" an unsure voice in the rushes whispered, apparently no wiser about speaking out.

"Forget it," Jeremy whispered back in a raspy voice, attempting to approximate the sound of the man he just killed. "I think he's gone. You spooked him by the looks of it. Come on out of there."

He stepped aside, out of plain view and waited for the other man to come to him. After a moment of rustling dry reeds, the sodden man emerged, swearing and trying to stomp the mud from his boots. "You surely took your time about deciding when enough was enough," he whined. "Next time you can be the decoy. Then we'll see if you like standing up to your waste in cold swamp water."

Once the "decoy" stepped out in plain sight, Jeremy stepped forward and confronted him, only inches from his face, the ornately etched pistol pointing directly at the frightened and pathetic creature's heart.

"James is no longer with us," Jeremy told him, his voice even but full of menace. "Your little plan didn't work. Now, how would you like to tell me what this is all about?"

The man stared at the pistol, barely able to comprehend that James' plan had not worked. "I – well, let me get all the way out of the water, will you – please?"

"I don't think so," Jeremy growled. "Perhaps a touch of discomfort will make you speak up a little faster. By the way, kindly remove your weapons and toss them behind you, well out into the swamp?"

The man did as he was told and then stood there speechless, dripping mud and water from his waist down. "What do you want to know?" he whispered finally.

"For one thing," Jeremy snapped, "I would like to know who you men are. And then you can tell me why you are trying to kill me."

"We're just a couple of businessmen," the man started lamely.

"Businessmen!" Jeremy snorted. "And what sort of business would have you running about in swamps and attempting to kill me? You surely can't be assassins. You're both much too stupid for that."

"Well…" the man started. He had apparently decided to attempt to ignore the question of who he was because he switched quickly to give an answer to the second question. "We weren't originally here to kill you. In fact, we don't even know who you are. We came to get the young fellow, to frighten him and get him to tell us what we need to know."

"And what would that be?" Jeremy asked, feeling he already knew the answer.

"I honestly don't know," the man whined pitifully. "We were just supposed to deliver him and make him willing to talk."

"Deliver him to whom?"

But the question would not be answered this night. Jeremy heard a sound immediately behind him and spun about to confront this latest possible danger, thinking it might be the third member of the assassin's party. But all he saw were the eyes of a raccoon that had crept up to investigate what strange creatures had invaded its territory. The creature scampered away when Jeremy made a shooing sound in its direction.

Just as Jeremy started to turn back, there was a light splashing sound behind him, followed by a larger splash behind the rushes. His prisoner had vanished back into the swamp. This time, he seemed to have gone directly or the more open water for his trail seemed to end there. Perhaps this one had not been quite as naive as Jeremy had thought, for he could not pick up the man's trail again.

★ ★ ★

Jeremy emerged from the brush onto the road, exhausted and wet from the knees down, to find Oliver waiting for him.

"Did you can catch him?"

"I found them," Jeremy responded tiredly, still rubbing at the blood on his hand.

"Them?"

"Yes. The man I chased was a decoy. I found another had been either following me or waiting for me and I was forced to sneak up behind and end his stalking days with my bayonet." Jeremy looked about at the darkness of the wilderness surrounding them. "The other bolted when a sound distracted me. He disappeared into the swamp. He did tell me, however, that there had been a third in their party, someone who had apparently hired these two."

Oliver looked about nervously, half expecting to find a musket pointed at him from the bushes. Seeing nothing but wishing to get away from here, he turned back to Jeremy.

"You look exhausted," he sighed, trying to take his mind off the fact that two of the three killers were yet at large. "I guess if we're going to set up camp, we'd best get going, before the other has a chance to collect himself."

"That won't be necessary," an almost patrician voice interrupted them. A tall man in uniform trousers, obviously a British officer, walked up to them.

"How is our new-found friend?" Jeremy asked. "I suppose he'll not be long for this world."

"He had no chance," the soldier replied, wiping blood from his hands, his manner as one who was much accustomed to such results. "At least it was quick. He bled to death in minutes."

Jeremy sighed, unsure if it was out of frustration or out of relief. "It may seem unsympathetic, but I've seen such gut wounds before, and he's quite lucky it's over. Death from such wounds can be lingering and extremely painful." His mind could yet produce amazingly fresh images of the makeshift hospital area at John DeCou's house following the battle at Beaverdams.

Then he realized what the officer had said upon his approach. "What did you mean that our camp would not be necessary?"

The officer looked at them dispassionately. "I'm Captain Howard Renforth, surgeon in the employ in His Majesty's service, Forty-Ninth Regiment, at present stationed at Burlington Heights and I'd heard you ask about Captain Fitzgibbon. I think you'd best come to the base with me and speak to the officers there about what happened here tonight."

"Are we under arrest, sir?" Jeremy asked, surprised.

"Not at all. But I'm sure they will wish to ask you some questions, such as why you are here and what your business with Captain Fitzgibbon might be," Renforth replied.

"I can answer that for you right here and now. I was asked to come here by one of his men, a Corporal Jack Devane, and I was wondering if you might know if Fitzgibbon was there. By the way, my name is Jeremy van Hijser and this is my cousin, Oliver Davidson."

A light of recognition lit in the officer's eyes. "Jeremy van Hijser! I've heard tell of you from Fitzgibbon. It seems you've had your hands full with Willcocks' scoundrels down the peninsula. You're getting to be almost as large a legend in this camp as James himself, perhaps larger since none but the Captain has ever met you until now." Jeremy surprisingly thought that he detected a glimmer of respect in the officer's eyes.

"Yes sir. I've tried hard to forget about my encounter with the Canadian Volunteers, but they won't seem to let it be," Jeremy replied solemnly. "They keep coming to my house and disrupting my life. It seems to have become somewhat like game to them."

"There's no doubt they're a nasty bunch," the officer said, shaking his head.

"So, sir, can you tell us? Is Fitzgibbon in camp?"

"He was the last I was there, two days ago. I've had what passes here for a leave, you see," Renforth confided, as if telling a military secret. "Wait while I get my coat. I'm afraid you'll still need to answer those questions."

Jeremy smiled grimly. "That would be fine with me, sir. I think the news I bring should be heard by the other officers as well. I would appreciate it, though, if I could be allowed to speak to Captain Fitzgibbon first."

"If I can easily locate him, that should be perfectly acceptable," Renforth nodded. "Now, if you'll follow me, perhaps we can find you some lodgings in the camp as well. That will afford you some measure of protection from the man who escaped you, should he venture to try it again."

While Captain Renforth went inside the tavern to retrieve his uniform jacket, Jeremy and Oliver checked their minimal equipment to see that everything was in order.

"Right, then," the Captain announced as he directed them onto the road. "Let's be on our way, shall we? I'm afraid that I have already overstayed my leave from the camp, not that anyone truly pays attention to such details any longer."

With that, the three men start off in a generally north-westerly direction toward Burlington Heights. They chatted informally as they walked, all the while dodging wagon ruts and potholes along the way. Unfortunately walking the roads of Upper Canada, especially at night, required a fair measure of caution, so as not to turn an ankle or worse.

Their attention to road conditions this night was the reason none of the men noticed as a fourth fell in behind them and began to follow, staying close to the trees and shadows that lined the thoroughfare.

★ ★ ★

Once inside the British camp, Jeremy looked all about, but he could make out very little in the dark. There were a number of open campfires, around which huddled the overflow of soldiers, attempting to keep off the late autumn cold in the deepening night. Straight ahead, he could see the silhouette of the barracks, used primarily as a hospital for those who had managed to arguably survive various battles and sorties. The thought brought a shudder to his entire being.

To his right, he caught the glimmer of the quarter moon off the surface of the expanse of water that would have been named harbour or a bay if not for the narrow strip of land, known locally as Long Beach, which separated it from Lake Ontario. This body of water was known variously as Lake Geneva or Little Lake or Small Lake. He knew from experience that there was another, smaller body of water and, to his left, the marshes of Cootes Paradise, so-named because of a British naval captain who hunted there in the previous century. This body of water he could not see from his present position.

The three men approached the larger of a rank of tents that occupied the centre of the fortified position. An officer sat studying the top of a pile of papers, and he barely noticed the men enter the tent.

"Is the General on base?" Renforth asked, referring to the commander of the British forces in this part of the province, Brigadier-General John Vincent.

"No, Captain," the officer replied, his voice barely above a mumble. "A messenger rode in late this afternoon, with a summons from Kingston. He left immediately and didn't know when he'd be back."

"Who, then, is the officer in charge?" asked Renforth, somewhat annoyed that the man could not do him the courtesy of at least looking up when he spoke.

"That would be Colonel Halberson," the other officer sighed, apparently exasperated at this interruption that was distracting him from his paperwork. Yet still he did not raise his head.

Renforth led the three from tent and stopped a passing sergeant who wore the uniform of the Eighth King's Regiment. "Take us to Colonel Halberson, Sergeant," he ordered.

Chapter Six

Wending their way through the soldiers, tents and stacks of ammunition and weapons, Jeremy noticed a hint of listlessness among the men. No wonder, he thought. All the action was down the Peninsula, and here they sat guarding this hill to which they had fled when the Americans broke through. For some reason known only to those in command, here the army remained, though the enemy had been driven all the way back to Fort George after their defeat at Stoney Creek and then The Forty.

They were led to an office which sat at the end of the barracks. The sergeant rapped on the door and waited for a reply. After a short silence, they could hear a muffled "Come in" from beyond the sturdy planks.

The sergeant poked his head inside the door. "Captain Renforth and two, er, gentlemen to see you, sir."

"Very well," a deep voice replied from inside the room. "Show them in."

The odd group comprised of the blood-stained Captain, a woodsman that he felt he might know and a boy he that he definitely did not, filed into the cramped space. The Colonel looked them over in an obviously exaggerated manner, the distaste at this encounter evident upon his face.

"Well, Renforth, what have you dragged into my office at this hour?" he grumbled. "It's rather late for locals with complaints or requests, don't you think?"

Jeremy, slightly peeved at this dismissive attitude, stepped forward. "We have information for Captain Fitzgibbon from his men at Beaverdams," he stated with greater than usual assertiveness. "If you could summon the Captain for us, we'll be clear of your office and shan't trouble you further."

The Colonel looked up finally from his reading and sat back in his chair. "I don't care for your insolent attitude."

"It's a good thing that I don't serve in His majesty's forces, then," Jeremy replied, nonplussed. "If we could just deliver our message, we'll be on our way and my attitude won't be a further bother to you."

Colonel Halberson grew red in the face. He was not accustomed to such a lack of respect. "Sir, and I use the title loosely, let me make my position in your respect perfectly clear! This is a time of war and as ranking officer I am the de facto government of this district! Is that clear?" His voice grew louder as he spoke.

"Quite," Jeremy answered simply, although his body language betrayed a total lack of intimidation.

Seeing that this encounter was quickly getting out of hand, Captain Renforth stepped in, attempting to diffuse the situation. "I'm sorry, Colonel. I'm afraid these woodsmen lack any sense of military decorum. With your permission, I'd like to have Captain Fitzgibbon summoned and be rid of them."

Halberson looked somewhat mollified by the Captain's explanation and suggestion. "Please do so, Captain," he grumbled, "before I'm forced to give them a taste of our jail. And Captain, please take these two with you to wait outside for Fitzgibbon. You're dismissed, Captain." He immediately pretended to put his attention back to the documents on his desk, although the colour on his face had not yet normalized.

Having been summarily dismissed, the three left the office, closing the door behind them. Renforth ordered the sergeant to find Captain Fitzgibbon and bring him to the mess.

"Thank God we didn't all end up in the brig," Renforth groused, trying to maintain a stern expression as they walked toward the mess hall. "Was it quite necessary to antagonize the Colonel so?"

"I must admit that it would've been more worth if I'd given the pompous fool a fatal attack of apoplexy," Jeremy replied.

Renforth began to chuckle despite himself. "His face did turn a rather interesting shade of red, didn't it? It had quite reached the hue of my dress uniform and was threatening to go all the way to purple."

"I don't know," Oliver muttered, his voice still betraying his nervousness over the entire situation. "I don't think I'd have liked sitting in a British jail. You made him quite angry."

Jeremy and the Captain looked at Oliver's worried expression and then at each other, bursting simultaneously into laughter as they entered the mess. They picked out a table in the corner that would afford them some measure of privacy and sat down on the wooden bench, waiting for the Captain to appear.

★ ★ ★

"Well, look who's rejoined the War!" the voice boomed as Fitzgibbon entered the mess. "And I've heard that he's already ingratiated himself with the acting camp commander!"

Jeremy stood up to shake the Captain's hand. "I hate to disappoint you, James. I really haven't any intention at all of rejoining the war. I was about to teach my cousin here the life of a trapper when your man asked me to bring you a message if we're out this way. And also to tell you that George MacPhail died during the raid at Black Rock, so you may not wish to accept any further intelligence from him."

The trapper told Fitzgibbon what he had been asked to convey and then sat back. "Now, if you'll tell us where we can sleep, we'll be on about our business in the morning."

Fitzgibbon seemed he was about to say something, but then apparently decided against it. "Well, Jeremy, thank you for bringing me this information. I'll fill in the commander in the morning before I head back. It will certainly be interesting to see what it all means."

"I'm sure it will," Jeremy responded. "Now, at the risk of repeating myself, could you show us our sleeping arrangements, please? It's been a rather long and eventful day."

The Captain accompanied them to a part of the camp where other civilians were bivouacked. Many of these men were merchants who either did regular business with the army or used them for protection for various reasons. Some were trappers like Jeremy who brought occasional provisions to the camp and sometimes provided the British with what information they gathered in their travels, much as he had done in the past.

"I believe you'll feel right at home among these men," Fitzgibbon said, shaking Jeremy's hand once again. "I suspect you'll already be acquainted with some of them from your past travels, although many are from the York, Kingston, Montreal, or Chatham. I believe you'll find room about one of these campfires."

"Thank you, James, and good night," Jeremy said and then led his cousin toward the end of a row of banked fires.

"One would think that the army could provide us with better sleeping arrangements," Oliver complained petulantly, as they lay down for the night.

"The Army seems to feel they owe their spies some form of accommodation, but apparently do not wish to spoil us," Jeremy replied with a chuckle, by way of explanation. "It should still be greatly preferable to sleeping out in the wilderness where we might easily be found if we were to build a fire. Besides," he added, sweeping his arm across the camp, "why should we fare any better than those who have sworn their duty to His Majesty's Army?"

Oliver looked towards the soldiers' tents, not far distant from their fire. "Something to keep the rain off us would have been nice."

"Stop complaining so," Jeremy muttered, already being overtaken by sleep. "I've seen no sign of the rain of which you seem terrified, but at least we're on high ground, and the coals should serve to keep the night frost off us. We could be sleeping in the marshes – without a fire."

★ ★ ★

At three a.m., there was little discernable movement in the camp but for a number of shapeless dark forms moving slowly and silently from fire to fire in the area that housed the civilians. They stopped and looked at each sleeping man, then moved on. When the shadowy forms reached the final campfire, which was little more than glowing embers by this time, one of the shadows used a sweeping arm motion to signal the others that the object of their search had been found.

Suddenly, an unsuspecting Oliver's exhausted sleep was interrupted when a hand clamped roughly over his mouth and he heard a voice close to his right ear. He was aware of something sharp pressing against his skin just below his Adam's apple.

★ ★ ★

"Just keep quiet," the voice whispered harshly. "We don't wish to wake up anyone else, do we?" When the Oliver slowly shook his head, the man released his hold. "Good. Quietly now, come along. We need to have a talk."

Oliver climbed slowly to his feet, his knees trembling horribly. There were others with his assailant, who were watching the others who slept at the fire but they stirred not at all. He stumbled forward when his captor gave him an unexpected shove, intended to overcome the lad's inertia.

A small branch cracked underfoot, sounding in the silence of the night as loud as cannon fire to the furtive shadows. All stopped and froze in position, watching the other man on this side of the fire for a reaction. The man snorted and then lay silent once again.

The small party moved out once more, heading for the wooded cliffs that comprised the north face of the Heights, where they could question their young hostage without identifiable sound. As they approached the edge of the steep incline, they made certain to give wide berth to the soldiers manning the guns which faced out over Little Lake, knowing that at least one man on each crew would be on watch.

Oliver felt helpless. He dared not cry out for they would doubtless kill him on the spot. He had no hope of breaking loose and escaping for they had him surrounded and guarded him closely. What alarmed him most of all was seeing that they had left one of their own to approach the sleeping and completely unaware Jeremy and he feared what would happen to his cousin.

As his mind raced to think of a plan to escape, or give alarm without being murdered, he thought that he sensed the man behind him change places with another. That must be the man left to see to Jeremy, he thought. My God, what has he done with Jeremy!?

They reached the very edge of the embankment, then followed it eastward a short distance until they reached a slight downward slope. A small stream, the reason for the depression, ran down the shallow slope and then practically dropped off into the dark waters below.

★ ★ ★

Jeremy had been awake since hearing the threat whispered in Oliver's ear. He had carefully assessed the situation, moving his head as little as possible, deciding it would be foolhardy to attempt anything at this point in time. He knew he was being watched and the men around him would surely pounce at any sign of life from him, preventing him from being of any assistance to his cousin and likely resulting in his own death.

His main concern had been that the men might well decide to kill him even if he made no such attempt. In the soft glow of the banked campfire it was difficult to determine who these men were so he was unsure as how to assess the level of such danger.

He had momentarily considered sounding an alarm with the hope of enlisting the assistance of the men on the far side of the fire but had then shaken off the idea. For all he knew, these men standing about him might well be those from the far side of the fire. And even had they not been, they surely could have killed Oliver and been well off before anyone could fully respond from a state of sleep.

As the men moved off quietly with his cousin, Jeremy had waited a moment more and now his concern proved to be a reality as one of the assailants, who had waited behind, moved quietly closer. He could almost feel the breath of the man they had left behind to permanently silence him as the thug bent down, knife in hand.

Without warning, Jeremy's hand shot out, pulling his would-be assailant toward him while rolling onto his back himself. He grasped the man's throat firmly with his left hand while bringing up his bayonet with the right. The man's eyes flared wide with surprise and pain, but could not shout out a warning to the others, for Jeremy's grip had cut off air sufficient for sound. Any grunt that did escape would have sounded to the other assailants like their man had accomplished his task.

Jeremy pulled the man down and quickly rolled over, manoeuvring himself into a position where he was kneeling on the rapidly dying man. If any of this man's companions had looked back, they would have seen one indistinguishable shadow atop another, apparently finishing off the bottom figure. Then he had stood up and quietly followed Oliver's abductors.

Nearing the edge of the grounds, Jeremy had, with studied nonchalance, approached the last man in the group, still counting upon the anonymity afforded by the poor lighting.

This man in the rear-guard turned around in greeting, only to be pulled suddenly close and have a hand clamped roughly over his mouth. He had been released from the embrace just long enough for a bayonet to lunge viciously upward, ending his life.

Jeremy had lowered the man to the ground, counting on the brush and brown, dried grasses to aid the darkness in covering his deed. As he released the body, he had wiped the blood from his hands with the man's shirt.

Then he had stepped up close behind Oliver.

★ ★ ★

As they approached the depression, Jeremy studied the now smaller group of abductors. There were yet eight. One on each side of Oliver, one ahead of him and the apparent leader, out in front with a fifth. The balance stood clear, keeping a watch on the surroundings ahead of them.

Jeremy reached out with his left hand and grasped a fistful of Oliver's shirt. Without warning or explanation, he pulled back on his cousin, swinging him into the rear. He could hear the younger man hit the ground with a dull thud as he reached for the abductor on his right.

Taking a firm hold of his enemy's wrist, Jeremy swung the man hard toward the left. The man's counterpart was not quick enough to react and was struck solidly with the body of the swinging man. With a surprised shout both men, trying desperately to regain their balance, stumbled over the edge of the cliff, crashing on the way down through the brush which clung stubbornly from the slope.

The silence was now broken, but Jeremy moved even before the man in front of him could react. Using his momentarily to screen himself from the leader, Jeremy lifted his rifle and pulled the trigger. In less than the wink of an eye, hammer struck flint, powder ignited in the pan, and the charge in the gun barrel of the over/under hurtled a thirteen millimetre slug toward the still turning man. Because of the close range, the target was knocked entirely from his feet and pitched forward in the direction of the leader.

At that same instant the lead man in this group of brigands turned around and was bringing his own gun to bear on Jeremy. He handily side-stepped the man coming toward him and continued as though nothing had happened.

"I didn't think we'd meet again after Queenston," the man said smiling.

"I wasn't aware that we had ever met," Jeremy commented calmly as he heard his cousin approaching, apparently back on his feet.

"Likely not," the man growled. "You were much too busy dealing with my boss."

"So, you are one of Dorian Williamson's men, then," Jeremy replied conversationally, seeming totally unconcerned that this man held his life in his hands. He could feel Oliver brushing ever so slightly by his back.

The leader had noticed Oliver's movement. "No, you don't!" he snapped. "I want you two apart. Come now, move away!" he barked at the younger man. Then he smiled. "I want a clear line of sight on both of you. Keep you from any heroics, such as sacrificing yourself for one another."

Oliver reluctantly moved away from Jeremy, stepping a good ten paces from his cousin before the thug told him to stop.

By now his other men on point men had come trotting back.

"Didn't you see this man take out half of your Brothers?" he demanded of the newcomers, with menace obvious in his tone without being loud.

There was a good deal of commotion coming from the camp behind Jeremy by now. Everyone had been awakened by the shot, and the alarm had been sounded. It would not be long before they determined where the sound had come from and came running.

"You won't escape," Jeremy said calmly. "They'll be here before you can turn and run."

"Oh, I think not," the man grinned mirthlessly. "They are all yet trying to sort out where the shot came from. You'll be dead and I'll be gone by the time they get here."

"Can you tell me this, then?" Jeremy asked, stalling. "Before you send me to my grave with the information anyway? I can understand you coming for me. You scoundrels have not left me alone since you held me prisoner near Newark. But why kidnap my cousin?"

The Canadian Volunteer laughed softly. "Well, sir, that was our mistake. You see, we didn't know it was you traveling with the boy or we would have taken you too so we could have ourselves some fun."

"And just why is it that you want my cousin?" Jeremy asked now, his curiosity genuine.

Before the other man could answer, however, there was a solid click and a young voice spoke out. "I think you should drop your weapon."

The thug looked over at Oliver, to see that he had stealthily moved several more paces away and now held a pistol, which was pointed directly at him.

Oliver had removed Jeremy's previously loaded ornately engraved pistol, from his cousin's coat. The thug's order to move apart had been a Godsend, giving Oliver the opportunity to prepare himself outside of the man's direct line of sight.

With a quick glance in the direction of Oliver's voice, the leader dived clear of the young man's aim, removing himself as a target option. The man beside him reacted differently, however, and the musket immediately began to swing in the direction of Oliver's voice.

Seeing the movement of weapon toward him, Oliver pulled back on the pistol's trigger. There was a loud report and a kick that nearly knocked the unsuspecting young man off his feet. The last thing he clearly saw before the force of the blast interfered with his attention was a startled look on his target's face. When Oliver regained his balance, he saw the man slump first to his knees and then heavily to the ground, blood soaking his shirt.

In the same instant, Jeremy made a diving lunge for one of the others, handily knocking the man senseless. He grabbed for the man's musket, which now lay on the ground beside him and raised himself to one knee, gun already pointing in the general direction of the stunned kidnappers.

Seeing that the moment had been lost, the group's leader scrambled to his feet and disappeared into the darkness, his remaining men close on his tail.

"I guess I won't be getting an answer to that question now," Jeremy muttered, a hint of annoyance in his voice.

"I had to shoot." The words fairly exploded from Oliver's mouth, still shocked that he had so nonchalantly shot the one thug. "He would surely have shot me."

Jeremy shook his head slowly. "There's no doubt of that. He brought about his own end, but it is unfortunate his boss got away. I certainly would have liked to hear the reply to that question. That is, assuming the animal even knew the answer."

Chapter Seven

The officer of the watch came running up, half out of breath, a half-dozen soldiers in tow. He looked down at the bodies of the two men and then at Jeremy and Oliver.

"I mean to have an explanation for all of this," the officer demanded.

"Quite simply, these men tried to kidnap us and we managed to break free," Jeremy responded tiredly. "I'm quite sure they're some of Willcocks' men – Canadian Volunteers, that is." He turned back to return to their fire.

"Oh," he then added, as if suddenly remembering. "Besides this dead man before us, there's one in the tall grasses near the edge, surely dead. And if you look down below, you'll find two more. They are possibly still alive, if somewhat banged up. And there's yet another back at our fire, dead for certain." With that, he pushed through the crowd that was rapidly forming around their recent battlefield.

"Oh, and unfortunately a few escaped," he said, turning back suddenly, adding the words almost as though it were an afterthought. "Sorry we couldn't kill them all."

"I'm afraid I'll need more of a report than that," the officer said to his back, as Oliver left to follow his cousin.

Jeremy waved his hand at the soldier without turning. "It'll wait until morning," he called back, the exhaustion evident in his voice. "None of those men will be leaving any time soon, and we must be getting some sleep before we're off tomorrow."

★ ★ ★

"Your task was but to deliver two men and you fools allowed them to get away!" the leader bellowed once their remnants had collected a safe distance from the camp.

"What do you mean, we let them get away?" one brave man asked defiantly. "You were there with us. In fact, you were in charge!"

The leader walked slowly over to the dissident member of his small force. Quietly, he walked around the man, not answering but making the fellow extremely nervous. "You know, I don't appreciate insubordination from my men," he growled into the man's ear, making the hairs on his neck stand up in fright. "This is a military unit, even if we are not wearing uniforms. And do you know what happens to insubordinate men in the field?"

He did not wait for an answer. Pulling a large hunting knife from its sheath, he plunged the blade into the man just below the sternum and pushed up with all his might. Then he stared into the man's eyes as they went wide with the shock and pain. He held that position, holding the man up before his gaze as the man's eyes turned milky and the last life ebbed from the former human being.

The others stood about silently, shock and fear rendering them numb.

"Vengeance is mine saith the Lord," he cried, as though in the throes of some religious fervour. "And I shall call upon the vessel of my choice to wreak that vengeance! So saith the Lord! Amen, Brothers, amen!"

"Amen," the others responded weakly, too frightened to question.

"How do you expect to find your way to Heaven with your faith so weak?" the leader thundered. "I said amen, Brothers, amen!"

This time the small band, which was now one man smaller, answered in apparent rapture. "Amen!" they shouted, almost as one. "Amen, amen!" They then continued to shout it as they marched away from Burlington Heights ever further, avoiding the main roads, the expulsion of air required to shout calming their nerves and creating a balm for their collective conscience.

★ ★ ★

Jeremy may have succeeded in holding off being questioned by insisting upon getting their sleep. However their time of rising was not to be of their choosing. Shortly after the first light cracked the morning sky and long before the sun could be seen, both were roughly shaken awake by a pair of soldiers.

He was immediately awake and would have fought them off automatically but for a voice which announced, "You two are to come with us." The source of this voice was Corporal if Jeremy correctly saw his stripe.

"Colonel Halberson wishes to speak with you and wanted us to catch you before you leave."

The cousins gathered up their meagre equipment and, escorted as if prisoners, headed for the Colonel's office. None of the soldiers would speak so there was no inkling as to the disposition of the Colonel this morning.

When they were ushered into the small room where they had met the night before, they found Halberson was in a particularly foul mood. "I should have the two of you shot and then court-martialled," was the greeting that met them.

"Don't you mean that the other way around, Colonel?" Jeremy suggested unnecessarily, knowing full well that it would do nothing but irritate the man.

"Don't tell me what I mean!" the Colonel blasted. "My way is much quicker. I wouldn't wish you to be using that smart mouth in the face of a military tribunal."

There was an uncomfortable silence in the room as the Colonel paced back and forth in front of his desk, seemingly searching for the most appropriate words to use. Jeremy and Oliver stood stock still, not quite fully awake but each feeling some degree of apprehension.

"I will not have wild melees in my camp while I am in charge," the Colonel finally opened evenly. "You two were offered the hospitality of His Majesty's Army last night and suddenly the camp – my camp – is torn apart in the middle of the night!"

"Now wait there just one moment!" Jeremy interrupted, to his cousin's great discomfort. "We can hardly be blamed for some men trying to kill us in the dead of night."

Halberson's face turned crimson with anger. "Do not interrupt me!" he barked, pronouncing each syllable separately and distinctly. "And do not presume to tell me for what I can blame you!" He paced around to the back of his desk and stood in front of his chair, leaning on the desk with both arms. "Now, why are men so determined to kill you that they are willing to risk being shot or captured, or both, by the British Army?"

"That is an excellent question," Jeremy started, "and I wish I had an excellent answer." He watched Halberson's face beginning to darken once more, so he quickly added, "The truth is, sir, that we really have no idea why they acted as they did. In fact, we had just asked that question when one of them gave us no choice but to shoot him and the rest escaped."

"I've heard of your strange exploits down the Peninsula, Mr. van Hijser. It has even been rumoured that you somehow ended up allying with American soldiers and Joseph Willcocks himself to kill one of the latter's own men."

While no question was asked, one seemed to hang in the air, but Jeremy decided not to make comment on the Colonel's remarks. It would be of no advantage to try to explain the situation, which the Colonel had captured in essence, and Jeremy felt discretion to be the better part of valour.

"You have no explanation of why Mr. Willcocks men are now trying to kill you? Or why they would risk kidnapping you from an armed military camp?" Halberson demanded.

"None, sir," Jeremy answered simply, not adding that he had not been the actual target.

"How about you, boy?" he asked of Oliver suddenly.

Oliver looked at his cousin, hoping for guidance, but Halberson caught the look.

"You needn't look at him!" he barked. "Just tell me what you know!" The Colonel's exasperation was becoming markedly more evident now.

"I have no idea why we were attacked," Oliver said finally, believing this was the safest route under the circumstances.

"It is obvious that you have no intention of telling me what is happening here, but I cannot have this in my camp! The morale of my men is, for some reason, adversely affected when there is shooting in the very middle of the camp," he added ironically. If he was making an attempt at humour, even at the expense of the men before him, no one seemed to notice.

Halberson darkly studied the civilians before him. "Very well," he finally sighed resignedly, walking to the front of his desk and looking Jeremy directly in the eye as a final attempt at intimidation. "Corporal, come in here!" he shouted, still holding Jeremy's maddeningly insolent stare.

When the young non-com entered the office, he found Halberson once more seated at the desk affecting an image of self-control and dignity.

"Corporal, I want you to take our guests and escort them out of camp," the Colonel ordered in a level but slightly shaky voice. "They are no longer welcome here. And once they are out, remain at the guard post to be sure that they do not attempt to return."

With that, Halberson bent his head as if to resume paperwork of some importance. He raise his hand slightly and brushed them off to signal that he would waste no more time on these two and that the soldiers were dismissed.

The Corporal led the men outside the office and across the field to one of the guard posts considered to be a "gate". The camp was now stirring back to life and many stared in curiosity as they watched the odd escort party.

★ ★ ★

Once they had been unceremoniously escorted from the camp, Jeremy and Oliver decided to head back toward Niagara, their mission here completed, if not in entirely satisfactory manner. As they passed Smith's Tavern, they heard Jeremy's name being called quietly. They turned to see Captain Renforth, summoning them from the inn's main door.

"What would you be doing here at this hour of the morning?" Jeremy asked, surprised to see the surgeon off the base so early.

"I had some business to attend to. And I've come across something that I thought might interest you," he replied cryptically.

"Won't you be missed on the base? I understood that it had been closed for the time being because of the little incident last night," Jeremy said as he strolled to where the Captain waited.

"Yes, well, I am a Captain and a doctor as well," Renforth commented drily and then gave them a sly wink. "But the truth of the matter is that when there is little call for me on the base, I may answer some local requests for medical assistance from time to time. It keeps the locals on our side," he laughed. "As I've heard you might well know, we can't always count on the loyalty of some of our citizens in Upper Canada. So, when one of the locals came asking for me, no one thought anything of it."

Jeremy chuckled. "So, you've seen to the emergency, have you?"

"I was just about to do that," Renforth said. "As luck would have it, the call came from this very establishment. Someone came by here last night after we left," the Captain explained. "I had asked a pair of local gentlemen if they could offer the courtesy of the tavern to anyone who might show an interest in the two of you, especially after that shooting in front of here, and they happily obliged. They were then to send someone to the camp and tell them that they had a medical emergency. This is a tavern and they have such emergencies on a fairly regular basis."

"You have someone who fits that description now?" Oliver could not disguise his pleasure and excitement at the news. "Perhaps now we can find out just what those attackers might want from us."

Renforth led them to a back room of the tavern. As he stepped out of the way, Jeremy and Oliver could see a man seated uncomfortably on the floor, hands tied behind him around a post. Two men stood by, a keeping casual watch over him.

"Thank you kindly, gentlemen," the Captain said and handed each a few coins. "That should keep you in ale for several days, if you drink sparingly."

The larger of the two displayed blackened teeth through his unshaven face and laughed raucously at the remark. "There are many things we might do sparingly, but drinking isn't one of them." They were laughing still when they left the room and closed the door behind themselves.

"Just see to it that you don't become real emergencies for me to come and see to," returned Renforth under his breath.

Oliver had paid little attention to the verbal exchange, however. When Jeremy and the Captain turned back to the prisoner, the young man was already squatting in front of him, staring in disbelief.

"What is it?" asked Jeremy, a chuckle still evident in his voice. "Have you never seen a man tied up before?"

Oliver ignored his cousin's facetious remark, his fallen nearly to his chest. "This man…" The lad was obviously shock and spoke in a hoarse whisper so that the prisoner would not be able to hear him. "This is the man that took the document from the dead man's pocket at the battle at Black Rock and gave me the address so I could tell the man's family."

★ ★ ★

Jeremy walked around the prisoner several times, saying nothing as he circled and studied the object of his interest. His intent was to unnerve the man even more than he already must have been by virtue of being tied and held prisoner in a tavern. Once he decided that he had accomplished that particular objective, he squatted down in front of the man, and looked him directly in the eyes, staring curiously still without speaking. In return, the prisoner stared quietly back through the one eye that was not swollen shut, for obviously he had resisted his capture. He was apparently unnerved by the silent attention.

Finally, Jeremy's voice boomed through the silence and tension he had created. "Why have you been trying to kill us?" he demanded.

The prisoner's eyes opened as wide as each could and then, partially recovering, chuckled nervously. "Are you crazy, man? Why on earth would I try to kill any of you?"

"Are you telling me that you didn't fire shots at us in front of the tavern earlier this night? And that you're not connected to that event in any way?" Jeremy asked skeptically.

"If someone fired shots at you, I hope you find them," the man grinned humourlessly, not truly caring. He obviously just wished the nightmare would go away so that he could get back to what he was doing. He squinted at the two men. "I don't know either of you so why would I wish for you to be harmed? Besides, I had only just arrived when I asked about you and was rewarded for my troubles with this abominable treatment."

"Why should I believe you?" Jeremy demanded, once again starting to pace around the man. When he noticed that the man sufficiently nervous to try to look about to see him, he stopped. "Why would you be asking about us if you don't know us? And was there anyone who can vouch for the moment of your arrival?"

"There certainly was," the prisoner replied, answering the last question first, his confidence recovering. "I'd arrived here on a wagon which I had hired in Stoney Creek. A farmer, I believe, named Jergens. If you ask him, I'm certain he would have no reason to deny it."

If you hired him in Stoney Creek, he's likely half way home again by now," Jeremy said dismissively. "We surely can't go chasing back after him. Anyone else?"

The man concentrated hard for a moment, apparently desperately searching for something else to prove his arrival. "I know! There was a man leaving at that time. By the way he shouted orders back inside as he left, I would guess he was the employer here."

"Well, that should be easy enough to check," Renforth offered. "The owner is here now. He never leaves for long, since he lives here. Just

enough to walk the smell of ale from his nose, he says. I'll go get him."
The military surgeon rose and left the room, closing the door behind him
to dissuade a pair of curious onlookers waiting outside.

Several minutes later, Renforth returned, tavern keeper in tow. "Tell
us, will you? Did you see this man alight from a wagon just as you were
leaving for your nightly stroll?"

The businessman squatted down in front of the prisoner. "I remember
someone looking much like him getting down from Herman Jergens'
wagon," he said finally, and then stood up. "Herman makes regular
deliveries here and sometimes drops off passengers who are on their way
eventually to the camp. So, is that all that you wanted to know?" he
asked. "This place needs cleaning up before I open up for business for the
day and can't be spending my time chatting with you gentlemen."

"No, thank you kindly," Renforth answered. "You've been a great
help. We should be finished here very shortly. Thank you for your help
and the use of you room here."

They waited for the tavern keeper to leave.

Jeremy turned to his cousin. "Oliver, didn't you say you saw him
here last night?'

Oliver looked about sheepishly. "Now that I see how this man is
dressed, I don't believe he's the same one. I guess I'm just overly nervous
in light of all the things that have happened." Seeing a disapproving
look in Jeremy's eyes, he blurted, "But they could surely have been
brothers."

Jeremy merely shook his head in reply.

Chapter Eight

"You still haven't told us why you would ask about people that you don't know. Who are you and why have you been following Oliver around?" Jeremy demanded of the prisoner.

"I told you, I know neither of you. Why would I be following this chap?" he asked, sounding genuinely puzzled.

"Do you mean to try to tell us that you don't know Oliver? Then why were you asking about us?"

"I wasn't asking about you," the man declared convincingly, looking quite confused. "I had asked if anyone had noticed two men come through here. There were a pair of questionable types I recognized from home and I wanted to avoid running into them."

"And who were these men?" Jeremy asked skeptically.

The prisoner looked his questioner in the face. "I don't actually know them. I've seen them in Buffalo when I've been there on business, and they're known to be of poor reputation. They've been known to run special...errands, shall we say. For Joseph Willcocks." He sat silent for a moment, and then a thought seemed abruptly to come to him. "Say, you don't suppose they would be the men who tried to kill you, do you?"

Jeremy looked up at Oliver and Captain Renforth, both of whom shrugged.

Left alone for a moment, the man now squinted again, trying to focus his vision as he looked long and hard at the young man his interrogator had indicated. He leaned forward and studied Oliver some more. Finally a look of recognition appeared on the man's face. "Why, aren't you the boy from Black Rock? The one I gave the name and directions to?"

"Do you yet mean to tell us that you hadn't any idea as to this fellow's identity?" Jeremy asked, trying to keep a note of scepticism in his voice but betraying some level of confusion in the effort.

"Do you expect us to believe that you just happened to run into me here, so far from home?" Oliver demanded, not waiting for an answer to his cousin's query.

"I run into people I know wherever I travel," the man responded. "I can see nothing strange about that." He smiled at Oliver condescendingly. "I am a businessman after all. It isn't as though there are so many places to travel to that you might you mightn't run into folks anywhere."

Oliver seemed suddenly less sure of himself. "But this is the second time I've come across you since I left home," he said, forcing the words as he attempted to marshal his thoughts.

"The second time?" Jeremy broke in.

"On my way to see you, I stopped at Shipman's Tavern for directions," Oliver muttered vaguely. "I saw him sitting in the corner by himself, and he looked directly at me. This is the man I told you about."

Captain Renforth seemed somewhat confused by this turn in the conversation. Leaning over the prisoner and with his face a mere few inches away, he sighed deeply, as though exasperated. "Before we continue, your name, sir?"

The man looked about furtively, as if trying to decide whether to tell these men this piece of information. He seemed to conclude that there would be no harm for he muttered, "Sims. James Archibald Sims."

"Is that it truly or did you spend so long answering that you might make this one up?"

"No. That is truthfully my name," Sims answered. "I just don't want my name cast idly about here. My health may well depend upon it."

"Well, at least we have something to call you now. As for seemingly following Oliver here, once might be coincidence," Renforth grumbled softly. "But twice in a matter of days seems a bit much to explain." Before the man could reply, he added, "And you needn't have feigned surprise at seeing Oliver here if you were caught looking at him at Shipman's."

In spite of the gravity of the situation, the prisoner chuckled. "I'm sorry gentlemen," he started. "I don't mean to make light of the situation. I truly have no answer as to why we ran into each other twice in such a short time, but I believe I can well acquit myself in the matter of my recognition of the young man."

"This I must hear," Jeremy remarked sarcastically as he folded his arms over his chest. "Go ahead. What fantastic tale would you tell us?"

The prisoner looked somewhat cowed by the disbelieving expressions on the faces of the three men standing around him and there was no laughter in his voice as he began to explain. "Well, er, that is, I have a problem with my eyesight," he managed to force out. "I'm dreadfully near-sighted and I really can't see from here to the door with any degree of accuracy." He rubbed his eyes to emphasize his point. "You may have noticed that I had to sit forward as far as I could and then squint quite painfully in order to identify the fellow you call Oliver."

"If your eyesight is so bad, why haven't you any spectacles?" Renforth demanded. "You appear to be a man of greater than modest means."

Now the man chuckled once more, seemingly unable to control this nervous habit. "Well, they were destroyed in the confusion of that battle that the young man was at." Seeing the puzzled look on Renforth's face, he added, "I suppose you didn't know that this young man was an American combatant, did you?" He found he had to laugh at this in spite of his situation. Then, before the officer could reply, he continued, "Well, at any rate now you see, because of my eyesight, I may well have looked directly at the young man. But if he was across the poorly lit tavern, I wouldn't have even seen him staring at me, much less recognize who he was."

★ ★ ★

Renforth paced back and forth several times. "I need a moment to digest what I've heard. I'm still left wondering why you, an American, are traveling about Niagara, just 'happening' to be in the same places as Oliver here."

Then, looking directly at Jeremy, he added, "And I now I must ask why it is that you're traveling about with an American combatant, and bringing him into a British camp, no less, where he can see the details of our defences!"

Renforth was visibly upset, and Jeremy decided it would be best if he answered that question now, before it threatened to confuse the issue at hand. "Captain, Oliver isn't a combatant. He just found himself, a young lad, caught up in the moment. His mother sent him to find me, his cousin, to take him in so he wouldn't be involved any further." He stopped momentarily to catch his breath before resuming. "We were on the base because we were asked by Captain Fitzgibbon's man to deliver a message, as I've been known to do from time to time. Oliver is honestly no threat to the British Army."

Renforth paced about, his head down, appearing to be deep in thought. "You're probably right, van Hijser," he said at last. "But we'll keep the lad off the base for now, shall we? And mum's the word concerning his nationality."

Jeremy and Oliver both nodded in agreement, almost simultaneously.

"That should be no problem," Jeremy added. "I'm afraid your Colonel has banished us from the base for all time. It seems he took issue with our being used for target practice and, in his frustration, decided that it was entirely our fault."

Renforth turned about, once again facing their prisoner. "So! How is it that you, apparently also an American combatant, and not Mr. van Hijser's cousin, come to be wandering about Niagara. And why have you stopped here, so close to this camp?"

"I am not a combatant!" Sims declared with apparent distaste. "I was near the battle site in Black Rock speaking to the gentleman that was killed. Then suddenly all hell broke loose and the other man threw himself into the fray, unfortunately getting himself killed in the process. I merely stood and watched from a safe distance until it was over."

"And why did you not fight?" Renforth asked dubiously.

"I, sir, am a businessman," Sims replied, puffing up his chest in a semblance of dignity he did not quite manage to make convincing. "I carry on my commerce on both sides of the river and find the entire question of war distasteful and a dreadful inconvenience to my business. I would stand to gain nothing by taking up arms for either side. Besides," he added with a weak and nervous smile, "with my eyesight, how would I shoot anyone – Just pull the trigger and hope I didn't hit one of my own?"

Jeremy did not return the smile as he let Sims finish and then asked what seemed to him to be the obvious question. "And just what would be the nature of your business, Mr. Sims?"

The prisoner looked evasive once again. "I, well I deal in old books, maps, manuscripts, that sort of thing."

Renforth studied Sims a moment and watched him become increasingly uncomfortable under his gaze. "I get the distinct impression that you don't wish to tell us just what it is you are up to," he said in a low but steady voice. "And if you aren't immediately more forthcoming,

I shall feel duty bound to take you to the camp with me and let the men there ask you questions. I suspect you will be spending the balance of the war there if you aren't hung as a spy."

Sims now began to visibly perspire, but did not immediately respond. His eyes darted about, as if looking for an avenue of escape or attempting to rapidly fabricate a tale, and his fingers fidgeted even more than they already were. However, the prospects of sitting out the war in a British jail or having his neck stretched by a noose were most unpleasant to consider. Besides, he thought, they might be able to help him with the puzzles involved.

"Fine," he said at last. "I'll tell you, but on the condition that you tell no one else."

"You are in no position to set conditions," Jeremy pointed out, smiling slightly.

Renforth momentarily lost his composure. "Do not for one instant believe that you are dealing with fools, Mr. Sims!" he growled, anger apparent in his eyes as well as his voice. "You will find yourself sadly mistaken in that case. What if you were to tell us you were indeed spying? We should then be forced to let you on your way without repeating a word? "There is simply no way that I…"

Jeremy looked over at Sims, a grim smirk appearing at the corners of his mouth. "Well, Sims, what say we just set you out at the road and let out the word that you have something that those brigands who tried to kill us might be interested in?"

A panicked look shot into the heavy man's eyes, the fear spreading rapidly across his face. "Very well, then," he relented shakily. "I'll tell you."

★ ★ ★

Sims took a deep breath and looked about the room at the three faces that stared back at him expectantly. "I was talking to that gentleman before the battle began at Black Rock because he had something in which I had an interest. I was told he had a certain document of which I had heard from a young man who offered to pay me handsomely for it if I should be able to get hold of it."

"I assume all of you are familiar with the Canadian Volunteers?" he said, interrupting his explanation. The remark was truly more of an assumption than a question. Everyone on the Niagara frontier on both sides of the border was familiar with Willcocks, although he was hardly seen in the same light.

"Some of us a great deal more than the others, unfortunately," Jeremy remarked wryly.

"Well," Sims continued, noticeably annoyed at the interruption even though it was of his own making. "Well, there was a renegade band that was barely controlled by the leader, Joseph Willcocks. A man by the name of..."

"Dorian Williamson" Jeremy remarked, finishing the man's sentence for him.

"You're familiar with the man?" Sims asked, genuinely curious.

Jeremy looked off as if into a great distance and said nothing for a moment. His face was a study in simultaneous rage and grief as the man's name brought the past briefly back to life. "He destroyed everything I held dear," he growled at last, his eyes assuming a distance and depth that could not be breached by travel.

Driving his pain back to the farther reaches of his mind, where he could more easily deal with it, he refocused on the man before him and cleared his throat. "I'm sorry, Mr. Sims," he said hoarsely. "Please continue."

Sims continued to stare wonderingly into Jeremy's face, and then snapped his attention back to his explanation. "Anyway, I was told that the man I was talking to might be in possession of a certain map and accompanying instructions. It was said that one of Williamson's men had given to him after the well-hated leader died at Queenston in a run-in with American soldiers brought on by an extreme case of insubordination by him."

The man stopped his story and added as an aside, almost conspiratorially, "It was said Willcocks himself helped hunt Williamson down, and there was a Canadian trapper involved, too."

Renforth glanced sharply over at Jeremy. "A trapper it was. Say, that wouldn't have been..." he started.

"This is not the moment to be discussing that!" Jeremy snapped. He did not wish to divulge that much information to this man nor discuss the details of his relationship with that beast to any of these people. He turned back to Sims. "Just get on with your explanation. We haven't forever you know."

Renforth looked at Jeremy curiously, but said nothing further for the time being.

Sims ignored them and continued with his explanation. "No one seems to be quite sure, apparently, what the document was for, but it's thought that Williamson or someone close to him had hidden something in the place indicated in the letters. I personally heard a rumour that it was something of great value to anyone who found it."

★ ★ ★

"And this rumour didn't tell you more specifically what this treasure might be that Williamson supposedly hid?" Renforth asked skeptically.

"No, I don't really know, but he suggested that it was something that some person or persons of importance would be very happy to retrieve. I don't know the nature of this person. With what I know of Williamson, I'm sure you'll agree he stole plenty from persons of importance," he said, looking directly at Jeremy. "To make this long story short, the man who was shot was trying to sell me these instructions when all the trouble started."

"And if these documents were so valuable, why did you think that this man wouldn't just try to sell them to the right people himself?" Jeremy demanded, his eyes burning holes through Sims, obviously not believing the man's story. After all, he did not know MacPhail well, but this story did not quite ring true from what he did know of the man. "Did he happen to mention that particular detail?"

Sims turned away from Jeremy's penetrating stare for a moment. "I was hoping that the gentleman didn't truly know what he had in his possession, since he mentioned nothing of its originator or persons of power. I was trying to convince him that it was merely a curiosity that someone dealing in antiquities, such as myself, might be able to sell to someone of like mind."

All the while he spoke, Jeremy noticed, Sims had never returned his gaze to his own. He decided that he just did not believe this man. But those details were probably not important now, he decided. That could be better dealt with at a later date.

Now Renforth stepped into the interrogation. "And naturally, when he was shot, you decided you could now have the document for free," he commented sarcastically. Sims was leaving an objectionable taste in his mouth.

Sims seemed not to notice the Captain's tone of voice. "Naturally, I felt that there was no point in allowing the papers go to the grave with the man. No one else would know what to do with them, for they bear no title proclaiming their purpose."

"Of course, you could not have explained it to, say, his family could you?" Oliver sneered. "Do you know that someone thought I had it and may have tried to kill me on at least two occasions?" The lad was obviously becoming angry.

Sims merely shrugged.

"Well what is it that brings you here?" Renforth demanded of Sims, breaking in again and not yet satisfied.

"My ride took me as far as Stoney Creek before I lost my mount to a broken leg," Sims explained. "Indeed, I'm headed for the town of York and this was where the gentleman who drove me wished to drop me off."

"Why York?" Jeremy asked.

"Because that's where the clues in the instructions take me," he replied smugly, as if they all should have been able to guess that.

Chapter Nine

Jeremy studied their prisoner carefully for several minutes, allowing the tension to build. Then he asked Sims, "So. Now what exactly do you expect us to do with you?"

"Let me go?" asked Sims hopefully, fully aware that the chances of that prospect would be slim to none.

"Surely you jest," said Renforth with an ironic chuckle. "I'm still not fully convinced you aren't some kind of American spy, although you scarcely seem intelligent enough for that." He hesitated momentarily, ignoring their prisoner's weak protestations concerning his intelligence. "But you are most obviously a scoundrel and perhaps a criminal as well. In any case, we can hardly allow you the freedom of Upper Canada to conduct your quest, especially since the thing you seek is a possibly damaging packet of documents hidden by a known thief, murderer and traitor to the Crown. And on top of all those things, you are an American and quite possibly a spy, despite your protestations that you are merely a businessman conducting your business."

Sims sucked in a deep breath, apparently trying to head off an attack of panic. He looked from face to face to face, desperately searching for a way out of this hole he had dug for himself. "What if I were to let you share in part of it, whatever it is?" he suggested finally and almost frantically.

"What if we let you show us where it is and then we could then decide what its future is to be?" Jeremy suggested alternatively, purposely not looking at the man. It was immediately obvious that Sims was about to object, but he cut the man off before he could speak. "This certainly seems like a fair bargain in exchange for your neck."

Jeremy's eyebrows arched dangerously as he turned suddenly and looked deeply into the man's eyes and added, seemingly as an afterthought, "For that matter, what's to stop us from disposing of you here, relieving you of the document and then finding this treasure for ourselves?"

Sims seemed taken aback by the suggestion and he hesitated for the space of several heartbeats before he replied hesitatingly. "Well, you might well do the first," he started, obviously picking up confidence as he spoke. "The problem, however, is with the second. You see, I no longer have the document." He seemed to be doing his best to avoid the eyes of any of his questioners as he spoke. "I committed the information to memory. If you want to know the contents thereof, you'll need to take me along and I'll give you the information sparingly, as necessity dictates. Not that I don't trust you gentlemen," he added quickly with a nervously hopeful smile.

Sims closed his mouth, silencing the additional words that had been forming on his lips. Perhaps he should make the bargain and then watch for a future opportunity to escape. It was much better than the alternatives. He had no doubt that these men, especially the Captain, could arrange to have him hanged. He was an American after all, in enemy territory during a war. "Well, gentlemen? Have we struck a bargain?" he asked, inwardly quivering with fright at the possibilities if they should not to go along with his plan.

Before anyone could respond to Sims' offer, Renforth broke in. "Wait one minute! Jeremy, I think you and I must have another little talk."

Jeremy was followed from the room by Oliver and then Renforth. Standing at the back of the bar, which was as quiet as a morgue at this hour, Jeremy turned and faced the Captain.

"What is it you wished to discuss?" he asked in feigned innocence.

Renforth snorted in disbelief. "What do I wish to discuss? I wish to discuss why I was bargaining with an American national found on British soil, that's what!"

"Oh, is that all," Jeremy responded facetiously.

"Is that all?" Renforth sputtered. "Is that all?"

"The Captain seems at a loss for words," Jeremy said to his cousin who shrugged, not wishing to become involved in this particular exchange. Then, turning back to Renforth, Jeremy urged, "Come on, out with it. What exactly is the problem?"

Renforth looked at Jeremy in disbelief. "If it's discovered that I've known something of this magnitude without informing the appropriate officers, it could well mean my career, not to mention the possibility of my hanging," he said evenly.

"We wouldn't be setting him free to recover whatever the treasure might be," Jeremy pointed out. "But there is no question but that you shall have to accompany us in so doing." Noting the look of shock on the Captain's face, he quickly added, "To be sure of the security of the prisoner in the service of some of the Crown in recovering what might well be the property of some of Upper Canada's wealthiest and, I might add, most influential citizens."

A broad, mischievous grin had formed on his face as he spoke. "After all, Sims doesn't truly know what is in that cache. Knowing Williamson as I did, it could well be stolen goods from the properties of his enemies, the well to do of Newark, but I have a feeling, for reasons I couldn't explain even to myself, that it might be something much more important. Perhaps something that might affect the outcome of the war."

Renforth slowly shook his head, not in the negative, but in astonishment. "It amazes me the way you seem to be able to twist things to your advantage."

"So I believe you are in agreement, then?" Jeremy asked.

"I shall need to get permission from the camp commander, as you well know, or at least should know," Renforth said in reply. "I really don't know how he'll react to such a request, especially since I can't lie to him about something of such gravity. And I should hasten to point out that he isn't particularly fond of either of us at the moment." "There's no need to lie. Just be sure to put your request in the words I gave you," Jeremy answered. "I've not yet met many senior officers who didn't have their future interests and possible promotions in mind at all times. Perhaps you could put it so that it's his idea. That way he can take the credit with a clean conscience," he suggested.

Renforth slowly walked toward the door, softly shaking his head. "It just might be silly enough to work."

Before he opened that door, however, he turned back to Jeremy. "Just why are you so interested in chasing what might well be a wild goose?"

Jeremy thought about it for a moment, searching his own heart for the true reason. Many came to mind, but the one stood to the fore.

"I knew Williamson as well as just about any person alive," he replied slowly. "One thing about him stands out – the fact that he never did anything in secret. He murdered openly, he stole openly and he used his ill-gotten booty openly. If he went through this much trouble to conceal something, you can wager that it must have been of some importance. It may just be important enough to affect a great many people and I think we should try to find out."

Renforth considered the answer a moment and then nodded. Without another word, he went through the door.

Then the Captain took a deep breath and walked out, leaving Jeremy once again wearing that same grin and Oliver watching on in open-mouthed astonishment.

★ ★ ★

A formless hat slouched low over his face, the man walked nonchalantly up to the sentry at the south guard post of Burlington Heights Army camp. There he left the simple message that he had to immediately speak to the officer who he specified. All the while, he tried to maintain a disinterested pose while he made certain that his face remained in the shadows. It was important not just to him but to the officer as well that no one get a good look at him. When the sentry returned in short order with the requested officer, he left the two men to speak momentarily and then watched the man quickly walk away.

Fourteen minutes later, the officer was seen walking alone and leaving the camp by way of a different sentry post. Well away from the prying eyes of the camp, he met up with the anonymous man in a secluded location.

"This had better be extremely important," the officer growled. "You're playing a dangerous game, summoning me at the sentry in that manner. Well, what is it?"

The man looked the officer coolly in the eyes. "I just overheard a conversation that I thought you would be more than interested to hear."

The officer stamped his feet impatiently. When the man did not explain immediately, the cold, his possible exposure and his impatience got the better of him. "Well? Get on with it, man!"

"The boy from Black Rock doesn't have the instructions," the other said quietly, noting with a measure of satisfaction that the officer's face displayed obvious confusion.

"Where is it then, or don't you know?"

"A man named Sims, who the boy thought was following him, apparently had it."

The officer paced about and then stopped. "Well, there's nothing for it," he sighed at last. "Follow this man Sims until you find the opportunity to kill him. Is he traveling alone?"

"He was," replied the other. "But now it seems he'll be with at least the boy and the other man, the trapper."

Just then, they saw Captain Renforth walking by, his pace suggesting a sense of purpose.

"That officer was at the tavern when they were questioning Sims," the spy pointed out. "Has he been to report?"

"Yes, he came to request leave for a special mission on behalf of the influential citizens of Newark as he put it," the officer replied. "To go with a locally known scout named Jeremy van Hijser on this quest. No real details, mind you. The answer was put off for an hour while for full consideration, likely with an eye to turning down the request as foolish. Do you suppose that Sims is the mission?"

"It most assuredly is. Van Hijser is the trapper that the boy from Black Rock is travelling with. Perhaps you could see if you can go along instead of Renforth?" the informer suggested. "Then we'll have a man on the inside, so to speak."

"You know I can't do that," the officer snapped. "That would seem rather odd, don't you think? A man in my position taking his leave to go adventuring about the colony?"

"You're right, of course. But do let them go or the mission might end there, for surely Renforth will have him brought in. Sims is an American, you see? I don't know why they wish to go to York in this regard, but perhaps I can find out by following closely. I have managed to do so quite easily to this point, but their numbers are growing as they continue. Perhaps I'll see my chance if I can hire some more men to help me. If not, I'll just see what I can do."

"I have an idea that may help," the officer said suddenly, as a thought occurred to him. He outlined his idea to the informant. "I'll make the necessary arrangements and have someone contact you. But be sure that you get it. We don't want to run the risk of anyone else knowing."

"Don't worry. It may take some time but rest assured, the papers will be mine." The man turned to leave, a grin of maddening self-assurance on his lips.

"Before you go," the officer said, seemingly as an afterthought. "I've dealt with you several times now and have no name by which to call you. It would be easier to converse if I had such a name."

The informant turned slowly back to the officer as if he were thinking. "Very well. You may call me Wolf."

"Wolf?" the officer responded, his voice a mixture of puzzlement and annoyance. "That's it? Just Wolf?"

"Just Wolf," the man repeated without explanation.

"Oh, and one last thing," the officer added as Wolf was almost away. "He's in the area – you know who I mean – with his band of madmen. He actually came onto the base last night and tried to kidnap the boy and his friend. He's becoming very bold…or very desperate. Be sure to keep an eye out."

★ ★ ★

Renforth returned to Smith's Tavern three hours later and Jeremy was dismayed to note that the captain did not come alone. He was accompanied by a younger regular soldier.

"Who is this, Captain?" Jeremy asked without emotion although his annoyance at this sudden turn could barely be contained.

"Colonel Halberson said that it had been recommended that I bring along reinforcement," the Captain said by way of explanation, seeing the questioning expressions on the faces of the civilians.

"And what exactly was it the good Colonel wished to reinforce?" Jeremy asked. "There's nothing this boy can do for us except to get in the way. Why do I suspect that Halberson doesn't trust us?" he added sarcastically.

Renforth threw Jeremy a warning glance that let the latter know they could not speak freely in front of the enlisted man. "I would like you gentlemen to meet infantryman Davis Halberson," he said while lifting his eyes toward the ceiling in an expression of exasperation.

Jeremy said nothing but threw Oliver a glance that told them he too should keep any observations to himself. It was obvious that the Colonel had sent along someone who he felt he could trust implicitly, someone who would be sure to report everything that happened and was said. They would need to be extremely watchful of every word they uttered lest this lad, who was obviously a relative of the Colonel, report back something they did not wish the Colonel to know. This would indeed be uncomfortable he thought. It was certainly an unnecessary complication in an already complicated situation.

The young soldier glanced about the room from one man to the other, seemingly amused at the obvious discomfort of these strangers.

"Is there a problem with my being here, Captain?" he asked finally.

"Not to worry, son," Jeremy answered quickly, for Renforth seemed at a loss as to what to tell the young man without lying to him. "Do you mind if I just call you Davis?" The young man answered with a shake of the head, so he continued. "We just hadn't expected anyone else along. We must move lightly and quickly to achieve our end and an extra body just makes it that much more unwieldy."

The junior Halberson looked slightly perplexed. "Just what is our end, as you put it? That is to say, what exactly is our mission? I'm afraid my uncle told me precious little about this but to accompany you and report back to him. He wants me to report in great detail, I might add, something that I don't quite understand, but then I'm not an officer. But I just do as I'm told, so here I am."

Jeremy and the Captain glanced knowingly at each other, their suspicions confirmed. But, what should they tell the lad? And how far should they go in telling him? "We'll explain later," Jeremy said finally. "We really must be off."

"I am apparently under your command, or at least under the command of Captain Renforth," remarked the infantryman acidly. "But I think we should clear the air before we go." He looked from man to man with a challenge in his eyes.

"Well, go ahead then," Jeremy replied.

Halberson lightly cleared his throat. "I know what it is that's creating a certain stress between us," he started. "It's true that I am the Colonel's nephew. But I should like to make it clear that it is my father who is indebted to the old man. I feel no such bond to the Colonel. Whether you believe it or not, I have no intention of telling him anything of importance. At the least, no more than I shall be forced to."

Jeremy smiled. "I would dearly love to believe that. But, if you don' mind terribly, we'll reserve judgment on you until we know you better." He did not wait for a reply but started off toward the door to go.

One after the other the group, which was now five strong, filed out. They kept Sims in the middle for the purpose of keeping a close eye on him at all times. The tavern was filling rapidly with customers, none of them seemingly paying the small troop much attention, busy as they were with the matters that occupied men in such places.

Chapter Ten

As they neared the door two men stood up and to the wary group they seemed to be intent upon blocking their progress. Jeremy looked them over, taking their measure and looking for obvious weak spots. Both were large men and judging by their builds, no strangers to hard work. But instead of causing the group a direct problem, they started shoving and shouting obscenities at each other. The tiff moved them in their path toward the door until they completely blocked the way for Jeffery and his companions.

"Here now," Davis muttered loudly as he pushed one of the two none to gently out of the way. "A bit early in the day for that, don't you think?"

The man who he had shoved lost his balance and stumbled over a bench by the door, sending him sprawling across the rough planks. "What the devil?" he remarked, rising slowly and unsteadily to his feet.

The second man, who had been the opponent only moments ago, now pushed the infantryman. "Who do you think you are? Just because you wear the King's uniform, you think you can push people around, don't you. Well," he said removing his jacket and whipping it across the room, "let's see what you're made of then." He raised his fists and steadied himself, affecting a poor approximation of a fighting stance.

Davis leaned his musket against the wall and started to remove his own coat. He was game for a bit of a brawl, but Captain Renforth put his hand on the younger man's shoulder.

"If you're to accompany us, keep your gun handy and your temper in check, and never mind the local drunks," he said sternly. "We must keep our eyes open for serious attack and never mind this sort of tomfoolery."

Chastened, the younger Halberson his coat back into place and picked up his gun. Then he turned to the two drunks and showed them his fist. "Right lucky you two are. Next time it'll be the pigsty for the both of you."

With that, he turned and followed the others out the door, stinging from the ring of the drunken bullies' mocking laughter that resounded in his ears and his mind.

★ ★ ★

Once the men had walked clear of the tavern and those curious onlookers who sat just outside on a bench, Jeremy turned to Sims. "And just where is that we're going?" he asked evenly.

"To York," Sims replied ingenuously, knowing full well what the question had meant. "I had thought that we'd settled that some time ago."

"I'd appreciate it if you'd not take us for fools," growled Renforth. "Just where exactly in York are we going?"

Sims looked about at his companions faces, and flashed an infuriating grin. "If I gave you all the information I have, you would no longer need me, now would you?" he commented archly. "I told you that I know where we need to go and I'll keep the information to myself but for that which you need to know next."

"What makes you think we can't just kill you and take the information you're talking about?" Halberson suggested. "Not that I have the slightest clue as to what that might be," he added perhaps a little too quickly. "But then we won't need you at all."

Sims now laughed aloud and shot back, "I've already been through that with your companions, but I'll repeat it since they obviously haven't let you in on the situation. I no longer have the paper. That wouldn't really have been terribly smart, now would it?" He tapped his head. "The information's right next to here, so you had better keep me alive if we're to find what we're looking for."

The group had continued to walk as they talked and now had entered a copse of almost naked elm trees. Before Davis Halberson could reply to Sims' remark or to query his companions as to the nature of the "paper" or what the information might be about, two men stepped out onto the road before them. Both he and Jeremy raised their weapons.

"Yield the road," Captain Renforth ordered the pair almost off-hand. "In the name of the King."

"I think not," growled one of them, a large, red-faced man. His eyes, one of which moved more slowly than the other, shifted back and forth, as though extremely nervous. "Look behind you."

Jeremy turned his head partly to the side so that he could look about without losing sight of the two the before him. What he saw with his peripheral vision were three more men with guns at the ready immediately to their rear. As he scanned back slowly to the front, he noticed several more stepping out on either side of them.

All of the men who now surrounded them were dirty, unshaven and ill-clothed. Aside from their slovenly appearance, the only other things they seemed obviously to have in common were the fact that most seemed young and they all held Brown Bess muskets, the ubiquitous weapon that, known by various names, armed most men on both sides of the war.

"Who the devil are you and what do you want?" Renforth demanded, affecting a posture of control despite the situation.

A man who had remained purposely remained hidden until now stepped from the shadows and strode confidently out in before of the foremost men. Jeremy immediately recognized him as the leader of the thugs that had tried to kidnap them the night before. There was no mistaking this man's deep, sonorous voice, which seemed to issue forth from the tangled mass of dark and unkempt beard like a rumble of thunder. Surprisingly clear blues eyes seemed to almost glow which, along with his blondish hair, seemed to stand out in marked contrast with the beard. If Jeremy had had any doubts that this was man that almost killed him the previous night, they were erased especially by those eyes. They seemed to burn with the light of fanaticism, an impression that would immediately be borne out.

"Most people call me the Parson," the stranger replied, almost as if he were casually making for polite conversation.

"I've heard tell of you," Jeremy returned, equally conversationally, while attempting to quickly assess the situation and grasping for an answer to this dilemma. "I believe your real name is Phineas Billings, correct?"

The Parson stared at Jeremy from hooded eyes. "That's right, Jeremy. And have you figured out yet where you know me from? Apart from last evening of course."

"Last night you mentioned Queenston." It seemed the man wished to make a game of this. Very well, let's see where it takes us, Jeremy thought, still smiling.

"I have a feeling that was just the final battle against your brother-in-law," Jeremy continued. "What you really wish for me to remember is that you helped the bastard beat me senseless while I lay defenceless in the barn just outside of Newark."

The Parson's weather-beaten face broke into a cruel grin. "So you know that Williamson was my brother-in-law. Then you also know that I have every reason for a vendetta."

Jeremy smirked. "I believe that I am the one who bears a motive for a vendetta," he replied. "But if you are trying to convince me that this is about my killing your relative, I don't believe it for a moment. From what I've heard, you haven't the soul to care about anyone other than yourself. I truly doubt that anyone, even a relative, could have shed any tears over that animal's death. Why are you really here and what is it you want of us?"

There was a moment of silence as the two men stared, each taking the other's measure, while the men on both sides waited curiously and nervously to see what was to happen. The Parson began to pace back and forth ever more agitatedly and then, without warning, lunged at Jeremy, his hands reaching for the trapper's throat.

Jeremy knew that he could not allow the large, rough hands of the former miller to reach his neck for there was raw, primitive power in the man. Once he gained a hold it would be very difficult to pry him off. Jeremy quickly stepped forward into the opening created by his adversary's spread hands and punched him hard in the chest and midriff.

The Parson was quite taken by surprise. He was accustomed to his targets stepping back out of fear when he attempted to strangle them, not step in and deal him a flurry of blows from between his arms. Then the surprise turned quickly to rage, more due to embarrassment than from pain. But before he could act upon his anger, his men stepped forward and forced Jeremy back at gunpoint. This action effectively formed a shield between him and his adversary.

"Well," the Parson panted. "It would seem you've not lost the spirit I saw in you at our last encounter earlier this year. Would that some of these dogs had as much," he snarled, his arm sweeping across his own men, making it clear it was they to whom he was referring. He roughly pushed the closest of them away from him and stepped forward, at the same time delivering a crushing blow to Jeremy's abdomen.

Jeremy sank to one knee and looked up his assailant while fighting to regain his wind. "And you," he wheezed, then coughed and spit into the dirt. "You are still the same coward that helped beat me while I was tied up in a barn." He suddenly wretched violently and uncontrollably and vomited onto the Parson's boots.

The Parson stood motionless, livid at both the perceived insult and the fouling of his boots. Fighting to control himself in front of his men, he clenched and unclenched his fists, which hung straight down at his side. "I'll finish with you another time," he finally muttered through clenched teeth. "For now, I have other business to attend here."

Now a cruel smile broke out upon the brigand's face as he stepped over and stood directly in front of Sims, looking him hard in the eye.

For Sims' part, the sweat poured profusely as his eyes darted about frantically from his ruddy face. The short, round man was inwardly praying fervently for salvation from the beating – or worse – that he was certain he was about to receive.

"By the look of your countenance, I gather you know who I came to see," the Parson suggested with a deceptively light voice. "And since you do, you'll surely also know what it was that I came to see you about."

"N-no," Sims stammered, desperately trying to think of a way out of his predicament. "Wh-what on earth do you mean."

The Parson walked slowly around behind the terrified American until he stood directly behind the man. Slowly, intending to draw out the terror he knew he was causing, he put his mouth close to Sims ear and said softly, "The document, Mr. Sims. I want the document this instant!" He almost spat out the final word, causing Sims to start rather violently.

"I don't have it any longer," Sims blurted, the words rushing out so they almost blended into one long word. "I destroyed it before I crossed the border." All could see that he was now weeping openly. "Please don't hurt me, Parson," he begged softly. "I can't give you what I no longer have."

The Parson moved slowly around to stand directly in front of Sims, his body so close as to almost touch the trembling man as he seemed to slither around to his new position. Then, with a sudden movement that made his quarry jump once more, he pulled his hunting knife from its sheath at his side and pressed it lightly against the now-wailing man's throat.

★ ★ ★

"Why don't you leave the man alone?" demanded Jeremy, now back on his feet and trying unsuccessfully to ignore the pain in his stomach. "He told you he no longer has it, whatever it may have been. We searched his clothes ourselves and found nothing and nothing is all that he can give you."

The Parson turned his head about slowly. He said nothing directly to Jeremy, but simply said, "Robert."

At the command, the man who was standing closest to him pushed his musket up under Jeremy's chin and pulled back the hammer.

"This is a private conversation between myself and Mr. Sims here," the Parson said evenly, the underlying menace evident in his voice, although he no longer faced toward Jeremy. "I'll thank you kindly not to interrupt while we talk."

"Now, Mr. Sims," he breathed menacingly, turning his attention back to the quaking American. "Why don't you tell me all I need to know while I remind you of the wages of the sin of lying to me?" A thin trickle of blood was now making its way down Sims' neck from the point of the knife, staining his collar.

Before the probing could continue any further, Renforth broke free of his guards. He pushed one roughly aside, causing the surprised Volunteer to lose his balance and fall to the road. Before the other could react, he pulled the musket from his hands and levelled the bandit with a swing of the butt firmly across the face. He then pointed the weapon directly at the Parson.

"That will be enough!" Renforth barked. "Parson, tell your men to lay up their weapons or I will, without hesitation, send you back to Hell where you belong!"

The Parson looked about uneasily, trying to decide if there could be a way out of the situation. "You only have one shot," he said evenly.

"That's true," Renforth acknowledged. "But that one shot will be for you if I see any of your men so much as twitch while laying up their arms. And although I'm but a doctor, even I can hardly miss you at this range."

The self-appointed holy man lowered his knife from Sims' throat and turned to his men. "Alright, lads, you heard the man. Lay your guns slowly upon the ground. I don't fancy any new holes in my person."

One by one, the Volunteers placed their weapons down, and Jeremy and his companions picked up their own. Oliver went about under the Captain's orders, collecting the weapons and tossing them in a heap at one side of the road.

"What will we do with them now, Captain?" Davis Halberson asked, his eyes darting nervously from one prisoner to another.

"I suppose we must interrupt our expedition and bring these men back to the camp at the Heights," Renforth suggested. "Being who they are, I'm sure they'll be swinging from the gallows at Ancaster before the month is out. Move them all to the centre of the road, that we might have them together."

Before the Captain's instruction could be carried out, the man who had been guarding Jeremy dove suddenly to the road, pulling a second pistol from his coat. Choosing the man who he thought to be the leader, he fired at Renforth, striking him high and felling him.

There was no time for the others to immediately see to the Captain, for all Hell broke loose, as Halberson turned and almost reflexively fired his gun into the offending man. His weapon now discharged, it was now useful only as a club, or for its bayonet. Seeing his disadvantage, there was a mad scramble for discarded firearms.

Jeremy noticed that one of the Volunteers had decided to rush the embattled Halberson. With barely a second to aim, he unloaded the rifle of his over/under, seriously injuring the man while Halberson fought a desperate hand-to-hand battle with another of the Parson's men. Then the trapper removed a threat to Sims with a judicious throw of his tomahawk and felled yet another with the scattergun that his same gun sported.

Oliver found that there seemed to be no room to fire his musket here, as the battle turned quickly to a close-quarters brawl. He faced off against two of the Volunteers, knife in one hand and his detached bayonet in the other. Carefully, they circled, and Oliver could see that the two men intended to trap him between them, so he backed up slowly to a stand of trees which lined the road.

As it appeared that the two were about to charge him simultaneously, a move he felt in his heart he would likely not survive, another shot rang out. One of the two dropped, a surprised expression on his face, and

Oliver allowed himself a split-second to look over at Captain Renforth, who had somehow managed to pull himself up on one elbow and fire his pistol. The officer flashed Oliver a quick, weak smile and then slumped once again into the roadway.

Seeing that he was likely to lose more men of his men, with the outcome hardly guaranteed, the Parson called out, "Brothers, retreat!"

Like ghosts in the night, the bandits melted away into the surround brush. Only the crash of branches gave away their approximate location as they scrambled to evacuate what had only seconds ago been a battle site.

"This isn't over," the Parson growled as he stopped momentarily at the tree line. He hesitated only momentarily, looking at these people who had so disgraced him in front of his own men, before he too vanished into the brush.

"Of that you can be sure!" Jeremy spat back.

"Let's after them!" young Halberson shouted, heading for the trees.

Chapter Eleven

"Let them go," Jeremy replied wearily, putting out his arm just in time to impede the infantryman. "They can easily wait in ambush for us in there, especially if we charge in there willy-nilly. Besides, we truly must see to each other now."

Halberson stared off after the escaping Volunteers, frustration eating at his gut. Then, after but a moment's watch, he spotted one of the Volunteers about two hundred yards distant. The man had broken from the trees for the moment, no doubt feeling himself safe at this distance, and was now running at a greatly relaxed pace in the open.

The young soldier raised his firearm to his shoulder, braced his legs to fire and then carefully sighted the length of the barrel. He breathed in deeply and then slowly exhaled, squeezing slowly and evenly on the trigger. There was a loud report and a puff of smoke. In the blink of an eye, the Volunteer arched his back, his face visibly contorted even at this distance, and disappeared into the tall grasses through which he had been running.

Jeremy seemed barely to notice the nearly miraculous shot. He had hastened to Renforth's side, hoping beyond hope that that he could still help the man. But he knew well before he knelt that any attempted aid would be pointless. The Captain's body lay totally relaxed in the dark puddle that had so recently provided his life force. There was no movement to his chest, nor any sign of pain on the man's face. To be sure, Jeremy rolled him onto his back and held his ear close to Renforth's mouth and nose, but no air moved and no sounded issued from within the now empty husk that had been Captain Howard Renforth.

He rose slowly to his feet, still looking down at the man who had helped them and died so needlessly. Again someone he knew had fallen at the hands of the brigand group that had started with the Parson's brother-in-in-law, Dorian Williamson. And all led back to the traitor Willcocks.

"How is everyone else?" he asked absently, his mumbling voice barely above a whisper. His rage consumed him so that all else seemed to fade.

"I think he cut my throat," Sims whined, after Davis and Oliver had indicated that they had suffered no serious injury.

Jeremy experienced a sudden burst of anger that he would have been hard pressed to explain had anyone asked. He spun about and faced the man, his face dark with the fires of his emotion.

"I almost wish that he would have done!" he snapped viciously. "This good man lying here died saving your worthless hide, and all you can do is squeal like the pig you are over a slight scratch on your neck. Have you no honour?" He stepped toward Sims menacingly. "Now get up from the road and see if you can summon a bit of dignity, you damned coward!"

Sims straightened up and faced at Jeremy with something approaching defiance in his eyes. "He didn't die for me and you know it as well as me," he said tentatively. "He died trying to find out where the treasure is."

Jeremy's first instinct was to throttle the man where he stood but before he could take a step, Davis intervened and struck the little man full across the mouth. The blow was hard enough to drive him back down into the dirt of the roadway. Then, without a word, he glared at the American and turned his back in apparent disgust, stalking away toward Renforth's body.

"I suppose we had best bring the Captain back to camp for a proper burial before we go on," he suggested softly. "This man deserves a soldier's burial."

Jeremy suddenly became aware of their surroundings and the remaining peril in their situation. He scanned the woods and brush about their position and listened to the silence that seemed to pervade the scene. "I wonder why we haven't drawn any attention to this point," he said suddenly. "There are soldiers at the tavern and surely they must have heard the guns."

When they arrived at Smith's Tavern, there was indeed group of soldiers hanging about outside. "Did none of you hear all the shooting and yelling?" Jeremy demanded angrily.

"Certainly," answered one of the enlisted men. "But, when we suggested to our Sergeant that we go and investigate, he told us that it must be hunters and that we were to remain here."

Jeremy stared at the man in disbelief. "That must surely have been some hunting party," he suggested sarcastically. "For all the noise, you must certainly have thought that the game was fighting back. And certainly there would be no game left in all of Upper Canada had such shooting been necessary to bring it all down."

The soldier appeared ashamed at their inaction, so Jeremy approached and clapped him on the shoulder. "I'm sorry. I'm well aware that the decision not to act was not yours. But I would like a word with this Sergeant, if you can direct me to him."

One of the other soldiers who had closed in to stare at the dead officer and who now eavesdropped on the conversation decided to speak up. "He left, back toward camp immediately after telling us to hold fast," he said. "He seemed to be in some hurry."

"What odd behaviour," Oliver commented.

"Indeed," Jeremy muttered in agreement. "That is odd indeed."

It took the small party the greatest portion of the balance of daylight to transport the body of the fallen Captain back to the Burlington Heights base. They had attempted to have the soldiers at the tavern do it so that they could be underway, but those men understandably wanted nothing to do with the strange matter. Not able to find even a wagon for the task, Jeremy draped their late companion unceremoniously across the old horse of a willing farmer and headed back to the camp.

It was not the action of choice for Jeremy, who was certain there would be a confrontation with the Colonel.

"What do you think we should do with Sims while we're in camp?" Oliver asked as he led the horse down the road.

"You're quite right," Jeremy answered. "It probably would be best not to bring him with us, in case he should be recognized or wanted or something. Besides, the Colonel might decide to beat the truth out of him, if he even cares that is."

"What will we do, then?" Davis Halberson joined in. "Leave him tied up in the woods until we come back out?"

"Just a moment!" Sims protested from the rear of the procession upon hearing Davis' suggestion. "If you are concerned that I might bolt, you needn't be. After that little demonstration by the Parson and his boys, I have no desire to strike back out on my own. You may have noticed that I am not the strongest fighter hereabouts."

The snort of derision resulting from that ridiculously obvious conclusion seemed almost to issue simultaneously from the other three men.

"Very well, then," Jeremy decided. "Sims will wait for us outside and will rejoin us when we come back. Jeremy, you will remain to guard him from himself and others."

He could see that Oliver was about to protest this decision, so he raised his hand in a halting gesture. Then he turned to the American. "But just be sure you understand that I am a hunter, a trapper and an occasional scout. If you suddenly take it into your head to run, let there be no doubt in your mind that I will be able to track you and hunt you down. And I would be somewhat upset should that happen."

When the group arrived at the camp, Colonel Halberson showed little concern at the news of the loss of his surgeon. However, he did attempt to play the part. "Is this then to be the wage of your little adventure?" he asked of Jeremy with a sneer. "I give you one of my officers to accompany you on this fool's errand and you have him killed before he is out of sight of the base?"

"We had no idea that anyone would attack us in force, Colonel, directly under the nose of the largest garrison west of Kingston," Jeremy replied wryly. "Especially with soldiers nearby at the tavern. I would have certainly thought that the scuffle we had last evening would be the end of it."

Halberson leaned forward in his seat, the wood creaking under the effort. "Now why would you think that?"

Jeremy smiled tiredly. "Why, we were certain that any self-respecting and competent commander would have sent patrols to search the area for traitors around your own base," he replied, watching Halberson's face turn red as he spoke. "And we were equally certain that such activity would have cleared the area of all such villains by now. Whatever the case, sir, I fear that we must be on our way. There is little light left to us and I would like to be clear of Little Lake before we stop for the night."

"You, of course, may do whatever you wish, not being of the military," Halberson said sternly. "However, the man you were escorting and my nephew will remain here. My brother wouldn't be the least impressed if should be forced to tell him that his only son had died here in this backwater."

There was a curious lack of conviction to the Colonel's argument, Jeremy thought.

"Excuse me, Uncle. If I may speak freely?" Davis interrupted, to the senior Halberson's obvious chagrin.

"Go ahead, Private. Speak your mind," the Colonel replied.

"You had sent me on a mission which may be of advantage to some of the more influential members of Upper Canadian society," the nephew offered, stressing the word "influential", as though he had a good measure of the man before him. "Nothing has changed except that these brigands have proven the importance of our mission."

Colonel Halberson studied his nephew momentarily. "You will remember, of course, that you are a mere infantryman and I am your Colonel," he said evenly and without a hint of menace. "You will not argue with my decisions."

"You granted me permission to speak freely, sir," the young man pointed out. Then, seeing the threatening look in his uncle's eyes, he added "Yes sir."

"That's quite alright Colonel," Jeremy interjected, attempting to draw the heat from the young soldier. "I'll need to discuss the matter with General Vincent, I suppose. I understand he's expected back on base in the next day or two." A sly look became evident in his face as he added, "I'm quite sure that even a Brigadier-General can use a leg up from the colony's leading citizens."

The elder Halberson's face seemed to drop at this suggestion. "You will be quiet while I finish what I was intending to say," he blustered, trying to salvage the situation without openly losing face to these civilians. "It will make little difference to me to have one soldier more or less on base. I just wanted to be certain you understood the gravity of the situation." To his nephew, he added, "You have one month and then I expect you back here reporting to me."

As uncle and nephew spoke, Jeremy felt that he detected some undercurrent running between them. He shook his head softly and rubbed his eyes. You're getting tired, he told himself. Naturally there is an undercurrent. They are family and who knows what complications lie therein.

As they took their leave of the Colonel once more, Jeremy turned and called back to the officer. "By the way, sir, I would think you might like to find out who the sergeant was at Smith's while the fighting was going on. According to his men, he ordered them to stand fast while Captain Renforth was being killed."

★ ★ ★

Once more on the road away from the camp, Jeremy inspected Davis Halberson's gun with great interest. "That's an unusual weapon you have there," he commented, looking at the bent stock, which sported a raised cheek brace on the left side. "I've no doubt it's a fine piece, for I've seen you shoot it, but I don't believe I've seen the like."

Halberson unslung the weapon from his back to give Jeremy and Oliver a better view. "This is one reason why my uncle doesn't mind my absence," he said, laughing. "I'm one of several marksmen in the camp. There isn't much call for that particular skill in this crazy war and in this even worse environment. Not a great deal of opportunity to sight up a target in the types of battles fought here."

Jeremy thought little of the British decision to have marksmen in the Canadas even though they were not needed, so he made no comment. He had seen much stranger decisions and policies in the British Army since this war began than he cared to think about. What was one more?

"Perhaps, but I can still see the advantage of having the ability on hand should it be required. I see your gun seems to have the same lock as the Brown Bess," Jeremy observed. "But the barrel seems somewhat shorter."

"This is a Baker Rifle," Davis explained. "I steam bent the stock myself to keep the gun stable while shooting. A trick I'd learned from the man who taught me the marksman's skills. And, yes, you're right. The entire rifle is only forty-five inches long or at least it was until I bent the stock."

"Well, you say there's not much call for marksmen, but you came in handy today."

Davis smiled and shook his head. "There was no real point to killing the man. It did us no real service. I was just extremely angry and he had the great misfortune of deciding to break from cover."

"In any case, your talents might yet come in handy before this is over," Jeremy said soberly.

The four men walked on toward York in General silence, rounding Little Lake just as the late summer's night began to fall upon them.

Exhausted from the day's events, they ate quickly with little conversation, and bedded themselves down for the night.

★ ★ ★

The next night found them making camp beside the outlet of a small creek which emptied sluggishly into Lake Ontario. They gathered what dry driftwood they could from the small beach formed of silt washed down in seasonal runoff and put it to flame. As the resulting fire blazed and then burned down, it provided them with a solid bed of hot coals. Now they added greener hardwood logs Oliver and Jeremy had cut to slow the burn and increase the amount of heat.

They partook of a meagre meal of dried provisions boiled in a makeshift bark vessel. Jeremy had made Davis leave behind his British Army issued tin mess kit since they might be in need of stealth, either for hunting or for fighting. The tin simply made too much noise, even wrapped.

Once the evening meal was completed, they settled down before the fire, huddled close and tightly wrapped in their blankets to maximize the value of the wood's heat. Before retiring, each man excepting Sims had made certain their guns and pistols were loaded and primed and then placed within easy reach. They had experienced no further trouble the previous night but it always paid to be cautious out in the open like this.

All about were the sounds of the night. An owl hooted plaintively from a nearby tree, there was a scamper of unidentified small feet no doubt avoiding that same owl. Branches touched and rubbed in the breeze, creaking like loose floor boards. These and a million other noises to which Jeremy and Oliver were accustomed unnerved the more civilized Sims who, nerves finally stretched to the snapping point, suggested they post a watch.

"I don't think that will be necessary, but you may feel free to stay up by yourself if you would safer," Jeremy answered facetiously. "On my part, I sleep quite lightly because of the conditions in which I travel about by myself. Besides, we all will be required to walk all day tomorrow and you may wish to be rested for the task."

Jeremy heard a click come from Oliver's spot. "What are you doing?" he asked Oliver, calmly turning toward him.

"Loading and priming is well and good, but I want to be ready to shoot," the younger cousin replied. "I was just cocking the pistol you gave me to use. I intend to hold it right here in my hand while I sleep."

Jeremy chuckled mildly as he reached across and carefully took the pistol from Oliver's hand. "I would sleep much better if you were not to do that," he said. "I've seen you sleep and I don't know what it is you do at night, thrashing about as you do, but I don't relish having a hole blown through my skull when you twitch a finger." He lowered the hammer and handed the pistol, grip first, back to Oliver.

"Besides, if you haven't the time to cock the hammer, you haven't the time to shoot to any effect."

There was a bit more good-natured and sometimes nervous ribbing on all sides before they fell asleep, dreaming of little. So soundly did they sleep that even Jeremy's usually keen sense did not detect a pair of eyes watching them intermittently during the night, seeing to it that they were still in place.

Chapter Twelve

The late afternoon of the fourth day of their mission, the crew found themselves emerging from a wooded stretch of the roadway and suddenly at the outskirts of York. The Niagara Escarpment, which had always been visible to their left since Niagara, had faded off into the distance the early previous day, turning generally northwest toward Lake Huron.

The men were hungry and tired. There was no end in sight to a steady, cold, light drizzle that had been bedevilling them since it awakened them in the early morning. The previous night's frosty weather had turned to the even more frigid rain as the four men awoke beside the dead embers of their fire. They had been forced to begin their day already damp, despite their various coats and capes.

Much to the annoyance of Jeremy and the others, the walk to York took them as long as it had owing mostly to the lagging and whining of Sims. But they had finally entered the road that Davis claimed to know by the experience of a previous posting. He announced this thoroughfare to be Front Street.

Jeremy and Oliver did not know whether this was indeed Front Street, but there was no doubt they had reached York. Soon after they emerged from the trees, they found themselves walking past fortified batteries. Indeed, the road would take them on through the fortifications that Jeremy knew had been badly damaged when the magazine exploded during the invasion by the Americans that previous spring.

On they plodded through mud and puddles, their sodden footwear squeaking and squelching in protest, still following the Lake Ontario shoreline.

★ ★ ★

"Does anyone know this place well?" Jeremy somewhat testily asked of the others.

"I only know it to a degree," Davis offered. "We once stopped outside of town on our way through to Queenston, and spent part of the day at the market."

"And how does one reach this market?" Jeremy asked. "It would seem that any information we would need would be available there. Is it a large market?"

"Oh, it surely is. And quite busy too, especially on Saturdays I'm told, because no one may sell meat, fish or poultry in York on that day except at market."

"Fine," Jeremy said, turning to Sims. "Now man, give us cause to be happy that we didn't shoot you and leave you at the side of the road for the wolves. What are we looking to find out here?"

"I'll tell you in the morning, when we set out to ask for directions," Sims replied maddeningly, still electing to keep his information secret until the last moment. "You just may shoot me yet if you think you can find the documents without me."

"But we can't, can we?" remarked Oliver suspiciously, wondering at the form of Sims' remark, his disgust with this man barely disguised.

"No, you can't."

"Then why can't you tell us the next step now?" Jeremy asked tiredly, not really caring any longer whether Sims should answer or not. "And why must it wait until morning? Out with it, man! Surely if we can trust you, you can trust us with knowledge that won't end the quest anyway. You can't judge the whole world by your own slim margin of honour, now can you?"

"Tomorrow," was all Sims said in reply, failing to rise to the bait.

"If it's to wait until morning, where shall we sleep?" Oliver wanted to know. "Surely we can't just lay ourselves down at the roadside? Much of the land here is cleared and there isn't much shelter."

"Oh, I'm afraid I must admit to knowing quite unfortunately that the constable won't have any of that," Davis offered with a smile. "Of course, then you would find yourself sheltered in the jail which is conveniently to be found right next to the market. Unless my memory has betrayed me."

"Where then?" Jeremy wanted to know, at this point perfectly content on his part to take his chances with the local constable. "And how do you come to know of this?

Davis ignored the second part of the question. "There's a hotel right near the market. I don't know what the price might be, but most sleep in a common sleeping area on the second floor, unless you can afford a private room, and I don't think any of us can. I'm not at all sure any of us can afford the common area, come to think of it."

"I only know that I am penniless," Oliver replied miserably. When he bent his head the forward fold of his hat neatly poured water directly in front of his face."

"Nor I," Jeremy muttered, shaking his head. "But perhaps Mr. Sims can be of assistance in this. What say you, Mr. Sims?"

"Oh, no, no," Sims replied too hastily. "I have no money at all." But the expression on his face put the lie to his protestations.

"Well, then," Jeremy said, looking about at his friends slyly and then with a less charitable demeanour at the man who had been their bane since the adventure had begun. "It would appear, then, that we all must sleep outside in the rain once more, and chance the wrath of the local constable."

Sims turned away so that no one could easily see what he was doing and picked at the loose threads at the hem of his coat. Several coins fell out, each wrapped in cloth so that they would not give themselves away by striking together and jingling in their hiding place, as well as to disguise their shape should anyone inadvertently touch them.

"Here!" he spat out bitterly, tossing the coins roughly at Jeremy.

Jeremy fumbled with the coins, just avoiding dropping them on the muddy roadway. "Why, gentlemen," he said grinning at the two younger men. "It would appear that our man Sims is capable of magic. He can apparently make money appear where there was none before. Else we must believe that he is a liar." He let out a loud laugh, at which the other two joined in.

Sims scowled sourly in answer to this hilarity at his expense. "Fine, you caught me in the lie. Now, can we please take my money and find some cover from this dreadful weather before I catch my death?" he muttered miserably.

★ ★ ★

"What happened here?" Davis stood looking up at the blackened remains of a burnt-out ship. Its charred skeleton silhouetted darkly against the late day sky.

"The British soldiers stationed here burned it when the Americans attacked York in April," Jeremy replied. "I heard about it just a few weeks ago. They knew they couldn't defend against the overwhelming numbers coming in off the Americans' Lake Ontario fleet, therefore they burned it so the enemy wouldn't have it."

They trudged on yet further until, at last and as promised, they reached the hotel. It sat immediately beside the muddy road and, also as promised, from the middle of the street they could make out an open space that they assumed would be the market.

Only two storeys high, the white clapboard structure yet seemed to tower over the road. Despite its plain and functional simplicity, it beckoned to four sodden travellers, an offer of welcome haven from the elements. They pushed in through the heavy double doors of the main entrance and found themselves immediately opposite the bar, obviously the establishment's focal point at any time other than meals. Off to the right of where they entered, several people sat eating a late supper at one of the few plank tables that served the establishment.

The travellers were delighted to find that the price of lodging for the night included a simple meal and Jeremy and his party headed directly to a table. They each ravenously wolfed down a plate of stew served with a rough slice of semi-stale bread and washed it all down with a tin cup of ale. To a man such as Jeremy, accustomed to eating the ever-reheated potage at home, this was feast fit for lords.

As they sat enjoying this simple fare, Sims seemed to ignore his food in favour of several more cups of ale, payment for which appeared almost like magic. He grew ever more animated as fatigue and alcohol combined to loosen his tongue. In spite of the best efforts of the others to keep a rein on his mouth, his volume increased steadily and he began to boast of things that Oliver knew to be so much hot air. To hear him tell it there was no greater nation in world than the United States of America and none with a greater life for its citizens, a dangerous notion in the still traumatized Town of York.

"Keep your voice down damn it!" Davis whispered hoarsely. "York was burned just this past April and they probably won't take kindly to you singing the praises of the enemy at the top of your lungs!"

"Why?" Sims slurred, becoming louder still. "Doesn't everyone here secretly wish the Americans would win the war?" he added with a hint of sarcasm evident beneath the bluster. Then he stood uncertainly and, leaning heavily on the back of his chair, turned to the room which was fast filling with the evening's drinkers. "Come, come now. Don't you all secretly wish you were citizens of the United States of America so that you might enjoy the freedoms of our great democracy?"

Jeremy and the others noticed a marked agitation among the others in the room. The establishment had been filling with men who filtered in to enjoy a cup of ale before retiring and a belligerent undercurrent was fast building all about them.

There had been no reply to Sims' question, and Jeremy and the others moved quietly away from the table, wishing to sever any association with the short, stout loudmouth who obviously irritated the crowd so. After several failed attempts to drag Sims with them, they moved to the wall and watched as events unfolded, hoping against all reasonable hope that the fool would simply collapse before he could cause any real damage. But it was not to be.

Goaded beyond endurance, some of the men at the bar started to move toward the insufferable little man.

One man, apparently a local worker by his dress, shouted at Sims, "Keep your damned seditious mouth shut!" He was visibly angry and nearly as well ale-fortified as Sims himself.

Now others joined in and started to move toward Sims with cries of, "God save the King", Death to Americans!" and "We'll see you in Hell first!" But Sims could not be silenced. In fact, the shouting only steeled his resolve to speak his piece, claiming it as his God-given right under his Constitution.

Finally the dam of civilized self-control which had to this point held back the tension could contain it no longer. To Sims' apparent surprise, if no one else's, several men jumped on him and began to beat and kick him roundly. The hapless Sims' blustering courage evaporated in the face of a beating, and he squealed like a stuck pig, which seemed to have the effect of enraging the mob ever more. Now more men joined in the fracas and the savage beating continued long after Sims' voice could be heard no more.

As Sims was dragged toward doors his head lolled loosely, but he was yet sufficiently conscious in that moment that he could spot his travelling companions through rapidly closing eyes. He spit blood through swollen lips onto the wooden planks of the floor and then feebly cried out with hoarse voice, using what seemed his final breath, "Governor Simcoe! Find out where he lived here!"

"Don't you think we might offer him some assistance?" Davis asked, feeling a twinge of pity at the American's treatment.

"I don't believe we could stop this… or that it would be in our best interest," Jeremy answered. "We could do little to stem that tide," he said, indicating the mob, which was now joined by passers-by on Front Street. "At best, we'd be on the bad end of a beating ourselves."

Ever more voices voices joined into the fray. But before events could turn truly tragic, Jeremy, Oliver and Davis watched as a constable and two hastily deputized citizens pushed and occasionally punched their way to the epicentre of the disturbance. Finally reaching the senseless and quite bloody Sims, they picked him up from the floor and dragged him off to a course of "traitor", "sedition" and even less charitable words.

"Come," said Jeremy to his junior companions. "I think it would be best if we were to disappear from view altogether. We wouldn't wish at this point to be connected by the mob to Sims, now would we? We can try to straighten this out in the morning."

"Shouldn't we follow and see where he's being taken and maybe try to talk to him?" asked Oliver, wanting to do something.

"I think there's little doubt as to where they're taking him. The constable has him, so he's going to the jail," Davis replied simply. "As for talking to him, they likely won't allow it, even were we stupid enough to request it. Do you honestly wish to go before the constable and point out to them that we're friends of his?"

All about them the din gradually diminished to that of constant intensity and volume. The momentary excitement created by Sims was rapidly waning amid the anaesthetic effects of ale and rum. Although he had some limited experience of taverns, Oliver stared about, yet unaccustomed such surroundings. Never before had he been exposed to an atmosphere as the volatile mob scene here this night.

Only Halberson seemed in his element in this place, somehow finding the coin necessary to buy more ale for himself and his companions. He made his way around the room, chatting up strangers with his arm thrown freely about these strangers' shoulders and necks.

After a time, he returned with a youngish, somewhat attractive woman in tow. He pulled her unceremoniously onto his lap as he sat back onto his bench. "Gentlemen, I want you to meet this young lady I just met. The barkeep wanted to throw her out but I saved her." There was no doubt at this point that Halberson was well into his cups.

"Anyways Oliver, Jeremy, this is Roseanne."

Oliver blushed quietly as the woman stared openly at them in turn, a worldliness that he would have been at a loss to explain. Her bosom was pushed high in her bodice to what she surely considered best effect and her eyes showed a weariness that put the lie to the smile displayed upon the remainder of her face.

Jeremy looked at her and Halberson with mild amusement, as if party to a joke to which not all were privy, certainly not his cousin.

"And how do come to be the only lady in this establishment in the evening drinking hours?" Jeremy asked, knowing the answer. "I believe the women have a separate room."

Halberson grinned even wider, showing the spaces where a pair of teeth toward the rear of his mouth was missing. "This is no lady, Jeremy!" he thundered for all to hear. "This is a whore!" The nearby tables broke into raucous laughter.

"Here now! That's no way..." Oliver objected, but stopped as he caught the knowing look and slight nod from Jeremy. He knew that the term was applied negatively to certain women and he sat back to study the woman curiously. "I've heard of them," he commented wonderingly. "But as no one has actually it explained to me, what is a whore?"

Once an explosion of renewed laughter died down once more the woman, who had now been introduced to the entire room as Roseanne the whore, took the question in the innocence that asked it. "It means I make men happy for money, young one."

"Happy how?" Oliver followed up, his curiosity now peaked. Once again the room burst into laughter and he coloured deeply, wondering how his questions had been the cause such hilarity. Obviously, everyone else here knew something he did not.

Jeremy leaned over and, as softly as he could in the noisy atmosphere, muttered something quietly to Oliver. The younger cousin turned pale and turned sharply to look at Jeremy, then looked back at the woman, afraid to make eye contact.

"That's right, boy," said Roseanne, the amusement obvious in her face. "That's how I make a living! And judging by your reaction to all of this, I would suggest that you're in more need of my services tonight than anyone else here."

Another roar of laughter issued from the crowd, this time accompanied by cheers, whistles and lewd remarks.

Oliver turned positively crimson at this remark. He was not familiar with sexual contact between humans but was well aware of the procreation acts among his farm animals, and that there was a connection. He also knew that such things were forbidden, especially outside of marriage.

"But what my dogs do looks decidedly uncomfortable and even painful!"

There was a clatter as one man laughed so hard at this that he tipped his chair too far and crashed to the floor. He lay there howling and breathlessly repeating to his friends what Oliver had said, as if they had not all heard. The fellow did not try to rise, but stayed where he was, among the dirt and sawdust, too weakened by his amusement to get up.

"Then I'd wager your dogs aren't doing it right," Roseanne replied between giggles. "Perhaps I'll need to show you myself."

"Here now!" protested Halberson. "I didn't fetch you here to provide a service for him!"

"Do you have money?" she asked Halberson pointedly, tiring of this sport which seemed to be leading nowhere.

"Well, not right now..." started Halberson. "But I'll be able to get some in the morning."

Roseanne jumped to her feet. "I'll not be treated in this manner!" she shouted, loudly enough that the few tables in either direction fell silent. "I'm a working girl and have no time for charity!" With that, she hiked up her skirts off the floor and flounced indignantly toward the door, followed by more drunken laughter, jeers and catcalls.

Halberson sat with mouth open, at a loss to explain what had just happened. "Where's she going?" he asked plaintively, his alcohol-befogged mind struggling to understand.

Jeremy rose from his bench and stretched. "Well, gentlemen, I trust everyone's had their particular type of entertainment tonight except perhaps for you, young Halberson. Better luck the next time. What say you we retire and we can see what's become of Sims in the morning?"

Chapter Thirteen

With that suggestion, Jeremy started leadenly up the stairs, the others hard upon his heels. Reaching the second floor, they picked their way cautiously across the large common room, the establishment hosting a somewhat greater crowd than was their custom due to the combination of inclement weather and the fact that tomorrow was market day. They stepped gingerly over people in various attitudes of repose and various degrees of consciousness. At last, they managed to push their way through to a spot near the rear wall where all three could lie crowded together.

Jeremy lay there among the throng for some time for he could feel the panic rise in his gorge. Accustomed as he was to the solitary life, sleeping alone in his cabin or beneath the open sky the packed, odorous, wheezing and snoring mass made him feel like bolting for the door. It seemed as though the air was slowly being pressed from his lungs and he experienced a fear greater than that of death itself. But the dire warnings of arrest for sleeping in public kept him where he was. The mere thought of being confined by locks and bars brought on a panic that was much greater than the tightness he felt in this situation. At long last, however, his exhaustion overcame his fears and he joined his fellow travellers in slumber, still clad in rain-soaked clothing, holding tightly to his guns for fear that someone might make off with them in the night.

★ ★ ★

The sun broke through occasionally the following morning, although it provided no warmth in light of their circumstances. The three travelers made their way quickly to the street, hoping to discover the particulars of what had happened to Sims.

Jeremy happily inhaled deeply of the crisp, cold air and sighed loudly. "I think I would have much preferred the wet ground to that stinking crush of humanity," he declared, arching his back to remove the kinks.

"I'll give you no argument on that count," Oliver replied.

Davis looked at the two with amusement. "It's obvious that you two have never served in the army. We're constantly being stacked into tents, barracks and such. That was no worse."

Jeremy stopped stretching with and provided Davis with a mock expression of horror. "Me, in the army? Good God, no, man! I'm much too independent to have some dandy in a scarlet uniform screaming in my face first thing in the morning."

"That's the problem with you colonials," Halberson muttered through his laughter. "You expect the King's men to come and protect you, but you're too independent to join up yourselves. When it comes time to do battle, you fight until it no longer suits you or until harvest time, and then you simply go home."

For some reason, the young marksman's comments did not ring true, although Jeremy would have been hard pressed to explain why. With a mental shrug, the trapper ignored the feeling. Davis was a bit of a rebel where his uncle was concerned after all.

"And you've witnessed this yourself, have you?" Oliver asked, familiar with a measure of the same complaints from some of the few career soldiers in the United States.

"Several times," Halberson replied guardedly. "The Americans never would have been able to run us all the way back to Burlington Heights if the militias and the Indians had stood their ground," he replied.

"Perhaps they were but concerned about the families who depended upon them to clear the land and bring in the crops, and who would be here yet after the war, after the soldiers, whose families are safe in England, have gone home? All in the cause of deciding which flag is to fly over the land?" Jeremy looked up and away as the last of the previous day's clouds lazily drifted away. "And perhaps it wasn't worth it to die fighting a losing battle for some glory- and promotion-seeking English officer, just in the name of so-called battlefield honour, whatever that might be. Much better, as they say, to live to fight another day."

He cleared his throat and spit in the road. "When I fought at Beaverdams, purely by chance I might add, the Indians fought like the devil for the British soldiers that seemed not to arrive until the very end."

He looked hard at Halberson. "And the British apparently had known about the impending attack for at least two days, perhaps more, but they seemed quite content to let the Indians fight the battle for them. The only white men there were a handful of local settlers who fought side by side with those Indians against overwhelming odds trying to fend off the American troops."

"And the reason that they fought so well was that there was no popinjay screaming insane attack orders at us. We took the Americans on our own terms. It's true the Indians have a strange attitude for battle such as leaving the field for a break as they see fit, but they are incredibly effective. I fought side by side with such men and I'll have no man question the honour and courage of either the colonists or the Indians!"

Jeremy glared defiantly at the infantryman, daring him to challenge his remarks.

Oliver was by now becoming somewhat alarmed at the increasing volume of his cousin's voice as his heart went increasingly into his speech. "Jeremy, please! You're beginning to draw attention to us, even at this hour."

Jeremy looked about sheepishly and then turned back to his companions. "I'm sorry. I'm always somewhat upset by that type of slanderous remark against my friends and neighbours." He brushed the hair out of his eyes, eyes which betrayed a depth of sorrow that was not due entirely to the discussion at hand. "I've known too many good men on both sides of this argument, and on both sides of the war, who've died in the name of causes dictated by powerful men who wouldn't dirty their own hands."

★ ★ ★

They had by now reached the York Market, a bustling piece of land turned over to the business of selling all manner of produce and anything else allowed by those who dictated such matters. Today was Saturday, the square's busiest day of the week, with stalls of all descriptions for the purpose of selling the various wares on both sides of the small stream that ran roughly down the middle of the allotted property.

Farmers had come from miles around to sell the last of their crops for this year, and makeshift tables displayed fresh pumpkins, apples and pears, remnants of the corn crop, grapes, and gourds of many colours and descriptions, some dried for storage. One would scarcely believe by this display that vegetables were a scarce commodity to most in the colonies. There were live chickens, goats and sheep, and beef, both fresh and preserved in brine for those who wished to store it. There were also dried preserved meats, eggs, milk, and cheese, the most common form of dairy. One could purchase wool, hides, cloth, carved wood, and many other finished products.

Off to one side were the Indians, who were selling the fish which they might have peddled door-to-door on any other day. They also sold fruits and vegetables and handcrafted items.

As if the sights of the Market were not enough to test the senses, they were inundated by the smells of fish and fresh and rotting vegetables. The various scents associated with the people themselves; of sweat and body odours, and occasionally fragrances and perfumes when mixed with all the others, threatened to overcome those travellers unaccustomed to it.

Add to it all the sounds of the marketplace. The fishwives competed with those at other stalls for the ear of passers-by. Children ran screaming through the crowds in the joy of being temporarily free, or at least until one ran into an adult, which in turn often resulted in the boxing of ears. Then the squeals turned into cries of pain and sobbing.

All the activity in the market was enough to spin the minds of all who were unaccustomed to the bustle. This included both Jeremy and Oliver, since both were from small communities. The sights and smells melded about them and overwhelmed their senses.

Across King Street from the approximate centre of the market stood the whitewashed St. James Church, its brilliant clapboard standing in stark contrast to both the forest behind it and the blue sky above it. It was said to hold two hundred, fifty people, a number which was astonishing to those raised in Niagara.

At the west side of the market stood the jail, surrounded by a fourteen-foot-high stockade that stretched sixty feet in each direction, a reminder that they had yet to decide what to be done about Sims. They hardly missed his constant snivelling but he was the reason they were here. If they were to continue on their mission, it was imperative that they get the instructions for the map.

★ ★ ★

Jeremy's sharp eye picked out a man who, by his mode of dress and manner, obviously was not a member of the ruling class and yet did not appear as though he might be ignorant of the events which shaped this town.

"Excuse me, sir, but we saw a gentleman at our hotel being arrested last night, but we're not quite sure of the reason for it."

The man looked tiredly at this newcomer, an obvious stranger to York. "Well, I don't the man of whom you speak, but did he by chance cause trouble? Was he drunk and had he insulted someone's wife? For that they'll arrest you for drunk and disorderly conduct. They don't take kindly to that sort of behaviour here, and rightly so."

"Well, he was being a bit unpleasant, but he did nothing of the sort of what you speak. He was just talking rather loudly in favour of the American system, which understandably upset a number of people."

The man looked at the trio suspiciously. "I'd heard of some such scandal. You wouldn't be friends of this man, would you?"

Davis stepped to the fore and sneered at the man. "Sir, I am a soldier in His Majesty's army. Do you think I would befriend such a man?"

The man, completely chastened by Davis's invasion of his personal space, stepped back. "No, no, of course not," he blurted. "I don't know what possessed me to even suggest such a thing."

Jeremy smiled inwardly. Well done, Davis, he thought. The young soldier had managed to back the man down without actually lying.

"And they would have taken him to that jail?" Jeremy asked, thumbing over his shoulder in the general direction of the stockade of sharpened cedar stakes that sat ominously in view of all at the market.

"Aye, that they would. They'll hold him there until the witnesses to what he supposedly did and said can make their accusations before one of Reverend Strachan's committees of information," the man explained.

"Committee of information? I've never heard of that. Is it a court of some kind?" asked Oliver, confused as to why an arrested man might be expected to go up in front of someone who, by his title, was obviously a minister.

"No," the man replied evasively, looking about to see who might be listening. "The committees really are just groups of York's most upstanding citizens who took it upon themselves after the two attacks this year, to punish those who show any manner of good feeling toward the Americans and their system."

"And do they actually try the man in these committees?" asked Jeremy.

The man tugged at his collar, somewhat uncomfortable with this continuing line of questioning. "Not truly a trial," he answered finally. "They hear the accusations of any citizens wishing to speak against his neighbour or, in the case of the man you're wondering about, perhaps a stranger. Except in rare cases, the accused doesn't have an opportunity to defend himself against the accusations. Then the committees decide whether to recommend the man's arrest or punishment. Recommend is probably not actually the right word, because the local magistrate would be taking some risk with his position if he were to ignore such a recommendation."

"And this is allowed by the government of Upper Canada?" Jeremy wanted to know, thinking this all rather excessive.

"Who's to say otherwise?" The man gave the trio a wry grin. "These are people of stature with connections to the authorities."

"That hardly seems right," Davis burst in, upset by what he was hearing. "Is there no longer any rule of law in this colony?"

The man looked at the young infantryman and spit into the dirt. "If I were you, young sir, I would be careful what you say. The committees were set up for people to inform on their neighbours, with or without any proof. If you're called up before them, you'll be found guilty for sure. By way of a friendly warning, I'd suggest that you bear that in mind in future while asking questions or making comments, especially to strangers." With that, he looked slowly and carefully about himself to ascertain that no one had been eavesdropping on their conversation, and then casually sauntered away.

"What do we do now?" Oliver asked when they withdrew to the edge of the market.

"I think it would be best if we should forget about it," Davis offered in a tone that suggested he was discouraged by the discussion with the man in the market. "There's nothing we can do now. If we were to ask to see him, they likely wouldn't allow it but they certainly would become quite suspicious and if some come forward to say came to town with him, we could well end up in a cell alongside him."

"I believe Davis is right," Oliver agreed. "We don't really know what it is we're actually looking for, if it actually exists or if there is a way for us to find it. This might be a good time to admit defeat and go home."

Jeremy ran his right hand over the four days' growth of beard gracing his chin. "You're probably right, the two of you. But, as much as I question the value of it all, I am a stubborn sort and would like to have a closer look at the jail just to convince myself that all is hopeless."

"You aren't honestly considering breaking the man out of jail, are you?" Oliver asked in astonishment. "Are you thinking of getting us killed?"

"Let's just have a look, shall we?" The others noticed that he did not confirm or deny Oliver's accusation.

The three men sauntered casually over to the stockade and looked at the jail itself through the gaps between the stakes that made up the stockade surrounding the jail's yard. It was a simple square building of clapboard over squared log with double doors on one side. As they watched, a reasonably well-dressed man approached those same doors and stepped in. Jeremy could hear a bell sound as the door opened and closed, obviously so that no one could sneak inside without the knowledge of the guards.

With a casual air Jeremy turned to his companions, pointed at the stockade, and remarked loudly, "I certainly wouldn't wish to be in there. I'll wager that the conditions inside are not to betterment of a man's health."

A man seated upon the ground at one of the stalls spoke up, admitting that he had been a prisoner himself in that jail on at least one occasion on charges of being drunk and disorderly, a not uncommon offence.

"They have both prisoners and crazies inside there," the man explained. "We all slept on straw strewn about on the floor, although there were hard cots for those who were sick. At the time, we all froze since it was winter. They didn't do a thing to make us comfortable and fed us dry bread and water only once a day."

"Thank you sir," Jeremy said to the man. "I'll tell my young son that and perhaps it'll put an end to the some of the mischief he's been getting into of late. Say, if he doesn't believe me can I send him here to talk to you in person? Are you here regularly?"

"No problem in that," the man smiled, showing large gaps where his teeth were missing. "Wish my father had done as much for me. Could have saved me a world of grief." He spit onto the ground at his side. "As to your son, bring him by and be happy to put the fear of God into him", he added with a conspiratorial wink

Having played out the charade, Jeremy wandered away to rejoin his comrades. "There's no hope of us getting him out of there, that's certain," he said with a defeated air. "Let's stay about for a few days and see if by some luck Mr. Sims is set free. If we don't see him out by Saturday, I suppose we should be starting back toward Burlington Heights and then home."

Chapter Fourteen

S ims stumbled several times as he was shoved unceremoniously into the meeting room by a constable and then manhandled roughly up toward the front of the room. Directly in front of him was a sturdy table with several chairs all facing in his direction. At each end of the table was a standard with a Union Jack hanging from it and, on the wall behind all of that, were questionable copies of portraits of King George III and his son, the Prince Regent, the man who actually, if not officially, ruled the Empire in his father's stead.

A dazed and bruised Sims stood looking about the room, blood from the beating the night before still on his face and shirt, his ankles and wrists in chains. His clothing was filthy from the melee, to say nothing of the poor conditions in the jail, his condition poorly disguised by the buckets of water thrown on him that morning. He seemed barely to recognize that in the room behind him some spectators were being allowed in. They were claiming to be witnesses but actually were spectators come for the great sport of seeing another enemy of the Crown being righteously punished.

After a seemingly interminable wait a portly, half-bald man emerged from the back room and stood to the left of the table. In a strong, clear voice he called out, "Oyez, oyez, oyez…" Instantly the hum of voices in the room ceased and those not standing did so.

"This meeting of the Committee of Information is now in session," the man continued. "May all who have business before this august body come forward and be heard."

Finished his part the man, who was apparently serving as court crier and clerk in the proceedings, for he seated himself at the end of the table where paper, pen and blotter awaited him. There he waited while several men, who had pressed angrily toward the front, were held back behind Sims by the constable.

Still barely a sound was heard as the crowd waited for the next movement of this quasi-judicial dance. They were not to be held waiting long, as a group of distinguished- looking gentlemen filed into the room from the door behind the table and took their places in the chairs across the front of the room.

One of the gentlemen put on a pair of spectacles, read from a paper on his desk and then, removing the spectacles once more, addressed the crowd.

"This is an unusual circumstance in that we do not normally hear such testimony in the presence of the accused. But because of the particulars of this situation and the blatantly open manner in which he created the public disturbance caused by his alleged remarks, we thought it best to deal with this in this manner."

Then he turned and sternly faced the prisoner.

"James Archibald Sims, is that your name, Sir?" Sims nodded. "You are here this day because some of the citizens of this town have accused you of making treasonous remarks in a public place. How say you, Mr. Sims? Are you a traitor to the Crown?"

Sims raised his head up slowly, his blood-shot eyes trained contemptuously upon the men at the table. He knew why he was here, for he had been warned of the nature this farce by a fellow in the next cell. Through the fog in his mind, he hazily formulated what seemed to him to be likely the most plausible defence, a decision that he would come to rue.

"I can't very well be a traitor," Sims stated confidently, in voice that indicated that he would have them upon this technicality. "I am not a British subject." This remark drew a gasp from the crowd of spectators and a general hum of discussion.

"Silence in this court!" one of the other committee members bellowed. With the state of proper decorum once again returned to the room, he leaned forward on the table. "Well, Mr. Sims. That would certainly disqualify you from being branded a traitor."

Sims felt his hopes rising. Perhaps he could work his way out of this after all.

"If you're not a British subject, of what land are you a subject?" the same gentleman asked.

Suddenly, Sims was not so sure that he had set the right course. He stood there staring blankly, gaping at the committee while his confused mind tried desperately to determine what course correction should be made, if any.

"Come, come, Mr. Sims. Surely you know to whom you pledge your allegiance?"

Before he could think further, Sims blurted out, "The United States of America, sir."

One might have heard a pin drop in the moments immediately following his proclamation. Then the room exploded in a cacophony of disbelief and protest at the words that had issued from the prisoner's mouth.

The sound of a gavel hitting the table carried easily through the din. "Order!" someone at the table shouted.

The room went quickly silent once more as the constable moved menacingly toward them with his stick and the crowd waited in anticipation of what might come next. Then the man in the middle of the table, who had originally read out the accusation, once again spoke to the prisoner.

"James Sims, you have made this a very easy decision for us. We shan't even have need of the gentlemen lined up eagerly behind you to tell us what you supposedly said. Under the circumstances, in this instance your very own words, we have no choice but to recommend to the Crown that you be charged with espionage and the attempted subversion of loyal citizens to your cause in a time of war. In addition, we will be recommending that you be dealt with in accordance with the accepted treatment of spies and subversives."

The gentleman banged his gavel to punctuate his decision.

Sims was taken by panic as the enormity of what had just happened finally broke over his consciousness.

"Wait! I'm no spy! Just give me a chance to..." he cried as the constable and the man acting as bailiff took hold of his arms and began to drag him back.

But no one was listening. The august members of the committee had risen and filed out of the room. Now the small crowd that had come to watch could no longer contain itself and had begun shouting curses and epithets at him. One man attempted to physically assault him but was held back by the constable who stood between them.

In the course of his struggle, Sims somehow managed to break loose momentarily from the grasp of the attending bailiff. He ran for the door through which the committee had disappeared, feeling a surge of hope that he might escape his committee ordained fate, or at least convince the men he was following to reconsider their terrible mistake. Before he could reach it, however, the bailiff and constable caught him a mere two feet short of his goal. With a flurry of Billy clubs and fists, his assailants quickly relieved him of his recently reacquired consciousness.

★ ★ ★

As Sims was being beaten into submission, his former companions were leaving the market. Just as they rounded the corner, they stopped cold as they were confronted by a wagon which was approaching them on Front Street. It was a plain flat-bed wagon and being pulled by a single stout draft horse. Accustomed as he was to hearing the bells on horses' harnesses, especially in towns, where they would warn people out of the way, Jeremy wondered at the lack thereof in this particular case. Then he became aware of the people walking along with the wagon and the load it was transporting.

In the back was a simple pine box, stained with lamp black, unvarnished with plain wrought-iron handles. He immediately realized that they were witnessing a funeral procession and Jeremy and his friends removed their hats out of respect as did most others on the street.

"What's the point to it all?" Jeremy muttered softly but darkly as they watched the back of the small procession. "In the end, no matter who your masters or what your lot, it all ends the same; a box and a lot of cold dirt."

★ ★ ★

During the balance of their stay, the three companions would work off their stay at the hotel with whatever chores the innkeeper had available. They mucked out the stables, tossed drunks, unloaded supplies, and even put a fresh coat of whitewash on their temporary home.

On the morning following Sims' "trial", after cleaning up after horses who must by all evidence have eaten something particularly objectionable, they returned to the market and waited about there. They were hoping for Sims' release, as they would continue to do when possible for all of the following week. However, there was no word or sign of him and on Saturday they went for the final time.

"That's it, gentlemen," Jeremy sighed at noon. "While it has all been a diversion from sitting about my cabin, costly as it has been in terms of lives, I think it's time we admitted defeat and started for home."

His companions grumbled in agreement, loath as they were to give up. As they turned to leave, they could hear the bell ring as the doors to the jail opened. Thinking nothing of it, they continued on until, behind them, they heard a loud commotion behind the stockade at the edge of the market. As they turned, they could see a crowd forming, obscuring their vision, leaving them wondering what all the noise was about.

Curiosity overcame Jeremy and he turned back toward the gathering throng. "Let's go see what all the excitement is."

As they approached the edge of the crowd, there was a sudden roar as the mob voiced its approval over whatever was happening in their midst. Pushing and shouldering members of the mob, being berated and even struck as they moved to find a better vantage point, they suddenly came out to the very edge.

There were stocks set up here, a detail they had probably all noticed but had paid no particular attention to before this. A man hung there, head sticking out through a hole made for that purpose and his arms dangling from two adjacent holes in a visibly uncomfortable manner. Someone had already obviously thrown a stone or some such object, for there was an ugly gash in his forehead and blood ran down his face, dripping onto his filthy shirt.

Jeremy felt shame for the man as he abandoned all valour, whimpering, crying and begging for the crowd to leave him be. This just incited the crowd more and his entreaties were met with a hail of stones, produce and clods of dirt, some barely missing the man's guard, who stood off to the right side with a bored expression upon his face.

They could all plainly see that the man was not Sims, but the scene made all three uncomfortable. "This is ridiculous!" Jeremy hissed. "No man should be treated in a manner such as this. Surely a criminal must be punished, but this treatment isn't fit for beasts let alone a man."

Oliver looked over at his cousin. "There's not much we can do about it, I'm afraid. Even if we could overcome his guard, we'd surely be torn limb from limb by this crowd for removing their entertainment. Judging by this crowd, this does seem to be quite popular sport."

As members of the crowd launched their missiles at the miserable soul, they swore and called him all manner of low names. Each time they found their target, there was another roar of approval, but Jeremy began to notice a subtle change.

"I believe this mob is tiring of their diversion," he said, watching as the crowd began to disperse, as if they suddenly remembered the original purposes that each had for being in this place. "Let's see if we can manage to have a word with him, shall we?" He outlined the plan that leapt into his head.

Halberson, wearing his somewhat dirty and somewhat rumpled uniform, marched smartly up to the jail guard and addressed him, positioning himself so that the guard was forced to turn his back on the stocks. "Weren't you stationed in Kingston in the spring?" Davis asked

"I'm afraid you've confused me with someone else," the guard answered, though clearly pleased that this soldier thought him to have a military bearing. "I'm not a soldier but a mere constable."

"I'm aware of that, but you remind of someone I served with and thought that this had perhaps been your chosen line of work after you left the service." He knew full well that no able-bodied young man would be leaving the King's service in the midst of a war unless he had been injured or cashiered.

While Davis engaged the guard in conversation, Oliver positioned himself so that he was blocking the guard's view of the stocks in case he should look around.

Jeremy sauntered over to the stocks and stood close to the prisoner. "Sir," he said in a low voice.

The wretched man looked up at him, misery seemingly pouring from his very eyes. "Who are you? And what the hell do you want?" he asked, first blinking to attempt in vain to remove the blood from his eyes, and then squinting at the trapper. "Have you come to break me free? For the love of God, get me out of here, please! Please!"

"Would that we could," Jeremy assured him, feeling rather foolish and guilty for bothering the man. "But I simply need to know, is there a Mr. James Sims inside there?"

The man seemed to think it over momentarily and then let out a sound that was somewhere between a sigh and a moan. "You would torment me with questions while I hang here, treated worse that an animal?" he whimpered. "What manner of beast – or perhaps fool – are you?" He spit a wad of saliva and blood into the market's dirt, just missing Jeremy's left foot.

"Just tell me, quickly. I need to know, for he may be the key to ending all of this." Jeremy wondered what would lead him to offer the man such false hope. But maybe better false hope than none, he told himself.

When hope is desperately grasped at, logic is not a first consideration. The thought that telling this man what he wanted to know might free him from his misery overpowered any urge to make sense of it.

"I heard the guard call out something that sounded like that name this morning, I think. He was calling the man he was calling an American spy and taunted him with the news that he was to be taken to Ancaster for hanging in thirty days' time." The man in the stocks coughed wretchedly. "What are you planning? A jail break? Please take me if you do. I no longer care whose side anyone's one."

"Thank you. I'll do what I can," Jeremy muttered, barely able to spit out the words, knowing that there was in truth nothing he could do.

Suddenly, there was a cry from the man's guard. "You there, what are you doing so near the prisoner?"

Thinking on his feet, Jeremy smacked the prisoner with the flat of his hand. "We've no need of your kind in this colony!" he shouted.

The guard rushed forward and grasped Jeremy firmly by the arm. "Here then! Get away from the prisoner!" he barked, giving Jeremy a shove. "You're not to be that close, even if it is to give him a well-deserved blow." The guard gave Jeremy a conspiratorial wink and added by way of explanation, "I'm not to allow such behaviour!"

Jeremy shrugged as if in resignation and shuffled off into the market, with Oliver and Davis making their ways separately to where they were to meet.

"Well, what did he say?" Oliver asked anxiously, his hoarse whisper seeming barely quieter than a shout.

"Keep your voice down," Jeremy said evenly. He looked slowly and nonchalantly about to see if anyone was listening and then answered in a low voice. "He says an American spy is to be hanged in Ancaster. The spy they're speaking of is to be taken out tomorrow."

"Do you think that would be Sims?" Davis asked.

"I don't know that any more than you do, but I think that's a fair bet. The man in the stocks seemed to think that was the name he's heard. Of course, he may have been saying that just because he thought I could free him."

"Where would he get an idea like that?" Davis remarked wryly.

"I had to think on my feet. He'd as much as said that he wouldn't tell me anything unless we could help."

"Now what do we do?" Oliver asked, his voice betraying the hopelessness he was feeling.

"We should be near here early and follow them. Then we'll look for an opportunity to try to speak to him on the road, away from the madness of this place." Jeremy was truly beginning to dislike the Town of York, mud, stocks, crowds, and all.

"In the meantime, I suggest we find out where Governor Simcoe lived," he continued, not feeling much more positive than his cousin.

"Why would we need to know that?" asked Davis, his brow knit in puzzlement.

"I'm sure it leads to another clue," Jeremy sighed. "But I can't but wonder why Williamson, who rarely left Niagara's border area, would travel this far to hide his booty." He looked away across the market. "I wish Sims had let us have the balance of the instructions, but I fear the man doesn't trust us." He smiled tiredly at the obvious understatement and rubbed the bridge of his nose. "Not that I suppose I should blame him. There are far too many men in this war for whom honour is but a convenience." His words echoed silently in his head as he remembered his shameless lie to the man in the stocks.

Chapter Fifteen

The rail-thin, sparsely bearded disciple known to the others as Brother Jacob came back into their makeshift camp at a full run.

"Parson! Parson! I believe I've some news that you might like to hear!" he shouted, as excited as a schoolboy who had been told that school would be out early that day.

The Parson abandoned the warm fire and sauntered over to where the excited man stood waiting to tell his information. "Well, what do you think you have that would be important enough to disturb the entire camp, son," he asked paternally, sounding like he had much more patience than he actually felt.

"I heard that an American spy is to be taken to Ancaster for hanging. Do you think that would be the Sims fellow?" he asked, suddenly unsure. "He was arrested the other day, telling everyone at the hotel what a great place the United States is."

The Parson paced about, stroking his chin. That certainly sounded like a strong possibility. This might be the opportunity they had been waiting for.

"Hmm, it seems we must act before he reaches Ancaster. Whether he truly memorized the information or whether he still has the paper on him, we must have that information." He looked around at the faces eagerly awaiting his every word. "Either way, if he is hanged, we lose it. And the Lord will not be pleased. That information that my brother-in-law left behind is intended to be used for the greater glory of God!" he thundered. "Not for increasing the personal wealth of others!"

"Brothers, this is what we'll do." He set about laying out a plan of ambush for the men. Tomorrow, at the time that this idiot – useful, but an idiot all the same – had told them that the escort was coming, they would be ready.

When all had been explained, he turned to Jacob. "You've down well, Brother and God will rain his blessings upon you for it. Now, get back to the market and see if you can find out anything about the trapper and his friends or what they might be about."

Brother Jacob nodded quietly and beamed happily as he spun on his heel to return to town. He would do as he was told although he would dearly have loved to have something to eat. His stomach grumbled noisily as he stoically accepted his duty.

★ ★ ★

That night Jeremy was awakened by the sound of people moving across the floor upon which they were sleeping. The sounds meant nothing to him in his semi-awake state and he drifted back off to sleep momentarily, only to awaken once again to another disturbance.

"Go back to sleep or I'll put you to sleep myself," someone whispered hoarsely in the almost lightless room.

Such disturbances were not uncommon in this place, with the bodies all packed so tightly on the floor and some guests arriving in the wee hours after whatever they had been doing, which usually was drinking. Jeremy was much too exhausted to give it another thought and quickly fell asleep one more time.

But his slumber as not to last. The next time he awoke he was staring directly at a pair of military boots. Those boots were topped by the grey-white bottoms of a pair of breeches which in turn were attached to a soldier.

"Is this the one?" His mind barely registered the question as it struggled to attach importance to the remark. Then he heard a scraping and noticed that his companions were carefully backing away.

"Yes. That would be the man who was with the spy," replied yet another unidentified voice.

Now the significance of what his senses had picked up seeped into his clearing mind. He rolled away from the boots just as they moved toward him, surely to kick him awake. When his movement was suddenly arrested by the bodies all around him, he jumped to his feet and made a dash for the stairway, leaping over bodies that were staring to rise in the confusion and tripping over at least one.

In the Name of Honour

He gained the stairs and leaped down them several at a time while he fumbled for a weapon with which to defend himself. Although his rifle was yet slung over his back – a precaution against midnight theft by his rooming neighbours – he knew that he had not the room to use it in these close quarters. Reaching the bottom of the steps, he managed to free his pistol and turned to meet his pursuers.

Then his head exploded in a flash of bright white light and his world went blacker than the room in which he had been sleeping.

★ ★ ★

Jeremy woke up groggy. His eyes took some time to adjust and when they finally found their focus, his brain took even longer to fight through the pain which was centred on the knot that his hand found at the back of his head. Finally, however, he broke through the combined mental and physical haze and the gloom of his surroundings. The answer of his circumstance arrived when he looked toward the source of the little light and, even in the grey of the early morning, he could see the dingy squared logs which sported only a couple of small, barred windows.

As his senses cleared, a myriad of scents threatened to overcome him and imperiled his very equilibrium. Clearly identifiable in the abominable stench was the odour of human feces and vomit, and all was enveloped in the musty stench of rot. All about on the floor of this cell lay the scraps of previous meals and other unidentifiable trash.

There was one other in the place with him, lying on straw that had simply been strewn about the floor. There was no heat to speak of in this place and his roommate lay shivering in the cold. From another place in the building, he could hear a man giggling hysterically and then complaining loudly about a ball and chain and from yet another quarter came the sound of someone vomiting strenuously.

Jeremy knew where he likely was. No doubt this was the very jail they had been watching from the other side of the palisade for the past days. Well, he thought to himself with a wry inward grin, I had to ask what it looked like. Rather more detail than I'd hoped for.

As he looked groggily about, he felt the onset of the same level of despair that had nearly crushed him when his fiancée had been murdered and he had banished himself to the wilderness in hopes of dying. The unbearable oppressiveness weighed down upon him as though he had been buried under a mound of stone. He could feel the rising of the panic that would lead to what he believed was an inevitable spiral into the hopelessness that he had previously just barely escaped.

To say the least, he was not a man to be comfortable in captivity and his own mind could spell his doom if he did not pull himself together. By now the fear of this madness was greater than the fear of being hung.

Fortunately, he would have no further time to dwell upon what he saw as his greatest weakness. The heavy wooden door opened and two soldiers walked in. In a few strides, they covered the floor to where Jeremy sat on the floor, cursing and kicking at Jeremy's sole roommate, who had the misfortune to be sleeping in their path.

"You!" a voice barked out, followed rapidly by a foot, which caught Jeremy a glancing blow to the left shoulder.

Jeremy winced from the assault and then slowly raised his head to look up at the soldier standing directly before him. "Were you referring to me, sir?" he asked with feigned innocence.

"You know damned well I am. Why else do you think that I would have kicked you?"

"Perhaps for the sheer sport of it?" Jeremy was feeling unjustifiably cocky, but it took him no time at all to regret his runaway mouth.

The foot lashed out at Jeremy again, this time headed straight for his chest. Acting purely on instinct, he took hold of the boot just before it reached him and twisted hard, another act that he knew immediately he would regret as the soldier cried out from the sudden pain of his ankle twisting and crashed hard to the floor.

The other prisoner scrambled to get as far away from Jeremy as he possibly could. He did not wish to be associated with this madman and certainly was not foolish enough to try to help.

Jeremy was immediately set upon by the other guard, who Jeremy had not noticed. Together the two kicked and beat him until he felt his consciousness fading, but sweet oblivion was not to be his. They lifted Jeremy to his feet and held him up, to what end he did not immediately know, but then the livid face of the guard he had attacked rose into his line of vision. In fact, he could soon see little else as the guard positioned his face only inches from the hapless trapper.

He spoke slowly, in a voice that sounded more like the growling of a dog and so low that Jeremy could barely hear, but the meaning was clear enough. "This is what we do with unruly prisoners."

Before Jeremy could brace his already battered body, the soldier punched him solidly in the stomach, driving out what little air that he had in his lungs. His legs gave out and he sagged heavily on the arms of the one who was holding him and then the second punch came, almost exactly where the first had been.

By now Jeremy only vaguely felt the punishing blows. His mind had effectively shut down as it could no longer stand the brutal punches. He wondered almost absently when it was going to end when a new voice broke through the oblivion that was closing in quickly.

"Here now!" Jeremy heard the voice say. "What are you two about, then? I sent you to bring him to me so that I could question him. How many answers do you suppose I'll get if you kill him?"

The man that was beating Jeremy moved out from in front of him and Jeremy looked in the direction of the new voice through the slits that were his eyes and the heavy fog that was his brain. He saw a man who obviously was an officer, though he could not determine his rank.

"Come on then. Bring him along and let's see if we can bring him around to speak coherently," the officer said and led the two subordiantes and Jeremy into the outer office.

★ ★ ★

Unceremoniously they dumped him into a chair and pushed him back so that he did not simply slump forward and fall out. The officer sent one of his men to fetch water in a tin cup. When Jeremy braced himself for a splash in the face, the officer laughed.

"My, my, have they beaten you so soundly?" he asked, chuckling softly. "Water in a cup is for drinking."

Jeremy shakily took the battered tin vessel in both hands, barely able to hold onto it without sloshing all the contents out onto the floor, or himself. He took a sip and tried to focus his eyes more clearly on the man sitting across an old table that was quite obviously serving as the officer's desk.

"Right then," the officer started. "My name is Lieutenant James Denham. I am British Army, temporarily attached to this jail until they reorganize their constabulary. You've already met my men." He grinned once again. "I assure you they're not such a bad lot if you get to know them, and I really suspect that you did something to precipitate the punishment that you received."

Jeremy tried to smile, the effort aggravating his split lip. "I don't appreciate it when my attention is called by a boot to the body."

Denham raised his eyes to look at his men. "Yes, they can be somewhat uncivilized at times. But then, you must understand that this is hardly a civilized place and you are being accused of sedition."

"Sedition? I have scouted and fought on the side of my country all along. I've been held and beaten by Canadian Volunteers, had my house and barns burned by same, lost my fiancée to them, almost lost my limbs at the Beaverdams, and you accuse me of sedition?" Jeremy stared hard at Denham. "I'm not quite sure whether I should laugh or be supremely insulted at the ludicrousness of the charge."

"I wouldn't laugh if I were you. This is certainly no laughing matter. And I know nothing of your woes and they are by your word only." Denham leaned forward on his desk, his hands clasped together. "But we have a man who says that you were with the spy Sims the other night and that you were asking about the jail."

"Who is Sims?" Jeremy asked innocently.

"Come now, Mr. van Hijser," clucked Denham, the whisper of a smile on his lips. "This man saw you and even identified you, by name."

Jeremy was somewhat taken aback by the fact that this officer, whom he had never met, knew his name. He was even more shaken, however, by the fact that someone had identified him in a town he had never been in before."

"And who would this anonymous person be?" he demanded. "What manner of coward is he, that I have not met this man face to face?"

"That person, I'm afraid, shall remain anonymous."

Jeremy tried to stand up, only to be roughly shoved back into the seat by one of the men who had beaten him. He winced as he was reminded of previous injuries.

"And is there no longer any justice in this province? What of my traditional right to face my accuser?"

Denham smiled, more broadly this time. "Mr. van Hijser, I'm sure you can appreciate that these are trying times. War sometimes necessitate that rights become somewhat 'flexible', shall we say?"

"I would rather say nonexistent," offered Jeremy sarcastically.

"So, what were you doing with this character Sims?" the officer demanded once more, no longer smiling.

Jeremy looked Denham directly in the eyes and saw that there would be no quarter here. "Very well. I didn't feel at liberty to tell you this, but since there was no direct order against doing so, I might as well fill you in, if you'll remove these other two from the room." He indicated the two guards. "This is not for their ignorant ears."

One of the soldiers stepped forward, his hand raised to strike. "I'll show you ignorant, traitor!"

"Parrish!" barked Denham. "That will be quite enough! The two of you, wait outside."

Once the two guards had stepped out into the crisp air, he turned to Jeremy and shook his head. "You truly don't know what is good for you, do you? You may be here for some time and Parrish has no sense of humour whatsoever."

Jeremy rubbed his sore ribs. "Of that I've no doubt. But I've seen that they require no reason and I doubt that either has any reason."

Denham grunted in agreement. "But what of this tale you wished to tell me?"

"It's quite simple sir. We were sent here on a mission by Burlington Heights' Colonel Halberson to find clues to what may have happened to the items looted from Niagara citizens."

"Oh come now, Mr. van Hijser," Denham interjected. "Do you honestly expect me to believe that you came to York to find properties stolen from Niagara residents? That makes little sense to me."

"Nor to me," replied Jeremy. "But, according to Sims, this is where the clues lead."

Denham appeared puzzled. "According to Sims, you say? Are you telling me that you are blindly following this spy?"

Jeremy smiled, accompanied by an involuntarily wince as he as reminded of his split lip and he tasted salt. "I know how it sounds, Lieutenant, but he has the information and won't reveal the next clue until we reach the place of which this one speaks." He noticed Denham about to break in again. "And before you comment, let me tell you that we have already been attacked several times over this mission, we presume by Canadian Volunteers who know that there is a document."

"I see," remarked Denham, thoughtfully rubbing his chin.

He walked calmly to the jail's door without another word and called for his men. When they reported, he turned back to Jeremy. "Very well then. Your story seems odd, to say the least. But there is much oddness in this strange colony of yours and in the war itself, so I'll send someone to Burlington Heights to ask Colonel Halberson to corroborate what you've just told me."

"And until then?" Jeremy demanded.

"Until then, you shall remain as our guest here," Denham remarked coolly. Then he turned on his heel and, opening the door, stepped out without further comment.

"And now we can show you more of our brand of hospitality," one guard muttered grinning wickedly. His grin displayed a mouthful of yellow to brown teeth, with a number missing from their places in the stubbly face.

"Perhaps you could wait until your lieutenant gets word from Burlington Heights," suggested Jeremy hopefully. "He might not appreciate having to release an innocent man beaten beyond recognition."

The large soldier previously identified as Parrish laughed in a manner that might easily have been mistaken for good humour. "You don't honestly think we care what that prissy young pup wants, do you? We'll just say you fell down."

"How many times?" Jeremy asked ironically.

Now both men laughed uproariously.

"I think I like you, traitor," Parrish rumbled. "You have a good sense of humour."

Jeremy smiled, trying not to appear nervous. "Does that mean you no longer mean to beat me?"

Parrish laughed even louder. "No son, I'm afraid I still intend to do that. There's still the question of my man here who you nearly sent to the infirmary when you dropped him. And we still think you're a traitor."

With no further ado, the two soldiers set about beating Jeremy until, finally and gratefully, all went black once again.

Chapter Sixteen

Oliver and young Halberson knew that there was little they could to assist Jeremy at this juncture. Perhaps some grand scheme would come to light but in the meantime Davis suggested that they get on with the mission.

"That way," he explained, "if we should find some way to free him, or if he manages to free himself, we can all leave York in a hurry with at least this leg of our task complete."

"I have my doubts that there is any great advantage to it, but let's discover where Simcoe lived, shall we?" replied Oliver, surrendering his hopefulness to great misgivings. "Then perhaps tomorrow, we'll find a chance to ask why we've looked for it."

They set about their task by slowly walking through the market once again, subtly questioning people by way of engaging them in small talk. At last Davis came upon an older gentleman who he wagered must have resided in the area in the time when Simcoe lived in Upper Canada. Although he was obviously not a butcher, his was a meat stall and the still-draining carcasses of several creatures hung about where the fellow was seated on a low three-legged stool, intent upon sharpening a rather large knife with a whetstone.

"Excuse me, sir," Halberson said, declaring his presence. The man looked up at the three strangers, squinting momentarily as he focused his eyes upon them. He wiped his hands on his already bloody apron and stood up.

"What can I do for you gentlemen?" he asked, relishing the possibility of new customers. "What'll it be, then? Would you be after some beef?"

With the butt end of his knife he hit a side of beef of which some large chunks had been carved.

"No sir, just some information, if you please. We need to know where Simcoe lived here as Governor."

"Information?" the man spat more than asked. "I sell meat here. If it's directions you want, ask a constable." Without a further word, he sat back down on his stool and began once again to hone the blade of his knife.

Davis's temper flared at what he considered a display of rudeness. "Now wait here…" he started, but was cut off by Oliver's hand, pulling him away by the arm.

"We don't wish to make a scene, now do we?" he hissed. "We'll find someone else."

The woman selling fruit in the next stall caught their attention as they turned to leave. "Did you want to know where Old Man Simcoe lived?" she asked. When Oliver nodded, she continued. "It's quite simple, really. Just go up the Don River some miles, and you can't miss it. The Castle Frank, that's what they call it. My husband and I were in that area just a few months past and it's really quite the sight. It's made of logs and is named after Simcoe's son, who lives there still."

"You say Simcoe's son is still there?" asked Davis. The woman nodded. "Well, I must heartily thank you for your information. You are most surely more courteous than some here," he added, casting a quick glance toward the meat vendor's stall. "I think we should buy some fruit for our trip, eh, Oliver?"

Oliver paid the woman for the fruit they selected and thanked her once again for the information. They decided to call it a day for neither had any desire to travel up the nearby river and look at the home owned by the Simcoe family. In fact, the longer they thought about it the more ludicrous was the idea that Williamson might have come all the way up to York and then out to the countryside to hide his papers.

They turned to head back to their cramped hotel accommodations to await the morning, when Davis stopped his companion, pointing across the crowded market toward the church.

"Does that man seem familiar to you?" he asked, indicating a dirty, hungry-looking but otherwise nondescript young man who was, to all appearances, appraising the goods at a fish table. "He's been staring at us for some minutes now. Well now, he's seen me pointing and has turned away."

Oliver had not seen the man look over, but he was only paying partial attention, his mind on other matters. "Let's go talk to the strange man, shall we?" he said, taking off through the crowds as fast as the milling bodies would allow.

"I've lost him!" Davis called out when he reached the place at which the man had been standing. "Did either of you see where he went?"

Oliver shook his head while straining his neck to see out over the crowd.

"Alright then, split up!" Jeremy ordered. "We'll take each a side and look for anyone who may seem familiar. If you find someone of that description, cry out. Just keep looking and if you can't find hide or hair of him, I'll meet you in front of the church in a half hour."

Oliver worked his way across the market slowly, carefully but discreetly checking each person in turn to see if they might be their man. Frustratingly, there was no longer any vestige of him, and he headed for the church as planned.

Davis had gone in the other direction and as he stepped out from behind tinker's stall near the now empty stocks, he almost walked right into the object of his search. The young man looked at him with surprise and then noticed the expression on Davis' face, directed at him. The fellow started to run.

★ ★ ★

The young infantryman took but four or five long strides and then threw himself at the escaping man. With an impact that winded both men, they slammed into the muddy ground. Neither moved for several seconds and then the fugitive made a move to scramble clear and make a break for it. But he was not fast enough. Davis took hold of the man's ankle and gave it a hard twist. Having little muscle to his emaciated frame, the ankle gave easily and the man went down again, screaming in pain.

"What's the matter with you?" the man demanded, holding onto his ankle and wincing. "Are you quite daft? What is it you're after then?"

"You know or you wouldn't be running," Davis replied between gasps, still winded from his collision with the ground.

"I didn't take anything, honest! I don't know what that fishmonger told you, but I didn't take anything!"

Davis took a closer measure of the young man before him, who was close to his own age. It was obvious that he was hungry and scared and he continuously looked nervously at the stocks, in whose shadow they lay, before meeting his captor's eyes once more.

"Do you mean to tell me that's why you ran?" he demanded sternly. "Over some bit of fish?"

The young man now looked steadily into his captor's eyes. His own were wide open once he realized that something was not right with all of this.

"Of course. Why do you think I ran?"

"Because you were watching us," replied Oliver, uncertain now about the situation and confused at this turn of events.

"I wasn't watching you," the young man replied, obviously equally puzzled by it all. "I may have looked in your direction, but I ran when the other chap with you pointed me out. I thought he was fingering me." He stopped for a moment and looked about at the people who had pressed closer to see what the fuss was all about. "Why would I be watching you?" he asked.

"Now that I see you up close and hear you talk, it seems that it's a case of mistaken identity," Davis replied, unable to think of anything better to say. "We thought you were someone else."

The young man got off the ground, followed almost immediately by Davis. "Well maybe I should be calling a constable, then," he said indignantly, his courage suddenly taking on a life of its own. "You can't just go about throwing strangers to the ground without a good reason. I think you may have broken my ankle."

He hobbled about in a circle to illustrate the terrible injury he had suffered at the hand of this man. "You all saw it didn't you?" he asked the crowd, some of whom nodded in agreement.

Davis stepped closer to the petty thief and muttered in a voice too low for onlookers to hear. "If you want real trouble, just keep it up boy. I'm sure the constable would like to investigate the matter of the fish while he's here. I'll be more than happy to tell him that I saw you steal it and chased you down to turn you in." He pointed to his own uniform. "See this uniform? I'm one of the King's men. Who do you think the constable will believe?"

The young man looked steadily at Davis, apparently mulling this sudden development over in his mind. Then he turned to the crowd and took a bow. "Ladies and gentlemen, thank you for your attention. That'll be all for this day's show. Please come back tomorrow."

Davis smiled at the people as they turned to go. "I must give you this, lad," he muttered. "You certainly act better than you lie. Be off now."

The young man looked hungrily at an apple that had fallen on the ground from Davis' pocket. His hunger was evident in the lack of meat on his bones and so Davis nodded slightly. The fellow quickly snatched up the apple and walked off quickly – without a limp.

"Well, it seems he wasn't watching us," muttered Davis, sighing heavily. "Either that or he's a better liar, or actor, than I give him credit for."

Oliver had just then appeared through the crowd, having been attracted by the commotion and the possibility that Davis had found their man.

"What he said might well be the truth I suppose. It may be that he just caught your attention because he kept shifting his position, seemingly so as to not lose sight of us while we were asking questions," Oliver remarked. "By his appearance, I guessed that he might be one of the Volunteers we met on the road. He had the same furtive look and nervousness as a couple in that bunch."

Davis sat on a bench near the stocks and sighed once again. "Well, if he was lying, it's not likely that he found out anything by his watch," he said. "Right, then let's move along back to the hotel, shall we?"

★ ★ ★

The two young men headed down to the harbour and sat watching the light vessel traffic there, mostly small skiffs bringing local trade to market. Though an ideal harbour for just about any purpose they had discovered twice it was a difficult place to protect from American attack. Fear of such confrontation on Lake Ontario prevented much shipping by water as the navy tended to stay at Kingston, wanting to keep their ships ready for a major naval engagement. As a result, most goods were transported over the less than ideal Kingston Road.

"What do you make of what's happened so far?" Davis asked, crunching into an apple. "Doesn't this entire enterprise seem rather strange to you?"

Oliver looked out across the water. "I'm not much familiar with the history of your colony, but it would seem that your Mr. Williamson came a long way to hide the booty." He turned back to the infantryman. "I'm beginning to think someone has sent the lot of us off on a wild goose chase."

"If only we could find out from Sims what is next for the information," Davis muttered darkly. "I would surely like to know what his nonsense is supposed to lead to."

"I've been thinking even that Sims misunderstood something in the directions. But unless he tells us what the instructions say, we have no way of knowing for certain. In light of the impossibility of the task, I would suggest that we should leave for home in the morning were it not for Jeremy," Oliver sighed. "I think it highly unlikely that we shall ever find out any more from Sims. The fool has put the noose about his own neck, and I don't see how we can help him, or even if we should. Not even to find out his secrets."

They watched the harbour in silence, taking in the water and the wooded peninsula that gave this port such great protection from the elements. After a while Davis stood up and started slowly and dejectedly off toward the hotel, soon to be followed by Oliver.

★ ★ ★

Jeremy's senses once again revived in a cell. This one looked the same as the one where he had been before but, instead of his previous cellmate, the man he saw now looked very familiar. As he looked, the man cautiously peered in his direction.

"Sims!" Jeremy roared. "You bloody great fool! Look what you have gotten us into now!"

"At least you haven't been condemned to death," Sims replied morosely through split and swollen lips.

"Not yet at least."

"Why are you here?"

"Someone, and they won't tell me who, told them that I had been with you," Jeremy replied. "Unfortunate as that is, it happened to be true. However, I told the lieutenant that we were on a mission under Colonel Halberson and he's sending someone to ask if I spoke the truth. So we may yet be freed within several days."

"Hopefully, the lieutenant's man will return before my neck is stretched."

"With your behaviour the other night, you may have reason to hope he'll return before I choke you myself," grumbled Jeremy. "I should have followed my first instinct and stayed well the hell out of anything to do with this war. More the fool I."

Their conversation was interrupted as the door swung loudly open, slamming against the jail's log wall. There stood the soldier that Jeremy had injured shortly before, a sadistic grin showing on his face.

"Now then, let's see what you're really made of, now that I'm ready for you," he growled and then started forward menacingly toward Jeremy.

"And where is your friend this time?" Jeremy asked mockingly. "Are you not afraid that, without his help, you might be injured once more?"

"As I said, I'm ready for you now, and I'm bound to make you pay for what you done."

Jeremy was aware that, as the man moved forward, he limped and there was a slight grimace of pain when he placed his weight on the ankle which was bound tightly. Broken? Probably not, for he had returned rather too soon had that been the case. Nonetheless, it was causing the soldier some discomfort.

The great oaf of a man lunged for Jeremy, who lashed out almost instinctively with his foot and caught the man in the point of his greatest weakness. Jeremy could swear he heard a cracking sound as the previously injured ankle gave under the impact.

Jeremy heard the soldier roar with pain but he did not go down. In a frenzied panic, he lashed out at the ankle again just as the guard's hands reached for him. This time there he could hear the injured joint give as the man screamed in pain and went down on one knee, his hands now grasping automatically for the injury. Jeremy leapt to his feet and, taking careful aim, kicked his jailer under the chin with all the might he could muster. The man crumpled into the dirty straw and mud.

"Damn!" Jeremy cursed, trying to shake off the pain of the kick. "I think I might have broken my own foot in the process. Well Sims," he said, turning back to the man cowering in the corner. "Are you coming with me? There'll be no mercy the next time, if ever there was to be."

Sims looked out from behind his knees, wide-eyed with fear. "No. You go on if you will. I don't think you can make it out alive, but I've no desire to die with you."

Jeremy threw Sims a glare of unutterable contempt and then shrugged. "I'll try to come see you at your hanging then."

Chapter Seventeen

He ran from the cell and made for the door that would take him to freedom. He was aware subconsciously that Sims probably was right. But he had no desire to spend day after day being beaten by the thugs that served as guards. He had suffered enough of that at Williamson's hands the year before.

As he reached the door, a voice called out to him. Turning slightly, he noticed Lieutenant Denham sitting behind the old beaten desk in the corner where he had gone unnoticed in Jeremy's haste to escape. He was holding a pistol, the hammer cocked for service.

"I think you had best come over here," Denham said evenly.

Jeremy stepped cautiously toward the desk.

"Stop right there." The lieutenant motioned with the pistol. "I think you should go back in the cell and wait for the man you just reinjured to come around. Now put your hands on your head."

Jeremy did as he was told and he started back to the cell. As he crossed the sill between the rooms, he hobbled slightly.

"I believe I broke my foot on your man's face," Jeremy grumbled and reached for support from the lieutenant's desk.

"I'm sure there will be more broken than your foot alone when Terrigan has done with you," Denham replied. Once again he waved the pistol to indicate that Jeremy should proceed.

Jeremy had been watching carefully and, as the muzzle of the pistol reached farthest point in its arc away from him, he pushed with all his might at the desk. The heavy piece of furniture shot out and caught Denham across the tops of his thighs and threw him off balance.

Before the lieutenant could react, Jeremy leapt up onto the desk, landing on his knees. In almost the same motion, his right fist lashed out, catching Denham full on the chin while grasping the pistol with his left hand and deflecting the weapon upward. Wild shouting and banging issued from within the cell area, shouted encouragement to any who might be taking on the hated jailers, bringing the sound in the tiny jail to a deafening level. And then the pistol discharged, missing Jeremy's head by mere inches as the lieutenant staggered under the blow.

With the report of the pistol, the building went suddenly silent as the jail's occupants strained to hear the outcome, so that Jeremy was able to hear a scrape in the doorway of his recently vacated cell. He looked up to see the man Denham had referred to as Terrigan standing there looking out upon the scene of the scuffle.

Fear thrilled through Jeremy, realizing the man would now be coming after him, but then he quickly realized that the soldier had a look of pure astonishment on his face.

Terrigan stared without focus at the two men struggling at the desk and then looked down at his torso. He pulled his hands away from his chest to display blood oozing rapidly from a ragged hole in his shirt. Then his eyes rolled back and, without a word, crashed to the plank floor of the jail.

The lieutenant stopped in his struggle and stared at the body on the floor.

Jeremy relieved the officer of the now spent pistol, which he quickly realized to be his own by the engraving work. "If you have this, you must have my other weapons as well," he said to the shocked lieutenant. "I suggest you show me where they are."

Denham gave no immediate reply but glanced carelessly in the direction of cupboard which stood in the corner. Jeremy strode to the door and, with two blows of the pistol handle, broke off the padlock. There he found his rifle, bayonet and tomahawk, but his ammunition was gone.

"Where are the flint, powder and balls?" he demanded of the lieutenant, who had not yet moved.

"They're not here," Denham replied. "No loaded weapons are allowed on the jail property."

"It would appear that you don't follow the rules well. However, it's lucky that I had added this," Jeremy said with a half-smile. With a flick of the wrist, he twisted the butt end of the rifle stock, revealing a secret compartment. He removed a small piece of cloth which contained a spare flint and two cartridges, each consisting of ball, powder and wadding. With practiced ease, he loaded the over/under.

By this time, the shock of the pistol blast had worn off and the din in the jail increased rapidly once again. Jeremy heard the cheers and encouragement of someone who had obviously guessed the outcome of the fight, and cacophony reached a crescendo as the others realized there was a chance they would be freed. Unfortunately, there was no time to even go back for Sims. The other guard had not appeared and there was no way of knowing who may have heard the noise or what the response might be.

Jeremy opened the door and stepped cautiously out of the jail. With a glance in either direction, he walked off down the street and then broke into a run when he reached the road out of York.

As he passed the hotel in which they had stayed, he found Oliver and Davis sitting on the veranda. "Get your things and meet me outside of town near the ruined Government House!" he shouted out as he ran past. "I'll meet you there." And then he was gone."

Their mission now an abject failure, the three men spent the night hiding in the hulk of the charred vessel at the waterfront. The next dawn's early light found Jeremy, Oliver and Davis already on the long road back towards Burlington Heights. The plan was that at that point the cousins would part ways with the infantryman and then continue on to Niagara.

And for reasons that Jeremy could not fathom, Davis did not seem particularly disturbed by their failure. Just the adaptability of youth, he supposed, shrugging at the thought.

Well past the last of the farmhouses that could reasonably consider itself part of York, they came upon a farmer sitting at the side of the road. He stared forlornly at his wagon, which had somehow managed to break two wheels on the same side, leaving the vehicle listing uselessly to that side and dumping the man's goods out into the road.

He looked up slowly as the men approached. "Good morning to you," he offered without little enthusiasm, obviously not feeling the spirit of his words.

"Good morning," Jeremy returned. "Can we be of some help?" he offered, though not at all certain how.

"My son's gone back to the house for some tools and, hopefully, at least one wheel," the farmer answered, waving vaguely down the road. "He'll be back shortly, and I think the two of us can manage but thank you anyway. Damn these roads!" he added, almost to himself. "Thomson never keeps up his share of the road and this is the result," he added, referring to the regulation that all residents must make improvements and repairs to the section of road that bounds their properties.

"Have you spoken to him of it?" Oliver asked.

The farmer looked up at him with a tired expression displayed in his eyes. "Aye. Many, many, many times. But it seems as though I'll need to speak to the authorities if I wish to correct his ways. And I have no wish to involve government men in so small a problem, for they'll surely overreact and cause more problems than they solve."

"Well, good luck then, sir," said Jeremy, and the trio headed on once more.

Not far along from the encounter, they heard a disturbance behind them, and a voice rang out. "Make way for the King's men on the King's business!"

There was silence, followed by what may have been a reply that could not be heard from where Jeremy and his party walked. Then they heard the louder voice once again. "I said, make way! I don't care to hear of your circumstances. I have a prisoner bound over for execution and if you don't move, I'll have you join him!"

There followed more silence, or what seemed like it, and then the grunts of men exerting themselves followed by a clatter and a loud crash.

"I think by the sound that the gentlemen we spoke to has just had his wagon overturned," Oliver said in astonishment. "Do you think the soldiers would do such a thing? All they needed do was to go around."

Jeremy had seen his share of arrogant military officers in the past. "I'm afraid there's little some self-important men would not do to make themselves known," he sighed. "It could have been worse. The popinjay who leads that detail could have shot the poor man for obstructing justice or perhaps treason."

"That's why we in the United States threw the British out," Oliver declared self-righteously.

Jeremy offered a sad grin. "Do you not think that the United States still has men such as these, especially in time of war, when they can likely get away with their bullying actions?"

Oliver fought back an urge to deny Jeremy's charge but then finally had to admit that he knew from personal experience that his cousin was right. Chastened, he sighed heavily in resignation. "I suppose you're right on that account, cousin. I don't think we can ever be free of bullies."

"Not so long as there are those who are willing to give these types of men the power to act upon their odd sense of honour," Jeremy added. "I'm afraid there's no answer to that."

"Do you suppose those might be the men escorting Sims?" Davis broke in.

"It could well be. I don't imagine there would be that many others all on one day," Jeremy replied. "Especially at this early hour of the morning."

"Perhaps they'll give us the chance to speak to him momentarily, that we might ask him for the directions one last time," the marksman suggested hopefully.

Jeremy shook his head. "I suppose we might try. But by the sounds of it, the officer in charge is not the accommodating sort."

"Well, let me speak," Davis suggested. "Perhaps he'll be somewhat more reasonable with a man in uniform."

Jeremy had grave doubts, especially considering the condition of Davis' uniform. The officer might be more disposed toward shooting his companion for his slovenliness or he might assume that the sharpshooter was a deserter, a more common condition than one might assume. Nonetheless he merely gave the young soldier a resigned shrug. He sincerely hoped that it could do no harm to ask.

In mere moments, the beat of hooves on the packed dirt road announced the arrival of the prisoner detail. As they rounded the last bend before where they stood, Davis stepped carefully onto the road well in front of them and saluted to the approaching officer, who drew up his detail to glare at the odd group before him.

"And why would you be blocking my detail, soldier?" the officer asked, sneering.

"Private Davis Halberson, sir, on a mission from Colonel Halberson of Burlington Heights!" He completed his salute smartly and waited for the officer, obviously a Lieutenant, to reply.

The lieutenant stared at the soldier before him, pursing his lips as though deep in thought. "Well, private, I'm not familiar with your mission or, for that matter your Colonel, who seems by his name to be a relation of yours, but why are you in the company of this rabble," he asked, indicating Jeremy and Oliver, "and in this condition of dress?"

"These gentlemen are part of my mission, sir," Davis replied by way of explanation.

"Well, move your mission out of the way of my men, or your mission will be over!" the Lieutenant snapped.

"I'm sorry, sir, but I am required to request a moment with your prisoner. He may have information pertinent to the mission of which I spoke," Davis explained.

"I am under orders to stop for no one and to allow this man to speak to no one, do you understand?" the officer barked, his face turning red. "Now, stand clear, or risk being shot!"

The lieutenant was clearly losing his temper, and Jeremy stepped forward to pull Halberson away from the road. One of the soldiers riding guard, however, mistook Jeremy's sudden movement for an attack. He raised his gun and clumsily struggled to fire from his mount.

Davis, seeing that Jeremy was in danger of being shot, jumped in front of the soldier's horse and attempted to grab the horse's bridle. The animal panicked at the sudden movement from directly in front and pulled away, rearing up and throwing his rider onto the still-muddy roadway with a muffled thud.

The lieutenant saw his man go down and immediately overreacted. He drew his sword from its scabbard and, raising it high, ordered his men to fire upon the three in the road. It was an order for which the remaining three soldiers were unprepared. Jeremy and his companions ran forward screaming, panicking the horses and allowing them to get close enough to unhorse the men.

"Traitors and spies!" the lieutenant screamed maniacally. "Those men are traitors and spies! What are you waiting for? Shoot them! Stop them before they free the prisoner!"

The soldiers by now lay sprawled in the mire in roadway, however, and were in no condition or position to be shooting anyone. They found themselves staring up into the gun barrels of the men from Niagara, their own having been kicked out of reach.

The lieutenant himself found Jeremy standing beside him.

"I would kindly request leave to speak to the prisoner," Jeremy said evenly, although there was no suggestion of the words being a request. He pulled back the hammer on his gun to make his point.

The officer looked down on the woodsman from his mount and, for reasons that could only be known to him, decided that he was better than any colonial. Without warning, he slashed viciously downward, his sabre making a slight whistling noise as it travelled.

In the same fraction of a second, Jeremy pulled the trigger on his gun and was immediately rewarded with a burning pain across the front of his left shoulder. With the left hand, he released his grip on the gun's stock, automatically reaching across his chest to the source of the discomfort.

He barely registered the sound of the lieutenant slamming heavily into the ground as his fingers identified the warm, sticky feeling of blood soaking his hand. Out of pure instinct, he looked momentarily toward the officer and saw that there was no danger from that quarter and then turned to the others to determine their situation. All was as before, with three soldiers yet lying in the roadway under the guard of his companions.

Davis herded the British soldiers together well away from their weapons and then left them under Oliver's watchful eye. Then he went to the where the lieutenant lay and nudged the officer lightly with toe of his boot. There was a soft groaned but no attempt to move, so Davis reached down and rolled the man over onto his back.

"How is he?" Jeremy asked almost absent-mindedly, stuffing pieces he had cut from the officer's saddle blanket into his shirt to soak up the blood.

"You just grazed his skull. I don't know why he's just lying there as he is. Mostly just dazed, that would be my guess. You, on the other hand, are bleeding like a stuck pig. Are you alright?"

"Fine," Jeremy replied, wincing as he tied a piece of cloth across his chest, attempting to apply pressure. "He just grazed me as well. When we're clear, I'll have a closer look at it to make sure it's closing up. Now, where's Sims? I suggest we speak to him and be on our way before the lieutenant regains what little senses he has."

"He escaped off down the road while he had our hands full of this lot," Oliver' voice came in explanation. "I don't know if we can catch him, but he's still tied to his mount."

Jeremy reloaded his gun, wincing at the wound's reminder as he did so. "Well, let's be clear of this place. Perhaps we'll come upon him somewhere along the road."

Davis and Oliver removed the flints from the soldiers' muskets and shook the powder from the firing pans. It would at least allow the Canadians an opportunity to escape into the forest before the soldiers could install new flints and reload and re-prime their guns.

Chapter Eighteen

The Parson and his disciples waited impatiently less than three miles down the road from where Jeremy and his companions fought with Sims' guards. Split into two groups, they sat among the bushes which occupied the spaces between some of the many trees. The Parson's main hope at this time was that the fools would not shoot each other in the cross-fire. For this reason, he kept himself several yards further down the road from the intended arena of action.

It had seemed like an inordinate amount of time had passed since Brother Simon had come running back to report that Sims and his military escort were on the way and should arrive at any time. Since then, he had thought that he had heard a disturbance farther up the road toward York, possibly involving gunfire. However, it was impossible to tell for certain because the trees and terrain tended to muffle sound over even short distances.

"I thought you said they were right behind you?" he shouted over to Brother Simon, the man who had sounded the alarm earlier. The disciples were becoming increasingly nervous for it was obvious to all that the Parson had lost his patience completely. The man seemed not to believe now that they would be seeing the soldiers any time soon.

"They were only a short ways up the road," replied Brother Simon in a sound very close to a whine. "I honestly don't know where they went."

They were all deathly afraid of the mercurial leader they knew as the Parson. They had all seen the results of what could happen when mistakes were made. The Parson did not believe in mistakes, and errors were considered the work of the Devil. That was, of course, unless they were his own, in which case they were caused by the Hand of God, whose motives were wholly beyond their understanding and therefore brooked no blame. The holy man considered it to be entirely within his preserve to exorcise the Demon when mistakes were made. It was questionable which was actually greater; the fear of God that the preacher had put into them or the fear of the man himself. It was definitely the latter that kept them from running away at the first opportunity.

The Parson was about to give up on this enterprise and rose to declare the whole exercise a waste of his precious time when he heard the sounds of horses' hooves, coming on at a fast clip. That's odd, he thought. An escort to the gallows is usually a matter of great gravity, requiring a certain level of dignity and ceremony. This was done so that all they pass on the ride would know the seriousness of matter and it required that the escort ride slowly through the countryside. Ah well, he thought, perhaps something has happened to spook them.

"Get ready," the Parson ordered in a deep, steady voice. "Here they come."

The disciples all checked their muskets, as they were trained to do, to be sure that they were ready to open fire when the command was given. That having been done, they resumed their positions to await their targets. The tension of this final wait was palpable and all were perspiring in the cold before long.

Finally, almost anticlimactically after the stress of the wait, a number of mounted soldiers trotted around the bend.

The Parson arose from his place of concealment and stepped out into the road without warning ahead of the oncoming horses so that they would be in position to reap the crossfire. He held a Bible in his left hand and brandished a pistol in his right.

"Repent for the Lord shall be your salvation!" he cried out, the unexpected and undetermined obstacle causing the soldiers to rein in tightly. "All will be forgiven if you but repent of your sins!"

"Get off the road, you mad fool," ordered the officer in command of the troops. He was livid that this man should so interfere with his troops, nearly unseating the two men in front as their horses shied, the second such occurrence this day. "You are interfering with men on the King's business. Go peddle your wares to the ignorant rabble and clear the way." He had a strip of cloth tied haphazardly about his head, dark where blood had obviously seeped through.

"Then you shall all rot in Hell!" the Parson screamed and dropped the hand holding the Bible immediately before he ducked for cover.

As he jumped clear of the imminent line of fire, he thought about the speed of the horses once again and the fact that something was missing now grew into a certainty. Try as he might, he could not see the fat man they were here to get. The situation was not right, he realized. Too late, he shouted, "Hold your..."

Having seen the signal to fire – the drop of the Bible hand – from their leader and not able to understand what he was saying, the disciples fired. First one, and then the rest pulled their triggers and a cloud of smoke arose from both sides of the road as the first volley flew into the roadway.

One soldier fell from his horse immediately, his face showing a grisly partial grin where the ball had ripped away his left cheek. Unfortunately for him, he was still alive, though he would be of little service to his fellow soldiers.

With all the smoke drifting across the roadway, it was difficult to tell if anyone else on either side of the fight had been hit. Some of the horses shied at the sudden sound, having never been tested in battle, throwing two of the riders to the ground. The remainder yet seated on their mounts spun around in place, some looking for their assailants and others just trying to calm their horses. The air was filled with the sounds of screams, commands, musket fire, and the whinny of the horses, and it was impossible to sort out any of it.

The Parson's disciples reloaded as quickly as they could, but they were not trained and practiced military men and before they could fire another volley, the soldiers in the road had lain their horses down on both sides to offer some measure of cover. In seconds, musket and pistol balls were flying in all directions, with little success on either side.

The battle seemed frustratingly to be heading toward a stalemate, with no serious casualties on either side. The Parson fidgeted in place as his impatience grew with every passing second until finally he could stand it no more. He had ordered his disciples to fix bayonets in advance, before they had taken up their positions, and now he was tired of waiting for the British to make their fatal error.

He had been waiting for the British to empty their muskets all at about the same time. But they did not seem to be about to give him the opening he needed. They were cagier than to give the enemy a full volley. They continued to return fire in rotation, as regular as machines, making sure that there were loaded muskets behind their horses at all times while the others reloaded.

The Parson watched from his place of safety as a musket ball caught one of his men in the forehead. The man uttered not a sound and his face registered no expression as the ball carried through, driving splintered bone fragments into the man's brain and killing him. Ghoulishly his body, now without guidance, seemed to move to jump up and then dropped down out of sight. That was the third one, the Parson thought. If he was going to succeed, his disciples would need to take more aggressive action. He decided that, ideal or not, his men would make their move.

"Ready, men!" he shouted, when he was sure he would be heard by his men. "First unit! Now! Attack!"

As he last of the words issued from his mouth, the men did as they had rehearsed time and again. Screaming like the very demons of Hell they were told they were meant to battle, they sprang without thought or consideration of injury out of their concealment and rushed headlong at the enemy.

In the face of the fearless and mindless onslaught, the British soldiers finally panicked and opened fire on the screaming men all at once, not sure what to make of such suicidal behaviour but fearful for their lives all the same. The disciples seemed to stop almost in place, as though they had run into an invisible but unyielding wall.

But now the British were in the unenviable position of needing to reload all of their muskets at the same time, giving the balance of the Parson's disciples the time they needed for a quick charge. The remainder of the fanatics rushed out from behind their cover, firing muskets on the run and screaming at the top of their lungs as had the doomed rank before them. The Brits, having no time to reload, rose to meet them, bayonets at the ready.

The English officer in charge produced a brace of pistols and felled two of the ambushers. One dropped instantly still while the other screamed and writhed in the roadway until the Parson could stand the noise no longer and ended the man's suffering himself. The officer then threw the now useless pistols at another to slow him down while he picked up a fallen comrade's rifle and prepared to fight on with the bayonet. There was a dreadful clash as two sides met, which could now be plainly heard as there was no more shooting, all having emptied their weapons. There were several minutes where, because of the crush of bodies, the Parson had no idea which side, if either, was winning.

From his place at the sidelines, the Parson saw one of the British soldiers, covered in blood, stagger out of the melee and run feebly for the woods. By the time that he realized what he had seen and could react, the man was gone, although he could still be heard crashing clumsily through the brush over the sounds of the remaining battle. The Parson thought about chasing after him but, concluding that the man was in no shape to survive the freezing night without shelter or cover.

It would not be long before the fight ended. The soldiers fought valiantly and with superior training but, in the end they were overwhelmed by the fanaticism and sheer numbers that the Parson had thrown at them. Soon all of the redcoats lay dead in the roadway and the surviving disciples, exhausted and bloodied, stopped clubbing and stabbing even those who were already dead. There were but three of the Parson's original force left, and only one of those men had no discernable injuries.

The Parson decided that it was finally now safe for him to come out into the open again. If the man truly believed in anything, it was the theory that a commander killed or seriously injured in battle could not be of any benefit his men. To that end, he always took pains to make certain that he would meet neither of those ends.

He strolled casually out into the killing field, to where the bodies lay sprawled about in death, the dead horses among them as well. He went through the motions of saying silent prayers over the deceased on both sides, occasionally pulling them apart, looking to see who might be the target of this exercise. He had still not made out Sims' form among them, and he began to fear that the businessman would be dead and that then they would never find the paper he was seeking. It had been impossible in the heat of battle and the clouds of musket smoke to determine who was being shot. But Sims was obviously not still standing among them.

He carefully studied each of the British soldiers, turning them over when necessary, in case they might have tricked him by putting the prisoner in uniform in case of such a contingency. Finally the Parson admitted defeat. He threw his arms up in the air and looked at his men as if this was all somehow their fault.

"He's not here!" he bellowed at the top of his lungs and his men visibly shrank back out of reach, their fear of this man greater than that of the battle itself. "That bastard Sims isn't here! I thought the Brother said he was coming. So where is he?"

The disciples stood speechless. Many of their fellow disciples had just died in this horrible exercise and now perhaps it was all for naught?

"Where is the Brother that told me Sims was coming?" The Preacher stormed.

One of the others said nothing but pointed at a body in the road. Brother Simon had been chosen by the Parson to be one of the first to die in the initial charge and most of his face was destroyed as he was shot point-blank.

"That's him?" their leader asked, his tone coming down somewhat as a sense of hopelessness of this mission sank in and slowly invaded his being. The disciple who pointed out the body was too frightened at his leader's silence to do anything but just nod.

"Well good!" the Parson exploded. "He's lucky that he's dead. If he'd still been alive, I would have done worse to him for his incompetence!" He would not allow his men to think him weakened by any of this. Angrily, he looked around at the dead one last time, as if to convince himself that Sims was indeed not there.

Nobody spoke. Nobody dared. The Parson had killed for less.

The three surviving disciples and veterans of Battle of the York Road, as the Parson would name it heroically, just waited and then meekly followed the Parson as he led them soundlessly back down the road toward Niagara.

★ ★ ★

As Jeremy and his companions made their way along what could barely termed a trail which had been made by unknown others, they kept their senses attuned to any sights or sounds that might alert them as to Sims' location. They truly had little expectation of finding the man, fully expecting that even Sims could manage to escape his bindings and ride to freedom. However, it seemed that even such little expectation could foster hope.

"Do you think the soldiers will follow us in here?" Oliver asked after more than an hour, glancing over his shoulder nervously every few seconds.

"I doubt it," Jeremy replied. "They were tasked with delivering Sims and I imagine they are much more likely to attempt to find him than to venture off into the forest after armed men who could well ambush them, and allowing their charge to escape in the process." He winced as his shirt once again rubbed against the wound on his shoulder. It was beginning to dry and the chafing and the tight feeling that accompanied it was causing him some discomfort.

"I don't know. I keep thinking that I can hear a sound like something heavy stepping carefully along through the trees," Oliver persisted. "There! I hear it again!"

The three stopped and listened carefully. After a moment there was indeed a sound of rustling leaves and the occasional breaking twig as something moved in a direction approximately toward them, on a course that would intersect with their path almost where they stood. They left their path with the intent of intercepting the sound, whatever might be causing them.

At a distance of almost twenty-five feet, they came upon a wider path, much better defined and possibly once intended to become a roadway. And approaching slowly with a stop-start gait was a horse with someone slumped over the front of the saddle. They stepped out as one, guns held at the ready, blocking the oblivious animal's forward progress.

At the unexpected but not unusual sight of men approaching, the horse merely stopped in place and waited, flicking its ears in anticipation.

As Davis took hold of the harness and reassured the horse, Jeremy cautiously approached the slumped figure. He nudged the man and he slumped toward the far side without falling off, apparently held in place by his hands, which were lashed firmly to the saddle. Unsheathing his knife, he cut the bonds with two quick strokes and then pulled the man lightly toward him by the shoulder.

The body, for there was by now little doubt that the man was dead, tipped over and fell to the ground with a thud. Jeremy looked down to find a dead pair of eyes staring up at him from the forest floor.

"It's Sims," Jeremy muttered with a sigh. "By the looks of his corpse, I'd say the horse took him under a tree limb he didn't see coming. Broke his neck by the angle of his head."

Oliver looked slightly nauseous. "Why do you think the horse ended up in the woods? Wouldn't it have just continued on down the road?"

"Maybe gunfire or something scared it and it took an opening into the trees to get away," suggested Davis, having no other explanation for it.

"Will you look at that?" he blurted suddenly in surprise, now standing over Sims' body and unwillingly staring at the grotesque angle of the head. "The trees must have torn at Sims' collar, partly separating it from his coat!"

Jeremy's mind a momentary blank, overcome by more senseless death – something he never seemed to become accustomed to – his attention drifted where directed by the sharpshooter. Sure enough, the collar was now detached but there was something not quite right, he thought. He pulled free the rest of the collar from under the dead man's head and studied it.

"The collar's come loose, as you say," he began almost inanely in restatement of the obvious. He fingered the edge of the seam, its threads coming apart easily in his fingers. "It would appear that it was only attached to coat with a couple of threads to begin with."

"Another of Sims' money caches, do you think?" Oliver asked.

"I don't know. He seems to have been fond of using his coat for such."

As he picked more at the threads, the material of the collar separated to reveal a tightly folded sheet of paper. It would have been impossible to detect during the search back at Smith's Tavern, for most collars had stiffening of some fashion. It had likely been hidden there all along.

"What does it say?" Davis asked excitedly, already anticipating what it might be.

"Yes, come now, cousin. Are they the mysterious instructions we seek?" Oliver jumped in.

Jeremy ignored the two impatient young men as he carefully unfolded the document, more writing appearing from behind each fold as he continued. "This is it," he said quietly. "And unless I misunderstand, Mr. Sims truly should have let us see this earlier."

"Why? What have you found?" Oliver asked anxiously, craning to peek at the document in his cousin's grasp.

"Well, he got it quite wrong..." Jeremy started.

"I think I hear someone coming!" Davis interrupted. "I suggest that get away from here! I think someone must have followed the horse's tracks. They don't seem to be far off and I expect they'll be here very soon."

Galvanized in spite of emotional and physical fatigue, Jeremy jumped to his feet, anxiously stuffing the paper that cost Sims his life into his kit bag, which hung at his left side. "Come on gentlemen."

Chapter Nineteen

The three men ran as quickly through the woods as the natural obstacles would allow, heading in the general direction of Lake Ontario. Not entirely sure that this ruse would prove to be their salvation, they hoped the branches and fallen logs of the forest would cause even more problems for their pursuers. As they ran they looked about constantly, searching desperately for a solution more certain to be their salvation.

They ran on at what would turn out to be a tangent to the shore, their strength flagging with the effort, when suddenly they stumbled onto just such a possible solution to their problems. Just ahead was a ravine with a stony creek at the bottom. This was advantageous, but the best part was the configuration of the opposite side.

Jeremy scrambled down the slope and came face to face with to an almost sheer promontory nearly fifteen feet high, topped by a dense thicket of spruce which created a nearly impenetrable mesh of sharp, dry branches.

"Up here!" Jeremy cried down to his companions and the others climbed as quickly as they could through the growth on the slope and then up over the promontory. Once at the top, they stopped to check their rear for British troops.

"Do you see any sign of them?" Oliver asked his cousin anxiously as he flipped himself up over the side behind the others.

Jeremy searched the side of the ravine from whence they had come and listened carefully, willing himself to ignore the pounding of his blood in his ears to listen for an approach from any direction. "Nothing," he said finally. "They must not have an experienced tracker among them, because I don't think they've picked up our trail."

"We seem to be asking this question a deal lately, but once again, what shall we do now?" commented Davis, sorely rubbing a bruised and skinned shin he acquired bounding through the forest and climbing the growth below.

"I suggest we keep moving for a time," Jeremy replied, still searching intently for any sign they had been found out. "Even without a tracker, they'll pick up our trail eventually. We took no pains to make it difficult, and the ground is soft from all the rain in so many places." He looked about. "There," he said pointing to rocky ground. "Let's try to stay on stony ground for a time and our trail should dry up. They won't be able to search forever immediately with bodies to return to town."

★ ★ ★

The fugitives set up camp against the west bank of another ravine, no doubt carved by some now-absent stream, to break the wind and built a low and almost smokeless fire to warm their chilled bodies. Without proper sustenance, the cold was taking a greater toll than it normally would have. And then, as if the misery of being already wet, cold and hungry, in addition to being on the run was not sufficiently trying, it started to snow lightly just before nightfall. While it could not actually physically make them any colder, it was just one more thing to add to a long list of complaints and lower their already flagging spirits. The sight of the large wet flakes floating down in suffocating silence seemed the perfect crowning touch to an already dreadful day.

"Just what else might the Fates hold in store for us, or dare I even put the question?" Jeremy muttered darkly, wishing he dared to move closer to the fire without the risk of setting himself aflame. He pulled his damp woollen blanket over his face in the hopes that his breath would keep enough heat close to his body that he might survive the night. Thus shivering and mired in depression, he eventually fell into a deep slumber in time, the exhaustion caused by the tribulations of the day overcoming all other things.

The morning skies promised no better a new day than the old had been for the three men. When Jeremy awoke, he stretched stiffly in an attempt at loosening up his body from the tight ball he had pulled his body into while trying to stop the excruciating shivering which he had awakened to often in the pitch blackness of the wintry night. He had quite forgotten the shoulder wound until he stretched, but it now screamed an emphatic reminder.

He foraged about in the area around their makeshift camp, pulling at weeds and digging aside the snow with the toe of his boot, hoping to find the object of his search. At last he sighed with satisfaction as a plant stalk he recognized poked up from the ground. It was not the same as what Josef had used after Beaverdams, but his friend had told him that the root of this one would do in a pinch.

He carefully washed the root before mashing it up, although he was not certain why they needed to be so clean. Then, mixing the result with water from melted snow, he made a thin paste, which he applied over the entire wound. A cloth tied on as a bandage to keep it altogether and he was done.

Now he arose from the squatted position in which he had worked.

"Alright, gentlemen," he called out, trying to sound much more forceful and cheerful than he truly felt. "It's time we moved along once again."

Oliver and Davis were amazingly enough yet asleep and the latter groaned loudly as he rolled over, followed closely by a string of oaths as the physical privations of the night broke through to his consciousness. From Oliver, however, there was no response.

"Oliver!" Jeremy called out loudly. "Get your carcass off the ground!"

Still no response.

Panic began to creep up on Jeremy as he looked at his cousin. There was no visible sign of breathing and his skin displayed a pallor suggesting the worst. "Oliver!" he cried again, this time kicking out at the young man in fear. Again there was no immediate response and Jeremy began to fear the worst. It would certainly not be the first time that this transitional season in Upper Canada claimed someone to hypothermia. He prepared to lash out once again, when he saw Oliver stir.

"What's all the noise?" Oliver whined. "You're bound to awaken me with all that caterwauling." With that, he turned over as if to resume his slumber.

Jeremy, disbelieving his cousin's penchant for sleeping through nearly all disturbances, looked over at Davis, who just shook his head in astonishment, for sleep had not come easily nor passed well for him either. Jeremy looked back to his cousin, glanced skyward as though in supplication, and then flung himself bodily on the younger man, ignoring the protests of his shoulder as they wrestled.

After several moments of horseplay, they sat back winded.

"Are you awake yet?" he asked of a winded Oliver.

"Well, what are we to do now?" Davis asked, laughing at the two men who were panting from their exertion. "Have you gentlemen yet worked the childishness out of your systems?"

"Best watch yourself, boy," Jeremy chided, a glint of humour shining in his eyes. "Else the two of us may be forced to teach you your manners as well."

There followed a silence as the banter had reached an impasse, all three yet cold, stiff and hungry. They looked about at their surroundings and Davis rose to look back along their trail, not certain for what he was looking, but sure that he should be. Seeing nothing, he sat back down with his companions.

"He was right though, cousin," Oliver finally said. "What are we to do now?"

Jeremy pulled the letter from his kit, carefully smoothing it on his leg. "Perhaps this will tell us more than I noticed yesterday," he said. "Though what I saw there would give us a good beginning, there's no doubt."

"You said Sims had got it all wrong before we were forced to run for our lives. What did you mean?" asked Davis.

"Well, it seems the reason Sims urged us all the way to York was because of the first line of instructions," Jeremy replied. "There's a bit of angry preamble and mad ravings about the British Crown and Williamson's boss, Joseph Willcocks. Then that's followed by some dribble about his mortality. This seems to be a sort of last testament to one of his men in case of his death, although it doesn't stipulate which. And then the letter says 'You must begin this quest by starting at the east wall of Simcoe's second home.' That's where Sims made his error."

"Wait a moment," Davis objected. "Simcoe lived first in Newark and then moved to York. So, why was Sims wrong?"

Jeremy smiled. "I've lived around Beaverdams and Niagara all of my life. What you say is true. However many from outside the area, and even some within it, don't know that it is widely told that Simcoe lived in two places in Newark." He looked at the two younger men and explained. "I was quite young of course, but I remember my father mentioning that when Simcoe first arrived, there was no place for him and his wife to live without putting out someone living there, so apparently they started out in tents. While there, he had Navy Hall rebuilt and moved in when it was ready."

"Do you mean to tell us that Fort George's Navy Hall is actually Simcoe's second home, and the starting point for our search?" Oliver chimed in, at once excited and frustrated.

"It does make much greater sense than Williamson travelling all that distance to a point north of York to hide his booty," Davis said thoughtfully. "One would think he would want it close to the border."

"You're right," agreed Oliver, seeing the wisdom of the argument. "He didn't really know who would win the war…"

"As we still don't," interrupted Jeremy.

"And if the Americans lost, he would want to be able to retrieve his booty on the run," Oliver continued, ignoring his cousin's interruption.

"Fine, fine, then we're all agreed that Jeremy's reading of it is likely correct," Davis broke in, seeming a bit impatient. "Then what comes after that?"

"The next thing it says 'Take forty paces to the east and turn south. Through the arms of the Old Lady, you will see your next stop.'"

"The Old Lady?" Oliver said, puzzled.

"That's what it says," replied Jeremy, pointing to the line on the page. "Hopefully the meaning will become at least mildly obvious when we go the Navy Hall's east wall and walk off the forty paces and turn south."

"Then it goes on to say 'When you get there, you will see the Old Man's Oversight.'" Jeremy continued. "After that it gets into specific numbers of paces and directions that will mean nothing until we find the Old Man's Oversight."

"Old Man's Oversight," Davis mused. "To what would he be referring do you think?"

Jeremy shook his head slowly. "I'm afraid we'll not likely know until we get there. If then even. There is always a possibility that it's some manner of code shared by the group of bandits that Williamson led. Well, in any case, we won't solve the riddle standing in this place," he said, picking up his property and packing a few items away. "Let's be off, shall we? Perhaps we'll even find something to eat along the way."

★ ★ ★

As the three bedraggled men shuffled into a low defile several hundred yards from the main road, Jeremy suddenly raised his arm to signal the others to stop. His fatigue had given way suddenly to acute alertness and he cocked his head slightly toward some low shrubs ahead and to the left of their trajectory.

"What is it?" asked Davis in a hushed voice, his nerves on end.

"Quiet," Jeremy snapped in a whisper so low the two men could barely hear, despite having crowded in closely to do so. Silently he pointed to Oliver, signalling his cousin to circle around to the right, and then gestured in the opposite direction to Davis. He waited momentarily as they moved out and then slowly started forward, crouching low and stepping softly in the direction of the sound he was certain he had heard.

Oliver swept to Jeremy's right and hesitated momentarily, looking to Jeremy for guidance. His cousin urged him on with a barely perceptible nod.

Before anyone could react, there was an explosion of snow and evergreen brush. A body had burst from cover and grasped Oliver from behind, an arm around the young man's neck and a pistol to his head.

"The rest of you!" the man shouted desperately and hysterically. "I know there are two more of you! Stop where you are or you will be searching all the way to the lake for his head!"

Jeremy stepped out from behind his cover and stood openly studying the frightened man who had them at this disadvantage. Although military man by the cut of his clothes, there seemed to be little of the military left about him. His tunic was ripped and torn in places too numerous to count and it was coated in blood, dirt, leaves, and twigs. His head bore no hat and his breeches were in only slightly better shape than the tunic.

"I don't know who you are or what you mean here," Jeremy started slowly and softly, attempting to sound calm and reassuring. He was fully aware that his cousin's life hung in the balance, his fate in the hands of a man so frightened that his actions would be unpredictable and unreasonable. "We certainly mean you no harm, sir. Kindly let my cousin go."

The man responded by tightening his grip across Oliver's throat. His eyes darted quickly and frantically from Jeremy to Davis, who he could barely see, and back again and his breathing came in short, rapid, shallow puffs. The terror in his eyes shone at them from among the layers of dirt and blood that coated his face. Jeremy's soothing words only seemed to agitate him even further.

"I remember you three from when you ambushed us on the York Road, wanting to release the traitor," he growled nervously, as if hearing Jeremy's silent wonder at his reaction. "Where you shot the Lieutenant." He started visibly as Jeremy took a partial step in his direction, causing him to press the pistol more firmly against Oliver's head. "But he was alright, no thanks to you lot, and we reloaded and mounted up to try to find you and the traitor you freed."

"Did you find him?" Jeremy asked evenly, wondering if the soldiers had stumbled on Sims' body. "And where is the rest of your patrol?"

"You know full well, don't you?" the man screamed in reply. "Your friends finished them as well, only a few miles down the road from where you first ambushed us, and you know it!"

"Our friends?" Davis asked, puzzled. "You say our friends attacked you the second time. May I respectfully ask you what these friends looked like?"

"Don't try to confuse me!" came the shrill reply. The soldier took several steps back, swinging Oliver slightly from side to side as he did so, making sure that neither of the others could get a clean shot at him. "I lost all my mates! Lads I served with since France! Now the two of you will do as I say and lay down your weapons or you too shall be friendless."

Jeremy and Davis were aware that this man was quite obviously hysterical and that the man might do anything in his condition, including the killing of an unarmed man, something he would not likely do under normal circumstances. But there was seldom anything normal about this God-forsaken war, especially to a veteran of war on the Continent, so they slowly and carefully laid their weapons down upon the ground.

As the soldier watched the others lay down their guns, Oliver could feel his arm relax slightly around his throat and he sensed more than felt, the pistol being aimed slightly away from his head. Knowing instinctively that this was his opportunity and before the soldier could react, Oliver flung himself back into the man, throwing him off balance. Without hesitation, he slammed his arm back, catching the man solidly below the breastbone, knocking the wind out of him and bringing him to his knees.

Taking hold of the soldier's pistol arm, Oliver twisted hard and threw him the balance of the way to the ground and then just lay upon him, still holding onto the pistol with all his might, afraid to let go.

Jeremy had begun to run forward as soon as Oliver started his move and he now wrenched the pistol from the soldier's yielding hand. Nearly simultaneously, he drew his hunting knife and laid it across the winded man's throat. With the theatre of action suddenly still, both he and Oliver were surprised to hear the man crying. Slowly and carefully, the two men rearranged themselves so that Oliver could get up and Jeremy could find a more comfortable position from which to control the man.

Jeremy could do nothing but stare speechlessly at the crying soldier before him. He had fought a number of his men in his time, but he had never seen anyone surrender to great wracking sobs like this man had.

Chapter Twenty

"Pull yourself together man," Jeremy said softly, feeling mildly embarrassed for the man even though he believed that he understood what the man had been through. "We mean you no harm. The incident on the road with us was a misunderstanding. Your comrade-in-arms thought we had moved threateningly and the result was that senseless set-to."

The soldier, exhausted and spent, stopped crying and took a deep breath. He stared sullenly at Jeremy and then asked with all the challenge he could muster, "And what of your friends who waited to finish the job? And why have you tracked me down to finish me off?" His demeanour had become quite calm, almost fatalistic, as if he fully expected to die here and, having freed himself of his emotions through crying, was now prepared to do so.

"I don't know who these friends are that you speak of," Jeremy said thoughtfully. "And we certainly didn't track you here. We've been running from you and your party and now we've apparently stumbled upon each other. I'm not surprised that you might not believe this, but consider this: why would I lie to you with a knife at your throat? In any event, and if you would humour us, what did these friends look like?"

"Before this discussion continues, could you please let me up?" the soldier asked. "I feel less inclined to speak with my air crushed from my lungs."

Jeremy and the others laughed at this remark, dissipating the remainder of their adrenaline and a good deal of the tension hanging about them. Slowly, Jeremy removed the knife from the man's throat and backed off to allow him to stand. He indicated to the soldier with a gesture that Davis still held his rifle at the ready and then nodded at the man to go ahead.

"I paid scant attention to most of them. You colonials all look very much alike to me. That's not meant to be an insult, just a fact," he explained quickly and awkwardly. "It was but the one man who stepped out into the roadway ahead of us who held my interest, I'm afraid," the soldier explained.

"The man just stepped into the road?" Jeremy asked, the description giving him an unsettled feeling. "Did he say his name? And, by the way, what would yours be?"

"Mine is Johnson," the man replied, still a little suspicious. "What would yours be, if you could return the courtesy?"

"Jeremy van Hijser. And the other two are Davis Halberson and Oliver Davidson."

"As for the name of the man who stepped out in front of us, no, I don't recall him mentioning his name," Johnson continued. "But it wouldn't be possible to forget him. His voice rumbled right through you when he talked and he had long blond hair and a scar at the right corner of his mouth where the beard didn't cover it."

"The Parson," Jeremy muttered to his companions, who nodded solemnly in agreement.

"The Parson, you say?" Johnson asked. "Strange, I thought that the Bible in his hand was but an act. A ruse to stop us."

"It is an act, or was at least. But what did he say?" Oliver wanted to know.

"When he stepped out he was, like I said, holding the Lord's Bible above his head with one hand and a pistol in the other. When we drew up he started quoting scripture – at least it sounded like scripture – and demanded that we release the condemned man in the name of the Lord." Johnson's voice had a trace of wonderment in it as he described the man.

Jeremy smiled ironically. "That's the Parson true enough. But as for the scripture, he has a way of twisting it into a version that will say what he wants. He can't read very well, so he does it mostly from memory and only then if it suits his aims. As for it being a ruse, at one time it likely was, because he didn't use it as often in the past but, from what I've heard from others, it's become a part of him. I can't help but wonder if the man's gone crazy enough to believe the character he's created for himself."

"And he started shooting when you didn't produce Sims?" Davis offered, guessing at the balance of the story.

Johnson shook his head. "No. When he finished preaching, he just stepped back. He then shouted something and his men charged us from out of their cover on all sides and began shooting. One after another, men fell to their attack, with many dying on both sides." He looked away, tears welling in both eyes once again as he struggled to compose himself. "We were all killed, excepting for myself of course. I don't know how many of our attackers died." He fell silent, obviously reliving the experience.

"You say there were a dozen of them?"

"Perhaps more."

"I don't know where he keeps finding reinforcements," Jeremy said in wonder. "But he always seems to show up the next time with a like number of men. I didn't know this colony held that many traitors who were that crazy."

"They may not in fact be traitors," Davis suggested.

"If not traitors, then how would you describe men who fight for the enemy?"

"From what I saw of them, some at least seem to be deluded by the man's words," Davis suggested. "It is possible that they don't feel they are fighting man's war, but God's."

Jeremy looked at Davis, seeing him as possibly somewhat older than his actual years. "You may be right," he sighed at last. "The Parson seems to own their minds completely doesn't he?"

Davis shrugged. "It would seem so."

"How did you manage to escape?" Davis asked, turning back to the soldier. He spoke softly while taking great pains not to sound accusing.

Despite the marksman's attempt at tact, shame seemed to replace the grief in Johnson's face. "I'm afraid I panicked. As men fell all around me for the second time and the Parson's madmen screaming as they hacked and slashed with their bayonets, I just jumped up and ran," he muttered, barely audibly. "I was some distance away when I heard a great deal of screaming and shouting when they realized the condemned man they were looking for wasn't among us, although I don't see how they could have missed noticing it before the shooting started."

He swallowed hard, fighting off the urge to begin crying once again. "When they were gone I doubled back to the road, afraid they might see me, and stayed hidden in the bushes. I watched for some time but when

I saw none of my mates move I rose to my feet and ran as far into the forest as I could before fatigue felled me late in the afternoon."

"There was no shame in what you did," Jeremy offered reassuringly.

Johnson looked up, the tears coming unbidden once again. "I thank you for that. But I lost all of my mates on that road. And I escaped with my life." He looked away, his tortured face stricken with a mixture of grief, shame and an inability to explain any of it.

"Maybe the Lord was keeping you for another purpose," Oliver offered hopefully.

"Perhaps," Johnson whispered, clearly not believing it, and said no more.

"Were there no other survivors?" asked Oliver softly, disbelief evident in his voice.

"None," Johnson replied, his voice barely audible. "Like I said, after the Parson and his men had gone, I watched very carefully for any signs of life, but there was none. The Parson's men, they simply wouldn't allow anyone to live, such a frenzy they were in."

"And when you were ambushed, you didn't have Sims with you?"

"No. We never did find him," the man replied. "He must have left the road before reaching the Parson because they were looking about carefully to make sure they hadn't overlooked him."

"Right then," Jeremy said loudly, clearing his throat and trying to shake off the dangerous depression that seemed to be settling upon them all. "Let's move on, shall we?" Turning back to Johnson, he asked, "Did you happen to notice in what direction they were heading?"

"No, I kept my head down, but I did hear mention of Ancaster," came the reply. "But, to be honest, I don't know if they were going there or if they were only talking about where the condemned man was supposed to have gone." He winced and closed his eyes momentarily.

"Are you hurt?" Jeremy asked him, suddenly reminded by the gesture that the man had been in two battles in single day.

"I don't believe so," Johnson responded, coughing uncomfortably. "I may have hit my head a bit when I dove to the ground, but there's no blood." He coughed again, this time harder. "It would seem that the night in the cold woods has done my chest no good either."

Jeremy gave the man a concerned look. "Do you think you'll be able to travel with us, or do you wish us to take you back to York?"

"Oh, no!" replied Johnson emphatically. "I intend to find these men and avenge my mates, not to mention recover a bit of my honour."

"Yes, well, let's just put our minds to surviving for the moment shall we?" Jeremy said. "Now then, if they didn't find Sims' among your party, perhaps the Parson and his men thought they'd missed the escort party somehow and he thought that he could still catch up to them before they reached the jail there," he suggested thoughtfully. "Were they mounted?"

"Not that I saw," Johnson replied. "Perhaps they had horses hidden, but I heard no sounds to suggest that they did."

Jeremy pursed his lips in thought. "That means they'll feel forced to move quickly. And that, in turn, may mean they'll cut across country in places where the road curves. We'd best be careful lest we accidentally cross their path."

The small group gathered up their meagre possessions and prepared to set off again, now with an added member. They pushed up a nearby hill and filed off into the trees, their guns at the ready. Johnson could not be left alone for fear he may have been injured where it did not show so Oliver remained at the rear with him while Davis and Jeremy scouted on ahead, looking for possible enemy presence.

Every time they heard a sound that might have indicated the presence of their enemies, Oliver and Johnson hid, waiting to see if any foe materialized. Several hours after starting out, they finally all met up again at the western end of the strip of land which separated Lake Ontario from Small Lake, the strip known locally as Long Beach,. The foursome decided to make camp here before moving back into Jeremy's familiar territory of Niagara. They picked a spot near the water's edge, as always sheltering in the evergreen foliage of a stand of young cedars that bordered this part of Small Lake.

There had been no sign of their collective nemesis and they had made slow but steady progress. They felt that they were now clear of the danger of attack from the Parson's men, or at least hoped that was the case. If they were indeed about, they find out in the morning when they would need to move out into the open to cross the land bridge back toward Niagara. Tomorrow they could continue on, unsure of what or who lay ahead in this increasingly strange odyssey they had undertaken for the sake of – what?

★ ★ ★

In the very early hours of the morning, Oliver awoke to the sound of a branch snapping not far distant from their camp.

"Did you hear that?" he shakily asked Davis.

He received no response from the sharpshooter, who lay with his back to the others, completely covered by his thin blanket as though he were unconscious, not moving, not making a sound. Oliver thought better than to risk waking him up for the sake of his own nerves, so he lay back down, and soon drifted off back to sleep, despite his fears.

As he slept, and not far from their hidden encampment, a canoe was uncovered of the brush that hid it. It slowly slid out into Little Lake with but a single person aboard, gliding quickly across the partially, not yet frozen surface toward Burlington Heights.

★ ★ ★

The cold grey light of morning found them already most of the distance across the long isthmus that led back into the Niagara Peninsula and ultimately Newark. It had been nearly an hour since they had crossed the small wooden bridge that offered passage over the small channel that joined the two bodies of water. Not far from the other end of Long Beach, they came upon the charred remains of the King's Head Inn.

The Inn had originally been constructed by the Crown as a way-station on the long trip between Newark and York. It had been burned to the ground just this past May by American troops for reasons unknown. It held little strategic value for either side and it was assumed by some that the enemy had merely relieved their pique or frustration upon the unfortunate structure.

Sitting inside the ruins, on the downwind side of the largest portion of wall yet standing huddled two soldiers. They had obviously made their camp therein and not heard, or perhaps were ignoring the approach of Jeremy and his group.

"What is the King's Army doing in a burned out inn?" Jeremy asked of the soldier who first reacted to their presence, raising his musket to challenge them. The other sluggishly rose to cover his partner from among the rubble. Jeremy could not help but think that, had he and his friends meant them ill, they would have been long dead.

"We're here to ask you, what might be your business here?" the soldier replied in good humour, apparently not disturbed in the slightest at the strangers' sudden appearance.

"We're headed back to Niagara, actually," Davis replied. "We're on a mission from my uncle, Colonel Halberson."

"No need to pull rank, private," admonished the soldier, identifiable as a Corporal, laughing. "We're bound to ask, but there's little we two can do stop anyone of ill intent. We merely ask and report anything out of the ordinary." He laughed louder at the absurdity of the assignment. "That is, provided we aren't shot in the act of asking."

The four travelers followed the Corporal into the shelter provided by the partial wall which still stood obliquely facing the Great Lake. Hot water steamed in a small pot which sat nestled among the hot coals of the fire they had obviously been feeding regularly for some time.

"Care for some tea, such as it is?" the Corporal offered. "We haven't any way to strain it, so we put up with the occasional bit of leaf in the drink. Your friend there sounds as if he might be needing a hot drink," he added, referring to Johnson's cough.

When the newcomers readily accepted his offer, he added more water to the pot and, when it boiled once again, threw in a bit of tea leaves to join those already in the vessel. He set the pot aside on a rock for the roiling to settle and then poured each a bit in the tin cup each man carried with his kit.

"I must apologize for not warning you," the Corporal grinned, as he noticed the questioning look in the eyes of the visitors. "Tea is hard to come by in these days of war, and we've been forced to improvise. There's a bit of chicory mixed with it – well, actually about half and half – to make it last."

Jeremy nodded. "I've used chicory as a brewed drink on occasion, especially when I was away in the woods on a trapping expedition," he said. "Once you get accustomed to it, it's really quite good."

"Just a bit surprised is all," added Davis, who had never been exposed to chicory before and had quite expressively displayed his reaction to the unexpected bitterness.

"Yes, I've had chicory before, but never mixed with tea," Oliver said, smiling. "I just wished to make sure that you weren't trying to poison us. You did say that you were quite defenceless here, didn't you?"

"Unfortunately, one never knows in these times," the Corporal chuckled. "But I fear that, had it been poison, you have had sufficient time to kill us both by now. By the way, I'm Smitty and that," he said, indicating the other soldier who was now coming to join them, "that's Frenchy. Out of Lower Canada, he is, and his real name is Edward, with a 'W' the English way. No worry, though, because he speaks English, and not a French bone in his body. We just call him Frenchy because he's from Montreal."

The men sipped carefully at the steaming hot tea and chicory mixture in silence for several minutes. Jeremy found that he and his friends were quite content just to be out of the north wind that had been building all day long and which now threatened to reach a gale force. And the hot beverage and the company of men who did not treat them as enemies were pleasant indeed.

"I'd heard that the British admiral, Yeo, took his ships through the channel into Small Lake, riding on a storm surge, to escape the American fleet that had chased him from York to here," Davis said, looking back along the strip toward the channel. "Back in September, it was. Is there any truth to the story?"

"Not unless the surge also lifted the bridge to let them under," Frenchy laughed. "We were here and, although we have moved the bridge to let in or out the service sloop that supplies Burlington Heights, we didn't move it that night. In fact, the good admiral's ship would have been ground to a pulp by the time we got there to move the bridge. And I doubt a war ship could get through there in any case, surge or no. But it does seem to have become quite a popular tale since we keep hearing repeated by passing travellers."

"Where did the ships go then?" asked Oliver.

"Who knows?" responded Corporal Smitty with an exaggerated shrug. "It was a dreadful night and the ships probably went into the mouth of the creek just around from the Beach. Wherever they went, it served its purpose though," he added, laughing. "The Americans thought they'd smashed up on the rocky shore and left them be, and now they've heard this tale, they think that old Admiral Yeo's the best sailor in the entire world."

Jeremy and his companions could not help but join in to the laughter at this turn of events.

Chapter Twenty-One

"I wonder what manner of other fantastic tales will come from this war when it ends, as surely it must, some day," Jeremy asked wistfully, though he pessimistically wondered at times whether it ever would end.

"Can't say," Smitty replied, shaking his head slowly. "It would seem that there are those who long so for heroes to worship that they are willing to create them in their own minds if none are immediately available. It's amazing, but the human mind can weave fantastic tales if it's so inclined for whatever reason it may have."

Jeremy stared into his cup, as though he were trying to read the leaves therein. "In my limited battle experience, I've seen more than my share of heroes," he said sadly. "But some of the real heroes will likely never be told of. Men like Josef, the Caughnawaga who fought with me at Beaverdams and again against Williamson, and who used his people's knowledge to keep me from dying of infection when I was shot." He sat quietly again for a moment. "And the men who screamed while the surgeon cut off their limbs after battle and, indeed, the brave surgeons who were forced to perform their gory duty time after time after time. Men who will need to find a way of making a living, because I doubt the Crown will be of much help."

Smitty and Frenchy both looked up at Jeremy. The former thought to protest Jeremy's remark about the Crown out of habit, but he had been in the King's service long enough to know the truth of what the man had said. He had friends of his own who had been unceremoniously cast aside because they were no longer of any use to the King. And now they faced a bleak future of begging for a subsistence living in some town, where they would be looked down upon for their helplessness for all their remaining days.

★ ★ ★

"It's been some time since we left the shelter of the old inn. Where are we?" asked Davis after having trudged along the road for what seemed to him like an eternity.

Jeremy looked carefully about. "I don't often wander down below here at this end of the Peninsula," he replied. "My guess would be that we'll be coming to the Fifty Mile Creek in short order. From there, we'll follow the creek up to the Mountain and take a short break. Sounds like someone could use a bit of a rest," he said, glancing at Johnson.

"I'm more accustomed lately to riding, I'm afraid," Johnson responded, letting loose with another of his wracking coughs. "Afraid I'm a bit out of shape."

Jeremy eyed him with skepticism, fearing that the man might be seriously ill. However, since nothing he said would change matters, he continued to answer Davis' question. "At any rate, we'll then follow the trails up there back to my home near the Thirty. It's not a good idea to stay below much past the settlement at the Fifty. We're too likely to run into anything from the Parson to Willcocks and his Volunteers to American soldiers, although the last has seemed increasingly unlikely."

"And why would that be?" asked Oliver, he too tiring of all the walking.

"They seem to stay in the relative safety of Newark and Fort George, especially since the Battle of Beaverdams," Jeremy replied. "They generally let the likes of the Volunteers or Dr. Chapin's men patrol the more risky areas. Quite frankly, of the two, I'd much rather run into Chapin's men."

They reached the mouth of the Fifty less than a half-hour later. They proceeded to follow the wooded bank up toward the Mountain as Jeremy had said. Wherever possible, they followed along the dry portion of the rocky creek bed, which grew ever rockier as they approached the escarpment, as witness to the constant erosion of the rocky face. The occasional wisp of smoke through a break in the trees was the only sign they had that this area had been settled at all, though Jeremy knew there were several farms not far distant.

Approximately half the way up, they reached a bench, which would follow along for several miles. Here Jeremy stopped the group. "This would seem a good place to have a rest," he said, dropping his kit upon the ground.

He studied their newest member with concern. "Johnson, are you feeling quite up to this?" he asked now that they were reasonably safe. "You seem rather pale. How do you feel?"

"I'll be fine," the soldier responded, smiling weakly. He started to sit down on a fallen tree, when suddenly his eyes rolled back and he collapsed heavily onto the ground instead.

"Apparently he won't be quite alright," Oliver commented, realizing immediately that he was once again stating the obvious. He rushed to place Johnson into a comfortable position. "Dear Lord!" he exclaimed, as his arm brushed against the stricken man's head. "He's quite burning up, Jeremy!"

Jeremy came over and crouched beside Johnson, also touching the back of his hand to the stricken man's forehead. "He's taken a fever of some type. Something to do with that cough no doubt. Get some water from the creek and we'll see if we can't calm it down some."

While Oliver ran for water, Jeremy and Davis propped the man up and covered him with their blankets. When Oliver returned, they proceeded to bath his head and neck with the man's own kerchief, at the same time trying to keep from allowing the water to run down the stricken man's body. When some inevitably did anyway, Oliver hastened to dry it in the hopes they would prevent chilling.

"Jeremy, would you look at this?" Oliver said after opening the front of the man's shirt to dry him. The entire area of his chest that he could see from the bit exposed was covered with an angry rash.

"Help me raise his shirt," Jeremy ordered. "I was afraid of that. The rash seems to cover all of his body. Everything except his face and hands, in fact, so we couldn't tell."

"What causes it?" asked Davis nervously.

"I'm not completely sure, but I've seen it once before," Jeremy sighed. "I think they call it typhus, and it's no good for him being here, lying on the ground in the cold such as he is."

"Perhaps we can get him down the hill to one of the farms," Oliver suggested.

Jeremy nodded. "That's what we'll need to do. I don't know how anyone will take to our bringing a typhus-stricken man to their house. When he comes around, we'll see if he can get that far. In the meantime, let's build a fire and get him as warm as we can. He doesn't need a dose of the chilblains on top of all else."

The men had no sooner begun to build up a store of firewood to feed the modest flame they had started than Johnson came to with a moan and partially awoke to another fit of coughing. This sudden activity was followed immediately by a loud cry as he grasped his head, the cough obviously aggravating a powerful headache.

"He's awake," Oliver said impotently. "What are you feeling?" he asked Johnson.

Johnson looked toward Oliver with a distant gaze. He squinted, as if he was having trouble seeing him, and then began to shriek loudly. "No! No! Get away from me!" he cried hysterically. "You've got my mates but you'll not get me as well! Get away, or I'll have to shoot!"

Johnson pulled Oliver's musket over to himself and fumbled with the hammer, unable in his delirium to manage the mechanism.

"Get that away from him!" Jeremy shouted, and Oliver and Davis both lunged for the gun before Johnson could figure it out.

Oliver handed Davis his musket. "We'd probably best keep firearms out of his reach," he said, watching Johnson slump back down onto the ground.

Johnson calmed to a ragged sobbing and moaning, obviously exhausted from the effort of trying to defend himself. Then he seemed suddenly to relax, followed by the most frightening thing the younger men had seen. He suddenly arched his back, lifting his body completely from the shoulders to his heels well off the ground, an odd keening coming from his throat. Then he began to convulse violently.

"He's having what I've heard described as a fit," Jeremy said, awestruck. "They say that's what happens when a fever burns a man out."

"What'll we do?" asked Oliver, his eyes wide with panic. "Do we hold him down?"

"From what I've heard, that's not possible," Jeremy answered softly, at a loss for effective action. "We'll just have to wait and hope that it passes, as I've been told it does. In the meantime, see if you can get this between his teeth so he doesn't hurt himself." He gave Oliver a twig the thickness of his thumb. "Maybe it'll help him to keep from swallowing his tongue too. I've heard that happens with these fits."

In a few seemingly endless moments the seizure passed, and Johnson's body collapsed seemingly limp and lifeless to the ground once more.

Jeremy bent over and listened to his chest, hearing a barely audible rasping sound coming from deep inside.

"He's still breathing," he said tiredly. "But I don't think we'll be able to get him to help. We'll just have to keep him warm and give him water when he can take it." He turned away, the frustration eating at him. "I wish my Caughnawaga friend, Josef, were here," he muttered. "He knows all manner of natural cures for a great many ailments. I'll wager he could pick some plants and make a tea and have Johnson back on his feet in short order." He spat on the ground in frustration and walked away from the others to think.

For the balance of that day, the three men took turns caring for Johnson, who awoke from time to time to take water and return to his slumber. He had no further seizures, although they noticed his breathing becoming increasingly shallow and raspy.

At some point during the night, while Oliver and Davis slept, Johnson's breathing ceased completely. Jeremy tried to shake the man awake, but he knew it was a lost battle when first the fever cooled and then the body temperature plummeted.

Jeremy pulled Johnson's blanket gently over his head and then lay down on his own beside the fire, not seeing any point in waking the others. Death seemed to follow him wherever he went, he thought hopelessly. Then he turned his mind off of all thought and stared endlessly at the remains of the fire before he finally fell asleep, a single tear rolling down his cheek into the Mountain's soil.

★ ★ ★

They interred the unfortunate Johnson by sliding him into a shallow crevice and filling it in with rocks and soil. Following convention, Jeremy said the basic few words that he could remember from past funerals over this man they barely knew. Then the remaining three men resumed their journey along the trail that hugged the escarpment, staying on the bench until it ran out. From there the trail snaked roughly along the contours of the Mountain, snaking in and out of ravines and other obstacles. Over the varying terrain they hiked all of that day and after passing below the mill belonging to the Ball brothers situated at the falls of the Twenty Mile Creek, they descended toward the rear of Jeremy's home.

While yet in among the trees and just above the small field behind the cabin, Jeremy stopped the other two and whispered to them to be silent and to stay put. Something was not quite right down below – some sound, some feeling, he was not sure exactly. Slowly and cautiously, knowing this terrain as well as any other part of his world, he put one foot in front of the other, as he moved as quietly as possible toward his home. Then he stopped and watched.

From his position in the bushes on the rise to side of the cabin he took stock of the situation. There were British soldiers stationed on the road and in front of his property, and he could only assume that they must be waiting for him to return. Fortunately they were quite unaware that he rarely, if ever, approached his own house from the roadway, preferring the advantage of the anonymity of the forest behind it. This told Jeremy two things about those waiting for him.

First of all, they were obviously not local troops for those who commanded them all knew Jeremy and were aware of most of his various habits, as well as the reason for them. Second, he thought with a wry smile, these men were not particularly bright. One would have thought that even an inexperienced officer would consider having at least a few of his men watch the rear and sides of the property.

Jeremy made his way silently up to the back of the house. Peering carefully around and checking once more behind to make certain there was no one there, he then slid inch by inch along the wall until he was almost directly behind the obvious man in charge, who stood near the corner of the building, facing the road. He hesitated only momentarily when he recognized the sergeant who had escorted them to Colonel Halberson when they had initially arrived at Burlington Heights.

"Are you waiting for someone?" he asked suddenly, his mouth only inches from the sergeant's ear.

The sergeant started at the sound so close and at the sudden accompanying feel of cold steel of Jeremy's pistol pressing under his chin. He had heard no one approach and it quite caught him off his guard. "What? Where the hell did you come from?" he blustered, trying desperately to regain control of his composure, while simultaneously casting about in his memory to identify the intruder. "And just who the hell are you?" he demanded, his voice only slightly tentative.

Only a British sergeant could make demands of a man who held a loaded weapon to his head, mused Jeremy. "I might ask the same of you," he finally replied with a grin. "Especially since you are standing on my doorstep as if you owned the place."

The light of realization dawned upon the sergeant. "Van Hijser!" he shouted. "We've been waiting for you! Men!" he shouted to his troops, who were slowly turning to determine the reason for the disturbance behind them.

"Arrest this man!" the sergeant finally shouted in exasperation, seeing that his troops were too confused to act.

"What for, sir, for catching you and your troops dozing?" Jeremy asked, at the same time pushing the pistol muzzle more tightly to the sergeant's throat. "I fear I must ask you to kindly have your men lay their weapons down upon the ground." To emphasize his 'request', he pulled the pistol hammer back, something he had not wanted to do earlier lest the weapon accidentally be discharged. "Now," he added evenly.

The sergeant hesitated momentarily but in the end had no choice but to do as Jeremy demanded. "You'd better surrender, van Hijser."

Jeremy let out a genuinely amused chuckle. "I must be confused, sir. I was under the impression that it was my cocked pistol pressed against your head."

"You have the upper hand now, but if you don't surrender, we'll be chasing you for the remainder of your natural life," the sergeant said shakily, in part due to the fear of being shot, but mostly due to the anger at having been caught off guard and then taunted in such a manner by this criminal.

"I guess I can live with that," Jeremy responded, "especially if you display the same level of competence that you have thus far. I could have splattered your head back to Burlington Heights without you ever knowing I was here. Besides, I rather suspect that if I do go back with you that my natural life wouldn't last much longer anyways. At least this way I have an opportunity to take someone to Hell along with me." He pressed the pistol tighter again, causing the sergeant to wince. "And you'll be the first to go, to await my arrival," he growled, all suggestion of mirth now absent from his voice.

"Just as you did with the guard at the York jail and the prisoner detail sent with the spy Sims?"

"I didn't kill the soldier at the jail. Lieutenant Denham shot the man when his pistol went off accidentally, not that I can say I was truly sorry. But what would have you believe that I had anything to do with the deaths of some soldiers from York?" Jeremy asked, his mind reeling. What was happening? The bodies of Sims' escorts, those that the Parson and his men ambushed, must have been found on the roadway, but what made them think that Jeremy and his friends had anything to do with it?

"Don't bother denying it," the sergeant snarled. "You might at least admit what you've done, for we have a witness. One soldier survived your ambush and made it back to York. There he positively identified you, so they sent a rider to have us arrest you. We obviously missed you at Long Beach so we came here to await your return."

"And did this survivor identify anyone else?" asked Jeremy innocently, fully aware that no witnesses had returned to York. Johnson had sworn that there was no sign of life among the soldiers on the road at either battle site.

"They said there was another with you, and that you had kidnapped Colonel Halberson's nephew," replied the sergeant. "What did you do with him? Did you kill him too?"

Chapter Twenty-Two

"Jeremy kidnapped no one," a new voice interjected into the discussion. Davis entered Jeremy's peripheral vision and approached the soldier. "My uncle sent me to work with this man and I am working with him yet."

The sergeant stared at Davis open-mouthed. "We expected you were dead, young Halberson. What have you done then? Have you helped this man murder those soldiers?"

"Don't be ridiculous!" Davis snapped. "Those men were killed by the Parson and his men – the same men who tried to kidnap Jeremy and his cousin that night they were in camp at the Heights."

The sergeant stared momentarily at Davis and then slowly shook his head. "That isn't possible," he said, looking the younger soldier evenly in the eye. "It was reported that those particular brigands had tried to raid the stores at Beaverdams on that very same day, and not coming even close to succeeding, I might add. They couldn't possibly have been in both places at the same time."

Davis looked across at Jeremy, who shook his head and shrugged.

"In any case," announced the sergeant. "If you are indeed innocent, you'll have your chance to prove it when we transport you to York for trial. If you are innocent, then surely you'll go free."

"It doesn't sound as though the jury will have much opportunity for deliberation," Jeremy said, his voice as hard as steel. "By the sounds of what you have told us, the evidence has been carefully invented and rehearsed. Going along with you for trial would most certainly be an act of suicide for us all." He paused as he seemed to deliberate momentarily.

"Well, enough of this nonsense, Sergeant!" he snapped, seeing that the man was about to offer argument yet again. "There will be no more discussion of this matter. You and your men will march back down that road and tell your Colonel that we simply had no taste for military injustice."

"Just leave your weapons where they lie and line up in the middle of the road!" Jeremy shouted at the sergeant's men. "We have other guns hidden in the trees. I have no desire to shoot any of you, but necessity is a cruel mistress, so they say."

"There is no one in the trees," the sergeant remarked indignantly, suddenly feeling his courage.

"I don't know what makes you so confident of that, since you were unaware of my being there right to the point that I had a pistol pushed uncomfortably against your throat. Nor did you know young Halberson was there." Jeremy waited momentarily and then, seeing that the sergeant would not believe him, he sighed in exasperation.

"Men," he cried at the top of his lungs. "On my signal, fire one shot only!" He raised his arm and then snapped it down to his side.

From off to their left, a single shot reported from the forest and the dirt at the sergeant's feet exploded as the ball slammed into the ground, the gunner unseen by any of them. No one spoke or moved for several moments as the sound died. Then the soldiers slowly and uncertainly shuffled to the centre of the road, milling about and eyeing the high ground about them apprehensively.

"One man then," the sergeant blustered uncertainly, but there was no conviction left in his voice.

"Do you think that I would order them all to empty their guns in demonstration?" Jeremy laughed, masking his concern that the sergeant would call his bluff. "If you want any more shots fired, they will be into the bodies of your men. Now place your hands upon your heads!"

When the men complied with the order, Jeremy and Davis walked along the line, patting them down for further weapons, keeping the sergeant as a shield the entire time. The search turned up three pistols and a number of blades of various descriptions, and all were tossed into the grasses growing at the roadside.

"Now, march on back to Burlington Heights and don't turn around," Jeremy growled, pushing the sergeant to the head of the line. "Men, follow them from the cover of the woods and see to it that none has the idea to attempt any heroics!" he shouted into the trees. Then, to the soldiers lined up before them, he added, "I have seen each of your faces. The next time I see one, I shall put a ball into it."

"Now, move out!" he screamed, and the line headed down the road away from them at double time.

★ ★ ★

Jeremy and Davis stood watching the last of the soldiers disappear around the curve in the road.

"Do you want me to follow and see that they keep going?" Davis asked.

"No. Oliver is already doing that and there's no doubt in my mind that they'll be back as soon as they can rearm," Jeremy replied, looking at the sky, which was fast darkening. "I doubt that they'll return in the dark, but I suspect we can expect them by first light. I think that we had best pack up and move out of here as quickly as we can."

"Where will we go at this hour, and in the cold at that?" Davis asked. "It'll be dark before we could reach anywhere.

Before Jeremy could reply, they were interrupted by the sound of an echoing musket shot coming from down the road. Both men looked in that direction as if they might see what was happening.

"Ours or theirs?" Davis asked.

Jeremy shook his head. "It's impossible to say. In either case, the fact that a shot was fired doesn't bode well. I suggest that we get moving and be ready to leave on a moment's notice."

As the two men turned to head toward the cabin, Oliver appeared racing along the road toward them. "They're coming back!" he shouted breathlessly.

"What was the shot we heard?" Davis asked him, an anxiety sweeping over him.

"That was me," Oliver gasped, and swallowed hard. "Just a mile or so down the road, they stopped and began to mill about. I wasn't sure what was happening at first, so I fired a shot over their heads in an attempt to keep them moving.

"Then I realized that they had come across four men on the road who could only have been Volunteers at this hour. They had some spare weapons and, as the soldiers re-formed, I ran back here as soon as I could safely leave the trees."

"They took weapons from Volunteers? Was there a confrontation?" Jeremy asked somewhat curious about this new twist.

"No. No confrontation. They just spoke to the men on the road and they just started to hand over weapons to the soldiers."

"That will bear more investigation later. Davis, I think that my desire to pack quickly has just taken on somewhat of an air of urgency," Jeremy suggested. "Let's go, the both of you!"

They dashed into the cabin, at first just milling about indecisively, wondering what to take, since neither of the younger men was a woodsman. It was left to Jeremy to organize them into action.

"Take powder and shot, blankets, some jerky and whatever other food might come in handy and that will fit into a small pack. Other than that, take anything you feel we might need that you can carry through the forest on a long trek. That last is important, for you may be carrying it for some time. And as you pack, have a mind of the weather."

They gathered supplies as quickly as they could and Jeremy retrieved a pair of spare pistols from behind some loose stones in the fireplace. All the goods they felt they could move easily were then made up into three packs and they ran from the cabin in time to see the sergeant and two of his men round the curve two hundred yards down the road.

The sergeant spotted them at about the same time, and immediately opened fire. The soldiers with him were quick to follow suit. From that distance and in the rapidly waning light they were wasting their shot and only one ball made it to the vicinity of the three men. It bounced harmlessly off the cabin wall and dropped to the ground, its momentum spent. At that distance a direct hit upon a man might have caused a painful bruise or even lightly broken the skin, but would not likely have been deadly. All three soldiers stopped momentarily to reload but now the balance of the troops came into view.

"Quickly!" Jeremy ordered. "Back up the Mountain!"

He herded his two companions through the back into the trees as fast as they could travel, though neither really required prodding with the sound of military footwear echoing from the roadway behind them. Once clear of the cabin's small back garden they followed an upward-sloping, barely perceptible path that Jeremy knew intimately. They could hear sounds of pursuit behind them but the intensity seemed to drop off as the soldiers lost the trail in the darkening woods. Jeremy and his charges kept moving, however, not trusting that their pursuers had given up.

The bare trees alone would have been unable to dim the late afternoon light, but a heavy covering cloud, which had been creeping steadily across the sky for a time, was now firmly in command of the sky. Oliver and Davis were finding it difficult to discern the pathway even with Jeremy leading the way, seemingly following it with ease. They raced first up, then across, a little down, and back upward once again, slipping often, bruising limbs and scratching their faces with the branches they could not see until it was too late.

★ ★ ★

Two figures moved furtively through the forests of north-western New York. It was late afternoon and there was no sign of anyone about as they passed more closely than they would have liked to a small farm. By their movements and their dress, it would have been reasonable to guess that they were Caughnawaga Natives from near Montreal, which they indeed were. Their people were reluctant allies of the King of England in this war, yet it was unlikely that they would be seriously challenged by the New York farmers, for their people carried on a great deal of trade, sometimes legally and sometimes not.

They had been moving for most of the day and, contrary to popular folklore, they were becoming quite tired. They just did not allow their exhaustion to interfere with their intention to reach their destination. Instead, they drank lightly whenever they crossed a stream and ate sparingly from bags strapped about their waists while they travelled.

The two men had left the area around Sackets Harbour about a week previous and had travelled hard by day and slept hidden in the forest at night. Now they were on the final leg and their goal was to reach Niagara before nightfall, where they would be finally able to relax and regain their strength before travelling the last of the distance to their destination.

★ ★ ★

Night settled on the Mountain with the finality of tomb. It was becoming extremely hazardous to continue under these conditions, but they had arrived at last at a deep ravine which cut back into the escarpment in a long broad curve. They climbed as they worked their way inward and finally reached the descendant of the once powerful river that had carved out this natural excavation. At the very top of the ridge, in the notch of the slice into the escarpment, a now modest stream flowed over the edge and dropped off into the darkness below by way of a surprisingly impressive waterfall.

The three men followed the ridge until it fell away toward a point, not far to the east of the waterfall. They climbed down the steep slope to a modest ledge, hidden by cedars and cedar boughs which hung down from above.

"This will do for this night," Jeremy announced, wearily dropping his kit to the ground and allowing his body to follow suit.

The others did likewise and a manner of camp was erected there against the side of the ridge. Its major charms were due to its positioning. The fact that the bulk of the ridge sat to the northwest of them afforded them a reasonable degree of shelter from the elements and an excellent vantage from a near-invisible position. With but a little room to spare after all three lay down comfortably, they soon fell asleep in spite of the cold and residual danger, exhaustion easily trumping their concerns.

At some time before dawn, the wind picked up and shifted rapidly to a northerly direction. Before long a mixture of wet snow and icy rain assaulted the trio, soaking them thoroughly in no time. They were now in the worst danger of the Canadian winter wilderness; exposure and hypothermia. The ledge, which had been a haven just a few hours before, had turned into a miserable and slippery hazard.

"Let's get topside and try to seek shelter from this misery," Jeremy shouted at his companions, trying to be heard above the noise of the wind, which had acquired an eerie quality as it whipped around the edges of the ridge and across the face of the cliff behind them.

In single file, they started gingerly along the ledge and then off it, retracing the steps they had taken to get here. Visibility, which had seemed almost nonexistent when they arrived, was now actually worse as they were blinded by the blowing, stinging precipitation. Davis slowly but successfully pulled himself up the rocks to the top and waited for Oliver, who was next.

Oliver would not immediately follow, however. So cold and numb that he could no longer feel his hands and feet, he could not find his way and missed a step in his climb to the second level. Before either of his companions could react he slid over what little there was of the ledge at this point and vanished into the darkness with only a barely audible exclamation of surprise.

Jeremy had heard even that tiny sound and became immediately aware that his cousin was no longer following. Taking one tiny step at a time and holding tight to a small cedar precariously rooted in the wall of the cliff, Jeremy move cautiously toward the edge. Despite the urgency of the situation, he moved first one foot and then the other in a sort of sliding shuffle to reach the edge. Finally negotiating the distance, he looked over for his cousin but saw nothing.

"Oliver!" he screamed, more in despair than hope. The sound seemed flattened and absorbed by the wall of frozen and semi-frozen particles that blasted his face. He listened intently for some manner of reply, yet holding out little hope. He knew this section dropped off for nearly one hundred feet before ending in the pile of sharp stone rubble formed by the quarrying action of years of freezing and thawing.

"Do you hear anything?" Davis asked anxiously as he slid carefully to Jeremy's side.

"If you'll shut up, perhaps I might," Jeremy snapped in reply. Immediately, he regretted his behaviour. "I'm sorry. But you'll need to be quiet."

"O-li-ver!" he shouted again, separating and drawing out the syllables.

An indistinct, muffled sound seemed to reply to the call this time.

"Oliver! Is that you?" Jeremy called out, barely daring to acknowledge the slight hope stirring in his breast.

Again he heard the sound over the moan and howl of the wind and the cadence of ice pellets against the rock wall behind them.

Jeremy lowered himself carefully to his hands and knees and visually searched in vain for some sign of his cousin. The darkness and the lashing ice made visibility a nightmare.

"Oliver!"

"I'm right here, below you!" a voice replied. "I climbed to here, but you'll have to get me the rest of the way up. I can't hold out much longer."

"Below me where?" Jeremy called, not yet able to see Oliver. He turned to Davis. "Hold my coat. I'm going to look over the edge."

Davis took hold of Jeremy's coat with one hand while bracing his foot against a rock and grasping onto Jeremy's cedar as firmly as his cold hands were able. Jeremy looked over the edge of the cliff using one free hand to shelter his eyes. There, approximately three feet below and two feet to the right, he believed he could barely make out his cousin's form.

Oliver had miraculously managed to stop his fall and had now hooked his arms over a rock which protruded upward at an angle from the face of the cliff. He must have swung out from where he had been standing however, for his entire weight was pulling down on his arms since there was nothing below to rest a foot upon. It was obvious that the others would need to recover him quickly, or Oliver would soon careen down the escarpment face to meet almost certain serious injury.

Jeremy looked around and up at Davis. "I will have to climb down to the rock that Oliver's holding onto and try to pull him up onto it," he shouted. "I'm afraid you'll have to get down here on the ledge with me and if you hook your foot around the tree you should be able to lower me down. There's simply not enough to hold onto for me to do it myself."

Davis was quite happy that he could not see past the edge of their perch. He lowered himself to his hands and feet while Jeremy moved himself into position directly above Oliver's position. Lying flat upon the rock ledge, he held onto Jeremy's ankles while the latter carefully slid over the lip. That was the easy part of the task. Retrieving him with the weight of Oliver holding on would be a miracle. This rescue was becoming more difficult with every moment as the mixed precipitation froze upon contact with the ground.

Chapter Twenty-Three

Davis' hold on Jeremy was not sufficient to slow his descent by very much. With a bone-rattling jolt, his left shoulder painfully smacked the rock that his cousin held onto. He grasped wildly at the offending stone and then off into the darkness below, terrified of pitching off into the invisible abyss. A primitive reflex made him kick out as he automatically tried to use his whole body to stabilize himself. Davis' grip held him firmly in place, even though he was now almost entirely off the ledge he had dropped from. Then he started as the thought occurred to him that all his movement might have dislodged Oliver's hands and knocked him off.

"Oliver, can you hear me?"

"Yes," replied Oliver in a faint, strained voice. "Hurry...up!"

Jeremy cautiously felt around the edge of the rock that held his cousin, feeling along the forward edge for Oliver's hands, terrified that at any moment he might pitch headlong into the silent void. Although the young man must be very close by he could see nothing for, in the darkness, ice pellets stung his eyes as the wind lashed his unprotected face, the wind's speed having increased as it whipped about the point of the ridge.

After groping for what seemed an eternity, his frozen hands encountered something that his mind could only interpret to be a wrist. "I have you," he shouted into the wind. Leaning forward so that he lay on the icy rock, he locked his hands about Oliver's forearms. "Now, one arm at a time, let go of the rock and grasp my arms."

Oliver did as he was instructed first grasping Jeremy's arm with his left hand, which was no longer hanging on. Then, swallowing his terror

| 174 |

at having to release his anchor to the earth, he reached for Jeremy's other arm.

"My hands are slipping!" Oliver screamed. In truth, he could not tell whether they were slipping or not, as his hands had no feeling whatsoever. It just seemed to his confused senses that he was sliding downward.

"Just hold on tighter! As tightly as you can!"

Jeremy pulled slowly, achingly, to bring Oliver up. He could feel the tightening about his shoulders as Davis pulled back more on his trousers, and his leather suspenders pulled at their buttons.

As Jeremy pulled at Oliver, Davis in turn pulled at him and suddenly Oliver's feet found some purchase on the side of the cliff, relieving some of the weight for his rescuers. He began to climb, though slipping often on the ice-coated stone, each time jerking Jeremy's arms and his own. When his shoulders broke the plane of the rock which had been holding him forever, both he and Jeremy took a second's rest. In truth, neither felt they could possibly go any further, numbed with cold and drained by exhaustion.

But in matters of life or death and like most on the verge of surviving, they plumbed the depths of their reserves to find that they indeed did have just a little more.

"When I count three, I'll pull you up with all my might," Jeremy panted, now seeing Oliver's face through one partially opened eye. "You find any purchase you can and push for all your worth with your feet for you'll have to heave yourself over the top."

"One...two...three! Push!" Jeremy screamed.

He pulled with every fibre of his being and the last of his strength, forgetting momentarily that he needed to stay on the rock himself. Inch by inch Oliver moved up and, with each rise, Jeremy moved his grip to reach farther up his arms, until he found he was pulling at Oliver's belt. He could feel a lurch in the pit of his stomach as the sensation of losing his balance struck him, but Davis' grasp held.

Then Oliver lay on the outcropping with him, his legs yet dangling but the trunk of his body now supporting him. For a long time, the two stayed in this position, hanging on for dear life, Jeremy holding Oliver and Davis holding Jeremy to keep both from sliding off their perch.

Jeremy called up to Davis. "Now pull me up so that Oliver can have the rock to himself!"

When Davis had finally managed to get Jeremy's centre of gravity back above the ledge, the latter shouted down to Oliver. "Now, cousin, stand up by pulling yourself up the cliff face. We're not but three or four feet down from the ledge, so keep hold of me. I'll pull you up as far as I can and then Davis will do the rest."

When Oliver had been successfully pulled up, he in turn was pulled the rest of the way back by Davis. The three of them now sat collapsed, panting and in utter exhaustion while now thick snow and wind swirled about them. All were oblivious to the elements since all had long since been soaked to the bone and frozen numb by their exposure. Then the last bit of sense that remained was taken by the exhaustion that resulted from the crisis and its resolution.

After several minutes, Jeremy was the first to speak. "It's still dark and I don't think that trying to climb back up to the top would be a great idea. I couldn't go through that ordeal again. We'll have to wait out the balance of the night here."

Oliver and Davis grumbled at the prospect of remaining the night in this exposed position but agreed, seeing the merits of the argument. In any case, neither had the strength to attempt the climb again now. They all huddled closely behind the overhang of cedars that initially made this hiding place seem so attractive. This at least cut the bite of the wind slightly, and they all hoped privately that they could hold on the few remaining hours to dawn. Not one was at all certain. For the balance of that endless night they fought a constant battle against the sleep that threatened to overtake them. They all knew that in their exhausted and frozen conditions they might not awaken should they give in.

By the time some light finally began to seep into their world, the wind had begun to back off little by little. And with the decreasing winds the blasting white abated as well, eventually slowing to gentle snow flurries.

"Let's get out of here," Davis suggested finally.

"I hope we can," muttered Oliver, not feeling his fingers despite having held them in his armpits all the while to keep them warm.

"We'll have to start by getting up and getting our blood flowing," Jeremy said as he struggled to his feet that no longer felt present. He began to wave his arms and stomp his feet to that end.

Finally, the sensation began to return to his extremities and they arrived with all the force of a runaway bull. Surely, he thought, this must be akin to amputation without benefit of rum. Despite himself, he first moaned and then cried out as the agonizing pain proceeded through his hands and feet, building in intensity until the tears rolled freely down his cheeks. Through the haze of his suffering, he could see that the others were faring no better than he was. The only comforting thought that peeked through the torment was that they must at least be thankful that they were all three still alive to feel it and that the feeling had returned at all.

Eventually, though it seemed an eternity, the pain decreased to bearable levels and they climbed back up to the top of the escarpment. Since the dawn had fully come by now, they felt free to build a modest fire to ward off the cold. Though the smoke from the damp wood quite exposed them to discovery, they succumbed to the fatigue that they had been fighting and feel fast asleep until near midday.

★ ★ ★

They started eastward in the morning, now somewhat refreshed if incredibly stiff and sore from the previous night's exertions, toward the shallow valley that was a major part of the drainage area for the Twelve Mile Creek. An expansive area of rolling hills, ravines and streams, they decided that this would be a good place for to go to ground until they could decide what their course of action would be.

They picked out a deeply cut, winding ravine nearly three miles back from the Mountain's lip. There was a slow clear stream along the bottom of it to provide them with water. Using broken limbs, they carved a depression out of the clay of the eroded downwind hillside that made up the outside of a bend in the stream.

The next step was to cut two branches, leaving a fork at the end of each to create a seat for the roof poles to come, each of which were each about fifteen feet long. Two of these were jammed as far into the bank as possible and lashed to the crossbar and two more from the bank to the crossbar. Then lighter branches were tied across the poles sticking from the bank.

Evergreen boughs were gathered from nearby and placed across the lighter poles and woven through them to prevent them from being blown away in a wind. More of these boughs were then piled against the sides and tied to the top edge pieces. The final touch to the actual construction was to pile high the portion of the roof that wasn't covered by the hillside with more cedar branches to make to provide reasonable cover against rain and snow. To make sleeping more comfortable, they each made a bed of yet more cedar branches.

Across the opening a few feet from the opening to the shelter, they constructed a short wall of logs almost the entire length of the opening to their shelter. On the side facing the shelter they dug a long, narrow fire pit. The logs would allow them to build a fire of hardwood the length of the pit and the heat would be reflected into their sleeping area. At the same time, they would limit the amount of light scattered to the area, making their site less visible to anyone who might be sufficiently daft as to be wandering about in the woods in the dark. Jeremy had learned this method on hunting trips with his father when he was very young and had proven its worth countless times. It was remarkably effective even in very cold weather, and even if the fire burned down to mere coals overnight.

They would have to be cautious in building their fires and not only because they could burn themselves out. There was always a danger that the glow of a large campfire could be seen for some distance some nights in the lightless sky. There was lumber mill on the waterfall but a few miles distant from their lair and Jeremy was not very familiar with the owner or his loyalties. With low fires they would likely remain undetected for at least several days in this deep ravine.

That night, the three fugitives from what seemed to them to be the entire world, ate a spare meal and then sat and watched the fire burn down to coals. Jeremy added some green logs down the length of the pit which would burn slowly and hotly, generating heat with little light for most of the night. However, anyone who awakened during the night would need to check and add more if required.

"I don't know what I'm to do now," Davis remarked as he settled in. "I've shown my face at your cabin, so they know now that I'm in league with the pair of you. Now I truly can't return to base."

Jeremy chuckled humourlessly. "I've the notion that it really wouldn't have mattered," he said sadly. "Your uncle knew that we hadn't abducted you. Something more is happening than we know about."

"If you do manage in some way to figure what that might be, please let the two of us know," Oliver muttered. "In the meantime, I guess we must decide what our next step is to be. We're being chased by the Parson and the Volunteers and at least our own army."

"Well, the main thing we have in our favour is that neither of them knows exactly where we're now headed," Jeremy replied thoughtfully, rubbing the several days' growth of beard on his face. "How could they know, since we don't even know ourselves," he added with a humourless chuckle. "Williamson travelled about in quite a large territory, so he could have hidden his treasure anywhere. Perhaps though, it might be best if we were to go to ground here for a short time and let our trail grow cold."

Oliver and Davis grunted their agreement and the three settled in for the night.

As they lay, feeling sleep steal slowly over them, Oliver was overcome by a stray notion. "There are Indians around this part of Niagara aren't there?"

"Yes, there are," Jeremy replied sleepily. "Though most aren't from this area. They're just here for the war."

"What will happen if they find us here in the night? Will they kill us, do you think?"

Jeremy laughed out loud in spite of himself. "With all who threaten us, you are afraid of Indians?"

"If they should stumble upon us, they might murder us in our sleep," Oliver shot back, his pride wounded by Jeremy's obvious light-heartedness concerning his fears. Davis grunted in agreement.

"You needn't worry too much about that," Jeremy reassured them. "The Indians I know aren't overly fond of travelling at night. They generally have a healthy respect for the spirits that come out in the forest at night. They are also very practical and know that it isn't terribly wise to go stumbling about among the trees in the dark."

Oliver looked darkly toward the place where he knew Jeremy lay, though he knew that the latter could not see his face in the low glow of the fire's coals reflected into the shelter. "Do you know many Indians?" he asked, changing the subject.

"No not very well," Jeremy replied thoughtfully. "I've been among many different tribes but never truly came to know them. However, after the Battle of Beaverdams, I became very good friends with a Caughnawaga named Josef DuLac. He saved my life with his knowledge of herbs and such after my injury became infected."

"I've heard these Caughnawagas are vicious fighters and that they're not from this area," Oliver commented.

"Many people are vicious when they're in battle. The Caughnawagas are no worse than others. And, yes, they are from Lower Canada. Actually, they're Mohawk Indians and Caughnawaga is the name of their clan. Oh, and by the by, they're Christians."

He lay back on his cedar bed. "I wish Josef were here right now," he muttered wistfully. "He was a great man to have around in battle or out."

"Where did he go?" Davis piped up. The others were not aware that he was yet awake.

"Home," was Jeremy's reply. "He went home to see his family. He'd had quite enough of the war." He sighed deeply. "He's a very smart man, my friend Josef. I had promised myself that I would stay out of the rest of it as well, but it seems to keep bringing itself to me in one way or another."

★ ★ ★

Their main concern during their stay was going to be food. While they had packed some dried meat and beans, they would need fresh food to keep up their strength in this winter weather, especially food with fat in it. The next morning they each set out separately to solve the problem in the way he knew best.

Jeremy spent the better part of the morning studying the patterns of the tracks of the smaller animals such as rabbits and squirrels. He set about setting a variety of snares to trap them – ones he knew would work best with each. Davis set off looking for deer, intending to make use of his marksman skills. Oliver, in the meantime, scoured the thin frozen snow for signs of edible plants to be eaten separately or added as an ingredient in some dish.

Jeremy had found rabbit tracks at the edge of a clearing in a small valley where two streams came sluggishly together. While it would be marsh in the spring, for now it was a dry and snowy field waste-high with the dried remains of teasels, milkweed, and other plants. Since many of these varieties had food value, he had had to wave off Oliver, who also came to hunt here.

The rabbit's telltale footprints exited the field at a mix of low brush that edged that particular part of the field. This was obviously a regular route for the long-eared rodent, for the pathway here through the weeds and brush formed a virtual tunnel just slightly smaller than the rabbit. Jeremy had found the location for the first snare, setting the loop of the thong on small forked twigs so that it was held open, to snare the animal's head from either direction. The other end, he tied firmly to a shrub as an anchor.

Checking his work, Jeremy then set off to find other spoor. There was no guarantee that any snare would capture anything, or that the captive animal would not chew his way through the thong to freedom. It was therefore necessary to set a number of snares and check them often in the hopes that one would provide a meal.

Chapter Twenty-Four

While his cousin was setting these traps, Oliver had wandered about a quarter of a mile up one of those same two streams. His arms were gradually filling with plants that the three men could use, hopefully as ingredients or supplements but, in a pinch, even as an entire meal. Tiring from the stoop labour involved, when he stumbled upon a small clearing, he sat down on fallen tree to pick the usable roots, stalks, and seeds from his haul to reduce the load's bulk.

Engrossed in his task, he nearly did not hear a barely audible, unidentifiable sound coming from farther upstream from his perch.

"Davis, is that you?" he called out clearly.

At first, there was no response from the dark, strangely silent forest. Then the sounds of approach resumed, continuing to grow ever more distinct. Oliver could now pick out more than one set of footsteps coming toward him. He picked up his gun and checked that it was loaded, for the ball would sometimes jar loose of its packing and roll out, as he had found out when he first met Jeremy, much to his great chagrin. There were few things more embarrassing – or potentially more deadly – than having your musket produce a great deal of smoke and noise only to find that it was all for naught.

Having checked that the gun was loaded, the firing pan primed and the flint in place, he positioned himself behind the log upon which he had been sitting, facing in the direction of the yet indefinable noise. Now the sounds came toward him more slowly, almost cautiously, as if sneaking up on something. He had the terrible sinking feeling that the something was him. He could hear indecipherable whispers and increasingly frequent twig snaps and leaf rustling, moving ever closer.

"There's no point in sneaking any longer," he called out, his voice displaying a level of confidence he did not feel. "I can hear you so come out where I can see you. And keep your weapons held high above your heads."

There was a final flurry of unintelligible whispers and then a voice cried out. "We're just hunters like you," the voice shouted. Oliver could detect laughter in the voice as if the person at the source of the speech were telling a joke, or playing a prank – or mocking him.

Now what could be so amusing about this situation, Oliver asked himself, just as two men stepped from the trees into the open? With a start Jeremy realized that he recognized them both. They were two of the Parson's men, whom he had seen near Burlington Heights. But what did they find so funny…

Oliver's thought was cut short by the sensation of something brushing past his head and down to his shoulders. It was a rope, he realized, as a noose rapidly tightened about his neck, cutting his wind and making it impossible to call out for help. He stood up almost reflexively, the fight or flight instinct in him taking over. This only served to pull the noose even tighter and he coughed weakly while pulling futilely at the rope. In a matter of seconds, his vision darkened as there was no longer sufficient oxygen to support his brain's basic functions and he dropped to the ground unconscious.

★ ★ ★

Jeremy stood stock still, listening for a repeat of the sounds that had reached him on the breeze just moments earlier. He thought he had heard Oliver's voice, eventually mixed with sounds of others. Cautiously he made his way up the smaller of the two streams from whence the sound had come, eventually catching Oliver's tracks. He knew that Davis had been nowhere near his cousin's position and it could not have been him that the other young man was addressing in so loud a voice. He looked carefully about the area but saw no one. Not even Oliver.

He twice circled a small clearing, as Oliver's tracks seemed to lead directly to a fallen walnut and he had noticed a small pile of plant parts there on the ground. Someone had obviously been stripping them for their useful portions quite recently. He came upon several sets of footprints but, seeing no sign that there was yet anyone around, he approached the fallen tree and looked around for other clues.

As he stood there, looking about in exasperation, Davis came back downstream, interrupted from his task by the same set of circumstances. "I thought I heard a loud voice from down here," he said, looking about but seeing nothing.

"I'm certain that it was Oliver," Jeremy replied, his face betraying a measure of dismay as he carefully studied the ground about the fallen tree.

"I didn't hear a shot fired," Davis offered. "What do you think happened here? Are there any signs of a scuffle?"

"No," Jeremy answered slowly his eyes never leaving the spot he was examining. "But it is clear by these marks that whoever was sitting on this log working on the husks – we'll assume it was Oliver – got behind the log on his knees, facing toward the wood toward the south." He pointed to the slight but telltale knee imprints in the light snow. "And there are two sets of footprints approaching the log from behind, then a hodgepodge of confusing footprints, and then but one set leaving along with the two sets that approached from the north, head-on to the log. We'll assume that at least one set that go right to the log are Oliver's, since no prints approach from any other direction."

Davis went off to the trees on the south side of the small clearing and looked about. "There are two sets of footprints here," he reported. "But they're out in the open, with no apparent attempt to hide. It's as though they wished to be seen."

Jeremy nodded. "That's probably because they were but decoys. The one set of footprints behind the kneeling man's position were being somewhat more stealthy than were our friends on your side, judging by the way the edges of the footprint cut into the snow. Those same trackers go back with a great deal more weight on them as you can see here by the increased definition of the print. Carrying Oliver, I would guess."

"So they probably clubbed Oliver from behind or some such thing and took him prisoner. Is there any indication of who they might be?" Davis asked.

"It's difficult to say," the tracker replied, looking about slowly for anything he might previously have missed. "The tracks would suggest that at the very least, the person who came up immediately behind him wore military boots. But that in itself means little, for many other than military have them, including Oliver himself. Some were issued, some removed from the dead in battle, and some were sold by men who stole them from military stores."

"Do you think they're still about?" Davis asked, suddenly nervous at the thought that they might be standing targets for ambush.

Jeremy shook his head. "I think we'd have been attacked by now. It appears that whoever took Oliver was satisfied with just him and didn't wish to stay for a possible fight." He stood staring at the trees to the rear of the fallen tree, stroking his chin as though thinking. "My guess is that our nemesis just might be the Parson and his lads came for Oliver specifically, although I'm hard pressed to figure how they knew he was here."

"What will we do? Follow the tracks?"

"I see nothing else we can do," replied Jeremy. "Their tracks are plain enough. So, as you said, we follow them."

They quickly gathered their meagre possessions from the shelter they had spent so much time constructing, along with the items that Oliver had left behind. Then they returned to the scene of the abduction and began to follow the trail. About a mile from the site they found a number of hoof prints, but it was obvious by the tracks that not all members of the party were mounted. It was also obvious that the horses were being held back as they were followed by a number of sets of footprints.

Before long, they reached the road that ran along the top of the valley. The footprints they had been following quickly vanished in the melee of other prints. In places the telltale prints of one of the horses became obvious as it stepped off the beaten path, but that too seemed to disappear as other minor paths and trails met with the road.

At least they had a general direction which they could follow.

"This is odd," Jeremy remarked finally, staring at a print in the snow, where another road turned off.

"What's odd?" Davis asked, looking in vain at the marks on the road that Jeremy was studying. These marks had long ceased to mean anything to him, not having the other's tracking skills.

"They've turned onto this road," Jeremy explained. "See this hoof print? It has a chip on the outside. For some reason it's not been shod, so it's quite obvious. That's what I've been watching for and here it is turning away to the left."

"What's so remarkable about that?"

"This trail east to west, toward the Twenty and beyond," Jeremy said. "If that was the Parson and his men that we've been following, one would have expected them to head back toward friendly territory to the east. Instead, they're heading directly toward enemy territory."

★ ★ ★

Oliver's eyes slowly regained their focus. Carefully, not at all certain of what had happened to him or of his present situation, he raised his head just a little and looked about. The motion created a sharp burning sensation about his neck and he tenderly felt there to find his skin had been rubbed raw and, indeed, broken in spots.

The sensation brought the events of capture rushing back into his mind. Simultaneously, he became aware that he was seated astride an old sway-backed horse, jostling him with every move.

"Look!" someone shouted. "The boy's awake. Now I can have my horse back."

A familiar voice called back from the front of the column. "You'll get no credit for patience, Somerville. But if he's conscious, you may certainly have your old nag back. Just make sure the prisoner's secure."

Before Oliver could fully place the voice, he felt himself being dragged unceremoniously from the beast's back. No one steadied him but, in an automatic attempt to arrest his fall, he noticed for the first time that his hands were tied. With a thud he landed on the road and lay there dazed.

"Get up!" bellowed the man named Somerville. "You'll be getting us both in trouble lying there."

Oliver just lay there, thinking that he was obviously in enough trouble already and, if he might cause this brute to take some small share of misery, it would surely be worth it.

"Suit yourself," Somerset grumbled and quickly tied a rope through Oliver's bonds.

Oliver did not immediately recognize the significance of the action. For the pace of a heartbeat, he stared dumbly at the new addition and then followed it towards its other end. Just as he realized what had been done, the rope snapped taut and Oliver began to be dragged unceremoniously along the roadway, his frozen body seemingly striking every rock and branch on the slushy, poorly kept thoroughfare.

With all the strength he could muster, he managed somehow to get his legs beneath him. He now continued along behind the horse, feeling every new injury to his body and hoping desperately that he would not trip and fall back down for he had no idea how he had managed to rise and was certain he could not manage it again.

★ ★ ★

The two Caughnawaga men approached the waterway from the east as they stole silently up to the water's edge. They scouted about cautiously for nearly a half hour before finding what they had hoped would be there – a dinghy used by one of the locals for fishing the river.

Although they would have preferred to wait until they had the cover of darkness, they fell prey to their elation at their proximity to their goal and their sense of caution lost in the moment. They quietly shoved off into the current and rowed across with all the stealth they muster what with the splashing of the heavy oars and the creaking of the pins in the oarlocks.

After what seemed an eternity, the two reached the west bank and, with no one in sight, pulled the dinghy up onto the shallow shore. They retrieved their equipment from the boat and started up the laneway past the village of Queenston.

"Both of you stand where you be!" rang out a command from among the trees lining the lane. "Lay your weapons down and step away from them."

Several men emerged from the brush, their muskets aimed at the two men. There was no hope of overwhelming or escaping them, so they crouched slowly to lay their weapons upon the ground as commanded.

"Well, well, look at this, gentlemen – Indians." A tall man with several days' growth of stubble stepped forward from among them and sneered, his face a mask of contempt. "I thought you Indians were so talented at moving about without being seen," he snarled. "We watched you coming most of the way across."

The Natives said nothing in reply, but merely stared at their captors, their eyes expressionless.

"Where you two headed off to so fast?" the man demanded.

His query was met with the same, almost indifferent, silence.

The man paced slowly across in front of the two. Then he withdrew a pistol from his jacket with a show of drama and waved in their faces.

There was still no reaction. Not a word.

The man moved even closer, until the Natives could smell the results of his poor hygiene. As he paced past the first of his captives, he suddenly made a quarter turn back, bringing the pistol across the first one's face. His victim staggered and bled from the fresh gash in his cheek but said nothing.

"Do you know who we are? We're Canadian Volunteers and you'd better talk or we'll take you to someone who won't be so kind!"

The only sound which followed was the hawk as spit and one of the bully's companions cleared his throat.

"One of you talk or I'm going to be forced to shoot someone!" the man screamed suddenly, his forced patience so quickly exhausted. His face glowed with a bright, ruddy hue as the rage boiled within him.

The two Natives did not seem in the least intimidated and there was no response.

Suddenly there was an explosion as the man pulled the trigger. One of the two prisoners dropped silently to the ground which began to grow crimson with the blood that poured from the man's violated chest. There were a few strangled gasps for air from the already unconscious man and then a barely audible rattle as his body gave up its last feeble efforts at survival.

"Now maybe you'll answer my questions, Indian," the man snarled at the one remaining prisoner.

The Native merely looked him directly in the eyes and said nothing, although his own eyes spoke volumes of the pain and anger behind them, had the man possessed the sensibilities to read them.

The self-proclaimed Volunteer sighed heavily, his bloodlust spent with the execution of the first man. He lowered his pistol and motioned the others forward. "Alright, let's take this one with us. Maybe someone at the camp knows a better way to make him talk."

Chapter Twenty-Five

Oliver and the Volunteers had travelled less than an hour in the punishing manner they had adopted for the prisoner when a lone man, farmer by all appearances, stepped out onto the road in front of the ragged column. "Parson!" shouted the man. "I have word from Willcocks."

The Parson sat arrogantly astride his horse and waved the messenger over. "Well, then, what is this great news you've interrupted our travel for?" he demanded haughtily.

The messenger seethed with obvious distaste and annoyance as he looked up at the Parson towering over him, but wisely said nothing of his treatment. "He says the British are on the march and that you should meet him in Shipman's Corners before nightfall tomorrow. Failing that, you are to go on to Newark to catch up."

The Parson looked across at one of his men, appearing to ready himself to make some comment, but then seemed to think better of it. He looked down once more upon the messenger farmer – literally and figuratively – and snarled.

"Are we to run away from every fight then?"

The messenger did not reply. He was well aware of this man's mercurial temper and had no intention of trying it.

"Which route did he take?" demanded the Parson.

"I don't know. I didn't actually see the man himself. A rider came to the Twenty and sent three of us out on this errand, one on each road to meet up with you if you should come along. The rider said Willcocks started off along the lakeshore road but might switch to another because he figured he was being followed by the enemy." As if the enemy would be unable to follow over two hundred men in Niagara, wherever they went, he thought.

The Parson wheeled his horse about to face his "troops", the messenger already forgotten. As the latter quietly melted away, the Parson shouted out, "Those of you with horses, come with me. And bring the prisoner with us. He'll have to ride double with one of you, but I'll not chance his escaping."

Oliver's arms were nearly torn from their sockets as the horse that had been towing him suddenly wheeled to face him. An arm reached down and grasped his wrists, pulling him roughly up behind the saddle.

"Hold tight, boy," the rider growled at him. "If you fall off, you'll still be tied to this animal and we'll be moving much faster than we have been. It'll not be pleasant if you should bounce on the ground and then are dragged."

"As it's been such a pleasure so far," muttered Oliver ironically.

The rider turned half about on his saddle. "What was that, boy?" he growled threateningly.

"Just agreeing with you," Oliver replied quickly, fear overcoming his burst of bravado.

★ ★ ★

Light snow flurries drifted almost aimlessly, seemingly undecided as to where their final destination would be on the ground, as Jeremy and Davis approached the main road that skirted the base of the Mountain. The road curved along following the hilly and uneven terrain, bordered by trees and brush on both sides. It was therefore almost surprising that they heard the hooves and knickers of horses long before the animals could actually be seen. They slid into a small tree-filled gulley just below the level of the road and knelt there behind cover, watching quietly to see what would appear around the corner just ahead of them.

Before long a large contingent of men rode by, not seeming to notice anything around them. Most of the searching they were doing seemed to be over their shoulders. It seemed to the two men watching that these others were behaving as though they thought were being followed. They were not in full flight, and indeed they could not be without leaving behind the many that were on foot. Jeremy was certain though that, if it came to an all-out attack upon them, the riders would make a run for it while the others scattered to the trees. In any case, they definitely seemed to be trying to put distance between themselves and whoever or whatever might be behind.

"Who are they?" Davis asked quietly.

"I don't know yet but I think they may be Canadian Volunteers. There aren't many civilian groups that large," Jeremy replied, still watching for a familiar face.

He would soon be proven correct. Once those who were no doubt intended to the advance guard passed their position, it would be mere moments before a very familiar face materialized among the crowd.

"It's Willcocks," Jeremy muttered angrily, his words almost lost to Davis.

The anger for this man that had built up over the previous year was brought to a boil as he watched the traitor ride by protected by his most trusted men. The frustration of knowing that there was nothing he could do but watch his enemy pass threatened to overcome his common sense. His body tensed up and prepared to leap out into the road at the man, apparently attempting to exercise a will of its own, independent of his much wiser brain.

But his survival instinct prevailed in the end, and he watched as they rode noisily by.

By this point the vanguard containing the leadership had passed from sight around the next bend but the procession yet continued to pass. Once the last of them were gone Davis muttered, "I figure over two hundred and fifty."

"I believe you're probably right. That would be about normal for the Volunteers these days although I've seen them number close to four hundred at times. It would seem it's much easier finding men to plunder their neighbours than raising a militia unit to fight for the Crown. Did you see Oliver among them?" Jeremy asked, hoping that he had merely missed noticing his cousin.

"No. Nor did I see the Parson or any of the men I saw with him at Burlington Heights."

"Nor I," Jeremy answered reflectively. "Perhaps they've not met up as of yet. But I've little doubt that they will at some point. If the British are on the move, the Parson is too big a coward to risk going up against them with his own few men. He'll want himself shielded by as many of other men's bodies as he can possibly muster."

"It didn't seem so by the account that Johnson gave of the Parson's attack on the road," Davis replied doubtfully. "He told of the man you call a coward stepping onto the road in front of armed soldiers."

"Yes, but he also mentioned the hero stepped back and waved his men forward to attack when the British decided to take the fight to them," Jeremy argued, his voice dripping with irony. "And don't forget, when he stepped out, he assumed that the soldiers would surrender in the face of overwhelming odds."

"Perhaps…perhaps… In any event, what will we do now?"

Jeremy stood there by the roadway, pensively stroking his chin, seemingly deep in thought His eyebrows were close knit in consternation. Then suddenly he announced, "We follow them of course."

"We follow them?" Davis queried. "Don't you think that the way they continuously look back, that they might notice us if we strolled along behind? The only other option is to follow alongside them, but we won't be able to keep up among the brush and trees."

"You're likely right, but I suspect I know where they're headed, and so do you. Just think about it. Those men acted as though the Devil Himself were on their trail, for all the relaxed airs some put on. The horses and those men on foot looked exhausted and not one stopped or slowed down for a moment."

"What does that mean? Is our army on the move, do you think?"

"Well, maybe," Jeremy offered hesitantly. "But I've seen too much holding back on both sides to hazard that guess. But perhaps he has run into Merritt and his men or some such group that rides in the forward areas. In either case, he has his men all together. That means they were planning something major, such as a raid perhaps. Yet it must have been foiled, else they would have split up again when done."

"You seem to know a great deal of their tactics," Davis offered wonderingly.

"Well, I've lived here throughout this strange war all along," Jeremy replied, regret obvious in his voice. "And I've been a captive of these men, if one can call them such. I've also seen Willcocks and his separate bands in action over the past year or so."

"Well, how do we catch them?"

Jeremy chuckled grimly. "I suspect they're headed back toward Newark. They'll try to avoid Shipman's Corners because the late Lieutenant-Colonel Cecil Bisshop's former troops are stationed there. At least, he did the last I heard."

Jeremy squatted onto his heels and began to draw a map into the slushy snow that had thus far accumulated on the ground.

"Here is Shipman's Corners. Here is Newark. Now, the road winds about following the terrain to cover the distance in a manner like this," he said, inscribing a long, snaking road from where they were to end up. "That winding is to our benefit."

"How so?"

"We can cut across country on trails that horses can't ride," Jeremy explained, looking up at his companion. "They cover rocky and steep portions that are impossible for the beasts. If we head out at a trot, we can probably catch them before they reach Newark."

Davis expression betrayed a level of disbelief, not to mention despair at the thought of running all day. "And, just supposing that we do catch up to them after running along bad terrain all day – and I'm not convinced that we, or at least I, can do it – then what will we do? We're just two men."

Jeremy shook his head slowly and smiled. "You are a Doubting Thomas, aren't you? We've the entire distance running there to think of something."

"Do you mean you'd have us chasing them across the country only to possibly find a solution along the way?" Davis asked, astonished.

"Yes, exactly, so we'd better get moving," Jeremy replied, starting off at a trot down the road. "Else we'll arrive there to discover we've thought of a plan for naught."

The two jogged several hundred yards along the road before turning off to the left onto a trail that Davis didn't even see until he was entering it. And they were off on a plan revolving about Jeremy's assessment of the situation and what he considered to be Willcocks' likely intention.

That assessment would prove to be only partly correct. And the part that would prove wrong threatened to be disastrous to him and the young soldier at his side.

★ ★ ★

Late in the day, with the sun glowing low on the horizon behind them, Jeremy and Davis approached Shipman's Corners from the along the Twelve Mile Creek. They followed the laneway that cut across the side of the deep ravine all the way up until it ended opposite Paul Shipman's Tavern. They headed straight for Bisshop's camp to the rear of the town, hoping to be provisioned and perhaps given a few men. As they drew up behind the settlement, they saw the military tents through the gloom of the early dusk.

"There they are," Jeremy announced rather tiredly. "Much as they were the last time I was here. Although there do seem to be rather a lot more than at that time."

He had a sudden thought. "I think you'd best let me go on alone, until I can determine the situation. If they're ready to arrest me to send me back to Burlington Heights, you make your way on to Newark to try to figure out the rest." He picked up his gun and headed for the camp.

The wind began to pick up again and the snow that had been drifting softly down for the past hour was whipped into a frenzy and swirled across the open area he was crossing. Visibility had been reduced to such a degree that Jeremy had great difficulty to so much as make out the flag flying atop the pole they passed by a mere twenty feet. Heads down, he pushed the last few feet into the encampment.

"Well, well, look what we have here," a familiar voice announced. "A face familiar to us all, I should think." A burst of laughter followed. "He must have so enjoyed our hospitality the last time he was our guest that he has returned for more." More laughter from the author of the apparent jest was followed closely by the snickers of those around him.

Jeremy lifted up his tired head and, with a violent start, was met with the vision of Joseph Willcocks grinning at him. He tried in vain to swing his gun around in defense but he was immediately surrounded by Canadian Volunteers.

"I don't think you want to shoot anyone here," Willcocks said in the mocking tone with which Jeremy was so painfully familiar. Then, to the men who had now surrounded the trapper, the leader of the traitors added, "Take his gun. And don't miss the pistol beneath this one's coat. Oh, and the tomahawk behind his shoulders as well, and the bayonet and the knife at his side." he added with a toothy grin.

Jeremy was quickly disarmed and then pushed roughly toward a nearby tent. As he stumbled through the partially opened flaps that were the doorway, Jeremy was aware of others sitting or standing around him. He recovered from the initial stumble and regained his balance and looked about, recognizing the mark of the New York Militia on one shoulder.

At the end opposite of Jeremy, a table had been set up, with a vacant chair behind it. Jeremy was pushed roughly ahead until he stood immediately before this lone set of furniture and then their captors stepped back, all but Joseph Willcocks.

"What are you about, Willcocks?" growled Jeremy. "Are you going to pretend to give me a trial? It wouldn't be like you to actually practice your mouthed belief in liberty and justice."

"Not I," Willcocks replied, smiling enigmatically. "This is war and there is another way of dispensing justice at such times, beyond my power. If it were up to me, we'd discuss what I want to ask you somewhere private."

"And what do you mean by..." Jeremy started, but his question was cut off before he could finish.

"Attention!" a guard shouted from the doorway and then stepped aside to make wake way for an officer.

The military man, looking tired but haughty, made his way the length of the tent in a few strides and took up a position just to the right of the chair. "Gentlemen, General McClure!" he snapped.

Since this was now apparently an American post, a bit of news that had not reached Jeremy, he assumed that this man before must be Brigadier-General George McClure. This officer strode purposefully forward without a glance to either side or any acknowledgement of anyone. Without looking up he took his seat behind the table.

"At ease, men!" announced the adjutant once the General was firmly seated.

"What have we here, Willcocks?" the General demanded tiredly after what he deemed an appropriate interval. "I haven't the time to be interviewing civilians tonight."

Willcocks cleared his throat. "Not a civilian, sir. This man is a spy. He's the one I've told you about before; the man who helped Captain Smythe and me when we were battling the renegade Dorian Williamson earlier in the year. He has been a sore in the side of the American campaign for some time."

"If he fought with us, how is he an enemy?" McClure asked in a bored tone. In fact, the General seemed quite disinterested despite the question.

Willcocks cursed under his breath, realizing he had made an error in mentioning the battle against Williamson. "Well, sir, he was only doing so in his role as a spy against us. We just caught him sneaking into the camp. For all we know, he was sent here to assassinate you."

McClure studied the man before him. He doubted Willcocks' story, having had some experience with the man's politics in the past. Still, the General was known more for his bluster than his actual courage and he felt he should investigate further if for no other reason than to avert any criticism that might be levelled against him.

"What say you to this charge?"

Chapter Twenty-Six

Jeremy studied the General and then replied. "To be honest General, I had no idea that this was an American camp. The last time I was here, this was British Colonel Bisshop's post. I didn't sneak in here at all, but merely strolled in with my head down against the wind. If there were meant to be sentries posted, I suggest you speak with them over their laxness."

"I see," the General remarked, cocking his head to one side. "So, what you are telling me is that you do have connections to the British military."

"Only inasmuch as I supply them occasionally with fresh meat," Jeremy replied, not a lie exactly as he was primarily a trapper and hunter, if not just those things.

Before the General could ask another question, Jeremy had a sudden thought. "If I were a spy for the enemy, sir, do you not think that I would know that the camp was now in your possession? And furthermore, would a spy walk boldly into the middle of the camp and risk being seen?"

He looked up at his adjutant, who remained stone-faced as he stood rigidly at ease beside the General. Finally, McClure sighed and addressed both men standing before him although it seemed to some that it was more for the benefit of his audience than in any real interest in what was right.

"Perhaps you are a spy and perhaps not," he pronounced tiredly, covering himself by boldly coming to a non-decision. "In either case, I think it not in my best interest or the interest of the U.S. Army to have you wandering about telling anyone what you've seen here."

"But I haven't seen anything, except for you," Jeremy said evenly. "I couldn't see a thing in that blowing snow, in fact. Not even Willcocks here, who I would have avoided like the proverbial plague."

"And that is enough to concern me, sir," replied McClure without looking back up at him. He nodded to his adjutant.

"Guards," the adjutant called. "Take this man and keep him under close confinement. Someone will come for him later for questioning."

Two soldiers stepped forward unenthusiastically and each took one of the prisoner's arms. They led Jeremy from this tent to a smaller one and roughly shoved him inside. Since it was but a canvas structure, the soldiers then joined the two more guards who were already there to provide coverage on all sides.

★ ★ ★

He paced about impatiently, wondering where the damned fool was. The officer from Burlington Heights was waiting in a farmhouse he had expected would likely be empty, since it had belonged to a now-deceased Canadian Volunteer. It was not far from Shipman's Corners and his being there was an unhappy situation but one that could not be avoided under the circumstances. As he waited, the blowing snow seemed endless and he shivered reflexively against the Canadian winter night.

He resumed his pacing in front of the fireplace, waiting for a knock on the door which would announce his expected guest. His spy knew he was to be here by now, and he should have reported at least two hours ago.

Suddenly and without warning the door flew open and allowed a gust of cold air through the simple clapboard structure. Even when the door was closed with a slam, the cold dry snow flakes swirled around about the cold floor like so much dust before finally settling and melting into insignificance.

The officer spun about, reflexively picking up his gun and cocking the hammer all in one economic motion. He almost pulled the trigger before realizing that this was the man he had been waiting here for.

"I thought I told you to always knock!" he bellowed, annoyed at the lack of protocol.

The guest laughed and unwound the scarf from about his head. "And I told you that I'm not good at following instructions. Rather an inherited trait I should think, if that were at all possible."

The officer swallowed his rage. It would not be long now and he would not need this man anymore. Then he would pay for all the demands and insolence.

The two had arranged to meet here on this night when the spy last reported to him. "Well, what have you found out?" he demanded, not wishing to stay exposed like this for long. His presence here would be difficult to explain.

"I'm afraid we have a problem," Wolf said. "Van Hijser was arrested tonight by the American military at Shipman's Corners."

"How is that my problem? Leave the man there to rot."

"Willcocks is there. And there's a good chance that the Parson is there somewhere as well, since they were seen riding away from the Twenty together."

The officer's face fell at that news. "My God, what if he gets their hands on van Hijser?"

"My thoughts exactly," the other replied.

"You must get van Hijser out somehow. Or kill him."

"And just how I am I to do that?" Wolf wanted to know. "He's in a tent in the middle of an Army camp and you just expect to order me to get him out or kill him?"

"Alright, alright, just calm down," the officer replied though he hardly felt serene himself at that moment. "I shall need to think on it for a bit. Perhaps my men can stage a raid or some such thing. I'll go back and talk it over with them and I'm sure we'll come up with a workable plan. You'll need to wait until tomorrow afternoon though, because I shouldn't be able to know before then."

Wolf sighed and turned for the door. "I'll go keep an eye on things. If Willcocks gets his hands on the man before tomorrow afternoon, I'll let you know. By the way," he said, seemingly as an afterthought, stopping in the doorway while still holding the door open, knowing it would how annoy the military man. "Where did you find these men? I walked right past two of them when I arrived at this house. They didn't even seem to realize I was there. If they're the best you have, I wouldn't advise you to attack the American camp. They'll all be dead before they reach the perimeter."

★ ★ ★

Oliver noticed dejectedly that he and his captors had reached, and then avoided, the settlement at Shipman's Corners even though it was obviously in American hands. That could only mean that, whatever the Parson had in store for him, it was to be kept from the man's so-called allies. That is, if the Parson actually had such that could truly be called allies.

After avoiding the main camp, they skirted the village and then descended into the valley on the other side, finally stopping at a clearing in the wooded bend of the creek which sat frozen at the bottom. The Parson set his men to pitching camp, erecting several canvas military tents and then having yet another erected below the sharp cliff that had been created by erosion in times of high flow. This tent stood all by itself on the side of the stream opposite the camp and was quite effectively hidden from view from most sides by trees and the cliff itself.

It was to this lone tent that Oliver was marched unceremoniously.

"In you go," one of his attendants grunted as he shoved Oliver hard into the tent. "Here you'll stay until the Parson decides what we're to do with you. I'm sure he'll want to have a bit of talk with you, pay you a social if you will." The man grinned wickedly, displaying yellowed and missing teeth. "Don't try to escape. There'll be guards on all sides but the cliff we're against and we'll shoot you if we see so much as a finger appear outside of that canvas."

Oliver shuffled dejectedly deeper into the tent, squinting about in the diminished light in an attempt to determine his surroundings. He was quite alone in here and all they had left him was an old blanket.

"It'll be a cold one tonight," he muttered, wrapping himself in the blanket to conserve as much heat as possible before it was allowed to dissipate.

He sat quietly on the floor of the tent, depressions and hopelessness washing over him in waves. The despair threatened to take away his will to live, for his cousin might not even know he was gone, much less what had happened to him. He was totally at the mercy of the animal that had brought him here, for whatever purpose he had in mind.

Suddenly there was a commotion as he heard splashing in the creek and someone obviously struggling. There was the sound of a scuffle followed by a dull thud and then a grunt, as though the air had left someone's body.

"Prisoner, stand back from the flaps," a voice rang out. "If you're there when we open them, you're dead."

Oliver stepped back to the rear and the tent flap opened, just long enough for a body to come crashing through, landing heavily, face down on the ground near Oliver's feet. Oliver knelt down and put his hand under the man's chest just long enough to determine that his new roommate was indeed yet breathing.

Oliver pulled off his blanket and wrapped it about the unconscious form that now shared his prison with him.

"Well," Oliver muttered ironically as he sat back against his heels, "at least I won't be alone."

★ ★ ★

After being vigorously and painfully questioned by Willcocks and his men, Jeremy was escorted to a tent and thrown in, adding more grief to the injuries that said questioning had produced. An indeterminate amount of time later, Jeremy heard a scuffling outside of his canvas prison and then the flap flew open.

Jeremy watched as Davis was thrown rather roughly into the tent, presumably already having been questioned by the Americans. Now the two men lay shivering together on the ground in the inadequate protection of the tent. They had only one thin blanket each and there was no heat provided.

"What happened?" Jeremy asked needlessly.

Davis cleared his throat. "When you didn't come back, I moved in for a closer look and saw the American flag. I carefully crept about and saw this tent being guarded by four men and thought you might be in here. Then I withdrew to try to figure out if I should go on or try to free you."

"I told you to go on," Jeremy broke in.

Davis smiled sorely. "I told you that I had a problem with authority. Nonetheless, when I was withdrawing, I withdrew directly into a rather large man who had his friend with him and, before I knew what had happened, I was questioned by a pair of soldiers and tossed in here with you."

"What did they ask of you?" asked Jeremy after the guards had nearly thrown Davis back into the tent.

"Just the same questions, over and over, mostly questions to which I had no answers. They decided that surely I'd slip up and give them different answers I guess."

"I'm sure that I can probably expect the same from them then," said Jeremy, nodding unseen. "Were you beaten in the course of the questioning?"

"No. No beating. An occasional slap with an open hand, nothing to leave any marks. Any bruises I bear are from the rough handling I received at the hands of the two civilians who arrested me." Davis' spirits were apparently greatly dampened by the bad turn of luck that had landed them in this situation. "How do we get out of this?" he whispered.

"I don't know," Jeremy admitted equally softly. "If we're to do so, we'd need to find out where they put our guns and kit. We'd freeze to death in the wilderness without them. Once we know that, or if we at least know how to find out, we would then need to get hold of a weapon and overcome the guards surrounding this tent."

"Doesn't sound like too much to ask," Davis remarked with a smirk that Jeremy could just make out in the gloom of their prison.

The trapper ignored the sarcastic remark. He was about to suggest the germ of an idea for action, when the flap to the tent opened and someone entered. Jeremy squinted, trying to identify the approaching silhouette.

"I'll save you the trouble of guessing," a familiar voice rang out, just as the tent exploded in what seemed like brilliant light, although it was but the illumination of a suddenly lit lantern.

"Parson," Jeremy muttered, trying to sound nonchalant. "I knew that with Willcocks retreating, a coward such as you wouldn't be far behind."

Then, unable to contain himself, the venom now obvious in his voice he spat out finally, "To what incredible turn of evil luck do we owe this visit? Have you come to have a laugh at our expense or do you feel you haven't killed enough people yet? Or have you perhaps come to minister to our poor spirits?"

The Parson laughed out loud, apparently genuinely amused by Jeremy's remark. "Now, now, Mr. van Hijser, why the ill will toward me? This is a war, and in a war people die. And as for your spirit, I'm sure it could use some ministering to."

"I'm happy to hear that you take the loss of human life so lightly," Jeremy responded wryly. "So what have you done with my cousin?"

"Oh, he's quite comfortable, don't you worry," the Volunteer replied with a grin. "We take quite good care of our guests, quite unlike the army, apparently."

"You mean he isn't here?" Jeremy asked with alarm.

"Of course not. They know nothing about the lad. This isn't military business."

"What kind of business is it then?"

The Parson's face visibly darkened. "Don't play games, Mr. van Hijser. You know precisely what kind of business this is."

Jeremy stared at the man blankly. "I'm quite sure I don't know what you're speaking of. Do you, Davis?"

"No. I thought we were being accused of being spies, which is quite the military accusation as far as I know," the younger man replied. "Do you mean to tell us that your superiors don't know what motives you might think you're hiding?"

The Parson was silent, his eyes flashing as if on fire.

"Yes Parson. I think that the General might not really care if your interests lie elsewhere, but what does Willcocks think of all this?" Jeremy added, playing upon Davis' ploy.

"He isn't aware of what Oliver is doing here either," the Parson snapped and immediately regretted telling this man that much.

"Don't you think he might take offense at your keeping secrets from him? It would be a shame if he were to learn that one of his Volunteers' had been keeping secrets from him and that his brother-in-law now held the answer to a great treasure but wouldn't share it with him. I understand that the great Mr. Willcocks is looking for a real military commission from the Americans." He smiled archly at the Parson, who by now trembling with rage. "And I'm also taken to understand that the man has very little sense of humour."

The Parson said nothing but continued to stare at him with a murderous stare, apparently trying to get himself under control. Then his resolve collapsed as he seemed simply to surrender to his baser passions.

"You bastard!" he screamed unexpectedly and lunged at Jeremy.

While the scream had been unexpected, the attack had not. Jeremy had been waiting for the man's legendary mercurial temper to get the best of him. When it came he reacted quickly and rolled from his spot on the ground, leaving the Parson to land hard on the bare, frozen ground with an audible thud.

Davis, who had also been watching the baiting exercise with interest, jumped up and dived on top of their enemy as he hit the ground. He was happy to be able to react for the first time since they were so embarrassingly easily captured and began to punch the man beneath him with all his might, the released frustrations adding to his fury.

The Parson weakly cried out for help. "Guards!" he croaked, obviously panicked by the sudden onslaught, caught in the sudden turn of events.

As Davis repeatedly struck the Parson, Jeremy noticed that the man's pistol had come free and lay unprotected on the ground. He snatched it up just as a guard entered the tent to see what the commotion was about. Jeremy quickly cocked the hammer and fired wildly in the direction of the tent flaps.

Chapter Twenty-Seven

Luck was with the pair finally. The ball found its mark somewhere in the vicinity of the guard's shoulders and he dropped back from the impact. He fell backward, but his musket dropped in the other the other direction, flying forward into the tent. Jeremy scrambled to retrieve it and aimed the gun just in time for two more guards to stick their heads in through the flap. Again Jeremy let loose a ball, catching one in the leg.

The second guard ducked back and waited. Two shots had now been fired from within the tent he was guarding and he could not help but wonder how much weaponry the prisoners inside had at their disposal.

Davis checked on the Parson. During the melee, he had fallen silent and now lay unconscious on the floor, his face bloody. Davis crawled over to the back wall of the tent and, lifting the bottom, carefully looked outside.

"There's no one back here!" he whispered frantically.

Aware that the guard outside could not be expected to wait forever, the two men rolled from the back of the tent and ran bent at the waist to the woods nearby. As the alarm was sounded, the pair had reached the steep slope to the Twelve Mile Creek below and scrambled down a short distance as quickly as their stiff and frozen bodies could move. Hiding there in the bushes and the darkness, they could plainly hear the commotion above.

"Let them go," the McClure was heard to say dismissively. "They're of no real consequence to us anyway. I never really believed Willcocks' rot about their being spies. At any rate, there's no way we can track them before dawn, when they'll be miles from here."

As the two men sat precariously and shivered in the unshielded wind on the steep hillside, they heard the commotion above slowly dissipate. The voices faded away as soldiers and Volunteers alike returned to their previous positions, some on guard and the rest off to sleep once more before it would be their turn to take the watch.

★ ★ ★

Oliver started awake from his restless sleep at the sound of a groan coming from his fellow prisoner. It was completely dark outside now, and he could barely make out the form of the other man as he groaned once more and then pushed himself up onto one elbow.

"Are you alright?" Oliver asked the man, the question sounding quite ludicrous even as the words left his lips.

"Eh, what?" grunted the other turning in Oliver's direction, obviously trying to see from where the voice had come. "Who are you?"

"Name's Oliver. How did you end up here?"

"I was captured by Willcocks' men and he sent me over to that Parson fellow for safe-keeping. They seemed to take offense when I tried to escape. How long was I unconscious?"

"I have no idea," answered Oliver. "There's little to keep track of time in here and I dozed off for a bit while you were lying there."

"Well, thank you kindly for the blanket," the man said, and Oliver the rustle of cloth. "I'll be fine now. You can have it back."

Oliver was about to turn down the offer but, in truth, he had become quite chilled since he had slept and he took it gratefully. "What might your name be?"

His companion was about to reply, but suddenly stopped. "Shhh," he cautioned. Then, in a bare whisper, he explained. "I think I heard something."

★ ★ ★

"Well?" panted Davis, perspiring in spite of the cold night. "I assume you have a plan. It's as you said earlier. We have no protection from the cold and are no closer to finding Oliver."

Jeremy smiled. "You'll surely think me quite daft, but I say we have no choice but to go back up to the camp."

"You're right. You are quite daft," the younger man replied. "Somehow, turning ourselves back in to the Americans doesn't seem the sanest answer to our position."

"We're not turning ourselves in. We're going to find my cousin, and our weapons, if we chance to discover what's been done with them. If not, mayhap we can replace them with others we find in the hands of those we have less than a great deal of affection for."

Jeremy began to scramble back up the hill to the enemy encampment, wincing at every slide of gravel or snap of twig in the cold silent air. Reaching the top with Davis at his elbow, he stayed to the brush and the trees that bordered the camp's clearing. They worked their way carefully back toward the tent where they had been held, arriving just in time to see a bloody and swollen Parson exit somewhat unstably and gruffly shake off a pair of rough-looking civilians who were offering to help him.

The trapper and his companion followed from a distance as the Parson blustered along in the slush and snow, holding his head and occasionally shouting obscenities at his escorts, who hung back at ever greater distance. They left the camp and crossed the settlement, heading for Shipman's Tavern. At the last moment, though, the three men turned and headed part way down the path leading to toward the smaller creek that fed into the Twelve. Part way, they left the path to follow the top of the bank of the creek, heading upstream to a group of tents almost hidden in the woods.

"It would seem that the Parson doesn't want his disciples corrupted by the common soldiers in the camp," commented Jeremy sarcastically. "Or, for that matter, their compatriots among the Volunteers. Or perhaps he just has something he doesn't wish to share."

"Do you think they have Oliver there?"

"I'd wager heavily on it. Let's see if we can guess where they're holding my cousin."

The two men moved carefully along just below the top of the ravine side which ran almost half of the way around the camp. They kept well hidden among the trees and brush that grew on the slope, maintaining an elevation which maintained their position just above the peak level of the tents below and above the eye level of anyone who might be casually passing by.

As they neared the three-quarter point of the curve, Jeremy stuck out his arm, stopping Davis dead in his tracks. He did it so abruptly and with such urgency in fact that he nearly knocked the younger soldier off his feet.

"What is the matter with you?" Davis started.

"Quiet!" Jeremy hissed. "Look down."

Davis did as he was told. Until this time, he had been looking almost straight across at the scatter of tents in the clearing immediately across the creek. Directly below them was a steep, badly eroded section of the slope they had been crossing. And but a few feet distant from the bottom of that slope sat a single tent, by itself on their side of the creek.

Jeremy pointed all around the tent. "There are five guards posted here," he whispered.

Davis followed the other man's finger. Indeed there were five men guarding this tent; two at the front flap, one on each side and a single guard who sat looking extremely bored on a log near the water. There was no guard in back because there was really no room between the tent and the slope.

"That particular tent seems to hold something of great import to the Parson and his men," Jeremy commented quietly. "They're taking no chances that someone might get in. Or that someone might get out."

"Why put it so far from the main camp? I would wager that the others can barely see it, if at all."

"My guess is that they don't want anyone, including their allies, to see what they're hiding in there," Jeremy replied. "It seems they have something valuable that they don't wish to share with anyone."

"I assume you mean Oliver," Davis remarked.

He shifted position that he might gain a better advantage from which to study the situation. As he did so, he stepped on a stone, which dislodged and rolled down the hill. The resultant clatter sounded like artillery in the still, frosty air.

"Who goes there?" a voice barked out from below. The man on the log seemed to have snapped out of his reverie and now stood ready with his musket pointing at the hillside, his eyes sweeping for the source of the disturbance.

Jeremy and Davis flattened themselves as much as possible to the slope. Fortunately they had not yet made a move which would have exposed them to view. Both men froze in their positions behind their meagre cover and held their breaths, as though fearing that their very respiration might give them away to the men below. Neither braved a glance to see if they had been spotted. They lay silently, waiting for the sounds that would tell them they had been discovered.

Now a second voice rang out in the dark, this one from the front of the tent. "It was just a raccoon, fool. Are you to jump every time you hear any sound at all? There's wildlife and weather in the wilderness, you know."

Jeremy and his companion allowed themselves to slowly and quietly exhale, listening for a change of heart below. When the only sound coming from below was the occasional restless shifting and some muttering from the man who had been called a fool, Jeremy signalled for Davis to follow him. The two men climbed up to a ridge about halfway up the slope. They now had a position from where they could almost look down upon the tent.

"I don't think they can hear us here, as long as we keep our voices low," Jeremy said, pressing against the ground. "And they surely can't see us."

"How do you propose we take on those five men?" asked Davis, the frustration evident in his voice. "We can't easily get around the tent to eliminate any guards without being seen or heard. And one shout from any will surely raise the main camp. As we just discovered, sound carries extremely well down there."

Jeremy was at a loss. "I'm sure I don't know," he muttered with a deep sigh. "Let's just study their habits for the moment and something may come to mind."

As they watched and listened, noticing nothing that would aid them in their task, a great commotion broke out from the other side of the Parson's main camp. The two listened in wonder as they heard Native war cries and the Volunteers' call to arms intermingle. Though they could see little from their perch, there were flashes from musket being fired and a sudden flare of flame as one of the tents caught fire and blazed brilliantly through the darkness. Occasionally through the trees they could see silhouettes and shadows running about, their identities indistinguishable.

Then suddenly a sound that was like music to their ears. Glancing down from their perch, Jeremy saw four of the five guards from below run across the creek, creating the splashing sound they had heard. Once the guards reached the opposite side, they ran with all apparent urgency toward the main camp to help their comrades.

"There's but one yet guarding the tent," Davis commented obviously. "We should be able to overpower him even if he hears us coming."

"Yes, and that's not likely what with all the noise coming from over there," replied Jeremy, flicking his head toward the sound. "Damn, I don't think they would even hear him if he screamed for help." Tossing caution to the wind, he rolled over to the edge of eroded portion and slid down into the extremely confined space behind the tent. "Let's go!" he called out in a still low voice.

When Davis joined him on the ground, Jeremy moved to the right side of the tent and signalled Davis to the left corner. On a signal from the trapper, the two quickly rushed for the front of the tent, one from each side. As Davis rounded the left corner first, he was immediately spotted by the lone guard, who was yet more vigilant than the two men had been expecting. The Parson's disciple snapped his musket to shoulder before Davis could reach him, stopping him dead in his tracks. The guard opened his mouth to call for assistance.

The call never came. The first attempt came out more like a hoarse croak and, by the time the guard had taken a deep breath to try again, Jeremy barrelled into him from behind. Winded by the unexpected blow, the guard released his hold on his musket and it skittered away across the now frozen snow to come to rest against a tree at the very edge of the creek.

Pain immediately shot through Jeremy's previously injured shoulder, causing it to bleed once again. He forced himself to ignore it while he collected himself once again. The injury, which he had kept dressed until now, would need to be bandaged anew.

Davis scampered to retrieve the weapon and pointed it at the guard's head from a mere two feet away. "Don't move and keep your mouth shut!" he hissed at the winded and completely astonished man.

"I'd listen if I were you," Jeremy suggested, approaching their prisoner. "He's a British infantry sniper, one of the best. I saw him take down a man from over two hundred yards away, so as you might realize, this distance would be child's play to him."

Deflated, the guard obeyed and allowed Jeremy to pull his arms back, lashing his wrists behind him. To make sure that there would be no further attempt at trying to summon help, the guard was also treated to rope being pulled roughly and tightly into his mouth. This rope too was tied securely.

★ ★ ★

"Let's see what you've been guarding that seems to be of such value," Jeremy muttered as he pushed the helpless disciple roughly into the tent. Davis tossed him the musket to act as insurance against any surprises.

As the guard stumbled in, Jeremy followed closely behind, squinting in an attempt to adjust to the extremely low level of light. What was almost immediately obvious was the presence of more than one person inside. As soon as he realized it, he reflexively raised the captured musket.

"Don't shoot us," Oliver was heard to say from the dim shadows. "All of us here are prisoners."

"Who is 'all of us'?" Jeremy asked. He looked about the tent at the other dark shape and then burst out laughing.

"What do you find to be so humorous?" asked Davis from the doorway, the annoyance apparent in his voice.

"I think I now know why we've been treated to an attack on the enemy by Indians just now," replied Jeremy. "It seems that the Parson had another guest in the lodgings and I believe they may have come for him." He ducked inside the tent.

Davis quick anger flared at Jeremy's cryptic answer. This was certainly no time for riddles! "Well, since you've brought up the matter of the Indian attack, perhaps you haven't noticed that it's quieting down somewhat," he remarked sarcastically. "So if you don't mind, please dispense with the laughter and let's be under way before we find ourselves guests here."

"You're quite right." Jeremy emerged from the tent with two men in tow. One was his cousin, Oliver, but the second was completely new to Davis although it was apparent, even by the scant light available to them, that this new addition to their group was an Indian.

"Let's get out of here," Davis said nervously.

The four men scampered quickly up the embankment, climbing steadily until they reached the top. From there it soon became evident why the raid had broken up in such short order, as they could hear numerous additional voices approaching. As they watched, from their temporarily safe position, the small valley flooded rapidly with Volunteers and American militiamen. They screamed and shouted and fired their muskets but, as anyone who stopped to look could plainly have seen, the Indians were nowhere to be seen.

They watched for a moment and then turned to leave at Davis' behest. But as they headed away from the ridge to head northward, they suddenly found themselves unexpectedly confronted. Without a sound, four Indians had materialized from among the trees and now stood pointing their weapons at the escapees.

The Indian they had released stepped forward. "C'est bien," he said.

The others looked at the three white men skeptically. Once they were convinced, however, that the prisoner had not been coerced into reassuring them, they lowered their weapons. He exchanged several more words with his compatriots in what the others assumed to be French and then he waved at the white men to follow as they turned to leave.

Chapter Twenty-Eight

A half hour later the group, now eight strong, reached a safe distance from the Parson's and the Americans' camps and they stopped to rest and regroup. Although they found shelter from the wind, no one suggested they start a fire for warmth, although the cold was biting. There was as yet obviously too much chance that they might alert any enemy patrols of their location. Instead, they huddled together side by side with their backs to an embankment.

"So," said Davis, first to break the silence, "is anyone going to tell me what is happening here? Who is this extra prisoner and how did we end up with this Indian tribe?"

"This extra prisoner, as you describe him, is an old friend," Jeremy began, glaring at Davis disapprovingly. "And quite frankly, one I never expected to see again after he went home."

Oliver, having heard some of Jeremy's tales of his adventures earlier in the year, gasped as he caught on. "Do you mean to tell me that this is the famous Josef DuLac that I was sharing captivity with?"

"Who is Josef DuLac?" Davis asked, perplexed at being the only one who seemed completely unfamiliar with the situation, an unaccustomed position for him.

"Well, this is the man who saved my life and helped me bring down Dorian Williamson," Jeremy explained, ignoring a curious expression that appeared on Davis' face and then just as quickly vanished. "Haven't I told you about him?"

"No, you haven't."

"It's quite the tale, let me tell you. But it's a tale best told when sitting about a warm fire," said Jeremy. "Suffice it to say that Josef here is a Caughnawaga Indian from near Montreal in Lower Canada. I first met him just before the Battle of Beaverdams."

"And I assume these other men are of his tribe as well," Oliver joined in, not quite sure what to make of these supposed savages who dressed largely like white men. "I heard you speak French to them. Don't they speak any English?"

"Of course we speak your language," one of the others replied with mock indignation. "We found it best to learn it else we might shoot the wrong man. Or possibly the right one." This last comment drew quiet laughter from his friends. "Or the wrong man might shoot us."

"What are you doing here, my friend?" Jeremy asked of Josef. "I thought you had gone home to wait out the balance of the war with your family."

Josef smiled sadly. "And I had thought that you were through with the war yourself. But, in my case, I was called up when Montreal itself was under attack. I couldn't just sit while the Americans moved toward my home. Besides, my home is gone"

"What do you mean your home is gone?" asked Jeremy, not all sure he should ask the question.

"Just that," the Caughnawaga replied morosely. "As I've told you, our home is on the border of New York State. Well, one day about two months ago, while I was out hunting, my people were surprised by a Seneca raid. They burned my house and my family were inside. They didn't get out in time."

All was silent for some time. The news had been dropped like a stone into the discussion, sending ripples of silent discomfort through the gathering. No one knew quite what to say to the obviously grieving man, or if they should indeed say anything at all.

"What part did you have at Montreal?" asked Davis, breaking the silence, his curiosity overcoming all other considerations.

"I was first sent out with a group of Frenchmen known as the Devil's Own Battalion. There were not many Caughnawagas involved as many of our fighters were yet down here. But they needed a few of us to guide this group of white men because they're from a very bad part of Montreal and, while fierce, have few wilderness skills."

"Where did you guide them?"

"We were sent through the smuggler's region on the border, in the area of the Châteaguay River to meet the Americans as they pushed north. They were camped near a farm belonging to a family named Spear, but we had information from the local smugglers and drove them out. They retreated and then regrouped but they weren't prepared for the cold weather and withdrew after taking heavy losses, especially when they fired on their own men thinking they were British."

Davis chuckled.

"I don't see what's funny," chided Jeremy. "Many young lives are being ended and destroyed in this stupidity, some of whom I have known in my dealings on both side of the border. And every life lost is a shame, regardless of who shoots them." He turned back to Josef. "Was that the end of your service?"

Josef shook his head slowly. "No, unfortunately, it was not. They tried again, but this time the British, including the soldiers we know from here…"

"…the forty-ninth regiment. Brock's own and Fitzgibbon's regiment," Jeremy interrupted. "I'm sorry, please continue."

"Well, the Americans were met at Chrysler's Farm because they couldn't get up the St. Lawrence past the rapids. The British defeated them there, but I had little to do with that. Mostly I was scouting and I followed the Americans when they returned home. They tried to make a winter camp but didn't come prepared so, starving and hungry, they went home."

"But that was weeks ago," interjected Davis. "Have you been active since then?"

"And how did you end up back here?" added Jeremy.

"Afterward, my brothers and I were asked to keep an eye on movements around the American base of Sackets Harbor," Josef sighed. "By then, we were quite fed up with the military life and decided to take you up on your previous offer to come to your cabin, to sit about and watch the birds. But, when we crossed over to bring our information to the British, we were ambushed and, I'm ashamed to say, I was captured."

"Well then, I suppose that since I freed you, you'll forgive me for not affording you the comfort of my cabin?" Jeremy responded.

Josef frowned. "No. Your saving me was payment for me saving your life after the Battle of Beaverdams. You still owe me the bird watching."

"You two can catch up on old times when we're safely clear of this enemy territory," Oliver broke in. He thought about what he'd said and then chuckled uncomfortably. "It's strange to hear myself say that. I am an American after all."

"If I were you, I'd keep that under my hat," cautioned Jeremy. "Don't forget, you were captured in the company of an accused British spy and a British soldier and were freed by Caughnawagas, who are British allies. I hardly think that your countrymen would look kindly upon your place of birth under the circumstances."

"For now, let's set our sights upon leaving this area," said Davis nervously. "We must get back to Merritt and tell him that the American troops are at Shipman's Corners."

"Aren't you forgetting something?" asked Jeremy rhetorically. "We're wanted by the British for supposedly murdering their soldiers."

"Then I suppose that we must tell them for you," Josef offered. "You men stay near here and keep an eye on their movements while we find the British troops."

With constant glances over their shoulders and stops to listen to every wayward sound, the eight men finally made their way to Lake Ontario. From there, they proceeded westward as far as the mouth of the Twelve Mile Creek. The Caughnawagas carried on from there toward the settlement of the Forty, hoping to intercept Merritt. The three white men headed up the western bank of the Twelve to watch the enemy from the bluffs opposite the settlement.

★ ★ ★

The Parson was a study in barely controlled rage as he stood silently in front of the tent where his prisoners had so recently been held. To look at his face, one would think that he was calm and accepting of the circumstances, but those who knew him could tell that he was at his most dangerous.

"Who was guarding this tent?" he asked with feigned mildness.

The four guards who had run off to the aid of the besieged camp, leaving the prisoners in the hands of one man, hesitantly stepped forward. They stood silently facing their leader, muscles taut in anticipation of the Parson's fury when finally it struck. Neither man dared risk a word. They knew it was but a matter of time before the façade would crumble and then they all would pay dearly for their transgressions.

The Parson walked slowly along the line-up, stopping in front of each man in turn to look long and hard into his eyes. Then, shaking his head, he would move on to the next, never speaking. He just sighed deeply as he studied his silent victims, the wayward souls that had allowed the prize to slip from his grasp. And his fury built like the pressure in a tightly covered pot before the steam blew the lid off.

As he neared the end of the line, he turned on his left foot, so that he was facing down the line. Taking a deep breath, he saw the men wince in anticipation of the tirade – or worse – that they all knew was coming. Instead, he started walking back the other way, his head down this time, hands behind his back, as though in deep thought.

Without stopping or raising his head, the Parson began to speak in menacing tones. "Do you know what you fools have cost me?" His voice grew in volume as he spoke. "You have cost me the world!"

He spun about and faced all faced all four. Looking beyond them into the tent, he shouted, "Bring the fifth idiot out here!" referring to the guard he had purposely ordered left in his bound state. He smiled and continued just loud enough to be heard inside. "There's no reason why he should be the only one to miss the entertainment to come."

Time stood still while the man who had been tied up and gagged was brought out with the others. If the Parson was anything, he was a master of the psychology of terror, and he was greatly enjoying his own performance. In fact, it was all he could do to keep from smiling as he continued.

"Does any one of you have a valid reason for this betrayal?" he demanded and then stepped up the man at the end of the line. "How about you? Was there a very good reason for your disobeying my orders to guard the prisoners with your life?"

The addressee was visibly shaking despite his tough appearance and the Parson thought, with satisfaction, that he might be about to cry. "We heard all the shooting and…and we didn't want any harm coming to you, sir."

"I see. I see," the Parson thoughtfully, as though reconsidering. "And the rest of you. Do you agree with this man's opinion?" he asked mildly.

The others all nodded but one. The man who had been overpowered and tied up just looked straight ahead.

The Parson walked up in front of the dissenting guard, stopping with his face only inches from his. "I see you don't agree," he growled. "Were you not concerned about my welfare?"

Without flinching, the man replied, "Yes sir, but your orders were to guard the prisoners, so when the others left, I stayed. Unfortunately, there were too many of them for one man to stop and they overpowered me."

The Parson stepped back as if shocked. "This man followed orders to the detriment of all else," he said admiringly. Then he pulled out his pistol and, without hesitation, shot the loyal guard in the head from point-blank range.

The other guards and the remaining members of the Parson's stood riveted, the horror and senselessness of what they had just seen too enormous to comprehend. Two men stepped forward with the obvious intention of removing the body.

"Leave him there," the Parson growled and the men stepped back. "I want all of you to realize something. I have no place in my heart for traitors!" he screamed. "These four men," he said, indicating the remaining guards, "risked their lives to disobey orders to save the life of their God-ordained leader. That man not only ignored my peril, but then proceeded to brag about how he followed orders while the others did not! He was disloyal to me and to the men he was assigned with!"

The Parson stormed about now, screaming his words in the faces of all present, although no one could any longer understand what the screams meant, not that any were certain that it mattered, since his logic was unfathomable. No one was certain how to react to any of this, so they meekly stood and remained still. Finally calm, he turned back to the four remaining guards, who now believed they had been vindicated in their actions.

"These men, ten lashes each for disobeying me!" he shouted, and stormed off across the stream toward his tent, the only one of the main camp not burned to the ground or trampled in the confusion of the fight.

★ ★ ★

Jeremy and his companions watched the settlement at Shipman's Corners and in particular the area around Shipman's Tavern, from the point directly across the Twelve. As they kept an eye on movements there, they saw an assortment of characters come and go. There was no telling just who many of these people might be, for the situation in Niagara was incredibly fluid. People changed allegiances overnight, attempting to stay on the good side of whoever might be occupying their village or town, hoping to keep their families, farms and various enterprises safe for another day.

Between the militiamen, spies and civilians, no one was certain who was friend or foe at this point in the war. Even regular soldiers were wary of being shot by some farmer who had changed sides since the soldier was last there.

But as they watched, something curious was taking place. Jeremy knew for certain that the troops commanded by them at this forward point was far greater than that of the British, so he was surprised at what appeared to be happening. Men of the New York Militia were filtering out of the camp, apparently unnoticed by the command, presumably heading toward the border and home. No one challenged them or attempted to impede their progress.

Then, later in the day, the entire army began to pack up.

"What's happening?" Oliver asked. Even his almost nonexistent military experience told him that something was wrong here.

"I'm sure I don't know," Jeremy answered, puzzled by hat he was seeing. "This is an odd way to wage a war."

"Perhaps it's but a feint," suggested Davis. "Perhaps they're retiring to the flanks, hoping to draw the British into the centre. You did comment earlier that Willcocks and his men were rather intent on moving away when we saw them on the road. Perhaps the British were chasing him."

"Perhaps," Jeremy said, not convinced.

The three continued to watch as the preparations continued in the camp below.

As the afternoon wore on, Jeremy could stand it no longer. "I've decided that there's really only one way to find out for sure what the Americans are up to." He picked up the musket, balls and powder he had acquired in the camp. "You two stay here. I'll be back in short order."

"Are you daft?" asked Davis, although it was really more of a comment than a question. "If they capture you again, they'll shoot you on sight."

Jeremy grinned. "You know that if you insist on asking me constantly if I'm daft, I might just begin to believe that perhaps I am? Else I might eventually take offence at your remark and find that I have to shoot you to defend my honour. Anyways, they won't even know I'm there. With all the commotion and all the comings and goings, they won't notice one more stranger in their midst. Unless either of you two has a better idea as to how I'm to find out what's happening."

Neither Davis nor Oliver said a word. They watched forlornly as Jeremy disappeared down the embankment.

Chapter Twenty-Nine

Jeremy headed directly to Shipman's Tavern, a sense of dread hanging over him like a storm cloud. The last time he had been in that establishment had been in the late spring and the memories were anything but pleasant. A friend had died there and he himself had been taken prisoner, to be dragged off at the tail end of a horse to Newark and beyond. But he managed to force the thoughts from his mind as he pulled his hat down low in front, seemingly against the weather but in truth to shade his face.

He walked confidently up to the bar, not wishing to seem out of place. "Just an ale, please," he ordered from the barkeep.

The bartender looked at him strangely and then sighed deeply, apparently out of frustration. "Ale? You want ale? You and every other man in the area!" Jeremy hardly knew where to look in the face of this unexpected barrage. But the man continued. "Are you daft, man?"

"Apparently, as people seem to be continually telling me that I am."

The barkeep grinned, taken off his stride by Jeremy's comment. His manner softened slightly and lowering his voice some, as Jeremy had hoped it might. "With all these soldiers and whatnot here for days, I've been cleaned out of all but water. And I wouldn't be drinking that, if you understand what I mean."

Jeremy just nodded, looking about secretly to see if he had drawn any attention from those in attendance. Apparently he had not. "Everyone seems to have been very busy outside all day. Are they moving out?"

"I'm sure I don't know. And I wouldn't tell you if I did. This business has managed to survive through all these problems and I've every doubt that my employer would appreciate me getting involved now. If all you're going to do is ask questions, then be off with you."

Jeremy really could not blame the man. All this barkeep needed was for one of his neighbours-turned-informant to start the rumour that this tavern and livery stable was helping spies and the building might be instantly razed to the ground. Jeremy decided that his best chance in finding something out might lie in trying to get closer to the commanding officer's quarters. Perhaps he might overhear something of note.

He strode purposefully across the settlement toward the rapidly diminishing military camp, looking all the world as though he might have business there. No one seemed to pay any attention to him as they toiled at collapsing tents, harnessing horses and all the other one hundred plus duties associated with an army breaking camp.

Perhaps it would not be necessary to go any further, Jeremy thought. It was obvious this camp was breaking up and militiamen were leaving towards the border.

Without warning, General McClure came walking around the corner of a small house, nearly colliding with a startled Jeremy. The trapper stepped back into the shadows of an outbuilding associated with the house and waited for the officer and his retinue to pass.

"There you are!" the General called out.

Jeremy started, thinking that he had been discovered.

"Willcocks! Come here! I wish to speak with you now!" McClure barked without missing a beat, obviously having either not seen or not recognized Jeremy.

Jeremy looked about, a sudden feeling of panic all but knocking the breath out of him. Willcocks would recognize him immediately for they had been face to face on several occasions, the last of which being the previous night. But Willcocks must have been coming from another direction, for he saw no sign of the Volunteer leader.

"Yes, General," he heard Willcocks say.

"I hope you're certain that the British number between two and three thousand plus Indians." Jeremy heard McClure say, really more of question than a statement. "I've met with my officers and they agree that we can't withstand such numbers in open battle. My reputation and the safety of our nation are at stake here."

"I saw them myself," Willcocks replied. "They chased me from the Forty to the Twenty and I fear they're waiting for yet more reinforcements."

"I wouldn't have thought that the Brits had that many troops in all of the Canadas," the General muttered. "Although my scouts report that the British Captain Merritt is raising all the militia he can find just up the Twelve from here. They must be to bolster the ranks, I'll wager."

"Yes sir, General," Willcocks agreed, perhaps a bit too readily.

"Well, I suppose that it matters little now, Willcocks. It seems most of my New York Militia have gone home ahead of their discharge date. Nearly a third of my force is gone and I fear I've left Fort George defenceless against a British flanking attack."

The two men continued talking intently as they walked away out of Jeremy's earshot. He waited for several minutes and then turned to start back to rejoin Davis and Oliver. But, as he made his way through the rapidly dissolving camp he saw one of Willcocks' men packing something familiar.

The items that the man was packing were Jeremy's over/under, his engraved pistol, and his tomahawk and bayonet. He also had Davis' Baker Rifle, which he was placing carefully on blankets to roll up with the rest of the items, which Jeremy also recognized.

Jeremy looked about to see if anyone was looking in his direction. He was pleased to note that no one seemed intent upon anything but what they were doing at that moment.

Deciding that the prize was worth the risk, he walked quietly up beside the man and placed the muzzle of his stolen musket against the man's head, just below his ear. "One sound and be happy to take your head off," he murmured. "Now, as though I was with you, finish wrapping up those weapons and move over behind the tree."

The Volunteer did as he was told. He knew he was being robbed but he had no idea as to the identity of the thief. The man obviously wanted Willcocks' prize trophy weapons and he was not about to die for something from which another would benefit.

As they moved behind the tree, Jeremy pulled back the musket and swung it stock first into the unsuspecting man's head. The Volunteer collapsed like a sack of laundry and Jeremy quickly grabbed the bedroll full of precious weapons before they could even hit the ground.

As he moved to escape with his recovered items, he felt a hand roughly grasp his shoulder.

"Do you know what we do with thieves in an army camp?"

Jeremy resisted the force of the man's pull on his shoulder, rapidly weighing his options.

"I don't know, but I suggest you do whatever it is to this blackguard. He tried to steal these items from me. I was lucky to get them back."

The man who had a hold on Jeremy's shoulders stepped partly around him, trying to get a look at his face. "Wait a minute. I know you. You're the one we captured just the other night."

Jeremy's captor stepped back to sound the alarm so Jeremy moved quickly. Before the rather large civilian could finish taking in his breath for the cry, Jeremy slammed his elbow into his solar plexus. He could hear the satisfying grunt and expulsion of air as he spun about and delivered a solid blow to the man's head, swinging hard with hands clasped. But he did not get the intended result.

Instead of dropping unconscious to the ground the man, who Jeremy could now see was built like a plough ox, simply shook his head as if to drive away insects. His face darkened with rage at the same time as a momentary look of confusion melted away.

"I'm going to have to kill you now," he grumbled, almost as an aside.

"Damn!" Jeremy muttered under his breath as his hand reached into the bedroll.

The huge Volunteer lunged at Jeremy, who attempted to spin from his grasp. He failed. Powerful arms encircled him and began to squeeze him against the man's rock hard chest. Jeremy could feel first the wind, and then his consciousness, begin to escape. He knew with what remained of his consciousness that he needed to act quickly or he would die in the giant's painful embrace.

His arms were pinned to his side by the man's massive arms, so he could not raise them. Somewhere outside of lessening vision however, he could hear voices approaching and asking what was happening. Even if the big man did not kill him he would soon be captured again, an even more unbearable thought than death itself.

With his last vestige of strength, Jeremy swung his tomahawk, which he had managed to free from the bedroll, at the man's groin. For a split second, he wondered whether the act had had any effect on the man at all. Then a groan issued from the man's lips and his grip lessened ever so slightly. With a sudden surge of hope, however futile, Jeremy began to hack at the man's groin mercilessly with what little strength he could muster.

His swing was not hard enough to break skin at this point nor, for that matter, to even tear the man's trousers. But the repeated love taps between the man's legs were having the desired effect. No longer able to ignore the pain caused by the bouncing of his gonads, his grip relaxed sufficiently that Jeremy could twist free of the deadly embrace.

As he dropped the few inches he had been lifted off the ground, Jeremy pulled back his arm and swung with all the might he could muster. There followed a horrifying scream as the tomahawk blade struck the giant between the eyes, splitting his skull and showering Jeremy with his blood. Jeremy's assailant dropped to the ground, writhing in pain.

Jeremy spun about just as two other men were nearly in reach. Out of his peripheral vision, he noticed that others had been attracted by the scream of his victim and were moving in their direction. His advantage as yet was that the newcomers approached tentatively, unsure of what was happening. He would have to act quickly if he were to hope to escape from this situation in one piece and a free man.

Dropping to one knee, he pulled his rifle from the bedroll. Hoping that it was still loaded and, thinking that there was every good reason why it might not be, Jeremy pulled back the hammer and fired in the general direction of the first man moving toward him. He breathed a sigh of relief as the powder exploded, sending the thirteen-millimetre slug from the rifle barrel toward its target, which was only two feet away.

The man dropped to the ground, holding his side and writhing with pain. Blood quickly began to ooze from between the fingers that covered the wound.

The second attacker stopped in his tracks. He hesitated for a moment and then smiled. "Well, lad, I don't know why you point that piece at me. But you've exhausted your load on my friend there." He slowly began to pull a pistol from his waistband, seeming to relish the prospect of a kill.

Jeremy smiled back, wishing to seem as relaxed as the man before him, yet anxious at the same time. He could see others cautiously approaching now. "Well, if you look closely, you'll see this gun has two barrels. The second is loaded with scattershot. I think I'll wait 'til your other friends get a little closer and then I can shoot the lot of you at once."

The man studied Jeremy momentarily and decided to take the risk. He snapped up the pistol and made to pull back the hammer when Jeremy pulled the second trigger on his gun.

And nothing happened.

With a suddenly hopeless feeling, Jeremy realized that either the musket part wasn't loaded or the pan wasn't primed. Either way, he knew he was dead as he watched the triumphant grin steal over his adversary's face and he raised the pistol to shoot. Jeremy waited for what seemed like an eternity for the shot that would end his life.

There was a sudden loud report from the edge of the Twelve Mile Creek ravine, followed by another. The man in front of Jeremy pitched forward, a ball neatly lodged in the side of his head. One of the others who had been approaching likewise dropped o the ground, screaming that he had been shot.

"The British! The British are here!" someone shouted, and the camp deteriorated into utter bedlam as the cry was taken up by others. "I saw Indians!" shouted yet another, and men ducked for cover as a bugle sounded while horses trampled wildly to get out of the way.

I'd better move before they get organized, Jeremy told himself.

He scooped up his weapons and then, running in a zigzag pattern to the ravine lip, he jumped over the side not knowing if there was a place to land. For the moment at least he did not care. There was another double report toward the American camp from off to his left, so headed along the steep hill in that direction, soon coming upon Oliver and Davis, who were rapidly reloading.

Davis finished reloading just as Jeremy broke from the brush to his left. He swung the musket around but recognized Jeremy as he was about to pull the trigger.

"Good God, man!" he chided. "I could have blown your head off."

"I thought I told you two to wait on the other side," Jeremy scolded.

"And aren't you glad we don't follow orders well?" asked Oliver, getting ready to take another shot.

Jeremy pulled up his cousin's gun barrel. "I suggest we get out of here before those soldiers get organized and come after us in force. There's yet enough confusion to make our escape, so let's use it, shall we?"

The three men climbed and slid as rapidly as they could down the steep rock and clay slope until they reached the bottom. They could hear the American troops above rallying as they waded quickly across the half-frozen creek and worked their way back up the other side.

Oliver dropped to the ground when they reached the crest, panting.

"Farm life has made you soft, lad," Jeremy laughed. "I heartily suggest that we keep moving until we're well away from here though. You'll have to catch up on your breathing later. Besides," he started, pulling at his sodden clothes, "if we stop now, we'll freeze to death before the Americans can even get here."

★ ★ ★

"Halt! Who goes there?" The challenge made clear there would be no second one as Josef and his Caughnawagas just before they approached a bridge crossing the Twelve Mile Creek.

"Friends," Josef replied, stepping from the night shadows to show himself and his companions to the on-duty sentry.

"So say you," the sentry replied, his musket still at the ready. "What's the by-word?"

"I honestly couldn't say or even know," Josef replied lightly. "We've just come from Montreal by way of New York and we've been criss-crossing Niagara looking for Captain Merritt all day to give him news regarding the American troops at Shipman's Corners."

The sentry looked him over, uncertain as whether to believe the Indian. However it would be unwise for him to send away someone offering information so he called over two other soldiers.

"Take this savage…"

"Josef," the Caughnawaga asserted. "We all have names. And I'll warrant that, as unpleasant as I can be at times, I'm no more a savage than you."

The sentry ignored him. "Take this savage to Captain Merritt. The rest will wait here."

Josef shook his head at the man's ignorance. "And what makes you think you could hold off these four men by yourself while I'm gone?" he remarked, a mischievous glint in his eyes. Shaking his head in amusement, he then turned to the other two men summoned to escort him. "Well, let's go then."

In short order, he was standing before the man who commanded about fifty dragoons in His Majesty's service in the Niagara Peninsula.

His reputation as an adventurer was well known, and he was known often to do what he felt best with a general disregard for orders.

"So, what do have to tell me?" Merritt asked. "I'm trying to organize these militiamen I've drawn to together and it's proving no easy task. I was hoping to catch some sleep before morning breaks."

"Well, since you're here, I assume you know the Americans are at Shipman's Corners," Josef started. I estimate there are close to fifteen hundred men, including Willcocks and his Volunteers."

"That many?" Merritt commented. "I knew it was a large force from my view across the Twelve near the town. And you say that scoundrel Willcocks is with them as well? I would dearly love to wring his neck personally for imprisoning my father, not to mention his harassment of many of my friends."

"They're camped separately from the main force, or at least some are," Josef explained. "If you like, we can show you the way."

Before Merritt could reply, there was a commotion outside the old farmhouse the Captain was staying and was hoping to sleep in.

"What the devil is happening here?" he bellowed. "Doesn't anyone know that it's nearly two o'clock in the morning?"

A Corporal snapped to attention and saluted. "Sir, we picked this man up on patrol. He and his two companions were running hard through the woods as though the demons of Hell were on their trail. He claimed they were being chased by Volunteers." He shoved the man forward before the Captain.

Chapter Thirty

Merritt seemed somewhat surprised at the identity of the prisoner. "Jeremy van Hijser?" he said. "Do you know we're to be on the lookout for you?"

"Yes, I know," Jeremy replied. "Someone has been trumping up charges against me and I'm afraid I'm now running from my own side in this infernal war. In any event, I'm glad I ended up here because I wanted to inform you that the Americans are pulling back to Newark."

"So why were you running when my men found you?"

"As I tried to explain to them, I was being chased by some of Willcocks' men. They almost caught me listening in to their boss and General McClure discussing their withdrawal. It seems Willcocks somewhat inflated the numbers of British troops advancing on Shipman's Corners."

"I think perhaps Willcocks has lost the taste for true battle," Merritt mused.

"Perhaps, though I doubt that he has ever had it," Jeremy concurred. "But I also heard McClure say that it didn't matter at this point because a third of his men had decided to go home before their time was up."

The Captain raised his eyebrows at the news. "Perhaps I can yet catch Willcocks and his filthy Volunteers before they reach Newark."

Before he could give his militia the order to march, however, a shout came from the sentry on the west side of the camp. "Rider approaching hard!"

Merritt strode over to meet what was obviously a messenger. "What do you have, Corporal?" he asked before the rider could finish reining in his mount. "Colonel Murray sends his regards, sir," the Corporal said breathlessly, handing a document to the Captain. "He's less than an hour away and he intends to march on Shipman's Corners before the Americans can lay waste to it. They're stealing livestock, flour, anything they can lay their hands on as they prepare to leave."

"Tell him we'll meet him at the bridge then, Corporal," Merritt said, and turned to move his men.

"Begging your pardon, sir," the Corporal called apologetically after Merritt. "The Colonel wishes you to ride to Beaverdams to DeCou's mills to protect the flour there. The American General has sent men in that direction and you're to stop them."

Merritt stopped dead in his tracks. "Very well, Corporal, you may tell Colonel Murray that I'm on my way to Beaverdams." He stood quietly seething as he watched the rider head back in the direction from which he had come.

"Sergeant-Major!" he shouted, obviously frustrated by the order but jumping into action. When the also sleep-deprived man appeared at the Captain's side, Merritt continued. "Turn out the entire camp immediately and prepare to be under way as soon as possible. I will personally need riders, so have the dragoons report directly to me. I want the militia to remain here under your watch until Colonel Murphy's main body reaches here when you will join them in advancing on Shipman's Corners. Do you understand?"

"Yes sir!" the sergeant-Major replied smartly and ran off to spread the orders to wake the camp.

Merritt turned to Jeremy, anger and fatigue showing on his face at the same moment. "Well, Jeremy, it appears as though I'm riding away from the main battle. You'll be best to stay with these men."

Jeremy shook his head. "No Captain. I think I'll head into town to see what state it's in. If Murray catches me, he'll likely send me back to Burlington Heights for hanging. He doesn't know me and he just might decide to follow orders."

Merritt laughed tiredly and clapped Jeremy on the back. "Take care, Jeremy. Perhaps I'll catch up with you before the dawn somewhere."

Jeremy and Oliver and Davis headed out into the dark night, back in the direction from which they had just escaped. Josef and his companions decided to stay with the troops for now, in case they were needed as guides.

★ ★ ★

It was yet early when the trio reached Shipman's Corners once again, the dawn still hours away on this cold December night. The winds had shift to a generally easterly direction now and it beginning to snow softly.

Their previous suspicions had obviously proven correct. As they previously reconnoitred the settlement from its fringes, it seemed the Americans had gone. And now, standing in the settlement itself, they could see there were no enemy troops left here and all seemed relatively peaceful in Shipman's Corners. The only sign that anything untoward had happened here was the refuse left by the large number of people camping out on the land. They came upon bits of clothing, broken plates which had likely been stolen from residents, a wide variety of partially-eaten foods, and even tent pegs that yet remained in the ground.

"It's early yet to be checking to see if everyone's alright," Jeremy commented. "I suggest we go to the barn and sleep for a few hours before carrying on again."

"Do you think that's wise?" Davis asked. "As you pointed out to the Captain, Colonel Murray may not so friendly if he chances to meet you." A grin broke out on his tired and somewhat dirty face but a level of unease seemed to belie his argument. "Of course, I'm fine since I can just claim that you kidnapped me."

Jeremy lightly elbowed the infantryman in the ribs. "Or perhaps I should tell them that you kidnapped us."

"Let's just move along, shall we?" Oliver broke in impatiently, the fatigue and stress rendering his temper too short to play along. "We can continue with your tiresome tomfoolery and perhaps even catch some sleep in some place more suitable outside of town."

They marched on for a half hour, near exhaustion, until they reached an abandoned homestead about three miles east of town and halfway to the lake. Here they felt reasonably certain that the British army would not bother them as they were far from the main road. Initially they considered taking turns on watch, but decided that, since it would be light in a matter of a few hours, they would dispense with it this once. They had found blankets still on the one bed in the corner, no doubt left by someone in a hurry to evacuate when the Americans advanced or retreated.

They fell into a sleep approaching unconsciousness. And outside, unbeknownst to them, the war was taking a nasty turn.

★ ★ ★

After only two hours' sleep, Jeremy awoke to the sound of footsteps outside their shelter. He threw off the blankets, waking his companions in the process. With his finger in front of his pursed lips he signalled them to silence and then crept quietly toward the door, his gun cocked and ready.

The door creaked open just a fraction of an inch, as though blown open by the wind. As Jeremy waited in silence, the door moved a little more, by several inches this time. Then, without warning, the door crashed wide open. As the snow, which had now picked up considerably, whipped and swirled into the one-room cabin, a blood-curdling yell sounded. It was followed by another and then another.

In spite of his vigilance, Jeremy was caught off-guard. When two figures burst into the shelter, followed immediately by three more, each moving in a different direction, he froze in place. Somewhere in the back of his mind, he believed he heard the sound of muskets being cocked. He heard Davis shout something about Indians and then the room went momentarily silent.

Then the uncomfortable silence was shattered by the sounds of laughter – first one man, then others. From where he was now seated on the floor, Jeremy could not see clearly with the snow blowing into his face through the still-open door and he struggled to understand why there was laughter instead of gunshots.

"Here, get out of the snow," a voice said light-heartedly. "You look ridiculous sitting there." A hand reached down and pulled him up to his feet.

Jeremy cleared his eyes and looked at the man who had helped him up, and burst out laughing himself.

"Do you find my face so funny to look at?" asked Josef, a broad grin still evident.

"Yes, you bastard," Jeremy responded, still laughing, though likely more at the sudden release of stress than any real humour. "You could have been shot, you know."

"Not likely," the Caughnawaga chuckled. "Neither of you seemed to know what to do when we stormed through that door."

"I'm glad you all think that this sort of nonsense is funny," Oliver pouted from his place at the back of the room. "I thought I'd die of fright. Worse, now I've lost that much chance to get some sleep."

This remark brought on more gales of laughter from all but Oliver himself. He snatched up his musket and stormed out into the snowy predawn.

"I'd better get him back in here," Davis offered, sobering up.

"He won't go far," assured Jeremy. "He left his coat in here. Give him a few moments to cool down, if you'll excuse the pun." He turned to Josef. "How did you end up here?"

"We're scouting in advance of Colonel Murray's troops," explained one of the other Caughnawagas, an older man named Louis St. George that Jeremy had also met at the Battle of Beaverdams. "When Josef saw the traces of your footprints end at this cabin, he thought it might be funny to play this little prank. Of course, we agreed," he added with a grin.

"There was another reason for rousing you, although not necessarily in this manner," Josef continued. "Murray is dying to move on Newark. Until now he has been restraining himself, but I don't know for how long. I thought I had best tell you to get under way in the morning if you wish to stay out of his way."

"You know, I'm not as concerned as you might expect. I think that, as long as we let the Colonel pass, we could easily blend in with the army's militia," Jeremy said thoughtfully. "Knowing the types that will be around the town, I'd much rather not be out front as we approach. We've spent quite enough time in the hands of Willcocks or one or another of his men this year and I think it would be greatly preferable if the army were to go in ahead of us."

"In that case," Josef replied, grinning broadly, "do you have any food? We're quite starved you know."

★ ★ ★

They set out at noon, hoping that the snow would diminish before they left. However, it continued to come down, creating a smothering blanket which rose by the hour. The depth was already well over their ankles and wind whipped at the mercilessly as they walked, increasing in intensity as they approached the lake. In the open spaces the blowing created deep snowdrifts which impeded their progress as they pushed on. They had more eight miles of the distance from Shipman's to Newark left to cover, and they knew it would take much longer than the normal hour under these conditions.

"The only consolation is that our tracks are rapidly being filled, should anyone attempt to follow us," Jeremy shouted against the wind. "Although I know of no one who even knows to look for us at this point."

"What of the Volunteers?" Oliver shouted back. "Who knows where they might be."

"I expect that, with the American army headed back to the fort and the British on the march in this direction, the Volunteers will be the first to reach the fort," laughed Jeremy. "Whatever else you might say of our turncoat friends, taking unnecessary chances has never been their failing."

He could not tell if anyone understood or shared the humour in his remark, for most sounds where drowned out by the wind howling about his ears. Nor could he discern the expressions on the faces of his companions for he was blinded by the snow that was generally reducing visibility all about them.

On they marched until well past what they estimated to be ten o'clock. It was at about that time that Josef appeared at Jeremy's side. It was extremely difficult to determine precisely, for the sun had not been even vaguely visible all morning.

"Someone's coming!" he shouted, only inches away from Jeremy.

Jeremy jerked his head back at the sound. "The noise of the wind is quite strong, but I'm not deaf yet," he half quipped.

"Sorry," Josef replied at a reduced volume. "I've been quiet for so long that I somewhat overcompensated. But there are people approaching several hundred yards ahead and closing."

"Do you think they're American soldiers?" asked Davis with concern, having overheard Josef's report.

"No. I wasn't close enough to make them out exactly. They were but dark images in the wall of snow. But they have no military bearing, nor are they spaced out as soldiers would be. They're all huddled together, as for warmth, and they're of differing heights."

Jeremy turned and looked at his Caughnawaga friend. "What manner of fools would be out in weather like this, but for we imbeciles, if not soldiers?"

The question was answered in short order, as the shapes materialized out of the gloom.

"It's a woman and three children!" Oliver commented with great surprise, gaping at the strange sight, the four of them trying to huddle together within the blanket the woman had wrapped about them all.

Jeremy waited for their approach. "Excuse me Madame," he said suddenly, startling the woman, who had been so intent on protecting her children from the elements that she hadn't noticed the eight men approach. "Where would you be going in such inclement weather?"

"To my sister's house. I'm hoping I'm right in guessing that I'm not far off now," the woman shouted. "Are you Americans or British?"

"British," Davis replied. "Where have you come from?"

"From Niagara," replied the woman, using the official name for Newark.

"What has possessed you to undertake such a journey in this weather?" asked Jeremy, an uneasiness gnawing at his gut.

"They're burning everything!" The words were blurted out as if they had been held back by a dam that had suddenly burst.

"Who are burning what?" Jeremy asked, not wishing to understand what the woman was suggesting.

"That American popinjay, that General McClure," she replied bitterly. "He's in charge and he has a few soldiers helping him, but mostly it's that traitor Willcocks and his rabble! They mean to set the entire town ablaze!"

Jeremy looked around at each of his companions and then back at the woman. "When did this start?"

"This morning they came about and started telling us to leave, but three hours ago at the most. They said they were under orders to burn the town and we had to get out as soon as possible."

"And when did the burning begin?" Oliver asked, scarcely believing his ears.

"Shortly afterward," the woman replied over the complaints from her children of hunger and cold. "I really must move along," she said. "It will take me probably another half-hour to reach my sister's and I don't know if my children will last much longer."

Jeremy said nothing. There was no coherent reply to news such as this. He and the others quietly moved out of the way and let the small, pitiful group pass. As they disappeared into the gloom of the snow storm, they just stood and watched for some time, trying to accept and digest what the woman had told them.

"Let's go," Jeremy said suddenly, with a force and determination that caught the others unawares.

Without another word, they lit out in the direction of Newark, anger with the Americans and their thugs and genuine fear for the residents adding resolve to their progress, despite the fact that the snow now reached almost to mid-calf.

As they proceeded, they met increasingly more refugees from the beleaguered town. Another woman passed towing a large tea tray, upon which sat a young girl, no shoes upon her feet, crying and shivering and screaming that her toes were frozen.

An entire family, including a grandmother, parents and six children sat under a tree in the snow, apparently too tired to continue, awaiting death. Jeremy and his companions scolded them and gave them some jerky to chew on and their own blankets to help keep them warm. Then they sent them once again on their way, in the hopes that they would continue until they found shelter.

Many others passed quietly by in the snow, grey shadows of misery and hopelessness. Plodding along in various modes and levels of dress, young and old, poor and wealthy, all united in the common despair of their situation. They when they passed, they moved silently into the night, their tracks filling with the drifting snow before they even were out of sight, leaving no sound and no evidence that they had passed. In the coming months, Jeremy would learn that most of these people would make their ways in these conditions the entire eleven miles from their former homes to Shipman's corners. A few would not.

Chapter Thirty-One

At their increased pace, the men realized they were tiring much more rapidly but they could not allow themselves to slow themselves down. Before long, they started off along a less travelled trail to save time and the parade of humanity slowed almost to a stop. On they pushed, for how long, none knew, for time seemed to have flowed together into one long eternity. They had no idea what it was they could do that might make a difference, for the town had been emptying itself out all the while, but the 'what' would answer itself when they reached there.

Finally they reached a reached a lone house well away from the main avenues of travel. As they approached, it was apparent that there was some illumination inside, leading them to think that people were awake.

"Hello, the house!" Jeremy shouted as he approached, not wishing to be shot by some frightened or irate citizen taken by the surprise of eight men suddenly appearing at his house, especially since some were Indians and few could tell the difference between Indian nations. He walked carefully up to the door and knocked forcefully. There was no reply.

Josef came around the corner. "The light just went out," he reported. "They must have doused their lantern when you knocked.

"We saw the light on," Jeremy shouted through the heavy wooden door. "Please let us in. We've come from Shipman's Corners."

The door opened just a crack. "From Shipman's, you say," a man's voice asked, followed closely by the tip of a musket barrel, which was aimed roughly at Jeremy's throat. "How do I know you're not some of Willcocks' men?"

Jeremy looked around at his companions and then back at the door. He was at a loss to prove his loyalties. Then it struck him.

Taking Josef's sleeve, he pulled the Indian up in front of the crack in the door. "If you'll look out, you'll see my friend, Josef," he explained patiently. "If you know your Indians, you'll recognize him as a Caughnawaga from Montreal. Now I want you to think and then to ask yourself if you've ever seen a Caughnawaga, or any Indian for that matter, ever traveling with any of Willcocks' lot."

There was silence as the door opened just a tiny bit wider, ostensibly to study Josef. Then the door closed. The men outside could vaguely hear several voices from inside as the inhabitants apparently discussed their situation.

After several minutes of waiting in the cold and snow, the door swung open. Now three muskets were facing them from inside, two held by men and third by a woman.

"Come on in and move along the right wall until I can get a better look at you," the man who initially opened the door ordered, as someone lit a lamp, creating some welcome level of illumination inside. "Please move slowly as we're all very nervous. And please lean your muskets against the wall inside the door as you enter."

Jeremy and his company gladly obeyed the man's orders, moving slowly into the relative warmth and greatly increased dryness of the clapboard house. As they entered, they saw that the house was quite full of people, who stood or sat and stared as the new arrivals came in. They were of all ages and both sexes, likely several families, refugees who had sought the safety and comfort of this house away from the main road.

The man studied his new visitors intently and seemed to take a special interest in Jeremy himself. Then a sudden light of recognition flared in his eyes and he suddenly lowered his musket, at the same time indicating to the others to follow suit.

"If I'm not mistaken, I do believe it to be Jeremy van Hijser, Catherine," he said, turning to the woman with one of the other weapons. As he did so, the lantern's glow partially illuminated his face.

"John Dinston?" Jeremy asked. "I haven't seen you in some four years, ever since you moved away from Beaverdams."

He looked appreciatively about the room, noticing the furnishings were of reasonable, quality, if not extravagantly expensive. "It would appear that you've done well for yourself."

The man he had addressed as John smiled tiredly. "I can't take the credit for that," he said. "This was my cousin's house. He did quite well for himself and was becoming an important man in Newark when he died suddenly of some lung ailment…possibly the consumption. That's why I had to leave my farm in Beaverdams and come down here. I've taken over his business and done my best to keep it going."

"And has done a fine job of it," another female voice chimed in. An attractive woman in her mid-twenties stepped up beside John.

"Well, thank you, Martha," John said with a smile. To Jeremy he explained, "Not that it will matter much now. It looks as though there may not be a business or anyone to do business with when this is over." He looked off into the distance, hopelessness etched in his face. "But where are my manners? This is Martha Jacobs, my late cousin's widow. She's been a great help with the bookkeeping aspects of the business, an area where I've always been hopelessly ignorant. She also taught me the business and introduced me to all those who mattered commercially."

"I'm pleased to meet you," Jeremy said sincerely, doffing his hat and showering everyone in range with snow. "I'm terribly sorry," he added sheepishly as they each tried, in his or her way, to discreetly brush off the flakes. "Now, John, can you explain to me exactly what has been happening in this town? And why the U.S. Army would decide to burn innocent civilians from their homes?"

"I'm not at all sure that the U.S. Army was in control," John said with a sigh. "Since they've been here, I've gotten to meet some of the officers here in the course of my business. Brigadier-General McClure is not at all a military man. He's a politician who was given his appointment for political reasons, as seems to be the case with so many of their top officers in this war. This is, of course, a fortunate thing for the British, since their singular lack of leadership has given our side some rather miraculous victories as I understand it." He snickered at his understated analysis of the American military and their ability.

"But his actions this past day have been egged on mostly by Lieutenant-Colonel Joseph Willcocks…"

"Lieutenant-Colonel?" asked Jeremy, interrupting John's narrative. "Do you mean to tell me that blackguard has finally received the commission he has long been chasing? And he goes directly to Lieutenant-Colonel at that." He stood looking at his host in astonishment, mouth agape.

"I'm afraid so," replied John, sadly shaking his head. "The man's been granted the legitimacy he's craved for as long as he's switched sides. It's the title he was willing to sell his soul for. And likely did if I may hazard an opinion"

"But Willcocks has long been pushing the various commanders here to allow him to burn the town should the British assault reach Newark. His reasoning has always been that the homes could provide shelter for British troops when they reclaim the town and use it as a base from which to attack Fort Niagara across the river."

"You're sure it was him?" Jeremy asked.

"Oh, yes, assuredly. I was in town myself when McClure and Willcocks rode into town. The burning began shortly thereafter and they were accosted by Dr. Cyrenius Chapin, who was still here with about fifty or so men, some of the few irregulars still around. I think you've met him, haven't you?"

Jeremy looked over at Josef and then nodded in his direction. "I surely did, as did my friend Josef here. The Battle of Beaverdams might have been lost to us had Boerstler left Chapin and his men in the van during their attack. When he wanted the glory for himself, he sent Chapin to the rear and fouled up the attack."

"Yes. The American military commanders here have certainly had a penchant for lording their supposed superiority over the irregulars, to their own loss. Not that the British officers are much better in that respect. But, as I was telling you, besides the characters I mentioned, the others have long left, and McClure only has a handful of real soldiers left to him."

"When I chanced by on my way out of town, Chapin had begun to berate the two for their unconscionable act and it was mostly Willcocks who did the arguing, although the General did pull out a document which purportedly shows that this action was recommended all along."

"Aye," said another woman, from near the back of the room. "And after the argument, that beast Willcocks rode about cursing and threatening those of us who he passed along the way. That he could so callously treat his own neighbours in such a manner." The woman began to weep and there was a momentary silence in the room as someone tried to console her.

"I've seen many of the townspeople on the road," Jeremy said sadly. "It was a pitiful sight to behold, in particular the children. If I have any say in it, Willcocks will pay."

John smiled sadly. "I hope that's true, but I'm sure he'll find some way to escape retribution. He has to this day."

"Well, I appreciate your information and the hospitality of your home and fire," Jeremy said. "But we'd best be off and see what might yet be done."

"I'm not sure that anything can," replied Martha glumly. "These people have been here almost two hours already and the town was in flames then. But perhaps you can catch up with that demon, Willcocks. And, if you find him, put an extra ball into him for me," she said bitterly, her eyes blazing.

"If I can, I certainly will," Jeremy said, pushing his tri-corn hat back down onto his head. "In the meantime, I wish you all good luck."

"And God's speed to you, sir," Martha said, looking long and hard into Jeremy's eyes.

"Thank you," Jeremy answered lamely, inexplicably feeling like a school boy in this attractive widow's presence. He stood frozen in place looking into the woman's fiery eyes and thinking he might like to return here when his mission ended.

He shook off the thought, however, although he was not entirely certain as to why. Perhaps war had made me so callous as not to completely care, he thought, although he knew that could not be more than a small part. Perhaps it was guilt, since it was so short a time since Elizabeth had been taken from him. But then, perhaps the main reason was that he had already had two great, if short-lived loves in his life, and both had been taken so cruelly from him. Although he knew the thought was ridiculous, perhaps he would be condemning any other woman who became involved with him.

But then just as suddenly his reverie ended, and Jeremy and his team reluctantly gathered up their weapons and headed back into the cold. It was likely too late by now to do anything at all for the people of Newark. They had seen the refugees along the road from that town for hours already. But they had to try to stop what they could of this travesty upon the poor citizens of that town, especially now that they knew Joseph Willcocks was behind it.

★ ★ ★

Back on the trail once again, they now almost jogged toward town, a greater distance than they had believed, although perhaps it was just the fatigue that made it seem so. A futile hope coursed through them that they might somehow be able to save at least a part of the Newark from the flames. Yet each man knew that it was highly unlikely for, though they could not yet see Newark, they could make out the glow of the flames in the sky above where the town would be. The Volunteers numbered easily enough men to carry out the deed in several hours and the wooden homes would burn like matchsticks once lit.

★ ★ ★

When finally they did reach Newark, they stopped cold in their tracks. Volunteers rode about the street, still throwing flaming torches into the already burning buildings, seemingly determined not to allow a single stick to remain unburned. They seemed oblivious to the suffering of the townspeople who were still fleeing or seeking refuge from the holocaust, these unfortunates the former neighbours of many of the arsonists.

And in the midst of it all, Jeremy spied the man who had brought so much misery to his life, either in person or through the actions of his subordinates. Willcocks sat astride his horse, shouting orders to his men, kicking wildly at the odd townsman who happened yet to be near at hand. He was easily distinguishable by his fine clothes and the symbol of the Canadian Volunteers upon his hat: a green band with a white ribbon cockade which shone in the orange glow of the inferno he had set loose upon this town. His face was lit up in demonic splendour by the same flames, reinforcing the image that Jeremy had long ascribed to the man.

Jeremy's anger surmounted any sense of survival or plan of action. With a shout of "Willcocks!" he ran into the town directly at the object of his rage.

The other seven rushed after him but did not attempt to stop him. Each unslung his musket from his shoulder as they followed him forward, felling two of Willcocks' men who happened to notice their wild approach and seemed intent upon interfering.

They could tell that Willcocks had finally noticed their fevered approach, and could see him still shouting orders as they approached, although it was impossible at this distance and under these conditions to hear what he was saying. But the intent soon became obvious as each of the Volunteers visible to them dropped what he was doing and followed their leader away toward the fort.

Jeremy's party fired several volleys after the rapidly disappearing Volunteers, to no discernable effect. The smoke and flames and the men's own anger were all interfering with their ability to fell a target. Finally, they slowed to a walk in the midst of the ruins of the once fine town that was once the capital of Upper Canada.

"It would seem that the bullies had no stomach for a fight against men who would stand against them," Davis remarked disgustedly.

"Perhaps," Jeremy remarked thoughtfully. "But maybe they thought that we merely the vanguard of the larger British force it seems they were expecting."

Josef chuckled in a somewhat ironic manner. "It's probably best that they thought so," he said. "Else this group of eight fools might be lying dead in this street in short order. As good as some of us may think we are, there were too many of them for the few of us to defeat."

The others looked at Josef for a moment. Two of his Indian companions stood nodding their heads ever so slightly, the other two looked slightly surprised and Oliver and Davis seemed a bit peeved at the remark.

Jeremy, on the other hand, just studied his Caughnawaga friend for a moment and then burst into laughter, with the others quickly following suit. "No words were truer spoken than those," he uttered through the sudden release of tension.

"My God!" exclaimed Oliver suddenly looking about them at the devastation. He said nothing else, but just stood slack-jawed, staring at the burning ruins.

The laughter of the others died as they too stopped and came to a true realization of their surroundings. There was nothing but flame, smoke and ash wherever one looked. Nothing seemed to have escaped involvement and the roadway was littered with personal items and pieces of furniture that people had tried to save from their burning homes before they were chased off. The eight men looked around at each other in despair and disbelief. None had ever seen destruction on a scale such as this.

Now that the Volunteers had ridden off, a pair of citizens wandered aimlessly about the glowing, smoky street like ghosts seeking the doorway out of Hell. The wraiths coughed and wailed and seemed to pay scant attention to the newcomers in town, and eventually just seemed to dissolve from sight, as buildings collapsed in great showers of sparks and cinders.

Near the end of the street, Davis spied a man lying on the ground, trying desperately to hold onto something as another who was obviously a Volunteer tugged at the item. Then he noticed yet another walk up, pointing a pistol at the prostrate figure. There was no doubt of his intent to murder the fellow.

Chapter Thirty-Two

Although he could not completely have explained why, anger flared rapidly in Davis once more and he drew back the lock of his Baker Rifle and brought it to his shoulder. While resting his right cheek on the piece designed for that purpose, he rapidly and automatically computed the distance, wind and all the other elements that could affect the trajectory of the load. He began to squeeze slowly on the trigger, all the while blinking through inexplicable tears in an attempt to overcome the burning in his eyes.

When it reached the point of no return, the hammer was released, flint and frizzen met, the powder in the pan ignited. The resultant spark in the pan spread in less than the bat of an eye through the hole into the gun, and a much larger secondary explosion took place inside the gun itself. The Baker's .625 calibre ball flew from the muzzle, followed quickly by the flaming patch that had held the load together.

Because of the distance involved, Davis had a split second to lower his gun, just a fraction of an inch, to watch for the result of his shot. It was with great satisfaction that he saw his intended victim drop his pistol and clasp his chest with both hands. By the time Davis lowered his rifle completely in order that he might reload, the man had already fallen to the ground and his cohort had scampered away in fear.

"My God!" said Josef in awe.

"What a shot!" joined in Oliver.

"The problem with such long-range shooting is that one doesn't have the satisfaction of seeing the expressions on the faces of scum of his like," Davis grumbled. "Not that one could see much in this haze anyways."

The others said nothing to this, and started to walk forward once again, now looking carefully about themselves as they walked, alert to any possible ambush. As they passed, more people slowly emerged from their places of hiding, such as they were, for barns, houses, shops and stables all seemed to be involved or already smouldering heaps of cinders and ash. But a few emerged from a kiln, another from an outhouse, and several more from a dense copse of cedars which kept off some of the snow and wind.

An elderly man, blackened by soot, wild-eyed, his hair singed at odd lengths stared at the eight men and then approached Jeremy. "Is the British Army right behind?" he asked hopefully.

Jeremy looked the man in the eye. "I'm sure they are, sir. They've been not far behind all the while we were traveling here."

The man returned to the other townspeople that had gathered and evidently told them what Jeremy had said. Some began smiling tentatively, as though not entirely certain that the news yet warranted any hope, some of the men clapped each other on the back in celebration and two women started sobbing uncontrollably.

Jeremy could hardly blame any of them for their reactions. Although there was a slight promise of relief, they had lost everything in this one day. Many would not be sure where to turn while others were already planning how to rebuild and still others would be planning their vengeance upon those who they believed were responsible for all of this.

★ ★ ★

As Jeremy was answering the questions of the townspeople to the best of his ability and with as much hope in his voice as he could muster, Josef noticed one of the men who had guarded him at Shipman's Corners.

"That bastard disciple treated me rather unkindly," he said unevenly to no one in specific.

"You told me of no mistreatment," Jeremy replied, barely hearing his friend.

"There was another with us when we were captured. This man enjoyed killing him. It wasn't anything I wished to explain in great detail," the Caughnawaga leader muttered and then took off at a run.

The Volunteer who had been the object of Josef's scrutiny noticed the Indian barrelling toward him. No one could hear if he uttered a sound, but his mouth opened and then closed, and he took off as someone would expect of one who had seen the Devil himself coming for him. He glance desperately and frequently over his shoulder, each time to see the horror of the Josef closing upon him with murder in his eyes.

When he was mere feet away Josef removed a knife from his belt and, while still moving, made a slight hop, at the same instant throwing the razor-edged weapon at his intended target. The flashing steel, highlighted by the flames all around, almost disappeared into the man's thigh, causing him to drop to one knee.

The Parson's man stumbled forward, tried to right himself, stumbled once again, his momentum carrying him on until he seemed almost to throw himself into the blazing wall of the house he was passing. Immediately his shirt caught fire, followed in short order by the rest of his clothes bursting into flame.

Jeremy caught up and took hold of the stricken disciple's hand which protruded from the flames. Giving him a quick tug, he pulled the man free of the fire and flung him on the ground soaked with melted snow. He rolled the screaming man over several times in the water and mud and then stood over him, his face an unreadable mask.

Josef took hold of the hilt of his knife, which was buried deep in the man's thigh and, taking a deep breath, he yanked, freeing the blade. The result was an immediate gush of blood and a scream from the injured volunteer.

"Get up," Josef ordered the disciple in a voice at once soft and commanding.

"I – I can't," wailed the injured man.

"Stand up or die where you lie, dog," Josef ordered, still showing no emotion.

The man, bleeding profusely from his leg and with skin hanging in charred strips from his arms, slowly forced himself to his feet, using a lone-standing fence post for support. He weaved in place, weak from loss of blood and the heavy burns to his body.

Josef gave him his musket, which he had not yet fired. "Take this and shoot me."

The disciple looked at the musket in his hand and then up at the expressionless face of his adversary. "Why?"

"Just do it!" Josef snapped.

The disciple stared down at the gun again and then a smile crossed his face, his brain now no longer able to recognize the pain from his injuries. He pulled back the hammer and started to put the musket to his shoulder.

"I don't why you want this, but it's how we should deal with all Indian dogs," he spit through the evil grin he sported.

★ ★ ★

Oliver had slowly walked toward the confrontation between Josef and the man he seemed to hate so. He now stared with morbid fascination as the scene played out before him. He knew the Caughnawaga did not wish to die but he had seen Josef hand the man his musket. He could not help but wonder just what it was he was playing at.

Then, out of the corner of his eye, he saw another man moving stealthily toward the pair from directly behind Josef. Oliver called out to Josef to warn him but he could not be heard over all the noises of burning and collapsing buildings.

Fortunately for Josef, Jeremy had also noticed and, when the newcomer pulled up a musket of his own, he sprang into action. He quickly raised his own gun and fired but he had not taken the time to aim and the shot went off into a pile of furniture. Initially he was stymied, knowing that there was little he could do now that his gun was empty.

The shot had not been completely wasted, however, for the newcomer was momentarily distracted by the rifle report and the splintering of a chair nearby. He wasted just enough time looking about to find the source for someone to act.

And Oliver would be the one to do so. By then he had recovered from his momentary paralysis and galvanized into action without a coherent thought. He ran swiftly across the open space toward the man that Josef still not know was there. All that was between them now was someone's dinner table but he did not even slow down. With a hop he touched on the top of the table with one foot and then launched himself toward the as yet unsuspecting target.

Oliver crashed into the man at about waist height just as the man had noticed the motion out of his peripheral vision and had begun to turn to face him. The musket discharged harmlessly into the air as both men landed heavily against a roll top desk. They struggled momentarily on the ground, but Oliver clearly had the advantage since the Volunteer had broken his shoulder upon impact with the desk.

It was through the haze of rage and adrenaline that he was rapidly choking the life out of the man below him. Almost as though detached from him, he looked at his forearm across his windpipe and bore down with all his weight. In the moment of realization, he seemed terrified of himself and eased off.

The Volunteer, rolled out from under, pulled himself to his feet and hobbled away as quickly as he could, seeing perhaps his only chance to survive.

Oliver was quite aware that his quarry had fled but he felt unsure of what he should do about it. His anger had seemingly frightened him. He had never thought of himself as someone who could kill another with his bare hands and the ease with which it had almost happened was confusing him. It was one thing to shoot a man in battle, but quite another to watch a man's face while you slowly squeezed the life force from his body.

Remembering why he was here, he looked up toward where Josef had been dealing with his own enemy. He focussed just in time to see Josef's already gory knife bury itself in the disciple's throat, almost immediately changing the man's expression from a mocking sneer to terror as he tried to remove it.

While he was watching, Tomas had reached his side. As Oliver noticed he was no longer alone, Tomas offered the explanation that answered the questions that were screaming in the young man's head without Oliver asking him.

"The sixth member of our team was his sister's son."

★ ★ ★

Jeremy wandered through the obstacle course that was the downtown as if in a dream or, more appropriately, a nightmare. He had known many of these people for he had come here often in better times for supplies. This tragedy, on this scale, seemed all but impossible to him.

All about, the houses and shops with which he had dealings in the past now burned ferociously if they had not already settled into heaps of cinders. The court house and the stables, McCarthy's store, the soap factory...all gone.

As he walked along in this daze, he was barely aware that the heat of the fires that raged all about was singeing his skin. He had never before seen destruction on this scale.

He stopped dead in his tracks as one of the larger houses suddenly and quite spectacularly surrendered to the flames. With a mighty groan the building collapsed inwardly, releasing a storm of flames and a sparks that would have been dangerous to neighbouring buildings had there yet been any left that were not already involved.

Davis approached Jeremy, careful to come at him from the side lest he startle him and be shot for his troubles. For the longest time, he merely stood quietly beside the trapper, taking it all in silently.

"Quite unbelievable isn't it?" he said finally for want of anything else to say.

Jeremy did not reply. He just stared deeply into the white flames that burned in the heart of the rapidly disappearing house. A single tear rolled down his right cheek, drying in the reflected heat before the drop reached his collar.

"Did you know the people who lived there?" Davis asked. He was becoming concerned and wished to draw Jeremy out of the state into which he had sunk.

Jeremy nodded. "The burning of this house means more than the loss of a home for someone," he said in a voice so low that Davis almost missed it. "This house held the majority of the books that belonged to the subscription library, invaluable books that contained a wealth of knowledge beyond anything in the colony."

"Have you ever seen these books?"

"Yes. I wasn't allowed to borrow them for I hadn't the money to pay into the subscription, but I was allowed to read or study items I wished to know so long as I did so on the premises." He turned and looked sadly at Davis. "I had spent whole days here before the war trying to learn things about this world and its ways and the thoughts of learned men."

Davis looked at the former library in wonder. "Do you think the books were still there?"

"I don't know. I fear they were, but I truly don't know," Jeremy replied sadly, coughing to clear the smoke from his throat. "Let's hope that the people who lived here managed to get them to safety, that they'd been forewarned."

"How many books were there?"

"I'm not sure. New ones were purchased every year by the subscription committee and some were kept at other houses. In addition, I'd been taken to understand that many had already been stolen or lost since the Americans took the town. I couldn't even hazard a guess as to how many there were."

Davis asked no more questions. He was not well-read man. In fact, he could read only enough to understand simple instructions. Nonetheless he looked books as something special, a reverence bordering upon mysticism, and he believed he could well understand Jeremy's feelings of loss at the thought of losing a large number.

The eight men scouted around looking for yet more Volunteers who might be a threat to them or to the few remaining townspeople when Jeremy heard a cry coming from behind him. "The troops have been seen approaching the town!" The shouted announcement was joined in short order with a general cacophony of cheers and complaints that they had not arrived sooner to save the town.

When Colonel Murray did arrive, he seemed to personally ignore the local citizenry as he brushed straight forward toward Jeremy and his small band, leaving the problem of civilians to several officers of lower rank. As he walked along he could not avoid surveying the damage of the visited upon the former capital, however, and it was obvious to anyone watching his face that he was not nearly as callous as he seemed. Emotion at the senseless destruction showed in his eyes and at the corners of his mouth, but stoicism was the British way and Murray followed tradition to a fine point.

He opened his mouth to speak, but in the place of his voice, a tremendous explosion issued from the fort behind Jeremy and just beyond the town proper. The night momentarily lit up as bright as daylight, blotting out what had formerly seemed like a glare from the fires burning all around. Then that initial blast was followed by several more of the same, if of varying intensities, causing soldier and civilian alike to shield their faces. Then the sound and the light vanished as quickly as they had arrived.

"The magazines," Murray said matter-of-factly to no one in particular. "They must have been waiting to see if we truly were coming before the final evacuation."

The dark grey cloud from the explosions washed over them and mixed with the haze of the fires and the snow, which yet fell steadily, if now less dramatically since the wind had died to a degree in. Such visibility as there had been in this town that had been Newark was now reduced even more. It was relieved only by the occasional flare of brilliance as yet another section of building collapsed into the white-hot coals, providing them a new source of combustible fuel removed the claustrophobic oppression of the smoke.

A number of Murray's men ran for the river to attempt to stop the American evacuation, hoping to exact some measure of revenge. But they were already clear of the landing and the last of their boats could be seen being pulled up on the beach beneath Fort Niagara almost directly across. Several of the British soldiers filtered back to report.

One Lieutenant in stopped directly in front of the General as the smoke, slow to dissipate, swirled about the two men. "Begging you pardon, General," the man said, saluting sharply. "There's something I think you should see."

The General and several of his officers wordlessly followed the Lieutenant to the edge of town and beyond to the fortifications.

"The guns have been spiked, as one might expect," their guide explained, sweeping his hand across to indicate the various emplacements.

The General sighed. "I suppose you're right. That is to be expected, but it's a deuced nuisance all the same," he grumbled. "When the appropriate manpower moves up, have the guns drilled and the touchholes re-bored. We just may need them eventually. But surely this isn't what you wished me to see Lieutenant?"

Chapter Thirty-Three

B efore the Lieutenant could reply, the answer became obvious.
"I'd heard their excuse for burning the town was to deny
the army billets," Jeremy commented sarcastically as the General
looked with disgust upon the thing that had been so troubling the junior
officer within the walls and ramparts of Fort George.

There was no reply from the General. There was no need for any, as
they all stood now looking at the new barracks the Americans had built
since they took control of the fort. Also still standing near the almost
new structures was a number of new canvas tents to handle the overflow
when the fort was at full strength. Not a flame had kissed these walls nor
any shingle knocked loose nor singed canvas erected for the U.S. Army
in any attempt to destroy the quarters in the course of the Americans'
retreat.

"In addition, Sir, there are munitions and additional new tents still
in the stores, along with most standard supplies. Well, sir, at least we can
provision and shelter the citizens."

"The bastards!" Murray almost spit as he said it, his rage palpable to
the men about him.

The crowd about them grew as other soldiers and some civilians
ventured in to stare across the water at the enemy fort on the other side of
the Niagara River. It was the only presently visible piece of U.S. property
they could see under the conditions, the enemy's standard flying from
their flagpole.

After a moment of stunned silence, someone shouted out with
heartfelt venom, "They must pay!" Others took up the cry and calls for
revenge at those who did this to the town and those who dwelt therein

filled the air. Soon there was no sound at this side of the river but for the sound of voices belonging to women and men, soldiers and civilians, all demanding satisfaction for this travesty.

It was into this din that Captain Merritt strode, heading directly for the General. "General Murray!" he said, saluting. "There seems to be nothing left. A proper count needs to be done, but there must be close to one hundred buildings of all types, including public buildings and two churches, burned to the ground. They even fired the library, which I understand to be one of a kind for this colony. There were over four hundred people living here, sir, and I suspect that we shall need to find billets for those that are left, Sir."

The General turned around and looked at all the eyes that were fixed expectantly upon him. "Very well," he said tiredly. "Set up camp and take stock. Give the people who remain here the tents from the stores and meet me at the Naval Hall. We will plan and prepare to take the fight to the enemy's own territory."

★ ★ ★

While the military concentrated upon logistics and the townspeople upon salvage, rebuilding or relocating, Jeremy and his group quietly melted away. But before they actually left what remained of the town, they helped themselves to new blankets from the stores to replace the ones they had given to the family on the road and extra powder and ammunition.

The General had paid little attention to their ragtag band thus far but there was no way of knowing when he would be alerted to the fact that they were wanted. As tragic as these events had been, there was a distinct peril that remaining in the face of the military might lead to their eventual recognition and arrest. They withdrew to a deserted outbuilding which stood alone approximately a mile from the town.

"Perhaps we should have stayed to help those poor people," Oliver suggested, the guilt evident in his words mirrored in his concerned expression.

"I don't think we'd have been any more help than the army," Jeremy replied, although it was obvious that he did not completely believe his own words. "Make no doubt that if the items we seek are as important as Williamson appeared to consider them to be, we must reach them before they are found by either his brother-in-law or the Americans."

He sat silently staring into the ether for a time and then added, "I wouldn't have thought that civilized men could behave in a manner as dishonourable as have the Americans this day. For the first time in the course of this war, I shudder to think what the consequences might be should the Americans win."

"It appears we'll spend another cold night," grumbled Davis, ignoring the philosophical and political ramifications and concentrating instead upon the more immediate concern of creature comfort.

"Well, I don't know if they'd keep you much warmer under guard if you're recognized," replied Josef. "I say 'you' because, of course, nobody is looking for five Caughnawagas," he added with a grin.

"Never mind the complaints," Jeremy interrupted with fatigued annoyance. "Or the alibis," he added, looking specifically at Josef. "Do you intend to get some much-needed rest or do you wish to carry on with your inane prattle? If the latter, I promise that I shall use the last ounce of my reserves to personally toss you out into the snow."

"And after we rest, what then?" Oliver asked hesitantly, not quite cowed by his cousin's outburst.

"We'll discuss that in the morning," Jeremy responded. "We can see nothing now and we must be able to see to find 'the Old Lady' of which Williamson writes and the target to which she points. Now go to sleep!"

★ ★ ★

It was an overcast morning, with light grey clouds forming a solid but not impenetrable cover. The snow had stopped completely now, leaving the area with knee-deep snow and even deeper drifts. Had the fugitive treasure hunters the time to enjoy the beauty, they would have been struck by the layers of white on heavily laden branches. The ashes from Newark, which had been falling almost uniformly with the snow, was now hidden by the whiteness except in the odd place where drifting had created contrasting patches of grey.

"I'll go back to the Navy Hall and look for this 'Old Lady'," Jeremy told the others in a tone that brooked no argument. "One man will draw less attention than eight."

"But two heads are better than one," broke in Davis, attempting a mischievous tone but truly feeling that one man alone might miss something.

Jeremy seemed to think about that and then nodded slowly, "Of course you're right," he said. Then, barely noticing that Davis was shouldering his weapon in readiness to go, he turned unexpectedly toward Josef. "But I think it would be better if you were the one to come with me. If I'm with an Indian it will draw less of a reminder than if I'm walking about with Colonel Halberson's son."

The two waded back through the snow toward Fort George and mixed quietly with the milling masses, which contained a number of other Caughnawagas who had arrived in support of General Murray's troops. They worked their way to the back of the fort and carefully approached the Navy Hall, fully aware that this might have been the billeting choice of General Murray. If it was, however, they saw no sign of him.

Arriving there unchallenged, they took forty paces east, toward the river, and turned south, looking about for anything that might be considered to be an "Old Lady". More accustomed to the personification of nonhuman things, Josef was first to feel that he may have spotted the object of their search.

"I believe the exact words you read me from the instructions were 'Through the arms of the Old Lady...'?" Josef asked, seeking verification.

"Yes, those were the words," replied Jeremy and then he saw it, too. Approximately fifty yards away in the area cleared about the fort and its environs stood a large old maple tree. Even in its defoliated winter state they could see that it sported no branches but two which curved gracefully upward from a trunk that had been blasted away above where the limbs separated, possibly by some past lightning strike. Looking directly through the centre of the old tree's limbs, all they could see was the Mountain.

"What's there?" asked Josef, not nearly as familiar with the area as his trapper friend, who had grown up and lived in this region all his life.

"Well, there's a road bending toward the top," Jeremy replied thoughtfully. "The area below it is where we fought the final battle against Williamson, in the village," he added, looking at his friend.

Josef nodded quietly. "But what is there that would be referred to as 'the Old Man's Oversight'?"

"I'm not sure, but I do think we'd best consider it while walking," Jeremy responded, nodding his head ever so slightly in the direction of a trio of soldiers who seemed to have taken notice of them.

"Perhaps you're right," Josef said, at the same time pointing a finger across the field the way they had come, as if he had spotted something of interest.

The two men started resolutely back toward their shelter of the previous night. Just after entering the woods, Jeremy pretended to drop something so that he could look back under his arm. He noted with satisfaction that the three soldiers they had spotted had seemingly lost interest, no doubt coming to the conclusion that he and Josef were of no interest to them. At least the military were now the only ones they should need to contend with, now that the Americans and their traitorous allies had all retreated across the river.

★ ★ ★

Not all of the escaping Americans' allies had taken refuge with them at Fort Niagara after following them across the river. A particular man whose motivation was something less heroic than the fortunes of war had taken his men back across to the British side once night had fallen. There the Parson and his men had deposited the boat they had commandeered in a safe place by the river, out of sight of the patrolling British soldiers.

Now he and two of those men were watching closely and anxiously at what was happening in the area about the fort. And almost the first things that caught their eye were the trapper and his Native friend walking away.

"Are you sure it's safe for us to be so close to them?" one of the disciples asked nervously, his state of mind due more to a fear his leader's reaction to the question than of the perilous situation itself. "Some soldiers could come by here at any time and find us."

"Are you questioning my wisdom?" the Parson demanded, staring with a glare that turned the young man's blood cold. "We've no room here for cowards, and we treat them exactly as the military do. Besides, you know I have God's protection in all things."

"Yes sir, I know," muttered the disciple, eyes downcast with shame and fear for having questioned who he believed to be a holy man.

"There's no real danger, at any rate," the other disciple broke in, apparently attempting to curry favour after witnessing the treatment of his fellow. "We can push off this boat and row away at a moment's notice if necessary."

The Parson glared at this second disciple. "I have no more love for bootlicks than I do for cowards," he growled. "Now go follow those two men. Watch what they do and see where they go. When they seem to have found what they're looking for, probably by digging or something, come back and tell us. We'll be pulled ashore at that small landing up the river that I pointed out on the way down here. Do you understand?"

The disciple nodded and headed off in the direction that they had watched the trapper and Indian take only moments before.

"Don't get too close but don't lose them," the Parson called after him. "And remember you're on God's mission. Don't let me and Him down." The Parson looked skyward as he said "Him" to establish the authority of his orders.

The disciple had frozen in his tracks and looked back when the Parson started speaking again. Now, with the fear of God properly put to him, he swallowed hard and then nodded soberly. In a moment, he was gone from view.

"Let's get this boat off and make our way to the other site before we're spotted," the Parson ordered his remaining men. "I don't particularly wish to get shot while standing here practically out in the open."

"But, I though you said…" It was the same disciple who had just moments before received a dressing down for questioning the wisdom of their presence here.

"I know what I said!" snapped the Parson, wheeling menacingly on the young man. "God gives his commands as the situation dictates." He pointed his gun at the unfortunate sinner. "If you're to continue questing His Word, I'll just send you to meet Him now and you can discuss it with Him in person."

Realizing that it was safest to say nothing further, the disciples grunted heartily and, with a mighty shove, slid the heavy boat into the Niagara River's current with the Parson already seated, that he might not get wet. Then, with a mighty collective heave on the oars, they pulled out slowly upstream and against the flow.

★ ★ ★

Slightly ahead of his trapper friend, Josef stopped with no warning. As his bemused partner watched, he then stepped backward several paces, exactly retracing his steps. Putting his finger to his lips to forestall the question he saw forming on Jeremy's lips, he pointed to a place between two small cedars. Taking as large a step as he could, as close to the trees a possible, he almost immediately disappeared from obvious view. As Jeremy followed his lead, he was tempted to ask the reason for these measures, but again Josef put a finger to his lips.

Several heartbeats later, a short bearded man wearing rough homespun clothing came trotting down the same path they had been following, his head down as he apparently followed the tracks in the snow.

As the man came to a stop just past where the two men hid, Josef stepped up directly behind him. Intent upon the footprints he was following and not immediately understanding the likely explanation for their sudden discontinuance, the man did not notice anyone approaching. There was no sound in the snow-dampened wilderness until, without warning, he was startled by a voice that came from directly behind him.

"Have you lost something, sir?" The sound was as a cannon report in the crisp stillness of the morning air.

The man spun about at the sound of Josef's voice. At that precise moment, the Caughnawaga's fist flew directly at his head, connecting solidly with his chin. The force of the contact snapped his head back and he crumpled at the feet of the two men he had been stalking.

"Who do you think he might be?" Jeremy asked, looking at the man sprawled out on the ground. "One of theirs or one of ours?"

"I've seen him before and not so long ago at that," replied Josef slowly. "This man was another of the guards on the tent that Oliver and I were being held in, back at Shipman's Corners, in the Parson's camp."

When the Parson's disciple and Canadian Volunteer came to, he shook his head and sputtered because of the snow in his face. He looked around, dazed, and then spotted the two men squatting about ten feet from where he lay.

"I must give credit where it's due," Jeremy told him while pointing his musket at directly in his face. "You boys who ride with the Parson are either unbelievably brave or unbelievably stupid. I'm not entirely sure which it is, although I suppose stupidity in large enough quantities could surely make a man seem brave."

The Volunteer just lay on the ground, glaring in defiance.

"Why are you following us?" Jeremy demanded. "For that matter, why have you remained on this side of the river when your side in the war has scampered in so cowardly a manner across to the other side? Speak up and we'll think about setting you free."

There was still no reply so Jeremy let out a deep sigh and looked at Josef. He had not truly expected for one of the Parson's young men to so easily divulge information. "Do you think he was the only one following?"

Josef shrugged. "The only one I noticed." He looked back along the way they had come. "Maybe I'll go and have a look though." With that, the Indian was gone, leaving no trace but for light footprints in the snow.

Jeremy looked at his prisoner again, noticing that a healthy bruise was forming along his jaw line. "I suggest you speak to me, boy. If you do not, I shall be forced to turn you over to the Indian when we get back to camp." He could see doubt forming in the prisoner's eyes. "And, I must warn you, the Indian has four more friends at our little base to help him. I hesitate to tell you what they did to the last man they questioned. Let me just say that he couldn't ever go back home afterwards."

Chapter Thirty-Four

The Parson's disciple swallowed hard and tried to put on a brave face but failed horribly in that endeavour. "The Parson told us all that what we do is for the greater glory of God and that He rewards martyrs in Heaven," he said shakily.

"Perhaps," replied Jeremy with a sigh. "And I must admit I rather admire your courage. I just hope that the Lord can still look upon you when you arrive in Heaven. That is, if you're so certain that's where you'll be going when you die."

It was apparent by the expression that formed on the young man's face that it had never occurred to him to question where he would be going upon his death, so Jeremy decided to play upon his doubts.

"I don't know precisely what you've been taught but what I saw in Newark doesn't look like the work of angels. It seems to me that committing such evils against innocent civilians is hardly a saintly action." He gave pause to allow his words to sink in. "Besides, if I recall my Bible lessons, it seems that fire is the tool of Devil, am I not correct?"

"B-but...the Parson told us..." the prisoner sputtered.

"Well, I'm happy to see that your faith is unshakable," Jeremy said with another exaggerated sigh. "I'm sure your faith will put you in good stead when our Indians deal with you."

The prisoner sat silently in the snow, his eyes darting from Jeremy to the space in the trees through which Josef had vanished earlier. Jeremy could see the young man was visibly trembling and he had grown quite pale. He decided it would be best not to press the fellow further and allow him to stew in his own mind for the time being.

Almost fifteen minutes later Josef returned at a trot, his breathing barely betraying his obvious exertion. "I followed this fellow's tracks back to the river. There was no sign of anyone else being sent out to follow us since there were only his tracks, but it's obvious a boat was launched a short time ago."

"Where do you think they went?"

"Well, I wondered that myself. I decided that they likely didn't go downstream past the fort, so I went the other way. I eventually smelled smoke down below as I ran along and I spotted the damned fools down below, sitting out in the open as though they were at tea. There are six of them at the river by a boat and a small fire. They seem to be awaiting something. My guess is that they're waiting for this fellow to return and tell them what he discovers."

"We'd best hurry along, then," replied Jeremy as Josef helped him raise the prisoner to his feet. "We'll have to move everyone out before those men decide this one's not coming back. But we'll need to work out a way to cover our tracks, because our passage is quite obvious in this fresh snow."

"I think I can remember a few tricks," Josef said with a smile.

"That's good, because I promised this lad you and your Indians friends would show him a few to help loosen his tongue," Jeremy said straight-faced, winking so that the prisoner could not see.

Josef nodded. "Well, bring him along then. When we've found someplace where nobody's screams can be heard, I'll ask him your questions again for you."

★ ★ ★

The captive looked back and forth from the Indian to the white man, searching their faces to determine if they were serious. Beads of sweat broke out on his forehead and face and he began to squirm nervously. His fevered looks were returned with unreadable expressions.

"I was told to follow you and find out where you're going so that you'll lead us to Brother Williamson's treasure and then we're going to kill the lot of you!" the disciple blurted out suddenly, all the words spilling out in one breathless sentence. "Please don't let your savage torture me," he pleaded desperately, now looking as though he might collapse from pure fright.

Josef smiled. "Very well, son, I won't let him near you." He began to chuckle softly, joined in almost immediately by Jeremy. "But you needn't worry. He doesn't do much torturing himself these days. He prefers that my friends and I have some of the pleasure."

"I was talking to the white man," the Volunteer offered, hesitant and unsure of what was happening, with yet a measure of defiance at the same time. Why was the Indian addressing him in this manner when he had so obviously been talking to the white man? "Perhaps you didn't understand."

Josef locked the young man's eyes in a steely glare, his humour fading rapidly. "I understand only too well," he snapped. "And I will remember what you said if I am to have further dealings with you."

The young disciple looked from Josef to Jeremy and back, the puzzlement on his face betraying his complete lack of understanding of the Caughnawaga's sudden change in demeanour.

"What do you think we should do with him?" Josef asked softly, after they had both removed themselves several yards from the Parson's Volunteer. "I don't think it would be in our best interest merely to set him free, do you?"

Jeremy stood for a moment in quiet thought and then finally held up one finger, a signal to follow his lead. Still without a word he nodded his head toward the prisoner and they walked back to the young man who waited anxiously, apparently straining to overhear their discussion.

"You're damned lucky that this man didn't kill you for your remark," Jeremy growled disgustedly. "Personally, I wouldn't have stopped him." He paused for effect, pacing from one side of the prisoner to the other. "However, a bargain is to be kept as such, and I said we'd think about letting you go if you told us what we wanted to know. We've talked it over and decided that we don't need a troublesome prisoner to take care of. And luckily for you, neither of us is as morally free as your Parson to take a human life."

The Volunteer disciple, now emboldened, met Jeremy's glare head on if with a trace of hesitation. He looked as though he might speak but, in the end, wisely chose to give no response. He was a simple man and as such, believed in honour between men. But the premier thing that occupied his mind was that he was to be freed. He would not die in this snow-covered field as he had feared and expected.

"We intend to leave you here now," Jeremy continued, tying up the young man's legs with strong but thin rawhide thong he carried for repair purposes in his kit.

"Do you mean to leave me here alone in the cold?" the prisoner asked with a hint of panic in his voice. "I'll freeze to death here!"

"In the time it takes for you to reach this knife and cut your bonds," Jeremy explained, showing the young man his own knife and then sticking it into a tree twenty paces away, "we will be far gone from this place. I suggest you return home and thank God and Josef here that you were not to be one of His martyrs of which you speak so longingly."

His explanation complete, he pushed the prisoner down into the snow and the pair trotted off through the forest. Not wishing to give the man a sense of where they were headed lest their plan fail, they set off at a tangent to the direction of the previous night's shelter. They continued on in their false direction until they were well out of their prisoner's sight.

★ ★ ★

Jeremy and Josef sat upon their heels at the base of the steep river bank. They were surprisingly well hidden considering the near-total lack of foliage. However, what bushes were there had been coated with the frozen splash of river water.

Near their vantage spot, the two men could see half a dozen men waiting noisily about their small boat with almost total abandon, laughing and talking at the top of their lungs. One would think that it never occurred to them that they were in the midst of enemy territory.

The fire that Josef had spotted earlier now blazed brightly, with sparks shooting skyward with every collapse of a piece of firewood and the plume of brownish smoke rose from it was likely visible for miles. The two spectators looked at each other in astonishment, each considering the overwhelming arrogance shown by their foe's lack of any desire to maintain a low profile.

After several minutes of watching this odd behaviour, Josef tapped almost imperceptibly Jeremy on the shoulder and nodded in the direction of a solitary spruce tree.

As he turned, their former prisoner came into view, stumbling on through the snow drifts, obviously exhausted and shouting incoherently at his brethren. The disciples were now all staring at the newcomer, wondering what was happening and making ribald comments at his expense as he floundered in the heavy snow toward them. Then one man stepped forward.

"Shut up, you fools!" the man shouted in a voice that could surely be heard all the way back to Newark. "Let Brother Daniel tell us what he's found."

Brother Daniel staggered the final few steps into the camp, gasping for breath, unable to speak for several minutes. The Parson stood waiting, the necessity of doing so making him seem about ready to explode.

Jeremy and Josef were glad to see that the purposely poor job they had made of tying up the prisoner had worked and the bait has escaped.

Finally, the young man took a deep breath and began his report to an obviously impatient Parson. "Parson, they've headed back south-westward."

"I didn't tell you find out in what direction they were going, you fool," the Parson snapped, his voice even but with an obvious underlying violence. "I sent you to report their destination. If they haven't arrived, what are you doing here?"

Brother Daniel drew back from his leader as if slapped solidly across the face. "They captured me," he replied softly and plaintively.

The Parson put his hands behind his back and began to slowly circle the hapless disciple. "If they captured you, why are you here? Should you not be dead or at least a prisoner?"

"They said I would be a burden to them," Brother Daniel whimpered, frightened now for his life, perhaps more than when he had been a prisoner. "And the man you call van Hijser said he did not feel right about killing me."

The Parson stopped his pacing, deep in thought, weighing that which his disciple had just told him. "Well, from what I know of the man, that's quite likely. Jeremy is a trapper and mostly a loner. I can see that he might not wish to drag along a prisoner," he muttered, more to himself than anyone. "And, also from what I know of the man, he likely couldn't bring himself to kill a bound and unarmed man, for he is weak of spirit and therefore doesn't understand the ways of righteous vengeance."

"He isn't the holy man that you are, Parson," another disciple piped in.

"He's a fool as well as a sinner," the Parson responded. He turned to the others, throwing his arms in the air as if to invoke God Himself, his voice rising with passion. "And what has God commanded that we do with sinners?"

"Kill them!" the disciples shouted, as if as one being.

From their place of concealment, Jeremy looked silently at Josef, who shook his head in disbelief with the display before them. The Parson truly had these young men's minds under the control of his pseudo-righteousness.

The Parson paced about the fire in silence, obviously formulating and discarding various plans. His disciples stood about rooted to their very positions, afraid to move and even more afraid to speak. Finally the pacing stopped and their appeared to be a collective relaxing of postures that coincided with the imminence of a decision, whatever it might be.

"We will break up into two groups," the Parson said, barely loudly enough to be heard by the two hiding men. He seemed to be addressing no one as he spoke, just casting his thoughts and words to the wind, expecting each man to capture their obvious wisdom.

"One team of four will travel by boat to the Village of Queenston and wait there at river's edge for my arrival. I will personally lead the other team of three by land and meet you there." There was a collective groan as they each thought about the work that would be required to continue rowing the heavy wooden boat upstream, now with only four men.

"And where will you be going?" a tall, gangly young man with several days' stubble upon his face ventured to ask.

Without turning to face the questioner, the Parson faced toward Heaven to respond. "It would be best for us if I were to keep that to myself. If any of you were to be captured, it might not go well for my health." His voice was strained, as though the very act of replying pressed the boundaries of his patience with the children he commanded.

The Parson gathered together three of the strongest-looking disciples to accompany him overland. After a closely muttered set of instructions from the Parson, the rest pushed their tiny vessel off into the Niagara River. Then he set off without a glance to see if his disciples were following, in the direction from which Brother Daniel had come.

★ ★ ★

Once the Parson's men had vanished from their sight and into the trees, Jeremy slowly stood up. He stretched his muscles which ached from his sitting so long on his heels. It had been the best position from which to observe, not only from the point of height but also because they could spring to react to changes in the situation had it become necessary to do so. But it tested his body all the same. Only twenty-seven and already an old man, he thought wryly.

Josef watched his friend and began to laugh softly. "It would seem my white friend should be thinking of retiring before I have to start carrying him," he quipped, as if having read Jeremy's mind.

Jeremy thought of several retorts but resigned himself to the truth of Josef's accusation in the end, however much it was offered in jest. "It would seem you're right, if only these animals would allow me to retire," he answered with convincing sadness. "But my balance seems still better than yours!"

Before he could react to the obvious intended meaning of the remark, Josef found himself bowled over and lying in the snow looking up at his friend, who was now laughing as well. He started to rise and threw a handful of snow in Jeremy's face. With surprising speed, he launched himself forward and tackled the unprepared trapper, sending both men sprawling into a large drift, both men laughing like young boys at play, but softly so as not to be heard.

Josef stood up, brushing off the snow. "We had probably best save the child's play for later. We need to head off the Parson and his men before they reach the others."

"That part at least won't be necessary," a voice behind them said quietly.

In reaction, Jeremy eyes cast about wildly for his gun, which yet sat propped up against the icy bushes. Seeing it was out of reach, he pulled his tomahawk from its harness behind his head and took a knife fighter's stance, still searching for the author of the sound.

Josef, in the meantime, had begun to laugh softly, and stood quite relaxed staring off into the trees beyond the brush.

"What is it you find so humorous?" demanded Jeremy, annoyed that the Caughnawaga seemed to notice something that he had not.

"I think it might be you, cousin," suggested Oliver, who materialized from behind a tree with Maurice, the eldest of the Caughnawagas. "If someone were behind you with a gun, like we are, do you realize how ridiculous you would appear? And do?"

Jeremy ignored the ribbing. "What are you doing here? And where are the others?"

"They're right behind. We began to wonder what kind of trouble you'd gotten yourself into. Of course," he added with a grin, "we'd no way of knowing that the two of you were just playing in the snow."

Before Jeremy could reply, Davis and the other three Caughnawagas quietly filed down to the water's edge. "When you took so long in returning, we decided to go looking for you. Maurice here picked up your return trail rather quickly and we finally followed it here. What happened? We saw other footprints that came the other way, and even I can see there were many more here."

"It's a rather long story," replied Jeremy, shouldering his kit and weapons. "I'll explain it on the way. For now, suffice it to say that the Parson and three of his men set out to follow our tracks. If you could follow ours here, it won't be long before he realizes that Josef and I doubled back on his disciple."

"I say we go back another way and wait for them to come back, hopefully well before they realize that the trail leads back to where they started," suggested Josef.

"You're right," replied Jeremy. "If they come all the way back here, the Parson will only become angrier than he always seems to be. Besides, he'll then be following us again, and I don't relish having that demon at my back."

Chapter Thirty-Five

At a trot, or as near as they could come to one in the occasional drifts, the now eight men set off to find a suitable ambush site for the Parson. Maurice, who ran ahead, suddenly stopped and lifted his hand.

"I can hear them," was all the Caughnawaga said.

The others listened and they too could hear the approach of the Parson's men. In fact, it was likely that most of Niagara could hear them, for they were singing a hymn as they walked. The words were changed and the sound was horribly off-key, but it was a hymn none-the-less.

"Are they quite daft?" asked Davis, quite surprised at the noise. "How did they expect to sneak up on you making all that noise?"

It was true. Something not quite right was taking place here. While none doubted that the Parson was quite mad, he was certainly no fool, not even so much a fool as his brother-in-law had been. Why would he allow his disciples to make such noise while supposedly tracking a quarry? To flush that quarry out into the open or perhaps to make them run to tire them out?

Jeremy did not think that was the reason. "Everyone take cover. Maurice, you and Giles take a wide arc to our right. Gilbert and Tomas, go to the left. And keep your eyes open at all times. Watch for a flanking movement. If you detect any, just follow them until a battle breaks out. Or until someone aims to shoot us, of course."

As the four Caughnawagas set off on their flanking errands, the remaining four men took positions at the side of the original tracks that Jeremy and Josef had made. There they awaited the arrival of the singing disciples.

They did not need to wait long, as three men soon came into view.

"The Parson's not with them," Jeremy whispered while looking nervously over his shoulder. "I suspected as much. He's gone round to try to ambush us." To Josef, he added, "I surely hope your bandsmen catch sight of him before he places a ball in my backside."

Josef just grinned but said nothing.

As the three men walked directly in front of them, Jeremy softly said, "Hey!" As the disciples stopped singing, looking about for the sound. "Continue on marching and singing or die where you stand. Do not turn about or a half-dozen musket balls will make short work of your worthless hides."

Josef and the others winced visibly as the three young men started off along their intended path once more, again singing off-key, if a bit more nervously. At a signal from Jeremy, only Josef followed along after them, slightly behind. The others stayed where they were, hoping to spot where the Parson was positioning himself.

And then Josef spotted the man himself leaning casually against a large maple, his musket cradled loosely in his arms. There was a smile on his face and he seemed little worried that he could also see Jeremy, Oliver and Davis following behind.

Josef looked about wildly, sensing that a trap was about to be sprung on their trap. "Get down!" he shouted to the others, secrecy no longer an issue.

The three disciples, not understanding what was happening, also dove down into the snow, much to the Parson's chagrin. Then the world seemingly came apart in a wild and violent explosion of gunfire from the trees about them. There were now at least nine men opening fire upon Jeremy and his companions, since the disciples in the path had now recovered and had begun to shoot wildly even without seeing their targets.

Jeremy lay behind a log watching the muzzle flashes of his enemies' muskets as they went off, waiting for an opening. Two balls thudded solidly into the wood of his shield, but still he watched. Then one of the disciples left himself open while fumbling to reload. Jeremy took aim and squeezed the trigger of his rifle and the man dropped back and moved no more.

A man at the tree next saw that Jeremy had taken his shot and charged forward with his musket up to his shoulder, waiting to shoot until he was upon his target. However, what he had not counted upon was that said target's gun had two barrels. Jeremy pulled the second trigger and a load of heavy shot hit the onrushing man full in the torso, ripping apart the disciple's coat, shirt and the skin beneath. His musket flew from his hand and clattered noisily against Jeremy's log while he dropped to his knees, blood pouring from his chest and his mouth, which moved seemingly in breathless, soundless speech.

Jeremy grasped blindly over the log for the disciple's gun. As his fingers found it, he saw another who charging forward, also thinking to take advantage of the reloading time. Jeremy shot the man at point-blank range. Just as he saw two more men fall to shots from others in his group, he whirled about, hearing a sound behind him.

Raising himself to a knee to fire at Jeremy was one of the singing disciples from the roadway. Jeremy was now truly without firepower and he waited with a calm that surprised him for the impact of the lead ball.

The man smiled, displaying a mouthful of very badly rotted teeth and revelling in the victory he could fairly taste even before he had it. Then he heard a shout from his right and whirled to see Davis pointing his rifle.

Jeremy knew that Davis had just fired his rifle and therefore was pointing an empty weapon. The disciple had not lowered his but was swinging it in Davis' direction. Jeremy reacted without thought. He reached behind his head for his tomahawk and tossed it all in one fluid motion. The weapon flew silently across the short space and hit the disciple in the side of the head, immediately in front of the ear.

The disciple's cocky smile vanished almost instantly as blood gushed from the wound and the tomahawk buried itself in his skull. His index finger, however, which had been closing on his musket's trigger, continued on its pre-programmed task and fired the weapon.

It took a moment for the smoke to drift aside in the breeze and allow Jeremy to see. He spotted Davis' coat lying on the ground, his nearly slack face yet displaying a trace of what must have been a grimace of pain resulting from the musket blast. The body lay in deathly silence, both hands covering the mid torso near his right side as if in a desperate attempt to keep the gore from pouring forth.

Jeremy sat helplessly beside the body, the horrid truth echoing in his brain. Davis Halberson was dead and there was nothing he could do to prevent it now. A gut shot was always fatal – always. And it was all

Jeremy's fault that this fine young man had died here in the snow so far from home.

★ ★ ★

Jeremy no longer heard the battle raging around him. He did not hear it when the Parson and his men, sensing victory, decided to charge the three remaining men, one of whom was not even fighting any longer. And he did not hear it when a set of war whoops issued from the trees to the right of and behind the charge and the subsequent renewal of the firefight. He also did not hear the sudden diminishing of sound.

He was miles removed from the world and its violence as he sat just rocking on his knees. Darkness had settled over his mind and pushed him into the depths that only a mind can reach; hopelessness, despair and grief consuming his being as it had when first Sarah and then Elizabeth had been taken from his life.

As from another world, he barely heard Josef's voice as the Caughnawaga gently grasped his shoulders and pulled him away from the dead young soldier. "Jeremy. There's nothing that can be done for him. He's in the hands of God now."

Jeremy whirled about on his friend. "Whose God?!" he spat. "No God I could ever accept could be so uncaring! He wouldn't let one after another of my family and friends die like this through no fault of their own!" He seemed to sag suddenly in upon himself. "And he took the shot for me," he muttered, his torment tearing into Josef. "He called the man with no load in his gun."

"I'll not argue religion with you now, nor try to tell you it wasn't your fault," Josef replied softly. "But, right now, the Parson and two of his disciples have broken out and are running for the river."

Jeremy looked in the direction of the river, as if he could see through the forest and brush. A fire burned in his eyes and tears of anger gave them an otherworldly appearance. "Let's get the bastards," he said, jumping to his feet.

He looked quickly about to take stock of the force they had left. Besides Davis, two Caughnawaga warriors, Gilbert and Tomas, also lay dead in the snow. That left him, Josef, Oliver, Giles, and Maurice.

"Let's get them before they escape!" he shouted with an odd calm. "Give no quarter! All must die this time!"

No argument returned in reply to his command. With a cry, the five remaining men took off at a run in the direction of the Parson's flight, reloading awkwardly as they ran.

★ ★ ★

Not a hundred yards from the river, they caught sight of the Parson. He and his surviving two disciples were struggling to push their boat into the water. Although it was not a particularly large vessel, it was large enough to transport at least a dozen men, and it had been drawn well up onto the gravel.

"I think your foul mission has ended on this shore!" Jeremy called out.

The Parson spun about and, seeing the force arrayed against him, jumped spryly into the boat. "Push, damn you, while I hold them off!" he screamed at his men.

The disciples put their shoulders into pushing the vessel free, their own lives not nearly as important as the "holy man" they were protecting.

"Fire!" Jeremy shouted, and his men all opened fire at the men and the boat at once.

One disciple went down immediately, splashing face down into the Niagara River just as the boat slid free into the current. The second seemed to have been hit, but he raised his one arm up and the Parson pulled him roughly aboard. The latter wildly fired both muskets now aboard before he turned to the oars and began to pull rapidly away from his enemies.

The boat was already a good distance off when Jeremy reached the water's edge. He stared impotently at the receding vessel, which carried away his latest arch-nemesis, brother-in-law of his last arch-nemesis, to safety on the American side.

Before it reached the safety of the far shore, however, the Parson felt it safe enough to stop rowing. He shipped the oars and stood up in the boat, spreading his arms wide.

"The Lord won't let you heathens kill his servant," he shouted tauntingly.

"We'll see," Jeremy muttered to himself. He had picked Davis' Baker rifle up as he started off and he now brought the dead man's weapon to his shoulder. He had loaded it with one of its .625 balls and its greased patch to reduce the friction of the rifling. He flipped up the folding backsight and aimed along the rifle, allowing for windage and distance.

Then, just as he had seen Davis do a number of times, he took in a full breath, muttered "for Davis", and squeezed the trigger slowly and evenly as he let the air free once again.

The powder exploded and the ball and burning wadding flew from the muzzle. But the shot, which apparently would have gone wide and low, encountered an unexpected target. Just as the ball left the barrel, the Parson's injured disciple, arose from the boat for some reason. He grasped the right side of his head as the ball struck and he pitched in seeming slow-motion over the side of the boat.

Jeremy felt deflated and collective moan issued from his companions before the drama played itself out. Following the impact with the disciple's skull, the ball glanced off and struck the Parson in the face. Jeremy and his companions watched as the traitor and false prophet dropped into the boat just as it slid itself aground on the far shore.

However, no shouts of victory left the men's lips. They watched intently to see if there was any movement coming from the beached boat. There was none, but all were loath to take their eyes from where they saw the villain drop lest he stir.

"Surely the ball didn't have enough force after hitting that man's head to kill the Parson as well," Oliver said, breaking the silence. "Could it?"

"I don't know enough of such things," Jeremy replied, still staring across the water.

"What say we try to make sure of it?" Josef asked, raising his musket's muzzle to get extra distance. Before anyone could answer he fired, the smoke drifting languidly across the water.

The others quickly did the same. As some shots obviously fell short into the water, they reloaded, corrected for the distance and let fly another volley. But before they could loose a third shot, some men appeared on the far shore and fired back in their direction.

Jeremy and his group returned fire but fell back as the others began to find their range. It would take a lucky shot for balls fired from a musket to hit a specific target, but such luck was not unheard of and the Americans could have a marksman with a rifle among them. It was time for a strategic retreat.

"Now what do we do?" Oliver said at length, once well back from the Niagara's edge. As they turned to look back, they saw a group of men hoist the body from the boat and carry the limp form off to the foot of the trail that led up the other side.

"Let's get back to care for Davis' body," said Jeremy softly.

When they arrived back at the place where they had seen their friend fall in the face of the enemy, Jeremy stopped suddenly in his tracks.

"The body..." whispered Jeremy.

"What of it?" asked Josef, who now reached the clearing at his friend's side.

Jeremy sank slowly down to his knees, incomprehension evident on his face. "It's gone. Davis is gone," he muttered in puzzlement.

Just as he said, the body of Davis Halberson was nowhere to be seen. All that remained, other than the bodies of Josef's two clansmen, was a patch of blood-soaked snow. It was impossible to determine anything from the mishmash of footprints that littered the clearing, and Jeremy sank onto his knees at the spot where the blood melted the snow.

He looked up at Josef, confusion etched in his face. "Where...?" was all that issued forth when his mouth opened, the question answered with shrugs of those present.

"There are so many footprints about," Josef muttered, the tension of confusion and frustration filling his words. "It's quite possible that someone decided to take his body for some reason."

"What possible reason could there be?"

Josef shrugged. "I'm afraid I have no answer to that. Maybe someone found him and decided to bury him. They couldn't know that we'd be back."

"Then why didn't they take the others?"

Josef gave Jeremy a look that suggested that the last question was quite naive. "What, and violate consecrated ground with the bodies of savages?" he remarked ironically.

Jeremy just nodded in reply, having no desire to address the matter at this moment. He did not point out that the bodies of the disciples were there as well.

"Maybe it was one of the disciples that came for his body. Did we account for them all?" asked Oliver.

"I don't think anyone had time to do an accurate head count," remarked Jeremy with a sigh.

A last he rose from his knees and turned toward his cousin, looking directly at him. At first there seemed to be no recognition of his kinsman. But shortly the world seemed to return to him, his face tired and haggard, the pain of the loss of yet another friend reflected in his eyes. Unknown to the others, there was also a deep sense of guilt behind the weary visage, that he was ultimately responsible for the deaths of them all.

"Josef, I suggest that we and your tribesmen take care of your fallen in the manner that you feel is right, whether it be Christian or Indian."

"We'll bury them here," Josef replied gravely. "We are Christians you know."

Jeremy nodded in silent agreement and pitched in to help.

Chapter Thirty-Six

The officer from Burlington Heights was meeting once again with his spy, this time in Queenston. In a copse of cedars behind the Smithertons' barn, he had waited impatiently, the cold penetrating his stationary body, but he did not wish to stamp his feet and wave his arms for fear of attracting attention.

He had been kept apprised of the intended destination of van Hijser and his men since their escape at Shipman's Corners and now it was time for an update. This project had been going on too long, with too many complications and it had already cost him much of what he had worked so long to attain. This meeting would hopefully signal the beginning of the end of this nightmarish process as he was to find out how far the trapper and his friends had gone in deciphering the instructions.

Now his man was here and Van Hijser was off in Newark, apparently to attempt to solve the next step of the riddle. The trapper and his Indian friend had seemed to figure out this aspect rather quickly, for the two were now on their way back to the others.

The spy picked up a handful of snow and made a ball, then threw it forcefully at the tree nearest him. "It seems van Hijser's figured out 'The Old Lady'," Wolf said, picking up another handful. "But they've been side-tracked from their mission. It seems that the trapper and his Indian were being followed as they came back and went after the Parson."

The military man rose from the fallen tree on which he had been sitting and began to pace. "I was afraid of that. He's getting close. Very well, keep following them if you're able." He nodded at the blood. "When he finds them, and it certainly appears he might, we'll retrieve the goods instead."

The officer looked at his spy long and hard. It was obvious to him that there was something the man was not divulging and he hoped that it would not affect the outcome of this particular enterprise.

For his part, Wolf hid his excitement. He had thought of asking the officer why he could not just go and follow the trapper and his friends himself, but he sensed an opportunity opening up. Possibly he would get his hands on the prize himself and then his patron could burn in Hell for all he cared.

★ ★ ★

The late afternoon of that day found the five remaining men shuffling along, weary in body and soul, back to the shelter they had used the previous evening. No longer concerned that anyone would follow them from the fort, they built a small fire. Some fresh small game and the heat from the fire, as well as much needed sleep would replenish at least their bodies. The other was a matter for time.

In the morning they travelled the last bit of distance to Queenston. Here too the Americans had left their mark, burning many buildings along the way. The few people who were about waved to the passing men, since many knew Jeremy personally. But there were inquisitive looks aimed at his companions, particularly the Caughnawagas. Indians had become a common sight in the peninsula, but generally only in a military role. Although some knew of Jeremy's involvement in the Battle of Beaverdams, he was not considered to be military personnel.

Standing at the base of the Mountain beside the road that meandered upward, eventually to lead to Chippewa and then ultimately Fort Erie, they were at a loss as to what they might be looking for. There was nothing as obvious as the "Old Lady" that could be identified as the "Old Man's Oversight" to be seen.

As they stood and stared at the Mountain impotently, a man came out from one of what was left of the twenty-odd homes in Queenston and eventually made his way by them.

"Pardon me, sir," Jeremy addressed the man, and then introduced himself. "Have you any idea who about here may have been referred to as 'the Old Man', in particular on who may have been known to the traitors who belong to the Canadian Volunteers?"

The gentleman looked thoughtful for a moment, and then replied slowly. "I've heard General Brock referred to as such in the short time he was here. But that is a common way for soldiers to describe their superior officers. And the Canadian Volunteers might well have known him at some point, especially their leader, Willcocks. He was an agent for Brock in getting the Mohawk from the Grand River to fight against the Americans. That was before he turned his coat of course."

"If it does refer to Brock, to what might someone be referring by his oversight?"

"I'm really not sure."

"Were you here at the time the Americans came ashore here?" Oliver broke in.

The man nodded. "I certainly was. I helped fight them as they came ashore," he announced proudly. "We weren't many but we kept them at bay long enough for Brock to ride here from Fort George."

"Perhaps you could tell us what you know of the battle?" requested Jeremy. "Perhaps something of the tale might give us a clue as to what we might be looking for."

"Surely," the man replied, obviously as pleased to tell the tale as any old soldier might be. "We fought them off from above the landing from as long as we could. There weren't many soldiers here then, but the Americans had been firing randomly across the river for days already. Killed one of my goats," he said indignantly.

"But we were holding them off, keeping them from climbing up here, and the guns up in the redan there," he said pointing up to a flattened area on the side of the Mountain. "Those guns were make kindling of many of their boats in mid-stream. When Brock arrived, or soon after, he was up there himself."

"Could that be Brock's oversight? What was he doing?" Jeremy interrupted.

"I truly don't know. He was up there in his flaming red coat among all the smoke from the cannon and the muskets, seemingly shouting orders. Couldn't really see much through all the haze. Until just before some Americans appeared at the top of the ridge behind them and started shooting down onto the redan."

"How did the Americans get behind them?" Oliver asked, caught up in the story.

"I was told later that they climbed up the cliff from the water's edge around the corner. When Brock came down from the redan with his men, he took cover behind one of the stone walls there," the townsman said, pointing to indicate where the General had taken cover.

"I was nearby when he jumped over and I heard him yell at someone else for an explanation. It would seem that he'd been told that the top was secure." He stood silent for a moment, shaking his head. "Then he was going to lead his soldiers back up the Mountain, the man himself well in front like he always was. But before he even made the base of the Mountain, he was shot and killed. That's all I know of the battle."

Jeremy stood momentarily lost in thought. Then he realized that the man still standing there, apparently waiting for recognition of his tale.

"Thank you very kindly for your time, sir," he said finally. "You certainly tell an exacting story. And it would seem that you and your fellows appointed themselves proudly in the defence of this country. I don't know yet if your information will help, but it gives us something to consider."

"I hope it will be of some service," the man replied, starting to move off, "and a good day to you all."

Jeremy watched the local walk on down the road toward St. Davids. He sighed and turned back to the problem at hand. "Well, I'm still not certain what exactly the 'Old Man's Oversight' might be, though it would seem that it has something to do with Brock's defence of this colony. I suppose we shall still need to go to the top and see what we can of the battle site from above. Perhaps it will make more sense if we see it from the heights."

★ ★ ★

Jeremy and his band stood at the top of the road overlooking the village of Queenston.

"I can see where that redan down there would have kept off any enemy troops for quite some time," Oliver commented. "It quite overlooks the best part of the river to cross. Do you suppose that's what the 'Old Man's Oversight' might be?" he asked.

"It does oversee the battle unfolding blow," Jeremy replied slowly. "But the number of steps paced off here and the directions for those paces would put us out in the air. I'm not aware that Williamson could fly, even if he may have thought so at times."

"Well, what else could the oversight have been?" asked Maurice.

"What if the oversight isn't a place but an action?" Josef suggested suddenly.

Jeremy's head snapped up from its previously bowed position. "What did you have in mind? Have you thought of something?"

"I have many thoughts," Commented Josef drily. "But I have one in particular concerning this puzzle."

"Well, speak up man!" Oliver chimed in, impatience evident in his voice.

Josef laughed. "You must teach this little one to have more patience," he quipped at Jeremy, nodding his head in Oliver's direction. "The man below said that when Brock was behind the wall, he asked for an explanation, thinking that his back had been secured by others of his troops. Perhaps the 'Old Man's Oversight' was to not secure his position."

"And the site of that oversight was right where we're standing now," Jeremy said thoughtfully.

"Or maybe it's the point at which the Americans crested the hill from the river," Josef suggested.

The five men fanned out toward the edge of the hill which rose precipitously from the Niagara River below. They ruled out much of the lip as being impossible or at least extremely difficult to climb.

"I see what looks like a bit of a path down below!" Giles called out. He began to follow the poor but usable trail until he saw where it crested their level. "Here it is!"

They rushed to the spot Giles indicated, from where Jeremy turned to the east by southeast. The next line of the will said, 'From this point, count out one hundred and thirty paces to the east by southeast and turn to the south for twenty-three more, above story's end, red upon red.'"

He began to pace off the distance, counting aloud and hoping that he was moving in the right direction since he had no compass. Finally, he stopped.

"If I was going in the right two directions, this should be it, or at least close," he said. "Now what is the meaning of 'above story's end, red upon red'?"

"Maybe directly below is the spot where Brock died, although who knows? Not two years have passed and already there are a number of tales about this battle," suggested Josef. "But it might make sense that the writer of this thought so. The 'red upon red' could be his blood on Brock's uniform. That would surely be the story's end, at least for the battle and for Brock as well."

"Very good, if that is indeed the answer," Jeremy muttered, a bit miffed with himself that it had not occurred to him. "I certainly have no better, however so now on to the next piece of the puzzle." But something else seemed to be occupying the tracker's mind as he looked about thoughtfully.

"You look to be deep in your own head, cousin. What would seem to be the problem?" Oliver asked, noticing Jeremy's apparent inattention. "Are you having difficulty remembering the next line, or does it puzzle you so?"

Jeremy shook his head, as if clearing it. "It's neither of those. There is just something about this that doesn't seem quite right, but I'm not sure just what it is that's bothering me." He looked off at the surrounding trees. "Ah well. Let's get on with it shall we? It's probably just my mind playing at tricks, what with all the intrigue surrounding this hunt. Now the next line is 'From here the way to the rock where, if one could see so far, one could see the place where trees stand in water.'"

"And what is 'the place where trees stand in water'?" Oliver asked with a sigh, becoming obviously frustrated with the entire process. None of this was making any sense and his impatience was getting the best of him.

"I believe I can answer that one," Josef cut in. "In the Mohawk language, we have a word which means roughly that. It is, in our language, *tkaronto*. I believe the place the instructions talk about is York, for Fort Toronto is its old name. If York were closer, or the buildings much larger, we would see it from some places along the Mountain."

Maurice scanned quickly around. "I see the entrance to a path from here," he announced quietly, pointing to a spot where a depression suggested a regular level of travel.

"Very well, let's give it a go, shall we?" Jeremy said, pushing his concerns to the back of his mind before they could even fully form.

★ ★ ★

They followed the path that snaked along the edge of the Mountain for a short time, until they came upon a shelf of rock which jutted out over the edge. This roomy, solid expanse of stone offered a stunning view of the land below and the travelers could see farms dotting the wooded areas below.

Beyond the farms, one could see, even from this distance, wisps of smoke rising from the still-smouldering ruins of what had, only two days previous, been the town of Newark. And beyond that Lake Ontario, dark and seemingly endless.

"This would certainly qualify as a candidate for the answer the answer to that clue," Oliver commented. He was nearly breathless due to the combination of the height of this rock, the cold wind which reached them unopposed from the north and the spectacle of the vista before him.

"All that's left, then, is the final line. 'Under the roof, the doorway keeps the object of your desire.' What do you make of that?" Josef muttered.

"I'll bet this shelf of rock forms and overhang," Oliver offered eagerly. "That would form a shelter of sorts, with the rocks forming the roof!"

Jeremy chuckled inwardly at his cousin's enthusiasm, but it did seem like a reasonable guess. There certainly could be no harm in going down to have a look.

"But what about the doorway?" Josef asked.

"You might find that out if you go below and look," Oliver remarked snidely, feeling he had his revenge for the Indian calling him "little one".

Jeremy moved to the side and eased himself down alongside the snowy shelf of rock that gave them all a view of Lake Ontario, carefully sticking to a narrow path which cut in only a footstep wide along the base of the escarpment's bare limestone.

He clambered under the roof provided by the overhang, forced to hold onto protruding tree roots and rock due to the rubble slope which slanted down to the floor below. Finally, feeling more confident of secure footing, he bent down carefully, holding on now only onto the rocks of the shelf itself to maintain his balance.

It was difficult to see in the back under the shelf, shaded as it was by rock and plants and his own body. Carefully he felt about until he found a small, roughly round opening measuring less than a foot in diameter.

"Do you see anything?" Josef asked from above.

"Just a hole in the rock. If this is indeed the doorway, however, whatever it is we're looking for can't be very large."

Wary of being bitten by some sleeping animal, Jeremy reached further inside, now even more cautiously. Then he felt something.

"There definitely is something in here," he called up to the others.

"What is it?" Oliver shouted back.

"I...can't...tell," Jeremy grunted while slowly pulling his arm back out of the depths. "It seems to be an oil skin. It must be the wrapping for something of value, judging by the care with which it's been tied."

"What is it?" Oliver again demanded impatiently.

"I would be hard pressed to know that without opening up the oil skin, now wouldn't I?" Jeremy responded ironically. "If you don't mind, though, I'd prefer not to do so on my way to the forest floor below. If you'll just be patient, I'll climb back up and we can all have a look."

Chapter Thirty-Seven

He worked his way back along the face and climbed up to his waiting team. Squatting there on the outcropping, he opened the packet very carefully, not wishing to take a chance on destroying anything. At last Jeremy pulled out several documents, carefully unfolding each and passing them on to the others to hold while he attended to the next. They seemed to be maps and a report by the U.S. War Department commenting on the state of battle readiness of the place in the maps.

Jeremy turned to the others, who were peering hard at the maps. "Do you think that this information is important enough to both sides to be worth the cost in lives that have been suffered?"

None could answer his question since none had even looked at the report.

"Obviously someone thought so," Oliver offered.

Jeremy looked up suddenly, as though something had just occurred to him. "You know, sometimes when you deeply concentrate on other things for a while, you remember what was at the edge of your mind earlier." The others just stared at him.

"In any case, these documents bring to mind just what it was that bothering me earlier is this," he continued. "Since Williamson knew where he hid the documents, why would he bother to write down these instructions in so arcane a manner? He must obviously have been hiding this information from his brother-in-law, which is why the Parson has been trying to get the documents."

He collected the papers from his companions and wrapped them back up their oilskins. When he reached a place of greater safety and comfort, he would study them to determine what could be contained in them that would be worth all the trouble they had been going through.

"So where is this leading?" Oliver asked. He was annoyed at having to return the papers without studying them.

"I can't help but wonder exactly who these instructions were intended for. And who wrote them, since Williamson was barely literate and not nearly this poetic?"

"I think I'll handle this affair now," a familiar voice boomed from the bushes at the point where they parted for the pathway they had all followed here.

★ ★ ★

The sound snapped the five men about almost as a single organism and the small clearing quickly filled with red-coated soldiers. At their head was Colonel James Halberson, Davis' uncle, pistol at the ready.

"I think it best if you just give me those papers," he said with a smirk. "I'll see to it that these get into the right hands."

"Why not let us bring it back to Newark?"

"I wouldn't be able to strike much of a bargain in that manner."

The five stared at the officer, some more surprised than the others.

"Did you follow us here?" Oliver asked, confused.

"Someone did," Halberson said cryptically, smirking all the while.

"What's all this about?" Jeremy demanded angrily. "Why has there been so much death and subterfuge over these damned papers and, if you knew about them, why did you not retrieve them yourself?"

"Still have no respect for authority, have you?"

"And you are the very reason I do not!"

The Colonel laughed softly. "To be honest with you, I was at a loss to decipher some of this. Also, I was attempting to use this whole affair to flush out the vermin known as the Canadian Volunteers. I had hoped Sims would draw them out into the open where we could set up an ambush and be rid of their kind once and for all.

"But once you obtained the instructions, I was rather forced to try to follow you instead, especially when Sims was shot. But things were taking a wrong turn and you were tossing about my name to everyone and I had to try to stop you. My attempt to have you arrested would have done much to solve my problems. But now I have every reason to shoot you all for violently resisting arrest when my soldiers were sent to get you. And especially now that you've murdered my nephew, who you first kidnapped."

"Your nephew was shot while fighting the Parson and his men," Jeremy snapped.

"Yes, that crazy fool and his band of mindless followers," Halberson said, shaking his head and smiling sadly. "I was rather hoping that it would be Willcocks himself who would come. I underestimated the Parson's greed and lack of fear of his commander.

He held out his hand toward Jeremy. "Now, if you don't mind, and even if you do mind, I would dearly like for you to hand me the documents in your possession."

"What makes you think that I would merely hand them over to you at your mere request?"

Halberson smiled in a manner that one would mistakenly call polite. "It would seem to me that you have little choice in the matter." Halberson's face grew dark. "But now, I suppose you've gotten in the way. You and your band have caused me a great deal of trouble, van Hijser."

Oliver leapt forward and pleaded of the soldiers accompanying Halberson. "Are you men going to allow this? Haven't you heard what he's said?" He was waving his arms now, trying to make his point, as if the soldiers had not understood him until now. "Don' you understand? This man's a traitor!"

Halberson stepped up to Oliver and slapped him hard across the face – hard enough to knock him to the ground. Looking down on the stunned young man, bleeding from the right corner of his mouth, he sneered. "Are you such a fool, man? These men are with me! Most are British soldiers who quite rationally realized that the army was never going to make them rich." His face returned once again to its previous icy smile. "With the amounts I'll earn them with this information, they'll be able to retire. And they'll not find themselves dying for some stupid cause of the King's choosing."

Jeremy's eyes and mind cast desperately about for a way out of this predicament. It was obvious that they must try to get away for, whether they handed over the documents or not, Halberson would certainly shoot them all to guarantee their silence. But with all these muskets pointed at them, escape seemed quite hopeless.

"Just toss the papers over here," Halberson commanded, sounding every bit as pompous as he always had.

"If you want them, I suggest you come and take them," Jeremy replied evenly. He projected an outward calm that he surely did not feel.

Halberson hesitated momentarily, trying to determine what this man thought he might be able to do. Then, with a shrug, he took a step forward to snatch the documents.

Meanwhile, Jeremy noticed that his Caughnawaga friends had inched once again, toward the trees. They had been close enough to make a run for it all along and their chances were improving every time their feet moved, although they were making it look like they were only repositioning their tired legs. In any case, now more than ever, the soldiers were paying much closer attention to the paper that they had been told would secure their retirements.

Halberson now stood toe to toe with Jeremy, apparently in an attempt to prove his dominant position in this situation. Once a pompous ass, always a pompous ass, thought Jeremy.

As he waited for Jeremy to produce the documents, Halberson could not resist the opportunity to bait the man. "By the way, van Hijser, don't you wonder how it is that I've been able to dog your steps so well all this time?" Halberson was so close, he was breathing in Jeremy's face.

Jeremy did not reply, but switched the papers to his left hand.

"It was someone you know," Halberson continued while staring now at the objects of this unexpectedly complicated operation.

Jeremy slowly lifted his right arm to hand over the documents, watching the other man's eyes and movements all the while. He noticed that Halberson had become preoccupied with both his taunt and the moving documents. In addition, he was forced to shift his pistol to his left hand in order that he might take the proffered documents. But before the officer's hand reached its goal, Jeremy gave him a hard shove in the direction of the closest soldiers.

Halberson felt himself being propelled backward and it flashed through his mind that his men might try to catch him. But it was not to be. Seeing their boss flying toward them, the three most immediately behind him, stepped instinctively and nimbly aside to avoid a collision which might leave them at a disadvantage in the face of the enemy.

With the attention of all of Halberson's men now on either Jeremy or their Colonel, Josef and his Caughnawagas made a break for the trees. Moving in an irregular zigzag motion, Jeremy saw to his satisfaction that they were soon out of sight of the now confused soldiers.

"Shoot them!" bellowed the Colonel from his prone position in the pathway. His men as one unit pivoted on one foot and loosed a barrage of musket balls into the brush and trees in the general direction of that taken by the Indians, reacting to the shouted order.

With only one soldier still keeping watch on them and even he not with his full attention, Jeremy saw their chance. In one quick movement, he stuffed the papers into his shirt and grabbed for Oliver's arm. "Now, jump!" he said, almost shouting.

The two men flew from the ledge, not altogether certain what they were jumping to, only now caring. Both just instinctively knew that it was a chance, something they would not have in the hands of Colonel Halberson.

After falling for some undetermined distance, they struck the side of the escarpment at an angle. Oliver's feet landed almost squarely in front of a pair of rocks which immediately shot away, skittering and clattering noisily down the slope. Jeremy landed flat-footed on the frozen soil of the slope, seemingly jarring every bone all through his body. Both men immediately lost control and alternately slid and tumbled rapidly down to the narrow bench below, smarting at each impact with stone, branch or tree root.

Their downward progress was soon to end. They both found themselves momentarily independent of the Mountain's slope and, when finally they landed, they were each treated to a bone-jarring impact with rocks and branches when they landed. The slope was little more than a steep slope of gravel and dirt, the result of unknown years of erosion of the top layer.

They lay catching their breaths for several minutes before either could speak.

"I think I may have broken something," Oliver finally said softly.

Jeremy had been taking stock of his own body and determined that his injuries were confined to scratches, bruises and a cut on his right cheek. It gave him some mild measure of satisfaction that his shoulder wound had at least not started bleeding again. "You would have made more noise than that by if you had broken something. Anyways, stop whining," he added with a smile. "Look at this cut. How am I to dazzle the ladies with a disfigurement such as this?"

"I don't know what makes you think that the ladies would have looked upon that ancient face with anything but pity."

"Say, do you hear anything?"

"No. Do you? Wait. I think that maybe I do hear something."

Jeremy listened carefully, attuned to the very air around him, but could hear nothing. He was uncomfortable with the level of silence around them. "Do you still hear it?"

"No, nothing now, I'm afraid."

"Yes, and that's not right. Halberson and his men should be beating the bushes to flush us out by now. There should be a great din as orders are given and taken and all the other sounds associated with a desperate hunt."

"There it is again!" Oliver almost shouted. "It sounds like voices."

Jeremy listened carefully, but that really was not necessary, for the volume of the voices was rising in a steadily rising crescendo. "It sounds like men having a something of a set-to," he said, as the arguing became shouting.

"Do you suppose the Colonel and his men have had a falling out?"

"Could well be the case," Jeremy said almost cheerfully. "There is little honour among thieves and murderers."

★ ★ ★

"Right then, Colonel, if you don't mind, we'll take those documents from you now," the Parson said with a sneering grin that marred a face already sufficiently marred by the scar and the eye patch. "It is Colonel, isn't it? Colonel Halberson, I believe? You're a long way from your post, aren't you, sir? And, as for the documents, I know you just took them from van Hijser just now. We heard you shoot him.

The Parson and his men had quite unexpectedly appeared from among the trees, muskets at the ready, just after Jeremy and his cousin jumped from the shelf. It galled Halberson to no end that he and his men had been taken so unawares. What, if anything, was he cutting these men into the profits for?

"You bloody fools!" Halberson erupted, screaming at his men and the Parson at the same time. "They've absconded with the documents and they're making good their escape even while we stand here discussing it!"

The Parson smiled. "Colonel, how stupid do you take me to be? You want us to go running after that trapper while you run off with my documents." He gave Halberson a hard look. "Now, please no more nonsense. Hand over the documents!" he barked.

"Very well," said Halberson with an air of resignation. He reached inside his greatcoat with his left hand.

"Slowly!"

"Very slowly," repeated Halberson, muttering under his breath. Following the orders of the man holding the gun on him, his hand came slowly out of his coat clutching a set of papers.

At the same time, his right had closed on the small pistol in his coat pocket and very slowly and carefully cocked the weapon so as to make as little noise as possible. A toy, someone had said when he had purchased it in Montreal. But it would be quite large and powerful enough at this arm's-length range to kill the man opposite him. Wedged in between the papers, he brought them out together.

As the Parson moved to take the papers from Halberson, the small gun slid out from among them. Even in this low level of sunlight the brass plate on the gun's handgrip flashed as he brought the muzzle to bear on the Parson himself.

"No! Parson, look out!" screamed one of the disciples, as he launched himself through the air at Halberson.

As his great misfortune would have it, the Parson's man was directly in front of the shot just as the spark hit the pan. A startled look came over his face as the small-calibre ball hit him in the neck just below the Adam's apple. Gurgling from the flood of blood into his throat as he tried to gasp for air, the young man hit the ground with a crash.

The startled Parson looked for but a split second and then dove sideways for the ground as a firefight broke out. Two of his disciples, thinking that their prophet had been shot, dropped their weapons and ran into the woods screaming in terror. However the rest of them pulled their triggers, most without thinking – or aiming.

The man beside Colonel Halberson levelled his musket at the man closest and fired. At that range, no soldier could miss and the man still standing nearest the Parson fell to the ground, holding his chest and screaming with pain.

Another, whose musket was not in position for firing, swung it at the disciple closest to him. The disciple grabbed onto the gun and wrestled for it, afraid to let go lest the soldier stab him with the bayonet end. As they struggled, neither man saw how close they were getting to the edge. The disciple slipped on an icy patch at the very edge and pitched over the side with a startled yelp. The soldier, still holding on possessively to the weapon for just a moment too long, followed directly after him.

Standing near a tree, one of the Parson's men, more cool under fire than some of his comrades, took careful aim and pulled the trigger. Nothing happened. He checked that there was powder in the pan and fired again. Still no explosion. He realized with a start that he had not an opportunity to reload since firing two shots after the fleeing Indians. But before he had a chance to appreciate the gravity of it, he lay dead on the ground, a musket ball securely lodged in his brain.

"Withdraw!" screamed the Parson in panic. He was afraid his disciples would all be killed, not that he cared for their safety. He was concerned that there would be no one left to protect him. He led the retreat, leaving the few men he still had in the field to cover his fleeing back.

Halberson's men were quite willing to end the battle once and for all and they rushed up to take chase. Had it been left to them, not a single disciple would be left alive.

However, Halberson had more immediate and important concerns than trying to hunt down the likes of the Parson and his disciples. "Stand down men," he ordered.

They stopped and looked back at him, the disbelief showing in their eyes. Not all of them were real soldiers and had no moral code that would force them to show the enemy any sign of mercy. Even some who were military men had few morals left to them since throwing in their lot with the Colonel. Left to their own devices, they would hunt down every last man and revel in the bloodshed.

"We must find those two with the papers," he said evenly, although he was angry that he was forced to explain himself to this lot. "That is, if any of you wish to be paid for your services for those papers are the prize that will produce the money. I'm sure there will be another day for hunting vermin."

Put into those terms Halberson's mercenaries gave up the chase, but they continued to grumble as they made their way back down to the road. Suspecting that Jeremy would head away from the road which led here to avoid being cut off, Halberson guessed that he would stick to the Mountain until he felt it safe to come down. The Colonel led his hired army along the St. Davids Road in the hopes of catching the trapper emerging from the woods.

★ ★ ★

"I suggest we remove ourselves from this area quickly but as quietly as we can," Oliver had suggested. "With any luck, they'll not follow us now."

As they had risen to leave, a gun report had sounded and echoed across the face of the escarpment. Knowing that it would do them no good to wonder, they gave it no further thought however. They just wished to get as far away as possible from there before whoever it was should come looking for them.

Jeremy and Oliver moved off down the slope and slid to the narrow streambed. There they stepped along precariously for some time on the icy rocks to avoid noisy branches and to leave no trail. In this way also, they would also keep the protection of the eight foot high embankments as they went. If their pursuers should yet come across their trail after all these precautions, at least they would not be very easy to follow for a while. In that they were supposing that indeed there were any pursuers, for they had heard no more from them since the initial volleys.

As they neared the bottom, Jeremy stopped suddenly and extended his arm to halt his kinsman as well.

"What?" Oliver asked nervously. "Did you hear something?"

"No, I haven't. But if you were intending to head us off, you might be waiting for us at the bottom of just such a defile. In any case, they might be waiting for us anywhere down here but most likely where the road wanders closest. Waiting for us because we couldn't go up and the obvious best way for us to go is down."

"Are you suggesting we continue across?"

Jeremy nodded. "I'm suggesting just that. And we must do it quietly. So travel slowly if you must so as to prevent a slide of rocks or a snap of branches. We'll keep on until we hit St. Davids, where I have some friends who may hide us, especially now that the Americans have left Niagara."

Chapter Thirty-Eight

Wolf watched the two men cut off across the Mountain but decided he would now make his travel a bit lighter. Following the defile the balance of the way to where it became a ditch which ran under the St. Davids Road, he climbed up alongside the wooden bridge and onto the roadway.

"So, there you are," a voice boomed from directly behind him. In his exhaustion, he had not thought to look or listen for traffic on the road.

Wolf had been hoping that he could avoid meeting up with this man again but decided to make the most of the situation. He turned slowly about and pasted a smile upon his face.

"Colonel, I thought I might meet up with you if I came down to the roadway here," he said as if greeting a long lost brother. "We couldn't have planned it any better."

Colonel Halberson looked down his nose on the man from atop his horse and replied. "Yes, well, now that we have met up, have you lost the men you were to watch? Or have you somehow managed to get the documents away from van Hijser?"

"Get them away?" the other responded with another question. "But I thought that you had quite gone to take them from the trapper yourself. That's why I came directly down here to meet up with you."

Halberson reined in his temper as he considered the reply. He had little trust for this man but felt that his own resources were important enough to keep him in line. He hoped.

"Does that mean that we now have no idea where they went?" he asked, his voice barely controlled. "Why didn't you stay with them?"

Wolf was momentarily at a loss. "Well, like I said Colonel," he finally managed to utter. "I thought you had van Hijser and his gang. Besides, it was you who told me to break away from them and retrieve the documents. You're lucky I have any idea at all where those two men who flew down from the cliff went."

"I would too have held them, had that fool the Parson and his band of imbeciles not interrupted and given them a chance to escape," Halberson muttered absently. Then the final part of his spy's words finally connected in his brain. "You say you have an idea of where they may have gone?"

"I know in which direction they went."

★ ★ ★

After what seemed an eternity of sliding on snow, ice and rocks and tripping over roots and branches, the cousins reached the village of St. Davids. There had been no major incident along the way, and they no longer heard the sounds of earlier on – the occasional snap of a twig, the clatter of sliding rocks and even a moaned curse as though some unseen someone lost his footing.

It was impossible to tell for certain of course, for a frozen forest has countless sounds of its own. Branches rub together, twigs snap off with little provocation and the combination of seeping and freezing water sends stones and even, very occasionally, large boulders crashing down the Mountain. Combined with the wind sounds in the trees and hollows one could reach just about any interpretation of the sounds, like watching clouds on summer's day.

Finally arriving safely in the village, they hastened to the still standing shop of an old friend of Jeremy's. Jeremy knocked soundly on the door, as it had been closed for business for at least an hour.

A middle-aged man arrived at the door, holding a cleaver and splattered with blood. "What the devil do you want? Can't you see I'm closed?" He looked closely at the two and then opened the door wide for the two to enter.

"Jeremy. I didn't see right off that it was you bothering me in off hours. What brings you here? Have you brought me some fresh venison?"

"No, Michael, I'm afraid I've come to ask you to hide us," Jeremy said, getting right to the crux of the matter. "Some men will be looking for us, I'm fairly certain. They're British soldiers by their uniforms in fact, but in uniform only. But I'm afraid it's been something of a trying day and we've no more strength to travel."

"Why haven't you headed for the safety of the fort?"

"Truth be told, Michael, I'm not sure who in the military can be trusted. Besides, the men following us have made what was already a dreadful situation even worse than it already was by spreading tales that may get us shot should we approach the military."

"You never were one to accept the authority of others," the large merchant laughed. "And who would these soldiers be that are following you?"

"They're actually more renegades than soldiers. It seems they've struck out on their own to enrich themselves in the course of the war. But the officer is a Colonel Halberson, late of Burlington Heights."

"And what is he looking for, if I may be so bold to ask?"

Jeremy looked questioningly at Oliver, who almost imperceptibly shrugged his shoulders, leaving the decision entirely up to him.

"Some documents that might be of value to the British have recently come into our possession." Jeremy began his explanation. "We've been chasing them over all of Upper Canada, it would seem. Then when we found them, we were greeted by the Colonel, who has it in his mind that he can sell them to the highest bidder. He is quite certain that the Americans would sorely wish to retrieve them before the British see them."

"Is there no honour at all left in this war?" the shopkeeper sighed. "What with traitors for neighbours and soldiers who prefer their purses over their duty, I'm beginning to think not."

"I'm sure he believes that he has a type of honour of his own making," replied Jeremy tiredly. "In the time this war has carried on I've seen many definitions of the word, many tailored to the user's own choosing to suit his circumstances."

"Well, come along then," the big man said with a loud sigh after shortly considering Jeremy's words. His two guests followed him through the shop toward the back.

"I see the Americans were somewhat more selective about what they burned in this village than they had been in Newark," Jeremy observed. "You're very lucky to still have this shop."

"You're right there. I don't even know why they left my place. One would think that they might consider this shop as perhaps being useful to the enemy, but there seemed to be little thought involved. They appeared as though they were on the run and just hurriedly burned what got in their way."

Michael Somerset's shop was not a large one for this was but a small village. His place of business was next to a smithy, which had been burned to deny the oncoming British troops the smith's services. There were also a miller and a carter, although not adjacent to Somerset's shop. It served as all manner of shops might in the larger centres, though in smaller quantities.

As Jeremy and Oliver followed Somerset, they glanced about at the shelves. The shopkeeper carried a small selection of spices and condiments, candy, millinery, hardware, farm supplies, and household products. He had originally apprenticed as a butcher back in Ireland, so when he opened this shop, he did much of the butchering for his neighbours who were averse to doing it themselves.

The few baked goods he carried were made daily by the Widow Seaton, who lived nearby. He did not often have customers for them, but he enjoyed eating them himself, and he could afford the pittance he paid his neighbour for her labours. He felt that it was the least he could do for the widow of a militiaman who had fallen at Queenston Heights with Brock.

Jeremy and Oliver followed the shopkeeper through the dirty curtain at the back and passed through a narrow space obviously employed as both storeroom and abattoir. On one side were shelves stacked with items that either hadn't been put out or there was no space for, while on the other, around a butcher's block, hung a number of cuts of meat, ranging from chicken to pork to beef.

Jeremy pushed a side of beef which was partially blocked his progress. "It would seem that you eat well here."

"I usually only eat the cheaper cuts," Somerset growled, never liking to admit that he was reasonably well off. "The more expensive cuts often belonged to landholders who don't wish to get blood on their own hands and don't really trust their own people to do it right."

They proceeded straight through to back of the building and climbed the almost vertical stairs to the second floor, where he lived.

Jeremy looked about appreciatively. "Well, Michael, I must say you've done quite well for yourself. Can you believe this, Oliver? These are plastered walls and ceilings!" These comfortably furnished living quarters were a far cry from the Spartan existence to which Jeremy was accustomed.

"I'll thank you not to spread that about," Somerset growled good-naturedly. "Some might think me too well off and try to bring down my prices."

In the room that served as his bedroom, he stood on a stool and pushed open a trap door in the ceiling leading to the attic.

"You two hide up here until we see if you're being followed here."

★ ★ ★

Jeremy and Oliver reached up through the small opening and pulled themselves up from the stool. As each rolled clear of the hole, he lay exhausted from the final bit of exertion. Neither saw it when their host pulled the trap door shut but heard rather the rasp of the wood being pulled across the opening.

Jeremy forced himself onto his elbows and finally to a sitting position. In the extremely dim light of the attic he looked about as much as he possibly could. But because of the darkness of the interior, he was able to discern some light coming through cracks at what would be the rear-facing wall of the building.

"Do you see that?" he asked thoughtfully, staring at the cracks.

"See what?" Oliver muttered noncommittally. "All I see is the dark roof." He had just been lying on his back, quickly drifting off to sleep as he stared into the pitch darkness above his head.

"Never mind," Jeremy replied, smiling. "It isn't that important I suppose."

"No, I suppose not," his semi-conscious cousin mumbled.

Jeremy forced himself up to his feet and, stooping under the low ceiling and balancing on the joists, he made his way to the end of the attic. He pushed lightly on the spot and found that he had been looking at some type of service trap door to the outside, just under the peak of the roof.

Perhaps this had once been a loading door to the second story before the ceiling had been put in, creating this attic, he thought. The plank floor upon which they had landed when they came up only covered a small portion of the attic. Any others that may originally have been here were likely used for something else since. And there was no real use for the attic during this war, for he had little to store up here. Just an occasional sack or crate which he did not feel the least inclined to look into. The rest of the attic was bare.

His curiosity satisfied, Jeremy rejoined his cousin, who was now fast asleep. He made himself as comfortable as possible and settled down to drift off himself. Just as he was about to relax he reached into his shirt, immediately feeling that something was missing.

"Oliver, did I give the packet of papers to you, by chance?" he asked with a note of rising panic. He jumped to his feet, almost banging his head on the rafters and anxiously checked all his clothing for the missing documents.

"What?" Oliver responded, starting awake. "No, I've never had them."

"Damn!" exclaimed Jeremy, flopping back onto the floor in frustration. "They're gone. I must have dropped them on the ledge or maybe they came out of my shirt on the way down the hill. In any case, I no longer have them."

"There's little we can do about it now," Oliver replied rationally, too tired to genuinely care one way or another about the pieces of paper.

"You're right, of course," sighed Jeremy in resignation. "In a way, I'm just as happy to see the last of them. Perhaps this will all end now and we can just get on with looking for our mystery relatives."

"Good idea," Oliver muttered, dropping off just as rapidly as the first time.

Jeremy decided that he too had best get some sleep for they would need to set out on the road again in the morning. Using their own kit, they lay down, thankful for the residual heat that came up through the ceiling from the rooms below.

As he lay there and the exhaustion overtook him, in that netherworld between consciousness and slumber, heretofore unacknowledged thoughts seeped unbidden into his mind. Try as he might, he could not banish the question that Halberson had forced upon him.

Who was it that Jeremy knew that had been informing the Colonel as to their progress? It was a corrosive thought, put there by a man of questionable honour. Yet, what if it were true? Did they indeed have a traitor in their midst?

The question nagged at him to a lesser degree by the minute as he slowly succumbed finally to his utter exhaustion. The last thought he had in that regard before he fell asleep was that it really mattered little now, for the papers were gone and it no longer held any concern for him.

★ ★ ★

Somerset made his way back down to finish butchering the side of beef that Mr. Bannock would want first thing in the morning. He honed his large knife on the leather strop that was nailed to the cutting block and was about to make a cut when he heard a loud, insistent pounding at the door to the shop.

An authoritative voice immediately rang out from beyond the barrier. "Open up in His Majesty's name!"

Muttering to himself and somewhat apprehensive that this might be the visit Jeremy had been expecting, he drew back the large iron bolt that kept the door locked.

"What would you be wanting at this hour?" he blustered. "My shop's been closed for the better part of two hours."

"I come on the King's business," proclaimed a British officer, who looked very tired and somewhat bedraggled.

"Well tell the King he can wait for morning as must all my other customers. Now good night, sir, and be off with you."

The officer, accompanied by several other soldiers, pushed his way into the shop past Somerset, slamming him into the wall to get by. "I'm Colonel Halberson and I'm searching for men wanted for crimes against the Crown. Any attempt to impede me and my men will be considered an act of treason."

So, this was indeed the man whom Jeremy had been fleeing. "I assure you, sir, they could not have entered here without my knowledge." In this he was telling the truth.

"Well then, perhaps they entered with your knowledge," the Colonel said. "You men, search the shop and be thorough," he ordered the two soldiers nearest him. The men, who appeared to be no less dishevelled than their commanding officer, began to haphazardly throw items onto the floor, items that could have no possible connection to the finding of fugitives.

"Here now!" the shopkeeper exclaimed. "You can't merely come in here and destroy my stock in trade."

"But we have. So it would appear that you're wrong about that," Halberson replied archly. "The rest of you men, follow me."

The Colonel and the balance of his platoon climbed the steps to the second floor and began to toss about Somerset's property, as they had done in the shop below. Finding nothing, Halberson began to walk slowly about. He looked carefully at the walls and ceiling and occasionally tapping a section that he deemed, for whatever reason, to be suspicious with the hilt of his sword.

"Over here," he announced at length, pointing up toward the ceiling. "Someone take that stool and prepare to climb up to the attic that's obviously above us there. You!" he called to the soldier near the stairs. "Find a lantern that we might see all there is to behold. I suspect we'll find what we're looking for there."

The first soldier pulled himself up into the attic and then helped another up as well. The assigned man had found a lantern and lit it from the banked fireplace and handed it up to the others. For several minutes there was silence above but for the stomping boots of the two soldiers as they looked about.

"There's nothing up here, Colonel," one of the men called down.

"Are you certain?" Halberson asked, dumbfounded. He had been sure that he would find Jeremy and his cousin in this man's house. He refused to believe it. "Pull me up. I'll see for myself."

Chapter Thirty-Nine

S tanding on the plank floor of the attic, Halberson looked around. There was certainly no room for anyone to be hiding here. He held the lantern higher but could see nothing. Pacing about, he kicked the meagre few crates and sacks which were too small in any case to hide two grown men, but this also yielded nothing. Finally admitting defeat, he climbed back down into the house with the two soldiers close behind.

"Very well," he said, glaring at the shopkeeper. "I've been able to find nothing, but I still believe that you've seen them. In fact, one of your neighbours saw them enter here about two hours before I arrived."

"Would that be the neighbour to the left?" Somerset asked, knowing he would get no reply, at least not an honest one. "I'll have you know, sir, that the poor soul living there is a bit particular to the demon rum. Never know what she might see if she weren't half blind. In fact, I doubt that she could even see my house in the daylight."

Somerset followed as the officer and his men climbed down to the ground floor, feeling a profound sense of relief and a great deal of curiosity. Walking to the window, he looked down below to see the Colonel mount up, obviously furious, and then ride away toward Shipman's Corners, with his men trying desperately not to fall behind.

He scratched his head. He was certain that he had sent the two men aloft himself. Was he going daft? He climbed up onto the stool and looked into the attic himself.

"Good to see you again," Jeremy greeted him. Beside him was his cousin Oliver.

"I've known you to be good at trickery and even some sleight of hand for the children on occasion, but how did you keep them from seeing you?"

Jeremy laughed. "We managed by hiding out on your very slippery roof in the freezing cold. We had discovered the old loading door and managed to pry it open. Then we pulled ourselves up onto the roof, which is thankfully right above the door, hanging on at times by our fingernails at the edges of your shingles. It was by no means easy, I'll admit. There were more than a few times when I thought I might lose my grip and go crashing to the ground. But the real trick was in not laughing aloud when we heard the disbelief in the Colonel's voice."

"Why did he not see where you'd gone?" Somerset asked, still puzzled. "If you could find it, why didn't they?"

"We only barely saw it ourselves," Oliver explained. "Only a tiny bit of light filtered through the cracks, giving it away. We'd made certain that they wouldn't see it by stuffing snow into the cracks as best we could. And when they came up with the bright lantern, the light of it would have easily overpowered that bit of light from outside and caused them to miss it anyway."

Somerset began to laugh, in part due to the humour of the situation and in part due to the release of tension now that it was over.

"Well now, lads, perhaps you'll be so kind as to help me put my store aright before bedding down again. You've caused me a great deal of bother with all of this." He tried to look stern but then broke out in great guffaws.

"I must say that it does an Irishman's heart good to see an Englishman so well outwitted," he gasped between laughs. "Especially an Englishman in uniform, and even more especially because he was such a pompous ass."

The three men climbed down, sharing the laugh at Colonel Halberson's expense and set about to salvage what they could of Somerset's shop.

★ ★ ★

"Michael, I want to thank you once again," declared Jeremy enthusiastically as he clasped the large shopkeeper's hands in his. "And I also want to say once again how bad I feel about the damage done to your shop."

"It was nearly worth it to see the look on the Colonel's face when he found you weren't in my house, even after one of my neighbours told him that he'd seen you fellows go inside, especially when you were indeed there." Somerset laughed heartily for a brief moment, but then quickly frowned as he thought of the neighbour who had betrayed him. "I intend, however, to find out who it was, by the way."

"Well, you can't really blame your neighbour," Jeremy reassured him. "He had no way of knowing that the Colonel was no good. And whoever it was may well not have known me. I've met few of your neighbours after all."

"True enough," the big man agreed. "But a neighbour shouldn't be turning in his own kind at any rate. And you needn't run off. I'm more than happy to let you two stay here. I've grave doubts that they'll return here again now."

"Thank you Michael, but that won't be necessary or wise. While he may be back, I'm rather more concerned about what may have happened to the documents we found up in the cliff. I still don't really know what they are or their importance, but I show hate any information of weight falling into the wrong hands," explained Jeremy as he swung the strap of his kit over his shoulder.

"And I should hate it even more if one of the groups who has been killing off or terrorizing my friends should benefit from their retrieval."

★ ★ ★

The Parson and his men had run until they reached the place above Queenston where they had hidden the boat, slipping and sliding in the snow, tripping over rocks and branches. Bruised and a little bloodied, they reached the vessel to find one of Willcocks' men sitting in it, waiting for them.

At least it was a comfort to know that Halberson had set off in the direction of Shipman's Corners for he did not wish to risk running into the Colonel. It had been worthwhile after all to send one of his disciples down the road from the heights to watch him go.

"I don't know what mischiefs you lot of misfits have been up to," he said, smiling at the Parson's muddy, wet and dishevelled crew. "But I do know that Willcocks is furious with you for ignoring his orders to stand with the Volunteers. You're needed to scout about Fort Niagara to watch for invading Brits. I suggest you row us across right quickly because if he loses his military rank because of you he may well decide to shoot you himself."

They pushed off the boat and paddled wearily and painfully across the Niagara. The Parson glared at Willcocks' messenger the whole time. He could little help but think that, once they got their hands on those papers, they would no longer need that puffed up, self-important popinjay Willcocks.

★ ★ ★

Jeremy had decided to head back toward the place where they had jumped from the ledge, in the hopes that they might find the documents somewhere in the path of their fall. In spite of his speech to his cousin the previous night, he had come to the conclusion that finding the papers might be their only way to convince the British command that their mission had indeed existed. If it came to just their word against Halberson's in a military hearing, they would be hanging from the gallows the next morning.

On the road once again, Oliver heard a sound coming from the trees to his right when they were but a mile west of Queenston. He tapped Jeremy on the shoulder and signalled that he thought someone might be lying in ambush.

Jeremy looked away as if something far down the road and to his left had attracted his attention. Then, without looking again at his cousin, he spoke softly from the corner of his mouth. "On the count of three, we rush in. One...two...three!"

The two men rushed in through the brush, keeping low to avoid being shot. They immediately spotted several men on all sides and automatically dove to ground. From their prone positions, they brought their muskets to bear.

There was no one to be seen.

"Show yourselves!" Jeremy shouted in frustration, although he himself could hardly see any reason why they should, since they had the advantage in the present situation.

Finally someone stepped out from behind a large maple. Jeremy looked at them dumbfounded as he realized that these men were their Caughnawaga companions.

"Very well, Josef, you must be here as well," Jeremy shouted out peevishly, feeling the fool for being caught out in such a manner, especially since the Indians were smiling. "But I must say you and your friends play a dangerous game. We could well have killed at least two of you before we were to realize it was a prank."

Josef stepped out from his cover. "What makes you think you'd have had the chance?" he challenged. "You didn't even know where we were. The two of you, however, were lying there on the ground, in the open, making perfectly good targets for us anytime we wished to shoot."

Josef's words reminded Jeremy that they were still on the ground. Glaring at his Indian friend he rose to his feet, slapping at his clothes to rid them of snow and forest debris, seeing that Oliver was doing the same. But finally he found himself forced to smile as he developed the mental image of what the two of them must have looked like to Josef and his men.

"One of these days you'll make the fool of me once too often and then I'll be forced to take your measure," Jeremy grumbled. He tried hard to keep a straight face but then saw the humour of the situation. Begrudgingly he started to laugh.

"I see your group has grown," Jeremy said, changing the subject the subject by referring to all the new faces that had now materialized from the surrounding forest. "Where did you find these gentlemen?"

"They were scouting and raiding along the river from Chippewa. They were driving off stragglers from the hurried evacuation of the Americans and their allies. It seems the U.S Army has run short of boats in the process. And some of the American soldiers and such had been out on patrol when the main body left, leaving them with no avenue of escape."

"After escaping from your friend the Colonel, we ran into our brothers here over by the river," Josef explained. "We told them what had happened and they were interested in joining our little hunting party since we didn't know what had become of the two of you. We thought we might have to fight those soldiers to free you."

"We escaped at the same time that you did, while you were drawing their fire," commented Jeremy. "By jumping off the cliff. Where are you all going now?"

"I can't speak for my brothers, but I think I'll stick with you. I am curious to see how this all ends."

The other Caughnawagas, now eleven in number, nodded their heads.

"We thought we might have the chance to practice some of our fighting technique if we were to run into either the Colonel or the Parson's men, if any are left," explained Maurice.

"I don't know about the Colonel, for we saw him ride toward Shipman's Corners from St. Davids. As for the Parson's men, I would think that they would all be on the other side of the river, along with the rest of the cowardly dogs that run with that traitor Willcocks, since they 're his charge at least in name." Jeremy almost seemed to spit out the words. "When I think of all the evil things that he and his men brought upon me and mine, and then the way they burned out the people of Newark, it makes what seems the very fires of Hell burn inside me."

No one spoke for the next several moments. Then Jeremy broke the spell he had cast with the venom in his speech. He took a deep breath and quieted himself down. Then he explained what he and Oliver had intended to do with the documents should they find them.

"I think I should like to go along anyways," Maurice volunteered. "If that ends it all, I may see if I can get involved in any revenge attack that may be planned against Fort Niagara."

"Very well. We'll certainly be happy to have the extra fire power along."

"I see you Indians from Chippewa are carrying bows as well as your muskets," Oliver observed with interest.

A young Caughnawaga the others called simply Chevalier, without a Christian name, Replied to Oliver's implied query. "Our short bows are easier to use on the run, have greater range, they're more accurate, and take less time to reload."

"Then why even carry a musket at all?"

"That's because they're better for hunting," offered Maurice. "Arrows sometimes are not as…final, you might say." He smiled at his own choice of words. "A musket ball tends to make more of mess than an arrowhead, so that even a wound that's not fatal can be very damaging. In battle, though, they take long to reload and they're much less accurate over great distances."

"Perhaps, then, our military should start using bows and arrows."

"What, and admit that the savages might have a good idea?" remarked Josef.

They had now all reached the point in the road where they could see the end of the defile where Oliver and Jeremy had come down in their escape. Jeremy signalled the others and they all set off up the hill. When they came to the spot where the two had obviously landed, they all spread out and began searching for the packet of documents, climbing up the hill at an approximately arms-length distance apart.

They reached the point of the two men's impact below the shelf and all climbed up to the top of the ridge together.

"I saw nothing, did you?" Jeremy asked hopelessly.

His companions said nothing, but just shook their heads.

"Well, it seems unlikely that so many sets of trackers' eyes could have missed it if it were there," Jeremy sighed. "I must have dropped it up here in the confusion, which means that Colonel Halberson surely has it now."

"If he has the documents, why did he come looking for us last night?" challenged Oliver. "One would think that the man would just quietly fade away to sell the goods."

"Maybe he just doesn't want any witnesses," Josef suggested.

Jeremy stood thoughtfully stroking his growing beard. "Maybe," he said doubtfully. "Oliver, did you happen to notice how many men he had with him last night?"

"I couldn't see him any more than you could from where we were," his cousin replied. "Why?"

"It just seems that there were a lot of voices. And if his men were all or mostly with him, what was all the shooting we heard as we were escaping?"

He looked about at the disturbed snow, hoping that somehow the ground might give them an answer to his question. Nothing jumped out at him, however. There had been a light snowfall the night before and any signs there may have been were covered up now. There was nothing to do but move on.

★ ★ ★

They trudged wearily into the Queenston in the early afternoon and spied some soldiers down at the water's edge. They were apparently hard at work down by the landing in the Niagara River, although it was difficult at this distance to determine what exactly was happening.

"What do you say we see if we can find out any news about Newark or possible retaliations?" suggested Jeremy.

"Good idea. But, say, isn't that the officer we met at Shipman's?" asked Oliver, pointing to a man who seemed firmly in charge.

Jeremy could not identify the officer for he had turned his head away since Josef had spoken. However there was something familiar in the way he gave orders as a number of men towed and then pushed a boat to the very edge of the Niagara River. There it was lined up with others of various descriptions, ready to be pushed into the water.

The small band of travellers approached the officer, obviously a Captain. He did not seem to notice them, so Jeremy cleared his throat before speaking, concerned that he might startle man, a result that could get him shot.

"I saw you approach, Jeremy," the Captain said without turning around. "You there!" he shouted at the men pulling another boat along the shore with lines toward the others. "Put your backs to it! The General may want these at a moment's notice!"

"Captain Merritt," Jeremy said, not bothering to offer his hand. "We saw you working here and came to ask if you've any news."

"Concerning what, might I ask?" Merritt questioned, raising an eyebrow.

Jeremy smiled. This was to be a security game then. Very well, he could play. "Concerning just about anything at all. How's your father, sir?"

Merritt turned around and looked at the trapper and his men. "He's doing well, thank you. All right, come with me. I'd rather talk out of the wind. These coats the Army gives us are not meant for Canadian winters."

"Will all due respect, sir, but the men hauling the boats don't seem to be cold," Jeremy observed with a mischievous twinkle in his eyes.

Merritt gave him a look of pretended offense. He led them to a barn that he was using as a temporary headquarters and the filed inside.

"Do they all need to come in?" Merritt asked with slight annoyance.

"They might as well," responded Jeremy. "It's quite cold out there, as you pointed out. Besides, I'll be telling them anything that you tell me in any case."

Chapter Forty

They stood inside the barn door out of the wind and Jeremy looked about in the gloomy building. There were no furnishings of any type, save bales of straw where, judging by the detritus, the men sat to eat. There was no desk and, since the barn was not large enough for a loft, no place for one to be standing out of sight.

"Jeremy, we intend to attack Fort Niagara when all is ready," Merritt started off by way of explanation.

"I'd rather expected as much. Such infamy certainly deserves to be answered."

"While we are making preparations, we need such as yourself and these Caughnawagas to scout the area about the fort to determine their readiness," the Captain explained.

"Well, I'd be willing to do that, since I'm familiar with area," Jeremy replied. He looked around at the others. "But I can't speak for the others here."

Jeremy's concern was about his cousin in particular. Oliver was an American by birth and he could not really be expected to scout against his own. Some of the men in the fort might well be his neighbours. Naturally Jeremy could say nothing in this regard to the Captain, for he might not be able to turn a blind eye to such information at this time.

"I will go," offered Josef and was quickly joined by his fellow Caughnawagas.

All eyes now rested upon Oliver, who seemed understandably uncomfortable with the sudden attention, especially under the circumstances.

"I think he'd best stay here to help your men," Jeremy spoke up. "I'm afraid my cousin isn't much of a scout or even a tracker, so I think it best if he stayed out of this. He's liable to be injured if he starts poking about in strange woods with enemy all about."

Oliver visibly sighed in relief. Picking up on Jeremy's argument, he made himself seem to resign himself to his cousin's evaluation of him. "I suppose it's for the best. I'd probably just get in the way in enemy territory."

"I have just one question," said Jeremy suddenly. "Surely you know of the order for my arrest. What of that?"

Merritt seemed untroubled by the query. "Well, having you across the river will lessen the chance that anyone will be arresting you won't it?" he remarked, smiling. "In honesty, though, I don't think Colonel Halberson's word will carry much weight at the moment. For one thing, his nephew seemed to be travelling with you of his own free will when saw you beyond Shipman's Corners. For another, there is an order to arrest the good Colonel on sight if he is found. You see, it seems that he has deserted his post in time of battle."

Jeremy merely nodded.

"You wouldn't know anything about Colonel Halberson, now would you?" asked Merritt, an inkling of suspicion showing in his eyes.

"I thought I saw him riding with some men at St. Davids yesterday," replied Jeremy. "But since he's looking for me, I thought it best to stay out of his way."

Merritt nodded thoughtfully, but was obviously not convinced by the answer. Jeremy had not lied directly, but the Captain seemed to believe that there was more to the story. However, without any idea as to what had happened to the documents, he decided he had said enough for now. He carefully cast a warning glance at his cousin, who nodded ever so slightly to acknowledge the signal.

"Very well, then, you shall leave for the far shore after the moon goes down," Merritt said, feeling that it would be best not to pursue his line of questioning any further, at least for the present. "A man will come each night to take whatever information you have gleaned each day. His bywords will be 'The best books are saved" and your reply will be 'One must have a good read'. Will you remember that?" When Jeremy nodded, he added, "Good luck to you. That will be all."

With that, Captain Merritt left the barn and strode purposefully back to the river's shore to continue his supervision of the gathering of boats.

★ ★ ★

In the wee hours of the morning Jeremy and his Caughnawaga companions helped row the boat to the far shore. Landing roughly two miles north of Lewiston, they climbed out onto the opposite shore, climbed the slope and then vanished quickly into the dark forest on the American side. Barely waiting for them to climb ashore the dragoons who had rowed across with them departed, again as quietly as possible, hoping that no one had witnessed the landing.

A half mile from the bank of the river the new scouting party entered a dense evergreen thicket on the slope of a ravine bed running east-west. There the men bedded down for the night, using a low reflector fire for heat and rotating sentries for security.

For the next two days they set out in small groups, Jeremy's own platoon consisting of himself, Josef and Maurice. They agreed to meet in their same night time location each evening to compare notes and make any necessary decisions for the next day.

On the third day, the arrangement was changed. They decided they would all go out after nightfall and rendezvous at the river at about midnight. They would then wait for their contact who was to give the sign to those across the river that they should come and pick the whole group up. Jeremy and his team had decided that they had provided about as much intelligence as they were likely to gather, but for one outstanding item. This night their final objective was to discover where the American advance guard was posted at night.

Jeremy and his companions had not gone more than a mile before Josef stopped them.

"What is it?" asked Jeremy in low voice.

"I'm not entirely certain," replied his Caughnawaga friend. "I have this feeling that I can't easily explain that we aren't alone. It's like I can feel someone watching us."

Jeremy knew better than to discount Josef's intuitions. If he said he felt it, then somehow he did. "Have you any idea where they are?"

"None, only that they're not far away," Josef replied, casually looking about as if trying to orient himself. He did not wish for their watcher to be tipped off. After stretching his neck, he lowered his head and turned it side to side, rubbing his neck as though it was stiff. "To the right, just a little way behind us," he said softly. "When I looked around, I saw a blur of movement in that direction as though someone was ducking away to avoid being seen."

"See if you can work your way around behind and see who it is," suggested Jeremy, fighting the urge to look in the direction his friend had indicated.

"Well, it was good to see you again," Josef said suddenly in a louder voice, obviously meaning to be heard. "Please bring a greeting to your brother."

"I certainly will," replied Jeremy, playing along. Then, waving good-bye to his friends, he set off along the path they had been following.

★ ★ ★

Josef and Maurice set off back the way they had come. They were pleased to note that their tail had lost interest in them, apparently more concerned with Jeremy. He made no undue effort to keep them from spying his movement on a course parallel with that of the trapper, but keeping his distance.

The two men walked a little further, until they had almost lost sight of the ineffectual spy. Then they cut across until they came across the man's trail and began to follow it at a slow jog. They wanted to catch up to the man following Jeremy but did not want him to notice them coming up behind. If they went too quickly, the man might catch the movement peripherally as he watched his quarry. As well, both had to be cautious of stepping on anything that might make a noise as they closed in.

After several more minutes of this exercise, Josef hooted in a way that he knew Jeremy would recognize. He could see Jeremy react by slowly drifting toward his shadow even as he continued forward. They soon entered a stand of trees that seemed even in winter to shut out the little light available from the glow of the stars. At that moment, Josef purposely stepped on a twig, snapping it. When the tail turned in the direction of the noise, Jeremy disappeared from the view of even his friends.

The man who had been following Jeremy hesitated and looked about in confusion in confusion and desperation, fearing his punishment if he should lose his quarry. Did the man suspect something or was this situation merely a chance occurrence? Finally, seeming to deep a deep breath, he plunged in to attempt to pick up the trail, bending low to attempt to distinguish Jeremy's footprints from all the others.

Once he had gone, Josef and Maurice followed silently and soon discovered that they were close upon the heels of Jeremy's stalker. They could just make the man out in the gloom as he continuously stopped to try to get his bearings and then move cautiously and tentatively forward.

Without warning, he came to a dead stop and Josef heard Jeremy's voice, which seemed to boom in this closely contained world they walked in.

"Why are you following me?" Jeremy could be heard demanding of the man in an authoritative straightforward manner.

Josef and Maurice instinctively moved farther apart to provide coverage to the greatest amount of ground possible.

Jeremy's stalker did not even attempt an answer. Without saying a word, he turned and bolted, not knowing where he was running in the dark, with Jeremy hot on his heels.

Josef stepped out in front of the frightened man just he was looking back over his shoulder again. He braced himself as the stalker crashed into him, never realizing until that precise moment that there had been someone standing there. Both men crashed to the snow and the stalker dropped his musket. As Josef struggled to his feet, the other scrambled about on the ground, momentarily searching desperately in the snow for the weapon.

"Just get up on your feet," Jeremy ordered. "You won't need the musket."

Josef came up behind the man, still brushing off the snow, just as Maurice rejoined them.

"Tie him to the small tree over there," Josef told Maurice.

Maurice pulled the man by his collar, keeping him off balance until he had him firmly against the young tree. He produced a piece of twine and pulled across his prisoner's throat, tying him quickly to the rough bark so that he would be less tempted to struggle. Josef then pulled is hands roughly back and tied them.

Jeremy walked up and looked closely at the face of the man they had captured.

"Why, are you even old enough to shave, lad?" he asked, the note of surprise evident in his voice. "How old are you, child?"

"I'm no child," their prisoner croaked, the twine about his throat impeding his speech. "I'm fourteen and plenty old enough to kill you if you didn't sneak up on me like that."

"Loosen off the tie on his throat," Josef told Maurice. "The sound of his croaking is unsettling."

Maurice laughed and complied.

"Well man or child, whichever you may be, why are you following me in the dead of a moonless night?" demanded Jeremy humourlessly.

The boy did not reply but just stared at them with hatred in his eyes.

"I do believe this may be a disciple," Jeremy suggested to his companions, while still looking at their stalker's eyes. "He has the crazy look of a willing martyr."

Josef stepped up in front of the prisoner and put his face mere inches from that of the boy. "Is that right, boy? Did the Parson send you?"

The boy glared at him and then turned away, unable to hold the stare. "I'm not telling you nothing," he nearly spat at his questioner.

Josef did not move. "Look very closely at my face," he told the boy in level but strained voice that even made Jeremy shiver. "What do you see?"

The lad looked closely at Josef again, the hostility still evident. Then his eyes opened wide as the realization hit him. "You're...you're an Indian..." His confidence seemed to evaporate as he sputtered out the dreaded words.

The young man began to shake. There would be no need to beat information from this prisoner. His fear of Indians would be all that was needed to break his spirit and hopefully loosen his tongue, provided he did not break down in utter terror.

"I feared that devil was yet alive," Jeremy muttered without waiting any longer for a confirmation from their prisoner. "It seemed too good a thing for him to have died in that boat." He walked up beside the youth and put his lips almost to the prisoner's ear. "Tell me. Where can I find the Parson?" he said menacingly, his voice barely above a whisper.

The youth just stared at Josef and ignored Jeremy.

"Very well," said Jeremy after several seconds of silence. "It's obvious the boy would rather die a horrible martyr's death than talk to us. Josef, you and your friend can have him to dispose of." He started to walk away and then turned back to his friends. "Try to keep the lad's screaming to a minimum, though, will you please? We don't want him heard all the way back to Newark."

The image invoked by that suggestion broke the last bit of resolve left in the lad. "He's just outside the tavern on the road ahead. I was but to follow you and make sure you were headed that way and to let him know if you were going elsewhere," he blurted out, the words falling from his mouth in a torrent that was almost too fast for his interrogators to understand.

"How did he even know we were here?"

The lad shrugged and shook his head at the same time. "I don't know. Honest mister, I don't know. He doesn't tell us such things."

Jeremy looked at his friends. "It seems that the bastard never learns by his mistakes. This is almost exactly how he dealt with us across the river the day after the burning of Newark."

"I don't know about that," said a familiar voice off to their right. "Even a dog as old as I am can learn, if not new tricks, then at least variations on an old trick."

The Parson stood not fifteen feet away. At a signal from him, a flint was struck several times, lighting a torch. In the fresh illumination Josef could see more men in a half circle around their position. Some were actually in the halo of the torchlight and some outside of it, making it extremely difficult to determine exactly how many there were. Not that it truly mattered. There were definitely too many for the three of them to take on, especially when caught at such a disadvantage.

"Kindly lay down your arms." The Parson's wording sounded like a request but the tone was unquestionably a command.

★ ★ ★

Jeremy and his friends looked around at each other, looking for any one of them to give a signal. But it was obvious by all their eyes that there was no inkling of a way out of this from any of them. Each set his weapon carefully on the ground, attempting to keep the pan out of snow as they did so.

When he first made his presence known, the Parson had been mostly concealed by the poor light. Even when the torch was lit near him, they still could not make out his face because of the flare of the fuel and the distraction of the other men.

But now the Parson stepped purposely forward and stopped directly in front of Jeremy. He grinned wickedly at his nemesis, highlighting the addition of something new in his appearance. A broad gash, closed but not yet healed, crossed the left side of his face, starting just below the hairline and ending on the right side, at the corner of his mouth. Over the left eye, he now sported an eye patch.

"Well, it's good to see that my long shot wasn't completely wasted," Jeremy muttered with an insolent smile.

The Parson's eyes flashed with hatred and then just as quickly returned to normal.

"Disciples, this is the meaning of obedience," he said, sweeping his arm broadly across the front of his body to take in all the prisoners and their laid down weapons. "And this," he said with a sound that seemed almost like a grunt as he punched Jeremy hard in the stomach "This is how disobedience is treated."

Jeremy stood half bent over, recovering his breath after the unexpected attack. The Parson's years as a miller certainly gave him a great deal of strength. With that fact Jeremy had no quarrel. He tried to straighten up just as two men stepped forward and grabbed him by the arms, pulling him upright.

The Parson punched Jeremy hard again, this time toward the right side, knocking the wind completely out of him.

"And this is for killing my disciples," he ranted. This time, he did not stop at a single punch, but bombarded Jeremy with a flurry of blows to the body that almost drove the consciousness from the trapper.

The Parson now jerked his head upward in a signal. One of the men holding Jeremy's arms grabbed a handful of the prisoner's hair and forced his head back. Now Jeremy was looking directly into the Parson's slightly perspiring and red face full of fury.

"And this is the wage for making it harder for your Parson to read his Holy Scripture, that he might bring you the Word of God and give you His direction."

The Parson seemed to pull back with his right shoulder and then swung with all his might at Jeremy's face. The ham-like fist ploughed into his prisoner's face and, despite the hold that his disciple had on Jeremy's hair, drove his head backwards.

Jeremy tried to focus, tried to think, but everything seemed to be slipping away. He could feel his eyes rolling back in his head against his efforts, and then everything went black.

Chapter Forty-One

Josef watched as, at a signal from the Parson, the disciples holding Jeremy let go of his arms and let him drop into the snow.

The Parson now rounded on Josef. "Let's see if savages can take a beating any better." He nodded to the same two men who had held Jeremy now rounded on him.

Josef took a stance to fight them, but he heard the sound of musket hammers being cocked and decided that he had better take the beating. Then he saw something that lifted his spirits. Behind the semi-circle of disciples, almost invisible beyond the glow from the torch, he could see several men slowly creeping up behind the Parson's men. They made no sound and no one was looking in that direction, even those supposedly on watch, for they were all watching the great sport of the Parson's beatings.

Josef could not determine who these shadows might be, but whoever they might be, they represented hope in a hopeless situation. He rather hoped that they were his fellow scouts who had stumbled upon them for some reason. At the same time, he knew in his heart that it was not to be, however. The shadows did not move quite like Indians.

Then the answer arrived, and Josef's spirits flagged.

"Have you gotten an answer yet?" asked a voice with a British accent. Colonel Halberson stepped into the light.

The Colonel was not wearing his uniform, Josef noticed. But then, having a warrant issued for his arrest had left him little reason to do so. And the scarlet colours would grant him no stead on this side of the river. Indeed, they would probably mean the death of him with either side if he were spotted.

"So, we meet again," the Parson seethed. "I was hoping that last time would have been just that…the last time."

"I see their guns have been laid down," Halberson mused, purposely ignoring the Parson. "Well, that's certainly a good idea. In fact, I suggest that you and your – what do you call them, disciples? – lay yours down as well."

The Parson's face flushed with rage. "You fool! I was about to get the location of the documents from this savage!"

"I believe that you, rather, are the fool," the Colonel replied. "You see, the Indians weren't there when the others escaped with the papers. And it would appear that you've rather handily laid out the only one of these three men who could possibly provide the answer that both you and I seek."

The Parson looked down in consternation at Jeremy, who still lay prone in the snow. Damned if the British bastard wasn't right.

As Josef followed his glance, he saw the same thing that the Parson had. But he noticed something else as well. Jeremy had shifted his position a little, probably to get a bit more comfortable while awaiting an opportunity.

"Be that as it may," the Parson returned with a forced calm. "You have no right to the documents. They belonged to my brother-in-law and they shall be mine." The light of the torch was beginning to betray a flash of fanaticism in his eyes.

"Belonged to you brother-in-law," the Colonel repeated in the same calm manner. "You seem to lack an understanding of the meaning of war."

The Parson laughed humourlessly. "You mean you've suddenly become a patriot?" he mocked. "It's a bit late for that, don't you think?"

"I'm no patriot," Halberson growled. "That's an emotion best left to the fools of the world. What I speak of is the principal of war that allows one to keep whatever one has the strength to take."

"Do you think you have that strength?" the Parson asked insolently. Then he suddenly screamed 'fire!' and dropped to the ground.

With all the talk that had been taking place, no one seemed to remember that the Parson's men had been ordered to lay down their weapons. Halberson had also neglected to notice that the command had not been obeyed.

Suddenly, the forest was filled with the flashes of the lit pans and the explosions of powder and balls as the muskets were being fired. Screams and battle cries filled the air as the skirmish built in intensity, although hardly anyone knew at whom they were shooting or what, if anything, they were hitting. It hardly seemed to matter anymore. A bloodlust had taken the place of all sensibility and the two sides merely kept firing, reloading and firing again in the direction that they thought they had last seen an enemy.

Josef had dropped straight to the ground as soon as the shooting started and Maurice, he saw, had done the same. He crawled over to Jeremy and shook him, trying to revive him.

However, Jeremy was not unconscious. Much as Josef had suspected, if there had been any loss of consciousness, it had been momentary. He had been playing possum, waiting for a chance to make a move against their captors. It was no longer necessary and as soon as Josef touched him, he raised himself to his elbows.

Josef gave quick signal with his head and the three crawled to a set of low spruce bushes after recovering their guns. Then out of sight of the fighting parties, they allowed themselves the luxury of rising so that they were merely bent at the waist to keep low. They ran as well as they could in that position until they were completely clear of the battle and the wildly aimed ammunition.

★ ★ ★

It took Jeremy, Josef and Maurice close to three quarters of an hour to reach the Niagara River, held back by Jeremy's beaten and bruised state. When they arrived, only minutes before midnight, they sat down on a large fallen tree a good thirty paces from the water's edge. It was not long before they were joined by the others of their group.

"Did you hear shooting a while ago?" asked the Caughnawaga called Chevalier.

"Did you?" asked Jeremy in return. He was concerned because they had been told not draw any attention to themselves.

"I'm really not sure," Chevalier replied. "I suppose it could have been anything. The forest can be like that."

"You did indeed hear shooting. I just wanted to see if it was obvious." Jeremy then proceeded to tell the others of their experience.

"By the way," he started. "Where is our contact this morning? It's quite unlike him to be late for his report."

Before anyone could comment, they heard the sound of muffled oars in the water. As the group moved to the last cover before the shore, they saw an amazing sight. All manner of boats were crossing the Niagara River together. They made no sound but for an occasional creak from an oarlock. No one spoke nor coughed. No muskets rattled. Almost like ghost vessels, they slid quietly up to the shore and scores of men proceeded to climb out, taking great care not to splash as they did so.

Jeremy recognized a number of the men in the invading force. They were neighbours from different parts of the Peninsula, mostly Loyalists. Their faces were set in grim determination as they poured out of their boats and soon crowded the landing.

The man in front, who was surrounded by men in a manner unfamiliar to Jeremy, was surprised to find the trapper suddenly standing there before him and swung his musket forward, pointing his bayonet directly at the trapper's Adam's apple.

"Whoa! Hold there, neighbour!" Jeremy whispered. "I'm a friend." He whispered the by-words, hoping that the soldier would be aware of their mission.

As the men from the boats passed them in silence the lead man quickly explained. "I'm Colonel John Murray. These men are the Forlorn Hope and we're here to teach the Americans a lesson about treating our families as they did in Newark. I assume you're Jeremy van Hijser?"

Jeremy nodded. "We were supposed to meet our contact here. However, he hasn't come to bring us back across."

"He didn't return last night, and we've no way of knowing if he's been compromised," the Colonel explained. "And there won't be time to row you and your men across. We need to act quickly and quietly if we hope to succeed. So you can wait here until it's done, or you can come with us." He started to leave and then turned. "Oh, by the way, if you're coming, remove your ammunition and fix bayonets if you have any. Say, are those Caughnawagas up there with you?"

"Yes they are," Jeremy answered, slightly puzzled.

"Could you please send them on to Lewiston? We need some advance scouting there for there will be another invasion force headed there when we give the signal. Have them meet Major-General Riall a mile and a half south of Lewiston near the shore in about an hour and a half. Tell them to use the same by-words."

"They're not mine to command, but I'll do my best Colonel," Jeremy replied.

He went back to his group and explained what was wanted. Then all of the Caughnawagas but Josef started off toward Lewiston and Jeremy and Josef fell in with the invading force.

★ ★ ★

They followed the advance party for some distance before they reached a tavern that Jeremy and his friend had been keeping an eye on in the past few days. In spite of regular comings and goings of soldiers, there seemed to be little in the way of any organized action here. However, it was reasonably certain that this place, at least tonight, was being used by the American advance guard.

Although it seemed that, in this war's porous security, someone must surely have leaked the information of a coming attack to the Americans by now. However, the enemy appeared strangely lax in their security. The single guard outside the door was killed quickly and quietly. After signalling to Jeremy to keep an eye out for reinforcements, the others charged inside.

Jeremy and his companion could hear shouting coming from inside, but not a shot was fired. Suddenly all was quiet again and the Montrealers known as the Forlorn Hope exited from the tavern with blood on their bayonets. Silently they filed by, already steeling themselves for the next phase of the assault.

"Maybe twenty American soldiers in there," one man grumbled softly to Jeremy as he went by. Then his voice grew incredulous. "They were all playing cards!"

Not long afterward, the advance party reached the edge of the clearing where Fort Niagara stood. No one believed this would be easy, for this fort was one of the best fortified on the frontier.

Approximately four hundred soldiers occupied this fort, which stood silhouetted against the dark night sky. Three large towers looked over the landscape and Jeremy knew from his reconnaissance and from British reports that the ramparts were protected by almost thirty artillery pieces. The guns were aimed primarily in the direction of the water, since the fort had initially been constructed by the British to guard the entrance to the Niagara River.

The force waited until all the men, now numbering over five hundred, all positioned themselves around the fort. The tension built as the time for an attack grew closer, many knowing full well that there would be some not going home after this battle. But the hatred aroused by the burning of Newark and especially the turning out of women and children into a snowstorm overcame such fear as was present that night.

Then Jeremy saw the Forlorn Hope move out again, running up under the walls where those on the ramparts could not see them. They were to fight their way into the fort by getting the guard to open the gate just a little and then force their way in. But then the British were the recipients of the closest to what one might call a miracle.

Just as the forward men reached the corner of the fort around from its gate, the drawbridge came down! By pure chance, the British had arrived just in time for the changing of the guard! Scarcely believing their luck, the soldiers charged in through the gate, their muskets still not loaded, but screaming wildly as the pent up adrenaline demanded an outlet. Immediately the fort's defenders were awake.

Once again Jeremy and Josef, along with some others, acted as rear guard while a seemingly lukewarm battle was engaged inside the fort. They could not understand why the whole thing was going so quietly, however. They heard shouts of shock, and the occasional shot, but there was no real sound of battle until they heard a single cannon shot from one of the towers.

And then suddenly it was over. A cheer arose from the fort.

Some of the soldiers came out to relieve the rear guard and Jeremy and Josef headed inside. At one side of the fort was a stack of weapons taken from the American soldiers and on the end, on the green, stood the population of the fort, most looking bewildered and all seeming frightened.

A member of the Forlorn Hope recognized Jeremy and stopped for a moment. "They hardly put up a fight!" he exclaimed in obvious disbelief. "It seemed as though they thought it was peace time."

As the two men moved further into the fort, they heard a shout up ahead. "Look in here! I believe I've found the stores!" someone cried out excitedly.

Jeremy followed some others to the doorway into which the man was pointing. He stepped inside with two junior officers.

The room in which they stood seemed filled to the rafters with supplies, many of them identifiable as having been stolen from the Canadian side, especially Fort George, during the occupation. Hundreds of guns lined one wall, all seemingly in good repair, along with barrels of ammunition for them. Clothing and boots and provisions filled the shelves of the other walls – more than any of the men here had ever seen in one place.

They wandered about in amazement, checking the stored goods, until a senior officer entered and shooed them out.

"Have you heard?" someone near Jeremy shouted to another, just as the trapper came back out of the stores. "There's a rumour that Colonel Murray is willing to share the prize money with us all!"

Jeremy and Josef did not stay to join in the celebration. They had promised to meet the main invasion force north of Lewiston and decided they had best move on if they were to arrive around the time the British fired their single cannon shot to signal the Riall and his men that it was safe to attack.

But first, they had another short assignment to complete.

★ ★ ★

Jeremy and Josef joined a party sent out to reconnoitre the countryside for possible reinforcements which they were quite certain did not exist. Their three days of scouting had found no sign of any other troops or even so much as a hint that there might be any on the way. In the meantime, the main body of British at Fort Niagara set in as an occupation force.

"There's someone up ahead," one of the soldiers whispered suddenly, as the night began slowly to give way to another day.

Stealthily, Jeremy, Josef and a few soldiers, a Lieutenant with family from Newark among them, crept up on the clearing that the soldier pointed out. Jeremy looks carefully through the branches of a stand of cedar. These trees, meant to hide those on the other side, now allowed Jeremy to watch unnoticed. What he saw amused him, and a smile formed on his tired lips.

"Lieutenant, I think one of the higher officers might want to see this before we close in," he whispered.

The officer sent a soldier for one of superior rank, who appeared in the form of a Captain.

Jeremy took a quick look through the trees and then summoned the Captain over to see for himself. What the Captain saw were several men changing out of civilian clothes and donning British Army uniforms.

"What is the meaning of this?" the Captain asked. "Who are these men and why are they changing into our uniforms? Are they spies?"

"No sir," replied Jeremy. "Allow me to introduce Colonel James Halberson, late of Burlington Heights and a wanted deserter. He probably learned what happened at Fort Niagara and decided that he and his men could blend in by donning their uniforms and merely falling in as your force passed by." He smiled at the Captain.

"On three, men!" he whispered to the others. "If they resist, shoot them!"

On the other side of the cedar screen, Halberson looked up and then glanced about, as if he had heard something. Then, deciding that he probably had not, he returned to the process of adjusting his uniform.

Chapter Forty-Two

Suddenly, a large number of soldiers poured from among the trees and surrounded the half-dozen men which were all that remained of Colonel Halberson's original force. They already looked somewhat beat up, with bayonet wounds and the occasional musket wound to show for the previous night's set-to with the Parson.

"British soldiers!" he shouted, at first panicky. Then he saw his chance to play act his way out of the mess. "Thank God you've arrived!" We had just..."

The Colonel's words died in his throat as he saw the last two men come through the cedars. "You!" he cried, at a loss to say any more.

"Save your story for your courts martial," the Captain said evenly.

"What have these men told you?" Halberson demanded. "As your superior officer, I demand that you arrest these two!"

"Save it, Colonel Halberson. All of the officers have been apprised of the warrant out for your arrest. Now, kindly remain standing where you are while my men determine that you are unarmed."

Grumbling, the Colonel did as he was told and his men followed suit, resignation written on their pained and exhausted faces. Jeremy quickly stepped forward, eager to search Halberson himself.

Josef came running up, having set out on a bit of scouting of his own volition. After glancing with a certain amount of satisfaction at the Colonel and his men and flashing them a broad grin, he pulled Jeremy aside.

"The Parson and his disciples are coming this way," he said softly.

"Captain," Jeremy called out. "How would you like to make an even bigger arrest this morning?"

"What do you have in mind?" the Captain asked in reply.

Jeremy filled him in on the impending arrival of yet more guests and told him of the plan he had in mind. The Captain called his men to him and explained to them what they were to do as well. The exhausted soldiers were at first merely compliant, but when their Captain explained to them exactly who was coming, they became quite enthusiastic about the idea.

★ ★ ★

The Parson and his men were sneaking quietly away from the area of the fort. What a lot of fools, he thought to himself. It's a good thing they didn't want us low-life traitors in their fort with them or we'd all be prisoners by now. I even brought them the deserter I found wandering about. He told them the Brits were going to attack. But for some reason the idiots felt that, since it didn't happen the same night, the man was wrong and there was to be no attack after all.

Well, he wasn't about to suffer the fate of those stupid officers that wouldn't listen to him. He would get his men as far away from there as possible before the British moved on.

Then one of his men returned from a quick scout up ahead and reported something that changed his mind, at least for the time being.

The Parson and his disciples carefully approached the low fire the scout had smelled from some distance away. The first thing he saw was several British soldiers lying wrapped in blankets on the ground about the fire. But he could hardly believe his luck when he saw that his nemesis of the previous night, and the only one who knew of the papers other than Jeremy and his crowd, was sitting beside the fire, his back to the approaching men.

He ordered his disciples to fan out and sneak up on the unsuspecting Colonel Halberson and his oblivious men. This they did, although several of them also sported wounds from last night's fracas in the woods. Most were quite looking forward to getting even for that without apparently any danger to themselves.

Although he was not a particularly brave man the Parson decided that, under the circumstances, he would take the Colonel himself. Quietly he crept up behind the officer who, by his posture also seemed to be asleep. He pulled a pistol from his belt and, cocking the hammer, placed the barrel right behind the unsuspecting man's left ear.

"Don't move," he growled happily as his men moved into the campsite.

Still no one stirred, including the Colonel. Something was wrong.

The Parson gave Halberson a light shove and the Colonel tipped over, landing still unresponsive, in the snow. Then he moaned. The man had been unconscious!

"Pull out!" he screamed at his disciples. "Pull out now!"

But it was much too late. He noticed that dozens of muskets were pointing at him and his disciples, all hammers cocked.

"I suggest you stay still," a voice said evenly. It was a voice that the Parson recognized.

As he looked up, he saw Jeremy step forward from among the soldiers. The man sported a huge grin as he walked up and pulled the pistol from the shocked man's grasp. Then the man searched him – his pockets, his hat and his boots – and stepped back.

"He has no other weapons," he announced.

Then Jeremy turned to the soldiers surrounding the campsite, who had disarmed the disciples as well. "How many of you men have been affected by Willcocks' Canadian Volunteers?" he asked. Many of the men put up their hands.

"And how many of you were victimized by that bastard Williamson when he was alive?" he asked. This time almost a quarter of the soldiers raised their hands, wondering where this was leading.

"And just one more question," he announced. He walked across his prisoner's field of vision, his hands behind his back. "How many of you are familiar with the Parson and his group of sanctimonious misfits?" Most growled in the affirmative, many of them now suspecting the point of Jeremy's questioning.

"Well gentlemen," Jeremy said, looking about at the anxious faces about him. "This is Phineas Billings, better known as the Parson. You may not know this, but he was Dorian Williamson's brother-in-law, and he is a Canadian Volunteer." He looked around at the anger quickly rising to a boil. "That's right, gentlemen. This man is a neighbour of yours. He has a farm near the Twenty, although he hasn't worked it in at least a year. He has been too busy robbing you and making life miserable for everyone you know. And he was with Willcocks when the bastard burned Newark! I saw him there with my own eyes."

"Hang him!" someone shouted, followed by many more. Soon the forest was filled with the sound of men wishing to end the menace of the Parson once and for all.

"I'm dreadfully sorry men, I'm afraid he must go back and stand trial," the Captain shouted, if somewhat half-heartedly, trying to be heard above the voices of his men.

It was no good, however. If anyone heard him, there was no evidence that anyone was paying any attention. The militiamen had turned instantly into a mob with nothing but vengeance on their minds. Ropes were produced and thrown over branches on the trees and nooses were placed about the necks of the Parson and all his men, some of whom screamed for leniency. But, one after another, they were hoisted by their necks and a collective cheer arose from the throats of those the Parson had victimized.

When Jeremy and Josef walked away from the scene, Colonel Halberson were being revived and led away in chains which had been obtained from Fort Niagara. And the Parson and his men were still kicking the air in futile attempts to find solid footings.

★ ★ ★

Jeremy and Josef joined those who headed north toward Lewiston to continue the punishment of the Americans. They had promised that they would meet General Riall and his main force and, although neither had a watch, both estimated that it would be five o'clock quite soon.

They were but a few minutes short of the rendezvous when they heard the echo of single cannon shot from behind them. Quickening their step, they crept carefully to the shore to see an amazing sight, just as the rest of their Caughnawaga friends met them to report as well.

The five hundred or so men who had attacked Fort Niagara seemed like nothing at all to the two men as they watched boat after boat launch from the Upper Canadian side of the river. The first were already beaching, but still the Niagara seemed filled from side to side with all manner of boat, and still more were pushing off. Where Merritt and his men had found so many vessels was a mystery.

Jeremy had been told that there would be close to five thousand troops and another five hundred Indians, mostly Mohawks from the Grand River. He had accepted that figure without question, but the numbers meant little until now, as he watched them all cross the river.

As the first boat was completed being hauled up from the river, Jeremy and Josef approached the officer who was most likely General Riall. He was of the understanding that the man liked to lead from the front in such situations.

"The best books are saved," said a rather haughty Lieutenant, who intercepted Jeremy before he could reach the General.

"One must have a good read."

"Very well then. You must be our man," the General started, ignoring the Natives that were with him. "What information do you have for me? And kindly remember that we had no word last night."

"Yes, I know. I was informed when the men crossed to take Fort Niagara," Jeremy replied, and then he and the Caughnawagas proceeded to tell the General everything they knew about the American defences up ahead. The general gist of the news was that, aside from a small contingent of militia, there were no defences. The Americans had been depending upon the fort to protect this end of the river.

★ ★ ★

Before all of the boats had even reached shore or unloaded their cargoes of men and supplies, the vast column started forward. They had landed near a place that Jeremy knew as Five Meadows, but found there was no opposition from this place. And on they marched, in ranks, a never-ending line stretching back to the landing point and seemingly across the river to Queenston.

Jeremy and Josef had run on ahead and had already climbed the rise below Lewiston. From here they watched the approaches for several minutes. Seeing nothing of great interest to them, they ran off ahead to reconnoitre the town itself.

Nobody seemed to be awake yet. Scarcely a soul stirred and the two strangers just continued up the street, looking about in disbelief. At what they would soon discover to be the militia post there was no frantic activity or, indeed, any activity whatsoever. In fact, the sole militiaman sat outside the post, sound asleep.

"How can it be that they've not heard the word that the fort was taken and the British are on the march?" Jeremy asked, confounded.

"I don't know," Josef answered, looking up and down the street as though expecting a trap. "Secrecy is usually the dream of generals. I guess the Forlorn Hope truly prevented a single man from escaping."

"Would they not have a signal so that the fort could let them know of an invasion? A signal such as the one I heard fired near the end of battle at Fort Niagara?"

"Surely, one would think so. Maybe the fort was just taken too quickly. Or maybe no one is paying any mind."

They walked back toward the edge of Lewiston's main street just in time for the first British troops to come into view. There was nothing to tell the military as they approach so, to stay out of their way, the two friends continued on ahead to do some further scouting for when the British were ready to move on.

Alarms of every type began to sound as someone finally noticed their enemy approaching. People poured into the streets and began to run away in panic from the coming invasion. Every form of conveyance was used to try to escape and bring what little goods they could with them. As the two men watched, the heavy horse, buggy and cart traffic snarled before reaching the edge of town. Wagons overturned, wheels ripped from buggies and men were unhorsed as the frightening cacophony spooked the animals, often driving them of down the road without their intended loads.

People abandoned their goods in the roadway as it became evident to them that they could either escape or keep their belongings, but not both. Children became detached from their parents and stood crying in the street while the remaining horses and carts rushed perilously by them.

"This looks much like Newark did when we got there, doesn't it?" Jeremy said sadly to his companion.

Josef just nodded in agreement.

It was then that things became even worse. The British officers lost control of their men, who ran in and out of buildings, knocking down all who got in their way. They looted all they could carry and then someone set fire to one of the buildings.

Now screaming wildly to scare anyone who was not already completely terrified, the Mohawks accompanying the troops ran amok as well.

The town's militia, after firing a few desultory shots at the oncoming enemy, had turned and run, they themselves partaking of the looting on the way. The last of them now passed Jeremy, shouting, "Run for it man! Save yourself!" It never occurred to them that the two men might not be friends.

With tears forming in his eyes, Jeremy turned sadly to Josef. "I won't be a party to this," he said in simple disgust.

"Nor I," agreed Josef softly. "And you know it'll be little different from this for the balance of the way to Buffalo and beyond if given the chance."

Just then another building burst into flames, to the cheers of the men in the streets. This would be only the start of an orgy of arson as the uncontrollable men started throwing torches through already smashed windows.

Jeremy and Josef started walking back through town, through the madness and the smoke and the discarded property and carts filling the streets. A number of times, they stopped to help officers as they tried to prevent some personal crime or other. Twice they came across a Lewiston citizen being accosted by some soldiers and they stepped in long enough for the person to run away.

Finally they reached the north end of town where General Riall stood watching the fiasco, the disgust evident on his face.

"I told Drummond he could bring the Indians only if he could control them," he said dumbly as they walked by.

Jeremy could see the anger in Josef's face at the remark and headed off any retaliation by his friend. "I believe your problem is greater than just the Indians," he said evenly. "None of your men, red or white, is under control."

Riall turned his head to give Jeremy a dressing-down, but before he could say anything, Josef interrupted him.

"What makes you any better than the men who burned Newark?" he asked flatly.

Then, with a last glance back at the burning town, Jeremy and Josef headed sadly back to the landing where they could take a boat to get back.

★ ★ ★

When they reached the Queenston side of the river, they were immediately helped in beaching the boat by Oliver and several soldiers, all of whom had been posted here for just this purpose.

"How did it go?" Oliver asked with a mixture of dread and excitement as soon as his cousin was firmly ashore.

"It was quite something," Jeremy began, and stopped. He swallowed, trying to clear the lump in his throat, and then went into great detail explaining what had happened, including tales of both the heroic and the somewhat less than heroic aspects of the action. Afterward, they sat quietly on the shore looking across the river.

"Do you think any of this was worth the cost?" Oliver thought aloud.

"I don't think so at all," Josef commented, before Jeremy could reply. "It will take some time before all the destruction can be put behind both sides."

"Let's see if we can get something to eat, somewhere without quite so many curious ears," Jeremy said suddenly. He nodded toward the nearby soldiers who were busy pretending not to listen in. He had things that he wished to say that might not sit well with some of the more militant types in uniform.

"By the way, have you seen Maurice and the others?" Josef asked, trying to mask his anxiety over the welfare of his clansmen.

"Yes, they came across over an hour before you," Oliver answered. "They all managed to make it, although none seemed anxious to speak of it."

"We met them before Lewiston and perhaps they had the opportunity to see what we'd seen."

The three of them rose stiffly from the log they had been sitting on and headed for the road.

Chapter Forty-Three

They eventually reached the tavern just outside of the village of St. Davids, and there they stopped for a meal.

"Do you have a meal for three weary veterans of the battles at Fort Niagara and Lewiston?" he asked the tavern keeper, like others in the area, a man he knew. He was hoping to head off any objections the man might have to an Indian in his establishment.

Whether any objections were to have been forthcoming, they would never know, for the tavern keeper was eager to hear of the battles.

Jeremy told the innkeeper he tell him what he wanted to know after they had something to eat. After being told that their meal would be on the house, they eagerly ordered some of the stew they had smelled wafting from the fire ever since the moment they had entered. Along with a chunk of bread each and mug of ale, they finally relaxed and allowed the relative comforts of civilization to seep into their very beings.

"At least we needn't hide any longer," Jeremy commented as he took a large gulp from his mug. "Halberson is on his way to a hanging I suspect, and the Parson was hung on the spot. Other than Willcocks himself, who was last seen escaping toward Buffalo, we seem to have no more personal enemies."

Oliver swallowed the bread that was in his mouth. "There's only one thing that has me curious is what happened to the documents. You say you searched them both and neither had them?" he asked his cousin. "Could it be that they gave them to someone else to hold?"

Jeremy laughed ironically. "Those two megalomaniacs? Give something that important to someone else? I think they'd sooner trust the Devil himself than one of the cutthroats they travelled with." He took another drink. "At least, I know I would."

"As to what did actually happen to them, I really have no idea. Maybe we dropped them somewhere during our escape and they're still lying on the side of the Mountain somewhere. From there, they could have blown away or washed away or collected by the forest animals to line nests and dens. Any number of things could have happened to them." He looked around at his companions tiredly, from one face to the other. "Truth be told, I'm not at all sure that I even wish to know anymore. A few pieces of paper can't be worth all we've been through in the past weeks and I'm truly not certain that I want to help either side after what we've seen in the past few days."

Oliver and Josef nodded in agreement, both being overcome by their exhaustion now that they had full stomachs. Jeremy could fully understand for he was quite ready to collapse himself.

The tavern keeper knew Jeremy was aware of their activities as only a tavern keeper could. He noticed his nodding customers.

"So Jeremy, were you actually involved in the fighting over the river?" he asked eagerly. When Jeremy nodded slightly, he continued. "Well thank you from all of us who lost so much to those rogues. A good many folks lost their livelihoods from here to Newark when their properties were burned. Anyway, you and your companions look to be quite done in. Why don't you go have a lie down in the common room," he suggested, referring to the large room in which travellers all stayed together.

"Thank you, Aaron," Jeremy replied. "I think we just might take you up on your offer."

They slept the balance of the afternoon and all through the evening and night as well. When they awoke, they found someone had placed rough blankets over them to help keep them warm.

They went down to the ale room one last time for some breakfast before heading on to Jeremy's home at the Twenty. As they were about to enter however, Jeremy stopped suddenly, putting up his arm to arrest the forward motion of his companions as well.

"What is it?" Josef asked, immediately steeled for trouble.

"Do you believe in ghosts?" Jeremy asked distantly while staring straight ahead.

"Why?" Oliver piped in. "What's this about ghosts?"

Jeremy pointed to a table in the corner of the room and said, almost in a whisper, "Do you see someone familiar in the corner there?"

Oliver and Josef looked where Jeremy had directed. If there actually had been a sound for jaws dropping, the noise would surely have given them away. There, as large as life, sat a ghost. Few other explanations were possible, for the man they saw sitting there spooning preserves onto a thick slice of bread was dead. They had all seen it.

Slowly they walked quietly over to the table and Jeremy, Oliver and Josef sat down at the "spectre's" table, hemming him in so that he could not bolt for the door.

"Well, hello, Davis," Jeremy said conversationally, holding his true emotions in check. "You have exceptionally good colour for a corpse."

Startled, Davis Halberson looked up and sat speechless for several seconds. He had traded in his British infantry uniform for clothes more suitable to a colonial and he had started on a growth of beard, but it had not yet developed to the point where it could disguise his features. He looked warily from face to face and then, unexpectedly, he burst out laughing.

"I truly never expected to see you three again," he said and laughed even louder, a nervous edge easily detectable in the false sound. "Indeed, I sincerely hoped that I would not. But if only you could see your faces through my eyes."

Just then, four soldiers entered the tavern and sat down not far from the four men.

"I think you had best explain what you're doing here," said Jeremy firmly, throwing toward the soldiers with an exaggerated glance.

"What makes you think that I'd do anything of the sort?"

"It's over for you now," Jeremy replied softy but menacingly. "But if you tell us what happened, just to humour us, it may be that we'll but take the documents I'm sure that you somehow have in your possession. If, however, you would prefer..." He nodded in the direction of the infantrymen, allowing the threat to dangle in the air between them.

Davis thought about for about a minute, glancing nervously toward the military men, one of whom stared back. Apparently that one had become aware that there was something amiss at the nearby table.

"Very well, I suppose you leave me very little choice." He was no longer laughing. "When you saw me being shot, you'll remember that you set off after Parsons and never looked closely at the wound."

"Do go on."

"Well, while you were fighting the Parson, I used the opportunity to steal away. It was nothing more than that."

Davis looked at Josef and then at each of the other two. He positioned himself like he was going to straighten his back out in his chair but then suddenly tried to stand up as if to bolt for the door.

Jeremy and Josef each grabbed Davis by a shoulder and pulled him roughly back down. Jeremy leaned over took a handful of the "dead" man's shirt with the intention of giving him a shake. The soldier that had previously glanced at them turned around again and looked at them curiously.

As Jeremy had grasped Davis' shirt, however, he had felt something but skin there.

"Hello, what have we here, then?" he said softly, the item under Davis' shirt feeling vaguely familiar. Keeping one hand firmly on the young man's shoulder, he ripped down on the shirt with the other. A packet fell out into the former infantryman's lap.

They all stared at the packet where it lay, too stunned to move. Finally, Jeremy picked it up and held it under Davis' nose.

"So I was correct in assuming that someone had found these," he said, with more than a small measure of bewilderment, not having truly ever expected to see them again. "But how did you get them?"

Davis looked from one to the other, and then over to the soldiers, one of whom was looking directly at them once more and seemed to be getting ready to rise. "I don't know if it would be wise for me to tell you that."

Jeremy sat back, allowing Josef to keep a close eye on their prisoner. "Well, that's fine. If you like, those men in uniform there can interview you for the answers we'd like to hear. Or, if it suits you better, you can tell us later, after my friend Josef has a little talk with you in private."

Davis shivered visibly. "Very well, then. Although I've heard you make that threat to others but I've never actually witnessed Josef harming anyone, except in battle," he said without great conviction, his argument apparently not convincing even him. "After I played dead I followed you lot to the Heights from just below the edge and, after you jumped from the overhang, I saw you tumble by. And there I saw them, bouncing to the ground not ten feet from where I hid. You must have dropped them."

"So you were out to get the documents all this time. And were you working alone in this, or was it but a miracle that your uncle came along behind us?" Jeremy asked.

Now Davis was truly frightened. He was going to be forced to tell these men more than he wanted to impart. But a glance over at Josef told him that the Indian, although civilized, would be happy to convince him to talk. At least if he spoke here, he could wait for a chance to run. In the meantime it was unlikely they would physically harm him in the tavern.

For his part, Jeremy was tired of this man's dissembling. It was time to shake him up a little. "Josef, I think you'll be forced to have a little talk with this man. He seems reluctant to share his information with us and now we've caught him in a lie. Even if he talks, I'm not at all certain that he'll tell us the truth." He glared at Davis.

The infantryman blanched. Despite his earlier bluster, he had always been deathly afraid of Josef. "No," he almost whispered. "No, that won't be necessary. I swear that if you lie again, I'll go outside and shoot myself for you."

"You won't get off nearly that easily. Besides, you've already told us how you've tricked us that way once already," Oliver growled, catching the spirit of the interrogation.

"You needn't worry about that," Davis pleaded. His eyes darted anxiously from Oliver to Jeremy and coming to rest on Josef.

Jeremy could hear the panic in the young man's voice. It was a fear well beyond what was rational under the circumstances. While Indians made many people nervous, they did not usually elicit such terror. "Very well, once again, how did your uncle just happen along at that particular point in time?"

Davis seemed to resign himself to an explanation. Taking a deep breath to calm his panic, he began again.

★ ★ ★

Davis sighed, as if in resignation. These men seemed to pick up on just the right questions to ask. But, before he could continue, Jeremy broke into his thoughts again, and what he had to say struck him like a hammer blow.

"It might be helpful you to know that your uncle has been arrested and charged with treason," Jeremy said.

Davis looked at him open-mouthed for almost a full minute and almost seemed to break into a smile, which he seemed almost to swallow. Then, almost hesitantly, he asked, "And what of the Parson and his men? Do you know where they went?"

Jeremy thought this an odd question, unrelated to their discussion but he decided to just answer it for now. "They went to Hell, hanged outside of Fort Niagara." He watched the young man's face for reaction and was not disappointed. Davis seemed to suddenly pick up.

Davis sighed deeply, as though setting aside all else. "Very well, then. Colonel Halberson asked me to get the documents once you figured it out. You were already on the way to solving the clues so, when he realized where you seemed to be going, he sent me to follow from below, where I wouldn't be spotted. I was dead, you know?" he added ironically.

"Yes. We know," Jeremy said humourlessly. "Go on."

"Well, when I arrived you already had them. I heard the Colonel demand them from you and then I saw you two plummeting by my hiding spot under the ledge. For a moment, I was certain you'd seen me, but then I noticed you were both a little dazed when you landed. I momentarily entertained the idea of killing you both, but that would have been nearly impossible." He smiled. "Fortunately for me, I spotted the document on the slope where you first landed on the slope, only feet from where I sat. Before you two managed to gather your wits about you, I grabbed them and made my escape."

"And then you tried to follow us along the Mountain, didn't you?" asked Oliver.

Davis nodded.

"See, I didn't imagine it. I really did hear sounds of someone following," Oliver declared almost triumphantly.

"But we lost you at the St. Davids Road didn't we," added Jeremy. "So you told the Colonel that we'd gone on to St. Davids and he did the rest by questioning the locals. But we were too smart for a mere Colonel."

"You mean you were there after all?" Disbelief showed on Davis' face.

"We were on the roof until we saw your uncle leave," Jeremy replied, grinning. "But then, he didn't know that we didn't have the documents, did he?"

Davis looked away, and then sat back in his chair as if he were finished.

"I didn't think so, or he wouldn't have bothered to continue chasing us. But I think you should continue," said Jeremy quietly, looking down at his ale.

Davis feigned confusion. "What are you talking about?"

"Well," started Jeremy, leaning forward. "You explained how you came to have our documents…"

"Your documents?" Davis fairly exploded the incredulity heavy in his voice. "Those were my documents, by birthright!" He suddenly clamped his mouth shut, as if he'd said too much.

"By birthright," Oliver repeated. "Whatever does he mean by that?" he asked his cousin. "Perhaps you should have him explain that remark."

Jeremy nodded slowly. "I've had a very busy several weeks, Mr. Halberson, and not very pleasant ones at that," he said deliberately. "Suppose you explain all of this, from the beginning. I'm much too tired to draw all the facts from you, item by item, so I'll ask you only this once to explain it all, from the beginning. And if I suspect you're leaving anything out – and I must say you have a penchant for letting things slip – I'll let Josef question you until you sing every chorus without any prompting questions. Then you can go off with the soldiers over there."

He smashed the table with his fist, making Davis, and his companions, jump. The soldiers across the room looked over to see if there was a problem.

"I'm not Davis Halberson," the young man said, unloading the bombshell out of nowhere. "My name is Samuel Worthington. And I'm not Halberson's nephew. I'm the bastard son of Dorian Williamson. I was raised near Buffalo while he was over here, fighting." He sat back and allowed that information sink in while nervously eyeing the soldiers. "I was supposed to get the papers that Oliver saw being taken by the man who turned out to be Sims."

"So you see, those documents are my birthright."

The threesome opposite him was momentarily speechless. They exchanged glances, for this was quite unexpected.

"Well done," grumbled Jeremy. "If not for this very morning, we would likely never have known."

"But why are you connected to Halberson?" asked Oliver.

"I think I can answer that," replied Jeremy. "Davis…," he continued. "…pardon me, Samuel here must have known Williamson had left something and it had to do with those papers. For some reason and, at this point in time, it doesn't matter what that reason was, he approached

Halberson and convinced the Colonel that there were documents that were worth a great deal. He needed someone with connections to the British hierarchy in case he needed to sell the items, whatever they might be, when the time came."

"He somehow found out that Halberson was dishonourable enough to partner with him, so they teamed up to get it from Sims." He stopped and looked at their prisoner. "And the choice of cover was quite excellent. When the two realized that we might be threatening the operation, you joined up with us so that we might lead you to it. Who could be better than the rebellious nephew of an unpopular British Colonel?" He nodded his head in appreciation. "Very good. Am I close?"

"Near enough," was the almost whispered reply.

Chapter Forty-Four

Jeremy and the rest sat back and studied Worthington while they let the information sink in.

"But why did you ask about the Parson?"

"That bastard is my real uncle and, since he obviously knew about the documents, he felt that they belonged to him now since he travelled with my father while he was alive. The bastard was quite willing to kill me over them, or would have been, had he known my identity." He let out a forced laugh.

Jeremy nodded. That made perfect sense. It seems that the Parson was this man's enemy as much as he was theirs.

"So, please tell me why you decided to cheat your partner."

"I figured he was trying to cut me out when he told me to stay away after I faked my death, so I decided to see if I could help myself. Halberson, by the way, never knew my true identity either."

"Very well, then," Jeremy said, looking directly at the former infantryman. "I think that answers all the important questions. The only one left now is what to do with him. But first, I have one last question."

Worthington looked up expectantly but said nothing.

"Halberson surely seems to have known a great deal about our movements and intentions. Obviously that information was coming from you. But how did he get it?"

Worthington gave a snort that Jeremy supposed was meant as a type of derisive laughter. "There were all manner of opportunities to get away from you and talk to Halberson. Just think back of all the times we were split up or separated for a time. For instance, when we camped just before

Long Beach, I arose when everyone was asleep and made my way quickly to Burlington Heights across the water by a canoe I'd found hidden on the shore for some unknown purpose. That gave me the opportunity to tell Halberson all about the incident with Sims' guards and was back by morning."

He looked at Jeremy with an bemused expression. "When I was captured quite some time after you at Shipman's Corners, I came directly from Colonel Halberson. I would have allowed you to rot there, but I wasn't entirely certain that I or my 'uncle' could decipher the map and instructions on our own, and I needed to make sure that they not fall into anyone else's hands. I couldn't let them fall into the Canadian Volunteers' hands. And while I was looking for a way to free you, I was discovered and ended up joining you."

"Halberson thought that he could manage from that point and ordered me to kill you if I could, but then we were freed the same night and I really didn't trust Halberson. In any case, it worked out well. Because of the way events developed, I was able to get the documents for myself. And I thankfully no longer needed Halberson, as I found another who could sell the information for me." Worthington smiled sadly. "But then I understand that he, too, was killed in the attack on Lewiston."

"And who was that?"

"That's something that won't benefit you in any way and may harm his memory for his family. I've known the man all his life and do I owe his family some things."

"Did you have Sims killed yourself then, that we might look for the documents?"

"No. At first we considered you people to be a complication none of us had counted upon. But once that fool Sims brought you into it, we needed to keep an eye on you while you looked. We couldn't be sure that you didn't have more information than you were telling, or who else you may have told that we would also need to find," replied Worthington. "As luck would have it, you did a much better job of actually solving the clues than that fool Sims ever would have done."

"Tell me something if you will," Jeremy started, leaning forward on the table. "All those times we were under attack and when Oliver nearly fell off the cliff, you helped us. You could easily have used the opportunity to reduce our numbers and make us more manageable each time, yet you always seemed to be there to help. Why?"

Worthington was not sure of the answer to that question himself. To some degree, it had been reflexive to help those he was travelling with and it certainly would do harm in acquiring the trust of these men. But there had been something more. He had begun to feel a camaraderie with them as time passed, which was something he just could not explain. But he vocalized none of these thoughts.

"There was more than one reason, actually. In part it was because we were fighting a common enemy and it wouldn't have been to my advantage to shoot the very people who were helping me fight them off. Additionally, I needed you to get me to the documents and I didn't trust Halberson. I was sure that he'd betray me at some point as he had everyone else," the explanation came finally. "In short, I needed you to find it so I could get my hands on it." He smiled. "As it turns out that it was both a good idea and a bad one."

Josef leaned over and whispered something to the trapper and Jeremy nodded in agreement. The man who was Samuel Worthington tried desperately to hear what was being said and then went a ghostly white when his imagination thought it had an answer.

They were going to give him to the Indian after all!

Jeremy stood and looked sadly at their prisoner. "I'm sorry to have to do this, but we can't drag about a prisoner along with us and I truly don't want to set you free. You're too dangerous."

Thoughts of being tortured by the Indian had been eating at Worthington's mind and now he broke. "You're not going to give me to the Indian, are you?" he asked, his voice breaking slightly. "You told me you would release me if I told you all." A tear worked its way down his right cheek as the fear of what he considered to be the ultimate punishment ate at his very soul.

"No," Jeremy replied slowly. "We've decided to turn you over to the soldiers there."

Worthington looked desperately from Jeremy to the soldiers and back. "But, you promised! Where's your honour?"

Jeremy stared coldly at the man who had cost them all so many lives. "I said no such thing. I merely suggested that the soldiers were there if you chose not to speak. There was no promise of freedom if you chose to do so. You see, I too am capable of applying your peculiar sense of honour."

He hailed the table with the soldiers. "Gentlemen, I think this may be of interest to you. We have only just discovered that this man here is Samuel Worthington, a Canadian Volunteer and the son of the late Dorian Williamson. Although an American citizen, he has been masquerading as a British infantryman for some time and has been allied with Colonel Halberson whom, you may know, has been arrested on charges of treason. It would most definitely be a feather in your caps to capture him and bring him to Fort George."

Then he looked at the young man, equal measures of regret and anger evident in his eyes. "You have no idea how much it distressed me when I thought you'd been killed. I had considered you both a friend and a brother. But now it distresses me even more to discover that you're yet alive, and that you have so thoroughly betrayed my trust and the trust of these men with me."

Worthington looked up at the soldiers, two of whom had each taken an arm and were pulling him to his feet. His face wore an expression of near-relief as they pulled him from behind the table, the threat of being tortured by Josef now ended.

Jeremy noticed "I shouldn't be relieved if I were you," he said, walking up in front of the young man. "They hang Canadian Volunteers."

Worthington had no response as they dragged him from the tavern.

"Do you really think they'll hang him?" Oliver asked.

"No, not really," replied Jeremy. "He's not truly a traitor since he was born in Buffalo and he's technically an American citizen. That could change when I show the base commander the documents we've retrieved. I suppose he could still be hung as a spy, though the documents aren't British. In any case, I intend to allow the information to leak across the border. It might be a good idea for him to find passage to somewhere else if he is released as a prisoner of war."

★ ★ ★

Once the man they had all previously known as Davis was removed from the tavern, the three men sat back down and slowly finished, picking thoughtfully at whatever they had yet sitting before them. Neither of them spoke for the longest time, each lost in his particular questions, many of which could never be answered to anyone's satisfaction.

"Well, shall we have a look at what we've nearly gotten ourselves killed over?" asked Oliver, first to break the silence. "Quite frankly, my curiosity is fast getting the better of me."

Jeremy pulled the packet of papers from his shirt with a theatrical flourish. Adopting the mock sobriety and drama of a circus performer, he withdrew the papers and looked at them one by one.

"It seems to be a report accompanied by several maps," he muttered.

"But of what?" Oliver demanded impatiently.

Jeremy quickly scanned the first worded document he found and read the title. "It says, and I quote, 'Battle Readiness of the Nation's Capital and Needs Assessment - Summary'. It would appear to be a report from the United States War Department. At any rate, it reads as follows:

★ ★ ★

"It is expected that the British must surely attack from directly along Chesapeake Bay, being the most direct route. No defences have been constructed at Bladensburg and we recommend that we place none. Several gunboats patrol in Chesapeake Bay at all times, providing easy support to land forces.

To free the maximum number of regular soldiers to meet requirements on the main front, we are recommending that Washington be defended at this time primarily by militia, and that such be trained at the time of necessity. It must be noted that of the fifteen thousand men are available for militia duty in the area of the Capital.

For protection against upstart and rogue forces of Canadian irregulars, two cannon have been stationed forty feet apart to guard Presidential Mansion from the east.

Since it has been determined that it is highly improbable then that out Capital might be attacked as in the course of this war, and since Baltimore and Annapolis are much more strategic targets, we feel in the circumstances that these plans are sufficient to meet our root needs.

Dated the fourteenth day of July, eighteen hundred and twelve."

★ ★ ★

"There are additional notes on the other pages, concerning their troop strengths and readiness, munitions and the like."

No one said a word for some time, thinking about the words contained in the report.

"Does this seem worth a fortune to you?" asked Josef finally. "It doesn't seem like more than an outline of a report, as though no one took it seriously enough to do a proper one. Is this what people died for?"

"I honestly don't think that they have any value to either side," Jeremy sighed. "Only the attitude evident in the writing of the report is of any value, for they seem to think there is no real danger of Washington being attacked. As to the report and maps themselves, they are a year old and the information is out of date. But even if it was recent, the information herein could have been got with a quick visit to Washington. No need for all this nonsense."

"What of the numbers someone has scribbled across the bottom?"

The three men looked closely at the faded notation at the bottom of the page. They were indeed numbers and read, as far as they determine, "10 16 32 54 72 94 124 132 143 169 180."

"It looks like someone added it afterward and it's so awkwardly done, one might think they were written in charcoal."

Jeremy studied the numbers. "That's difficult to say. There seems to be no sequence to them, other than the fact they are in order from least to greatest."

"In any event, we'll give them to the base commander and let the military decide whether they have any value to them. Perhaps the maps of the areas about the city are worth something."

★ ★ ★

The three men finished their meal in silence and paid the tavern keeper what they owed. They walked out into the new day to find the gloom and snow of the preceding weeks had cleared, leaving a sky that was a crisp bright blue. The result was that they all were blinded by the brilliance of the sun, especially as it reflected off the snow.

"The Cree, who live in the north of Lower Canada, have an answer to this light," muttered Josef, putting up his hand to reduce the direct sunlight.

"We do too. It's called blindness," Jeremy quipped facetiously.

"No, no, they have blocks of wood into which they've carved slits. They then tie these things to their heads so they can walk about in the glare of the winter sun."

Oliver held up a hand and looked between his fingers. "Hey, it does work, to a degree!" he commented.

"Well, of course it works!" retorted Josef, with mock indignation. "What do think, that we're savages? Don't answer that." Jeremy and Oliver chuckled. "But the wood they use is thicker, so it works much better than your fingers."

Oliver suddenly separated from the others and ran back into the tavern.

"The sun can't be causing him eyes that much pain," Josef commented. "What do you think got into him?"

"I'm sure I don't know," replied Jeremy, staring wonderingly at the door through which his cousin had entered.

The answer soon became apparent as Oliver exited once again, now with "Davis'" sniper gun in his hands. "There's no point in letting this going to waste. Perhaps, with some practice, I can learn how to use this myself."

"For what?" Josef remarked wryly. "Hunting?"

★ ★ ★

Some way off, they heard a great deal of shouting and then a gun report.

"What do you suppose that was?" Jeremy asked, looking off into the distance where there was nothing to see but trees. There were no further sounds so he shrugged and started off once again.

They hadn't made it more than a few paces when Jeremy suddenly stopped in his tracks. He pulled the report from his pocket and sat down hard on the decrepit bench that seemed almost to lean against the tavern wall.

"Of course," he muttered, barely loudly enough to be heard by the others. "Of course."

"Of course what?" asked Oliver.

"The numbers," replied Jeremy, his eyes alight. "I think I may know what they are!"

"Well, don't leave us to wonder," Josef snapped, somewhat irritated by his friend's drawing out of the answer. "What are they then?"

"It's a code, as I think we all may have suspected. But it's so simple, none of thought of what it might be. I think it's a simple matter of counting."

"Well, count."

"Someone, find a way of writing this down somewhere," Jeremy remarked, looking about for a piece of charred wood or anything that would serve as a writing implement.

Oliver ran into the tavern and soon returned with a pencil he's borrowed from the tavern keeper.

"Now something to write on," Jeremy suggested. "If we're to turn these papers over to the military, we don't want the answer written on there."

"Here you go," replied Josef, who had anticipated the request. He had found a set of orders from the American Command to the people in the area posted on one of the doors of the establishment and ripped the offending document down.

Jeremy counted the words in the document, reading out the word that appeared every time he counted out the next number in the sequence.

When he was done, they all looked at what Oliver had written down.

"From the place of this fifteen feet east then in root."

"The place of this must be where we found the packet of papers," Oliver said excitedly.

"True. And then we follow the instructions. Whatever we're to find next is no doubt hidden among the roots of a tree this distance east of that." Jeremy sighed tiredly. "I had thought that we were done with this, but now it appears that we must carry on with treasure hunt for some time more."

Chapter Forty-Five

The three set out again, heading back into the Mountain and the path that led to the shelf rock. Once there, they followed the directions and came to an ancient cedar. The tree was not large in girth, nor particularly tall, but its age was apparent in the number of roots which anchored it to the face of the rock.

There was a gap between the bottom of the tree and separation of the roots, into which had been stuffed a number of stones. It was obvious now that they knew where to look but a casual glance would have created no interest. Loose rocks stuck in the roots of such trees were commonplace.

Jeremy removed the stones and reached in. Again he pulled out a packet and groaned.

"I don't know if I have the patience to continue this quest forever," he muttered as he opened the packet to find yet another piece of paper. He unrolled the latest in this string of documents, wondering what arcane message or set of instructions he might find this time.

As he did so, there was a clinking sound of something metallic hitting the rock at his feet and then continuing off the narrow ledge to the rocky slope below.

"What was that?" Oliver asked, looking over the edge but seeing nothing.

"Something fell from the document when Jeremy opened it," replied Josef. "It appeared to be brass, but I couldn't tell what exactly."

"Maybe this document will tell us," Jeremy said, turning back to the opened piece of paper in his hand.

This was no long-winded document and there was nothing cryptic about its message. In plain script, obviously written by someone barely taught to write, were the words, "The kee too the seller to the burnt down Harrow howse on the Chipawa Rode. Ye'll never need agin."

"I guess we'll be going to Chippewa then?" asked Josef rhetorically as he slung his meagre kit over his shoulder.

For the last time, Jeremy fervently hoped, they were off once again – the sometimes trapper, the Christian Indian and the American farm boy – almost reluctantly with the thoughts of the dangers they had already survived foremost in their minds. Weary and sore, they truly did not wish any more such encounters, but the promise of retrieving settlers' loot made them feel they must continue.

★ ★ ★

Just outside of Chippewa, they arrived at the house that was, not so very long ago, the home of the Harrow family. These unfortunate people had no interest in the war at all and had just wished to continue their farming activities in peace. The American troops themselves had left them alone but with Joseph Willcocks and his Canadian Volunteers they had not been so fortunate.

Earlier in the year, Willcocks had decided that he needed a new base of operations for his band. The Harrow homestead struck the man's fancy as fitting his requirements perfectly and the family was unceremoniously ejected from their home.

When the Canadian Volunteers left, they left nothing. They had eaten what little livestock the Harrows had owned and stripped their cold cellar and barn of everything edible. Then, after the men had removed everything they deemed to be of value to them, and Willcocks was ready to move on again, the buildings were razed to the ground. The fire had burned and smouldered unchecked for several days.

It was here that the three began searching for the door to the cellar, kicking at the snow and wood. They moved aside a number of charred pieces that seemed just bit too neatly arranged and found the blackened door beneath.

"This must be it," Jeremy said quietly, grasping the slot in the door and giving it a solid pull. Holding his breath, he looked inside.

"What do you see?" Oliver asked anxiously. "Can you see anything?" From his angle of view, the door was in his way.

"I believe I see what someone thought all those lives were worth," replied Jeremy softly, almost sadly. He threw the door wide open.

The three men stared down inside the opening. Inside were hampers and boxes of someone's fine silver and other items that would fetch handsome value when it could be sold. Jeremy climbed down inside, using the boxes to step down upon since there were no ladder or stairs. He opened a small traveller's chest and sharply drew in his breath.

"It seems Williamson or somebody was far busier than I gave him credit for," he muttered. For the sake of his companions atop, he scooped some of the contents, holding them up.

Gold coins caught the sunlight and flashed out at the two men looking down into the hole.

"Well, we'd best get a wagon and move this load back to Newark, from where they can attempt to determine who owned these things," Jeremy sighed tiredly.

"That won't be necessary," a familiar voice interrupted. "I can take care of that myself."

Josef and Oliver's heads seemed to snap almost in unison toward the direction of the voice. In all the interest over the loot found in the cellar, neither man had noticed Samuel Worthington creeping up on them. He now stood less than fifteen feet from them, brandishing a mismatched pair of pistols in their direction.

"Hello, Davis," Jeremy called from out of the hole. He could not see their former companion but had recognized his voice. "You seem possessed of more lives than a cat."

"Hello, Jeremy. It was very nice of you to find my inheritance for me. You see, I knew of the documents and thought that they were the treasure, but it appears that you have carried the search farther. I thank you for your efforts."

"I assume you followed us here then," Oliver remarked. "But how?"

"As they dragged me onto a horse to take me away, I saw you three sneaking away from the tavern, looking at the documents you stole from me. I decided that it bore looking into further it and, since I hadn't struggled against my unsuspecting guards, I easily broke free and did exactly that. They tried to shoot me, but I was well clear by then."

"I heard," Jeremy muttered.

He motioned to Josef and Oliver. "Now put your weapons carefully on the ground," he ordered. Then, looking toward the cellar opening, he shouted, "Van Hijser, come carefully out of there but leave your weapons below. Don't forget I am familiar with all of them. If you don't do as I say, I'll kill your friends."

Jeremy did as he was told. Pulling himself out of the hole, he stood up slowly and faced Worthington. "I thought we'd surely seen the last of you once again," he said, brushing his hair from his eyes. "I'll need to be much more careful and kill you myself next time."

Worthington smiled. "I'm afraid you won't get that chance again," he smirked.

He carefully watched the three men as he pulled his coat aside to reveal a third pistol. "You see, I came prepared to remove all three of you from my life once and for all. Something I should have done long before."

He stepped forward and placed the barrel of one pistol first against Oliver's head while training another in the general direction of where Jeremy and Josef stood. Both weapons were cocked and his index finger now slid onto the trigger of the one which would end Oliver's life.

A report rang out, but Oliver did not fall. Instead, Jeremy's cousin was showered by the gore of the portion of Worthington's head that was torn off by the mystery blast.

Almost instinctively, all three scrambled immediately for weapons, whichever were most immediately at hand.

"I don't think that's a good idea," someone said, as a group of men emerged from the trees and brush which were planted by the Harrows to protect the house from winds.

"Well, well," Jeremy muttered, as he recognized the leader of the group. "Joseph Willcocks. I must admit that, under the circumstances, at the moment I'm glad to see even you."

"Oh, stop your gushing, Jeremy," the Volunteer leader said with a grin. "It's most unseemly." He strolled casually about the scene, keeping a careful eye on the men who were now his captives."

"Are you to kill us now?" as Oliver shakily.

"Oh, no," Willcocks replied grandly. "Jeremy knows better, don't you Jeremy?"

"Do I? I've had occasion to see the brand of justice you've dealt your own men."

Willcocks' eyes flashed momentarily but quickly regained his almost lost control. Looking at Oliver, he continued. "Have no fear, young man. As long as you do as I say, you'll be free to go as soon as we remove the items Williamson obviously stole from me."

"Stole from you?" Jeremy snorted ironically. "These items belong to the citizens you and your men robbed."

"Apparently Williamson had his own private enterprise," Willcocks returned, ignoring Jeremy's claim. "I can honestly say he was damned fortunate I didn't find out when he was alive. It's a good thing that I had it on good authority that he had hidden something from me and I had Worthington there followed the whole time."

"The whole time?" Jeremy remarked, incredulous.

"Indeed. For example, that young man you apprehended in York Market was one of mine." Seeing the surprised look on Jeremy's face, Willcocks continued. "I was certainly pleased that Worthington escaped arrest from the soldiers you turned him over to, else I would have been forced to free him myself, and that would have tipped my hand."

"But enough of these pleasantries." He turned away from Jeremy and his companions, toward his men. "Gentlemen, kindly relieve these fellows of their weapons and remove them from the site. Then load up."

As Jeremy, Josef and Oliver watched from the edge of the house's perimeter, Willcocks men brought in and loaded a wagon with all the items from the cellar.

Once they were ready to leave, Willcocks approached and tipped his hat at Jeremy. "I'd like to say it has been a pleasure, but it has been somewhat bothersome," he remarked. "I probably should shoot you to keep you from bothering me, but I've come to like you too much."

"You say you like me?" Jeremy asked sarcastically. "You have an odd way of showing it."

"Well, our discussion that time outside of Newark and fighting with you against Williamson gave me a manner of respect for you and your Indian friend here. Let's just leave it at that." He smiled and turned to go.

Then, without turning back he added, "By the way, I'm leaving a few men here to watch you for a short while. By the time they leave, I will be well across the Niagara with these goods, so there will be no point in following. Have a good day otherwise."

When their guards finally left a short while later, Oliver asked, "Should we follow them?"

"To what end?" Jeremy asked, defeat evident in his voice. "All we could accomplish is to get into a fight with yet more men and leaving more casualties, possibly us, and all to no good effect. The loot is gone."

The three men and merely stood staring in silence down the road in the direction Willcocks and his men had gone.

"Who you really think wrote the numbers on there?" Oliver asked thoughtfully. "They seemed to be added as almost an afterthought. Do you think it might have been Williamson?"

"I don't think we'll ever know the answer to that," Jeremy replied. "That packet may have passed through a number of hands before getting here."

"True, we'll never know for sure," Josef said. "There just seems to have been one long line of cheats in this deal. And we can't ask anyone. Just about everyone involved in this is dead, including Halberson."

Jeremy looked like he was about to say something, but then changed his mind.

★ ★ ★

Finally it was Jeremy who broke the silence. "Well, gentlemen, what are you going to do now? I know I've had enough of this war. But then I've said it before and still find myself dragged in. But for now, I'll think I'll finally just give this left shoulder a rest for a while. It seems to be healing well, but it may not continue to do so time and again."

"I believe I've said it too," agreed Josef. "And I'll likely be involved again. It has become personal to me now."

Jeremy and Oliver nodded slowly in understanding.

"Well, why don't you come and live with Oliver and me until the next crisis?" Jeremy offered. "While the cabin is much too small for a family, there's plenty of room for three bachelors."

"I think that may be a good idea," Josef replied. He turned and looked at Oliver, who sat there quietly, thinking. "And what about you? Surely you don't want to become too accustomed to this war habit."

Jeremy interrupted before Oliver could reply. "Oliver will need to stay out of it for now."

"Why?' asked his cousin.

"Because you aren't really a British subject and if you're caught fighting on the American side of the Niagara, the U.S. Army will hang you as a traitor. I think it's best if you just resume your previous calling as a farmer."

Oliver started laughing at this suggestion. "And what exactly am I to farm?" he demanded. "I've been at your cabin, and there's nowhere to farm on your land. The only way would be to clear large tracts of trees and even then the soil would be only marginal, especially located on a slope as it is."

Jeremy nodded in agreement. "True, true. Well then you'll have to become a hunter and trapper like the two of us."

"We can discuss those possibilities later," Oliver replied, his mind elsewhere entirely.

★ ★ ★

Jeremy and his fatigued band appeared at Fort George at around noon that day. They explained that they had come to bring information about the Canadian Volunteer who had been captured in St. Davids that morning. Before long, they were standing in front of the Officer of the Watch, a Lieutenant Tanner.

With as little fanfare as possible, they explained what they knew of Samuel Wittington and his activities. Then they produced the documents that had been the aim of the men involved. The Lieutenant became excited and asked them to wait while they showed the papers to the acting Commanding Officer.

Although there was no explanation of why it should be so, there was a great deal of excitement over the report and maps. Jeremy and his friends at least departed the fort feeling that perhaps their mission might benefit someone after all – other than Joseph Willcocks, of course.

As they walked through the remains of Newark, they were stopped at the only house to survive the conflagration. Jeremy understood it to belong to a relative of Captain Merritt, but it was not the Captain who hailed them.

The sergeant who called to them was recovering from an injury and he hobbled over on a crutch to keep the weight off the still-bloody stump that had once been his left leg.

"Aren't you the fellow they call Jeremy?" he asked. "I remember seeing you at the Battle of Beaverdams and I heard you were scouting for our boys yesterday when we put the Americans in their place for what they'd done here." His free arm swept widely across the remains of a once vibrant town.

"Anyway, I thought you might like to know what happened since. I understand you had to leave the field at Lewiston for some reason they wouldn't say."

Jeremy merely smiled at the man and nodded.

"Well, that bastard Joseph Willcocks sent his second-in-command – I believe someone said his name is Mallory – he tried to hold us back with that turncoat army of theirs. But he didn't last long. We had them on the run before they could reload." The sergeant started to cough violently and Jeremy waited patiently for him to recover.

"We chased them and burned everything in sight right up to Fort Schlosser, right across the Niagara from Chippewa before we stopped because it was too dark to fight. Anyways, we're staying there for a bit before we move on to Black Rock and eventually Buffalo."

The soldier seemed to be positively glowing as he described the great victory he and the army had over the enemy. He was equally as sure that their punishment of the Americans was just as Jeremy was sure that it was a travesty.

Jeremy congratulated the sergeant for still being alive.

As they readied to leave, the sergeant had one other thing to add. "Oh, this isn't about the fighting itself, but it was interesting just the same." He was seized of another fit of coughing.

"Word has been leaking through that the American officer who was in charge of the town here, McClure I think they said his name was, is in trouble with his own people."

"What do you mean?" Josef asked.

"Well, it seems those on the other side who have been burned out have been blaming him for their troubles. They say it's his fault because he stirred the hornet's nest by setting torch to Newark first." He chuckled. "I even hear that Chapin fellow tried to shoot him."

"Well, there's some measure of justice in all this," Jeremy sighed. "Thank you for the news, Sergeant. We must be off, but I offer my best for a speedy recovery of that leg of yours."

"It's not going to recover," the sergeant laughed as they walked away. "It's gone." His paroxysm of coughing accompanied them all the way to the town limits.

"Do you think he'll be alright?" Oliver asked Jeremy.

Jeremy let out a deep, frustrated sigh. "He might live. It's hard to tell. If infection sets in to his leg he's done. And that cough of his sounded serious. But I guess the worst part is how will he do otherwise?"

"What do you mean?"

"Well, he'll have some hard time making a living like that. But the most damaging thing is, what has all this killing, burning and looting done to his soul?"

"I didn't think you believed in souls," Josef ribbed him gently.

Jeremy looked at him and shrugged. "Not in the sense they teach in church," he replied. "I just don't know what else to call that something that guides your decisions. After what we saw yesterday I hope his can survive the glory." He pronounced the word "glory" with a heavy accent of irony.

Afterward

Jeremy looked about at his snow-covered cabin and then at the deer he had roasting for days now over a slow fire behind the cabin. It was Christmas week and, while he no longer believed in the religion, he still rather enjoyed the social aspects of the season.

Oliver was out collecting holly, with which he wanted to decorate, and to make holly crowns to wear while entertaining. Jeremy laughed at the thought. Sometimes Oliver showed himself for the boy he still was. Hopefully he could hold onto some of that throughout all of this.

Josef was also out, but he was digging for edible tubers in a place that he had spotted in the summer when he was here before. He had ably demonstrated to Oliver since they returned that there was no need to starve when you had the gardens of nature growing all about.

This would be an especially memorable Christmas for the people living about the Twenty. Although the war seemed far from over, the militia were back at home for the holidays. The most celebrated aspect, of course, was that the Americans and their foul, traitorous Canadian Volunteers were gone from Niagara. Now they could end the year feeling relatively safe.

The British had burned Fort Schlosser to the ground along with any other buildings near the fort and thrown all their supplies in the river. Then they had withdrawn to Fort Niagara, where they had left but a small occupying force for the winter. No one knew what would be next, but it was best not to dwell on these things when there were celebrations to be enjoyed.

"Jeremy," he heard from the rise behind his property. Oliver had stopped his picking and was coming down the slope, musket in hand.

Out of the corner of his eye, Jeremy could see that Josef was creeping toward the road under the cover of the informal hedge that sheltered the west side of the cabin.

"What is it?" Jeremy asked as he reached for his own gun, which leaned against a nearby stump. It still paid to keep one's weapons close at hand.

"Soldiers approaching the cabin in the front," Oliver said calmly.

Jeremy marvelled at how much his cousin had grown up in the short time he had known him. But then, he knew from personal experience, hard times had a habit of doing that to a man.

"I wonder what they want," he mused, heading for the roadway with Oliver. "Are they here to arrest us, do you think? Did they look like they were here on official business?"

Jeremy could not but think that the soldiers were here to arrest them on the old murder charges. It couldn't be the kidnapping charge, he thought, because Halberson and his pretend nephew had both been exposed. With a jolt he suddenly thought about Oliver. Did they perhaps discover the young man's nationality and come to arrest him?

"Keep your weapon ready," he told Oliver. "Until we discover what it is that they want."

They walked slowly to the front of the cabin to find three soldiers knocking rather aggressively on the front door.

"Can I help you gentlemen?" Jeremy asked politely.

One of the soldiers, a Lieutenant, turned toward him. "Are you Jeremy van Hijser?" he asked in an officious tone of voice, his back ramrod stiff.

"I would be the same, Lieutenant. How can I help you?"

"I have a message for you from Captain Merritt. He asked us to express his regret that he could not come himself, but he felt this could not wait until he was free."

"Apology accepted. Please send the Captain our best and wish him a Merry Yule, Lieutenant."

The Lieutenant looked like he was going to correct Jeremy. After all, British officers did not apologize to civilians. It had merely an explanation which he, if he were in the same position, would not even have given. But the Captain had insisted that it be done this way.

"The Captain wished us to inform you that the Parson owned a small farm just two and one-half miles east of here."

"Yes, I'm familiar with the place," Jeremy interrupted. "But what has that to do with me?"

The Lieutenant glared at Jeremy, angry at being interrupted. He had been told, however, to expect such behaviour from this man. He forced himself to ignore the question since it would be answered in the next part of the message.

"I was instructed to tell you unofficially that a law is expected to be passed early next year which will deem the lands of traitors forfeit. I was also to suggest to you that you, as the man who captured the Parson, should lay claim to his land as the spoils of war, as it were. And since it would take some time for such requests to be processed, likely not until the war was over, he also suggested that you move onto the property and work it. He pointed out that such requests are almost always granted if the claimant is already productively working the land."

"Thank you Lieutenant, and give my thanks to the Captain as well. And how do I go about making the claim official?" Jeremy asked, somewhat overwhelmed by this strange turn of events.

The Lieutenant almost smiled for the first time. Reaching into his coat, he withdrew a document. "The Captain said for you to sign this and he'll send it through with his endorsement as a prize for your efforts." He looked at Jeremy with curiosity. "I don't know why, but it seems to me that the Captain has gained a measure of respect for you."

Jeremy took the paper and signed it. "Just one question, Lieutenant, if I may?"

"Go ahead, sir," the officer replied stiffly.

"Do you know if I have the right to transfer the land when I own it?"

"Yes sir, I would assume that when you own it, you may do with it as you please." Seeing that Jeremy had no more to say, the Lieutenant turned and, with the two privates in tow, set off down the road to where they had hitched their horses to a tree.

Jeremy had to laugh. "I would guess that Merritt suggested that they not approach too quickly on their horses lest we shoot them before they could introduce themselves," he chuckled. "It seems they went a step further and decided not to ride up at all."

Josef stepped clear of his concealment, musket hanging loosely at his side. "So, Jeremy, you're to become a farmer now?" he asked, somewhat incredulous at the thought.

"What? Do you not think I can still farm?" challenged Jeremy, his voice the model of one who has been slighted.

"No, I..." Josef started.

Jeremy began to laugh and then looked at the two men he had just gone through so much with. "No, I have no intention of being broken to the plough once again," he said, to Josef's surprisingly apparent relief. "Actually, my thought was that Oliver could become a farmer once again."

Oliver looked at him, a stunned expression on his face. "Do you mean for me to farm the Parson's land?"

Jeremy laughed. "Surely you don't expect two committed trappers to do so, do you?"

Josef started laughing too. "I've never been a farmer," he added. "I've spent most of my life trapping and guiding and even a wee bit of smuggling."

"Besides," Jeremy added. "When my claim is finalized, and you're old enough, I'll sign it over to you."

"Would that be allowed?" Oliver asked. "I'm not a British subject."

"Nobody ever seems to know that," replied Jeremy. "The Parson hadn't come here long before himself, seeking free land. Merritt knows you served in the Crown's interest at Queenston and, as for the rest, well, just don't make a point of mentioning it to anyone. Besides, when this accursed war is over – and surely, it must end sometime – I'm sure Americans will be welcomed here again, although no doubt reluctantly at first."

"I'll need to get word to my mother and get her over here," Oliver said, changing tack. The thought of a farm here instead of living with Jeremy and Josef was quickly gathering enthusiasm in his mind. "Maybe, if our little farm in Black Rock is still there, she can sell it and bring the money over for seed and such."

Jeremy laughed at the sudden dissolution of all reservations in his cousin. He hoped it would all work out for the best.

"I think you should let me take care of sending for your mother," he said. "I still have many contacts on both sides of the river and ways of getting messages across lines."

★ ★ ★

More than two weeks passed before Jeremy heard back from his contacts, and they came bearing bad news. Oliver's mother would not be joining him on the newly confiscated farm.

On the day before New Year's Eve, as they were about to evacuate Oliver's mother from Black Rock, the British attacked, catching the Americans off guard. They had sent almost two thousand men to fight the oncoming Brits, including Chapin and Willcocks with their men. But they had fallen easily to the superior tactics and discipline of the fourteen hundred arrayed against them, with many running when they saw the Indians that the British had in the fore.

Somewhere during the battle for Black Rock, Oliver's mother had been shot. Nobody knew whether her life had been taken by an American or a Brit, for the fighting near their farm was fierce and a stray shot could have come from either side.

In the end, the entire eastern shore of the Niagara River was now a burned ruin, including Buffalo. Refugees fled to the homes of relatives or friends well away from the river until they were sure the British were there no longer. Jeremy's contacts told him that now people were filtering back to their homes and already plotting revenge.

I'm beginning to fear that this affair might indeed never end, thought Jeremy morosely. He shook it off and set out to give Oliver the bad news with Josef along for support.

Oliver was understandably devastated. His mother was dead, his property destroyed. And, with all the businesses on that side of the Niagara destroyed, there would likely be no one to buy the now empty property for some time. Even his mother's funeral had been held without him there.

"I'm dreadfully sorry about your mother," Jeremy said softly.

"You never met her," Oliver said, his voice barely above a whisper. "You would have liked her."

"I'm sure I would have," Jeremy agreed softly, searching for something better to say. He had never been the type for sentimentality.

Oliver looked up, tears running freely down his cheeks. "Now I won't have the money for seed either."

"I do believe you'll be getting two pounds sterling for your involvement in the attack on Fort Niagara," Jeremy replied. "That's the share of the prize money all who had anything to do with the campaign are to get, including Merritt's men. I've reminded the good Captain that you were one of his on that day and he says he'll be sure to see you get your share."

"And, if it will help, you can have mine as well," chimed in Josef, who had been staying apart for the interaction until now.

"And mine," Jeremy added. "What would I do with money, anyway? Besides, it'll save my having to feed you as I would if you should be forced to return to my cabin to live."

Oliver smiled weakly at his cousin, who gave him a pat on the shoulder and then turned and walked off with Josef, leaving him there alone with his grief.

★ ★ ★

Again, thought Jeremy, as the two walked backed in silence. Again someone close to me has felt the sorrow that this war seems to be providing without letup. In spite of what I thought earlier, this insanity simply must stop soon, he though hopefully. Surely I was right when I told Oliver that it can't continue forever.

I know I shan't be able to.

CPSIA information can be obtained at www.ICGtesting.com
Printed in the USA
LVOW122034060312

271895LV00005B/29/P

9 781469 768878